They never dreamed that one little April Fool's prank could change their lives forever...

Lena Walsh was just *FOOLING AROUND* when she asked Andre Dumont out on a date from hell. She never guessed the joke would be on her....

Kate Randall is *NOBODY'S FOOL*. But even *she* is intrigued when she learns she has a secret admirer. Too bad it's not the one she wants....

Everyone knows that *FOOLS RUSH IN*— and Mark Lavin and Claire O'Connor are anything but fools. But when they find themselves victims of a radio hoax, they can't help rushing...right to the altar!

Sometimes love gets the last laugh...

Vicki Lewis Thompson has been a *Fool for Love*—Harlequin-style—since she published her first book in 1984. The roof blew off her career in June 2003, when her first mainstream novel, *Nerd in Shining Armor*, became a Reading with Ripa Book Club pick and she hit all the major lists—*New York Times, USA TODAY, Publishers Weekly* and Waldenbooks. Although bestsellerdom is sweet, it hasn't changed Vicki's basic recipe for happiness—living in Arizona with her hubby, writing hot romance and drinking coffee from her own pot. In other words, just *Fooling Around…*

Stephanie Bond fell in love with a man who was willing to make a fool of himself to get her attention: After declining offers to go out because she was seeing someone else, she returned from a trip to discover the determined man had driven to the airport to leave a card on the windshield of her car. Intrigued, Stephanie agreed to go out with him, and four months later he proposed. As of this printing, they've been married for fourteen years! Stephanie lives with her persistent and loving husband in Atlanta, Georgia. Visit Stephanie at www.stephaniebond.com.

According to **Judith Arnold**, April isn't the cruelest month—it's the coolest month! In April springtime sweeps into New England, along with Judith's birthday, and of course April Fool's Day is always a hoot. The author of eighty books, Judith writes for Harlequin and MIRA. She has been a RITA® Award finalist several times, and has won numerous awards from *Romantic Times* magazine. Her novel *Love in Bloom's* was named one of the eight best paperbacks of the year by *Publishers Weekly*. Judith lives in Massachusetts with her husband and two sons.

Vicki Lewis Thompson
Stephanie Bond
Judith Arnold

Fool For Love

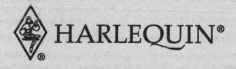

HARLEQUIN®

TORONTO • NEW YORK • LONDON
AMSTERDAM • PARIS • SYDNEY • HAMBURG
STOCKHOLM • ATHENS • TOKYO • MILAN • MADRID
PRAGUE • WARSAW • BUDAPEST • AUCKLAND

ISBN 0-373-83566-3

FOOL FOR LOVE

Copyright © 2004 by Harlequin Books S.A.

The publisher acknowledges the copyright holders of the individual works as follows:

FOOLING AROUND
Copyright © 2004 by Vicki Lewis Thompson

NOBODY'S FOOL
Copyright © 2004 by Stephanie Bond Hauck

FOOLS RUSH IN
Copyright © 2004 by Barbara Keiler

This edition published by arrangement with Harlequin Books S.A.

® and TM are trademarks of the publisher. Trademarks indicated with ® are registered in the United States Patent and Trademark Office, the Canadian Trade Marks Office and in other countries.

Visit us at www.eHarlequin.com

Printed in U.S.A.

CONTENTS

FOOLING AROUND

Vicki Lewis Thompson

For Lauri Thompson,
who loyally reads all my books and advised me
on this concept. Thanks, Lauri!

PROLOGUE

LENA WAS STILL chicken. Damn. She'd hoped the yearly ritual would get easier, but this March fifteenth was as scary as the others. Despite the butterflies, she walked through the door of the cozy Italian restaurant in north Scottsdale.

Tonight marked the annual gathering of the April Fools. Lena, Brandy and Mcg had bonded at a weekend motivational seminar, dished over sour apple martinis at the bar and vowed to accept the main speaker's challenge to blast through their comfort zones on a regular basis.

Lena's comfort zone was the size of a postage stamp. Her parents, Mr. and Mrs. Overly Cautious, had warned her from an early age that the world was a dangerous place, and she'd believed them. Reprogramming herself into a risk taker was a huge job. She desperately needed the prodding of the April Fools.

Every year during the ten-day period surrounding April first, each one of the trio deliberately made a fool of herself. To guarantee squirm-worthiness, the women dreamed up stunts for each other. Lena had spent her lunch hour last April first on a busy corner in downtown Phoenix reciting the balcony scene from *Romeo and Juliet*.

The year before that had been a little easier—going to a Suns basketball game wearing an evening gown and carrying opera glasses. She thought of her first task with nostalgia now—race-walking through a neighborhood park wearing a beanie with a propeller on top. Each year the assignments got tougher, which was why she was sweating tonight's meeting.

Still, she couldn't argue with the results. Each time, she'd sworn she would die of embarrassment. And, obviously, she hadn't. Even better, she was on the fast track for promotions and pay raises at Thunderbird Savings. Brandy and Meg had leaped ahead in their careers, too—Brandy in PR and Meg in accounting. Their strategy had definitely affected the way they projected themselves.

Inside the restaurant, Lena confirmed with the hostess that her friends had already arrived. Then she straightened her spine and walked through an archway into the dining room, passing hand-painted murals of Roman temples and Mediterranean seascapes. Since the April Fools had chosen the Ides of March as the day for assigning tasks, an Italian restaurant named Caesar's had seemed like a no-brainer. As a bonus, the food was great.

Both Meg and Brandy were drinking Chianti, and a glass of it sat at her place, waiting for her. Both women looked great. Since the club's founding, Meg had lost the extra thirty pounds that had plagued her, and she wore her red hair in a short and sassy style way different from the pageboy she'd started with. Brandy had ditched her frumpy suits in favor of flowing silks, and she'd colored her hair blond.

Lena hadn't changed much on the outside, maybe

because her parents lived in Phoenix and she didn't want to make them anxious. Her rebellious younger brother who'd pierced various body parts, moved to L.A. and formed a rock band gave her parents plenty to angst about. She couldn't bear to add to their agitation herself, so she still dressed conservatively, and her brunette bob was shoulder-length, as always.

Then again, she couldn't totally blame her parents for the way she presented herself. *She* skittered away from flamboyance, even now. Manicures and pedicures were about as exciting as it got with her.

And although she'd become more assertive professionally, when it came to her social life...forget about it. The same was true of Meg and Brandy, which was why they'd bonded in the first place— three cowardly lions. They'd decided to target their lack of a social life this year. If Lena's assignment was anything like what she'd helped write for both Meg and Brandy, she was in for a wild ride.

Meg glanced up as Lena approached. "You look petrified."

"I just need wine." Lena sat down and took a hefty swallow. "Okay, Meg's first, right?" She pulled Meg's envelope from her purse and handed it over.

"On an anxiety level of one-to-ten, this is a fifty." Meg stuck her table knife under the sealed flap of the envelope, pulled out the note and groaned. "Just shoot me now."

"Go on," Lena said. "Read it out loud. Brandy and I want to enjoy the moment."

"Okay." Meg sighed and held the paper up to the light of the candle flickering on the table. "I, Meg

Burney, promise that within five days before or after April first, I will ask Devon from accounting to go sailing on Tempe Town Lake with me. I will wear an itsy-bitsy, teeny-weeny yellow polka-dot bikini, and before the sail is over I will sing the entire theme song from *Titanic*.'' She gave a little whimper. ''I have to lose another three pounds! *Plus* I don't know all the words to that damned song, *and* I can't sing!''

''You have time to learn the words,'' Lena said, ''and voice quality doesn't count. Besides, Devon will be too busy looking at all that bare flesh to care if you're on key or not. And you do not need to lose another three pounds.''

''I'm a redhead. I'll get sunburned.''

Brandy snorted. ''Use sunscreen, Einstein.''

''I don't have an itsy—''

''Oh, yes, you do.'' Brandy produced a bag from under the table and drew out the contents, which she dangled in front of Meg.

Meg wailed again and snatched the bikini. ''I'll freeze my ass off!''

''This is Phoenix,'' Brandy said. ''It won't be that cold.''

''I don't want to think about it anymore.'' Meg handed an envelope to Brandy. ''I want to inflict pain on you, instead.''

Brandy's smile faded. ''Oh, goody.'' With a look of resignation she took her envelope, opened it and quickly scanned the contents. ''No way!''

''Read it,'' Meg said.

''I, Brandy Larson, within five days before or after April first, will kidnap Eric from the office and take him to my apartment where I will play the CD of

Bolero while I perform the Dance of the Seven Veils.'' She threw up both hands. "I can't dance! And my hair color's wrong. It should be dark, like Lena's, to pull off that kind of stunt.''

"Wear a wig," Meg said. "Besides, do you think if you're weaving around in some skimpy outfit that he'll care if your hair is right or you can dance a lick? You've been saying for weeks that you think he's interested.''

"Yeah, but couldn't I start with going for coffee?''

"Nope.'' Lena shook her head. "Not unless it's Turkish coffee served after the dancing. I have a feeling you'll both be feeling a little too *hot* for coffee anyway.''

Brandy turned bright red. "This is going to be so bad. You have no idea.'' She gulped the rest of her wine and put down the glass. "At least there's pay-back time.'' She took an envelope from her briefcase and handed it to Lena. "Now we get to watch you hyperventilate.''

Lena opened the envelope, her tummy churning. "At least you can't order me to snag a certain guy. I've never mentioned anyone specific.'' *On purpose.* Her crush on Andre Dumont, a top loan salesman at Thunderbird, was her little secret. Socially he seemed to be everything she was not—suave, self-assured, sexually magnetic. Maybe that came from his French background.

Brandy looked smug. "Meg and I worked around that detail.''

And so they had. Lena stared at her assignment. "I, Lena Walsh, promise that within five days before or after April first, I will ask the cutest single guy I know for a date. I will tell him it's for dinner, some light entertainment followed by dancing and to dress accordingly. Then I will take him for fast food, to a…*belly dancing lesson and goofy golf?*''

Brandy and Meg started laughing.

''Guys! You've got to be kidding, especially about the belly dancing. The other two things are bad enough, especially if he's all dressed up, but a belly dancing lesson?''

Meg seemed delighted with herself. ''That was my idea, inspired by your plan for Brandy's Dance of the Seven Veils. All you have to do is find a class and ask the teacher beforehand about bringing a guy.''

''But…but I don't know what guy to ask.''

Brandy laughed. ''From the look of terror on your face, I think you know exactly what guy. So that's it, then. We all have our assignments.'' She poured them more wine and raised her glass. ''To the April Fools.''

''Who are going to ruin my life.'' Lena touched her glass to Meg's and Brandy's.

Meg winked at her. ''We haven't yet.''

Maybe not, Lena thought as she took a hefty swig of rich red wine. But making a fool of herself in front of Andre Dumont was so far outside her comfort zone she might never find her way back.

CHAPTER ONE

OTHER THAN HIS NAME, there was nothing French about Andre Dumont. His mother and father had named him Andre because they'd been drinking Andre champagne the night he'd been conceived. Oh, sure, if some genealogy nut wanted to trace his roots, they'd probably end up at Versailles or Bordeaux. And he'd been told he looked French, all dark and brooding.

Perhaps if he'd learned French, he could have acted French. Women seemed to think a guy with French blood would automatically be great in bed, and that certainly couldn't hurt a man's image, he supposed.

Andre figured he was just as good in the sack as the average guy—and who could tell these things, anyway? But at least he'd finally figured out that when a woman asked about his French background he should simply smile and shrug, as if he took it for granted.

He'd picked up a few other tricks along the way. He actually did like to cook, which helped his worldly image, so when he invited a date for dinner, he served French wine and played French music on his CD player. He'd also tried to play up the dark and brooding thing, but other than letting his hair grow a little longer, driving a sports car and wearing Euro-styled shades, he didn't really know what to do.

He'd had a fair share of success with women, because he had a knack for selling anything, including himself. But he had yet to find the one lady he'd give up the single life for. However, there might be that kind of potential with Lena Walsh, a hot woman at Thunderbird Savings. She was on the management track and he was in sales, naturally, so they didn't see a lot of each other. Yet whenever they met, *va-va-voom,* his sensors went on red alert.

Unfortunately, Lena had never given him the slightest indication that he meant any more to her than the office furniture. He didn't take that personally because she didn't seem to give any guy encouragement. She didn't have some long-distance relationship going, either. He'd asked around.

Maybe she didn't like guys at all, which would be a crying shame considering her top-of-the-line packaging. Or maybe she was determined to make her first million before she turned thirty and didn't have time for silly things like dating and sex. Either way, she seemed immune to both his French charm and his salesmanship. He, on the other hand, was becoming obsessed with her.

He hadn't been out with any other woman in the six months he'd been at Thunderbird because he kept thinking he'd work up the courage to ask Lena for a date and he wanted his calendar to be clear. Then she'd bustle through with some management memo, efficiency and professionalism rolling off her in waves, and he'd lose his nerve.

Late on a Tuesday afternoon at the end of March,

she walked straight into his little cubby, giving him
the perfect opportunity to ask her out. He kept his
attention on her face and pretended not to notice the
curve of her breasts under her pinstriped suit jacket.
That was especially difficult because she was
breathing fast, as if she'd taken the stairs instead of
the elevator.

Be suave, Dumont. "Hi, Lena." He got up from
his desk and tried to look as French as possible.
"What's up?"

"I...um..." She paused and cleared her throat.

He stared at her. Never in the time they'd worked
together had he seen her at a loss for words. Her blue
eyes were filled with hesitation and uncertainty. He
had a horrible thought. "I screwed up with one of
my clients."

"No, no! Nothing like that."

"*You* screwed up with one of my clients?" He
found the idea inconceivable, but something had rat-
tled her. He noticed another strange thing—a fresh
coat of lipstick on her gorgeous mouth. Normally by
this time of day she'd be minus the lipstick and have
a cute little shine to her nose. Not today. Surely she
hadn't fixed her makeup for him.

"This isn't about clients." She fidgeted with the
button on her suit jacket. "Or anything to do with
the office."

He closed his mouth, embarrassed to discover it
was open. Suave French guys didn't stand around
with their mouths hanging open. They acted bored,
as if they always knew the score. But he didn't have
the foggiest idea who the players were, let alone the
score. He couldn't imagine what was coming next.

She twisted the suit button some more. "Are you...is there any chance you're...free on Friday night? I know it's short notice, so you probably have plans, which is fine, but I just thought if you didn't that—"

"You're asking me out?" He couldn't have been more shocked if she'd come to a company function in a negligee. "Why?"

She blushed. "Never mind. You probably have no interest in seeing me socially. It was just an idea. Forget it." She started to leave.

"Wait! I have lots of interest in seeing you socially. I didn't think you had any interest in *me*."

"Well, I do."

"I would never have guessed."

"I know." She took a deep breath. "I've been focused on my career recently, and it's not easy to— the thing is, dating takes time and effort, and I haven't been putting my energy there." She cleared her throat and looked extremely uncomfortable.

"I see. Well, that makes sense. I haven't really, either. Been putting my energy there, I mean." He told himself not to get too excited, but he was bubbling like a lava lamp at the thought that after a long dry spell, Lena had picked him. "But you want to put your energy there, now?"

She nodded.

"As it so happens, I'm free Friday night." He glanced at his desk calendar, as if to double-check, when he knew there was nothing going on besides catching a Suns game on the tube. "That's April second, right?"

"Right."

He grinned. "Good thing it's not the first, or I might wonder if this was all a joke."

"It's not," she said quickly.

Maybe too quickly, he thought as he studied her. Was this buttoned-down lady secretly into practical jokes? Nah, not likely. "What did you have in mind?"

She looked even more uncomfortable. "Dinner?" She made it seem like a question.

"Dinner would be good."

"And, um, some dancing, and…and after that, a little light entertainment." She sounded as if she'd rehearsed the pitch.

He controlled a chuckle and reminded himself that she didn't do this kind of thing every day. Of course she'd be nervous. According to her description, they'd probably be going to a supper club-slash-comedy club, a place where he could play the French guy really well while wearing his designer silk shirt and his best dinner jacket. "I'd love that. What time should I pick you up?"

"Actually, since I asked you, why don't I pick *you* up?"

"Uh, sure, why not?" He'd much rather drive. The driver was in the power position and, besides, Andre had a cool car. But he didn't want to come off like a chauvinist. "Let me give you my address." He grabbed a sticky note and scribbled it down, along with his phone number.

"Thanks." She took the note and folded under the sticky part.

Maybe he shouldn't have used a sticky note. Maybe he should have whipped one of his cards from the holder on his desk and put his address on the back of that. Much smoother. But she'd thrown him off his game, appearing out of the blue like this and wanting a date. Not that he was complaining. He needed to get his act together before Friday night, though.

She glanced at the address. "Great, you're not far from me. Is six good for you?"

"Six is excellent for me."

"Great." Her color still high, she smiled at him. "I'll see you on Friday night, then."

"I'm looking forward to it." He waited until she was out of sight before pumping his fist in the air. Then he ran his hand over the back of his neck. He'd planned to get his hair cut tomorrow, but he'd better not. Short hair would ruin the dark and brooding thing.

Fortunately his good shirt was clean, and the place on his chin where he'd nicked himself shaving had nearly healed. He was as ready for this date as he would ever be.

BETWEEN TUESDAY and Friday, Lena avoided Andre whenever possible. She realized that might seem weird to him, like she was some stealth dater, but she couldn't pull off this crazy scheme if she got to know him any better between now and then. Too much contact before the event and she might end up giving him some clue that the evening wouldn't be what he expected.

She'd duly reported her scheduled date to Meg and Brandy. She'd be the first risk-taker. Meg's sail on Tempe Town Lake with Devon was Sunday, and

Brandy was kidnapping Eric on Monday. They'd all decided to avoid April Fool's Day, so that the guys wouldn't get suspicious and think the women were deliberately pulling pranks on them with their crazy antics.

Lena could only guess how time passed for Meg and Brandy, but as for her, the anxiety level mounted daily. She battled it the way she always handled stress, by making lists. By Friday afternoon, she had almost everything crossed off. Manicure and pedicure, check. Haircut, eyebrow wax and bikini wax, check. The bikini wax was overkill, because she certainly wouldn't go that far on the first date, but doing it made her feel more confident.

She'd attended one belly-dancing class and coerced the instructor into giving a Friday-night lesson. She'd had to pay extra and get some volunteers, because the class normally didn't meet that night, but the prospect of having a guy join the group had whipped up the interest factor.

Departing drastically from her tailored clothes, she'd bought a flowing skirt and sleeveless tunic in a lightweight gauzy fabric. When belted around her hips with an iridescent scarf and accessorized with two bracelets and an anklet, it looked quite exotic. Yet she still could do all the activities she'd planned.

She'd let the saleswoman talk her into the scarf, bracelets and anklet. Meanwhile her mother's voice held forth in her head, reminding her that the bright stones were too gaudy and she might want to rethink the shimmering scarf. Lena had ignored her mother's voice and bought everything because they made her feel sexy.

Sexy was how she wanted to feel tonight, right? Instead she was scared silly as she imagined taking Andre out for fast food and then to a belly-dancing class. He would never want to see her again. Sheesh.

Her pulse jumping, she went back to her list. Car washed and detailed. Prettiest undies washed and waiting in her drawer. Andre would never see the black lace thong and low-cut underwire, but she felt more datable wearing them.

She'd covered everything on her list. Nothing more to do except go home at five, shower, dress and pick up Andre. This would be her first date since…wow, since last summer. Hank Mendenhall had asked her to the company picnic and in the course of that uncomfortable afternoon they'd discovered they had nothing in common besides work.

Hoping to distract herself from the embarrassing event she had coming up tonight, she tried to remember the last date she'd had before Hank. She was mentally reviewing her meager date history when her supervisor, Dana, called.

"I need to see you in my office before you head home for the weekend," Dana said. Something in her voice told Lena this was more than a casual FYI meeting.

"Be right there." As Lena left her office, she figured out what the summons was about. She'd been so involved in her dating plans that she'd forgotten about the promotion possibility. Yikes. This particular promotion couldn't have come at a worse time.

Dana Iverson, a blond in her mid-fifties, smiled and stood when Lena walked in. "Congratulations are in order."

"That's good to hear." Lena tried to look enthusiastic while she mentally searched for a way out of the box she'd put herself in.

"The promotion came through exactly as I'd hoped. As of Monday, you'll be supervising our six highest producers. I'm sure you already know who they are, but here's the list. Oh, and this is confidential until Monday. I wanted to give you a heads up, though, because I'm so excited for you. This will look very good on your résumé."

Lena nodded and took the list, but she didn't have to look at it to have her worst fears confirmed. On Monday, she would become Andre's boss. The company had a strict policy about supervisors dating those working under them.

The prudent thing would be to tell Dana now. And Dana might advise canceling the date. That would give Lena a legitimate way out of this nerve-wracking experience, and yet…she hesitated.

"Is anything wrong?" Dana asked. "You look worried about something."

Lena glanced up from the list, where Andre's name seemed to glow as if outlined in neon paint. Damn it, she'd spent her whole life being prudent concerning guys, and now, right when she had geared herself up to take a chance, this escape route had opened up. Whether she took it needed to be her decision, not Dana's.

"Nothing's wrong," she said. "Everything's terrific." Then she gave Dana a smile. "I'm absolutely thrilled about this promotion."

"LOOK, THIS DATE is already loaded with enough freight to sink it." Lena had managed to get Meg and Brandy on a three-way call. A girl needed advisors, even if the ultimate decision was hers. "How can I add in the job thing? If the date goes well, which I doubt, but if it does by some miracle, we won't be able to keep dating after tonight. That could be awkward if we're seeing each other every day. If it goes horribly, then the torture will be even worse."

"Do you want to cancel?" Traffic rumbled in the background as Meg talked from her cell phone.

"She can't cancel!" Brandy's voice echoed from the speaker phone in her office. "It's too late to come up with another stunt or even another guy. I say she goes through with it."

"And then what? I'm not supposed to tell him about this promotion, but for him to hear about it on Monday morning, especially if he knows I knew tonight, would be heinous."

"I agree," Meg said. "But you promised your boss not to tell anyone, so you have to wait until the last minute. I say give him a call on Sunday night, so he has a little time to prepare himself and yet not enough to spread it around and get you in trouble."

"He wouldn't spread it around," Lena said.

"Are you sure?" Brandy asked. "I thought you didn't really know him that well. And people get fired for being blabbermouths when they're not supposed to say anything."

Lena cleared her throat. "Let's just say I've observed him for some time. He isn't the type to—"

"*Observed him for some time?*" Meg's voice jumped an octave.

"You've had a crush on him!" Brandy cried out.

"And you never said! Bad Lena. Bad, bad Lena. If Meg and I had known, we could have put his name specifically in your assignment!"

Lena's head began to ache. "Well, you got him anyway! And that's not the point. The point is whether I should cancel this date on ethical grounds. I know that means I won't do the stunt this year, but I don't want to put either Andre or me in a difficult position."

"Let's think this through," Meg said. "Are you his boss yet?"

"Technically, no, but—"

"And you weren't his boss when you asked him out," Brandy added. "So you weren't breaking any company rules at the time."

"Right, but—"

"Theoretically you could have heard about this promotion on Monday," Meg said.

"But I didn't! And now I know that everything's about to change."

"Nothing's changed yet," Brandy said. "The way I see things, you might even be able to grandfather this relationship right into company policy. Well, unless you have a hideous time."

"That's what I expect," Lena said, visualizing the belly-dancing class and shuddering. "And then working together will be a nightmare."

"But you don't know that will happen," Brandy continued. "And if you two get along, then on Sunday night you can call and explain the situation. I bet Dana will make an exception if you want to keep dating each other."

Meg's cell phone crackled. "Yeah, and after Monday you wouldn't get away with it. So if you want to date this guy, you have to go for it now."

"Or I could turn down the promotion."

Both Meg and Brandy screeched in dismay.

"Ah. So you both pretty much hate that idea."

"Of course we hate it!" Brandy said. "The April Fools do not back away from success because it might make a guy uncomfortable. How could you even think such a thing?"

"I wasn't serious." She'd been semi-serious, though. Now that she and Andre had an actual date, and he'd seemed happy about that, she realized how much she wanted it to work out. It probably wouldn't work out, but if by some bizarre chance it did, then the promotion could really foul things up.

"This will be a blessing in disguise," Brandy continued. "You'll find out how he feels about dating a powerhouse woman."

"Who takes him to a belly-dancing class," Lena said.

Meg laughed. "God, I wish I could be there. Hey, where is the class? I should have thought of that. Brandy and I could—"

"Forget about it!" Lena shuddered. "As if I don't have enough problems."

"Relax," Brandy said. "So you're going to make a fool of yourself. So what?"

"Do *not* try to find that belly-dancing class, either of you."

"Whoops, gotta go," Meg said. "My turn at the ATM."

"And I have a call on the other line." Brandy coughed. "Have fun, Lena! Bye!"

"Wait! You both have to promise that you won't—" She stopped speaking when she realized she was pleading with a dial tone. Come to think of it, they could easily find out about the class by looking in the phone book as she had.

Oh, well, they were probably teasing her. They wouldn't really search out the class and show up there.

Like hell they wouldn't.

Suddenly her headache got worse.

CHAPTER TWO

AFTER LENA ASKED him out, Andre expected her to be friendlier at work than she'd been before. Instead she seemed deliberately to avoid him. Well, maybe she was super busy. It could happen.

Or maybe—and this would be sort of cool—maybe she was shy. He could build an entire scenario out of that. Lena had lusted after him for weeks, maybe even months, but she'd been too shy to let him know. Then, on Tuesday, she'd worked up her courage to make the first move.

All along she might have been covering her shyness and her attraction by putting on the busy professional act. He thought about that while straightening the papers on his desk late Friday afternoon. What fun it would be to use his well-honed sales techniques to put her at ease.

He'd schmooze her on the way to the restaurant, and once she'd had a glass of wine or two, they'd probably be talking away like old friends. He hoped they would be able to carry on a decent conversation about something unrelated to Thunderbird Savings. He admired her dedication to work, but if all they could do was talk shop, they wouldn't make it past a few dates. Andre enjoyed his work, but he liked to forget about it after he left the office.

Great sex was one way to forget about work, but even great sex wouldn't encourage him to hang on to Lena for more than a week or two unless they connected on a deeper level. Pure physical attraction used to be enough for him, but not anymore. His parents, veterans after marrying off his two older sisters, had predicted that he'd start thinking about stability after turning thirty. He'd laughed.

Then he'd turned thirty two months ago and sure enough, as if a switch had been thrown, he was sick of the singles routine. Here he'd had this significant birthday, and no particular woman he wanted to share it with. He'd spent the day with his family and watched his sisters with their husbands and children...and felt left out of something really cool.

He hadn't told his folks that, of course. Although he loved them to pieces, they had the potential to become the matchmaking parents from hell. He was a big boy, now, and he'd find his own serious girlfriend.

Tonight had the makings of a great step in that direction. The thought prompted him to start whistling as he tucked pending loan apps into a folder.

His buddy Jed Newman poked his head into Andre's cubby. Jed's blond hair and round face made him look cherubic. He was anything but. "You must be real happy about your date with Lena tonight," he said.

"What makes you say that?"

Jed leaned against the door jamb. "You hardly ever get out of here by five, and you're closing up shop with ten minutes left to go. *And* you're humming Springsteen's 'Dancing in the Dark'."

"So I like the Boss. And it's a good song."

"It's an I-have-a-hot-date song."

Andre laughed. "Okay, if you insist."

"I must admit I'm curious about how this will go. She seems a little too buttoned-down to be any fun."

Andre had wondered about that, too, especially after the way Lena had kept out of sight the past few days. "Hey, I'm a salesman. I'm up to the challenge."

"I'm sure you are." Jed massaged the back of his neck. "I think I'll hit the gym after I get out of here. Too much desk time. Which reminds me—are you shooting hoops with us tomorrow afternoon?"

"Probably." Then again, if tonight turned out well, he might ask Lena to go on a picnic. The weather was great for it. "I'll call you one way or the other in the morning."

Jed gave him a knowing glance. "Uh-huh. I get the picture. You'll play basketball unless you come up with a better alternative."

"Hey, cut me some slack. This is my first date in over six months."

"Which is why you need to take it slow. Rule of thumb—don't call for three days or she'll think you're too eager."

Andre closed his desk drawer and stood. "You know what? I *am* eager. And tired of playing games."

"Games? These are survival skills, man. Let your guard down and you'll find yourself picking out a silver pattern before you know it."

Andre gazed at him without speaking.

Jed shrugged and pushed away from the door

jamb. "Unless a silver pattern is what you're hankering for. See ya, stud. Have fun." Jed left quickly, as if afraid Andre's attitude might rub off.

Andre smiled as he grabbed his cell phone and headed out of the office. Jed was only twenty-six and the idea of settling down scared the hell out of him. Andre used to be like that, so he understood Jed's panic. He just didn't share it anymore.

On the other hand, he didn't want to come across as desperate. He *wasn't* desperate. As he drove the short distance to his apartment, he mentally listed all that was right in his life. He'd found a job that suited him. When he wanted company he could call up friends or head over to his folks' place in Paradise Valley where he'd play with the family dog and eat home cooking.

It was all good, but it wasn't enough. Inside his apartment he glanced around and admitted he had a comfortable place to live. But the guppies in his fish tank didn't really care whether he'd had a good or bad day. They didn't require much attention, either. Andre felt that, with all he had to give, he wanted a different lifestyle, a shared existence.

He shouldn't put too much importance on tonight's date, but he seemed to be doing that, anyway. After a quick shower and shave, he dressed in his imported silk shirt and best gray slacks. Then he brought out every damned tie in his closet. Should he go frivolous with the dancing bears or trendy with the Jerry Garcia? A power tie in red with gray stripes seemed too corporate, the paisley too feminine.

He had a subtle gray print already knotted around his neck when he changed his mind and took it off again. This wasn't a wedding, for crying out loud. Finally, muttering to himself, he grabbed one decorated in swirls of blue and put it on. Good thing he didn't have twice as many ties.

Maybe not the blue. He smoothed his hand down it and tried to decide if the swirls were distracting. Then the doorbell rang and he was out of options. He'd have to wear the blue unless he wanted to make her wait while he tried out the six he hadn't considered yet. Yeah, that would definitely start the evening off on the right foot.

He opened the door with a flourish while wondering whether saying *bon soir* would be laying it on too thick. As it turned out, he didn't say anything at all—just gawked at the eye candy on the other side of his apartment door.

The filmy outfit Lena wore looked so damned touchable his fingers itched to reach for her. And the scarf tied around her hips drew his attention to that part of her anatomy, and he began to get Big Ideas. He'd been thinking first date, so maybe a kiss at the door when the evening ended, if all went well. That scarf bumped his thoughts up several rungs on the seduction ladder.

She flushed. "Am I…is something wrong?"

"No…no!" He snapped out of his daze. "You look incredible, that's all. I'm used to the power suits, but this is…wonderful."

"Thank you." The flush on her cheeks brought out the deep blue of her eyes. "Are you ready to go?"

"Sure. Definitely." He started out the door before remembering his manners. "Uh, I mean, would you like to come in?'' He should have asked her that at least thirty seconds ago. His man-of-the-world schtick wasn't holding up under the pressure of seeing Lena in blue gauze that looked as if he could rip it right off her amazing body with no trouble at all.

''Maybe another time,'' she said. ''We should probably get going.''

''Right. I'll bet you made reservations.''

''Mmm.'' She looked apprehensive.

Damn, she was probably reading the contents of his fevered brain simply by looking in his eyes. He'd have to cool it or risk scaring her off for good. ''Does this place require a dinner jacket?'' he asked, trying to establish himself as a civilized guy who thought of such things.

''No jacket required. You'll be fine.''

''All right.'' This time as he started out the door, he checked to make sure he had his wallet and keys. ''Then let's go.''

''Nice tie,'' she said as they walked to the parking lot.

He glanced down, having completely forgotten which one he'd put on last. Then he compared the tie color with her dress and realized they matched. ''Well, if that doesn't look dorky. Want me to go back and change it?''

Her laughter sounded a little nervous, but she shook her head. ''I just thought it was interesting.''

''You don't care if we look like one of those sickening couples who plans stuff like this on purpose?''

''Um, it won't matter.''

''If you say so.'' He noticed they were headed for a silver Lexus and was glad he hadn't worn the teddy-bear tie. This woman had class oozing out of her pores. As she unlocked the car and he slid onto the leather bucket seat, he had a flash of how a gigolo might feel. The concept was fun to imagine, but in reality, he liked being the guy in charge, the one with the car keys and the reservations at a trendy restaurant.

Yes, she'd asked him out, and yes, he'd agreed to let her drive, but he'd be damned if he'd let her pay for five-star dining and wine at fifty bucks a bottle. And the evening was shaping up to be that kind.

As the Lexus purred to life, he cleared his throat. "Before we get to the restaurant, we need to have an understanding that I'm paying for dinner."

She pulled the car smoothly into traffic. "I asked you." She cleared her throat. "This…is on me."

"But I always planned to ask you out." Sitting here next to her and breathing her delicate floral perfume, he sincerely wished he'd taken the initiative a long time ago.

"You really did? You're not just saying that?"

"I really did. But you always seemed so…busy."

"Unapproachable is what you mean."

"Maybe a little bit. But you're focused on your career, and that's a good thing."

Her cheeks turned pink again. "The truth is I was scared of you."

Ah, so he'd been right. She was shy. "Then I must have seemed unapproachable, too."

"Not at all! More like you had it together."

"Which is exactly how I thought of you."

Her blush deepened. "If you're talking about my

career, then maybe. But when it comes to…oh, never mind. Let's not get into my insecurities.''

"You show me yours and I'll show you mine.''

"There, see what I mean? You can banter. I've never been able to banter with a guy.''

He was on more solid ground, now, feeling less like a gigolo and more like a supportive friend. "Sure you can banter. You're just subtle. Instead of saying Gee, your tie matches my outfit, and I think that's really strange, you said Nice tie. Understated humor.''

"If I hadn't been so nervous when you opened the door, I would have laughed when I saw the color of your tie.''

He grinned. "Maybe choosing the same color to wear tonight shows we're on the same wavelength.''

She shot him a quick glance and gave him a tentative smile. "Maybe so.''

"Let me buy dinner, Lena. It'll be so good for my ego to treat you to a great meal.''

"No! You see, it's not exactly…anyway, I'm paying.'' With that she flipped on the turn signal and pulled into the parking lot of a fast-food burger joint.

After the first jolt of surprise, Andre decided she might be one of those people who needed to have an iced tea or a soda going at all times. Maybe they had a longer drive ahead of them than he'd thought, and she wanted something to sip on. But when she parked instead of taking the drive-through lane, he was completely confused.

"Here we are.'' She didn't look at him as she unhooked her seat belt and reached for the door handle.

He laughed. "You're kidding, right?"

"I've, uh, been craving a cheeseburger all day." She didn't crack a smile. "You can have whatever you want—large fries, shake, the works."

She had to be pulling his leg. Had to be. She drove a Lexus, so he couldn't believe this was her idea of fine dining…unless she was weird.

He decided to act on the assumption that this was a joke and play along. Climbing out of the car, he joined her on the sidewalk that ran beside an indoor play area. It sounded like at least five hundred kids were in there.

"You bet I want a large order of fries," he said. "The fries are the best part." He reached out and opened the door for her.

She gave him an uncertain glance before heading inside. "I'm partial to the shakes, myself."

The interior was bedlam, crowded with families celebrating the end of the work week by taking the kids out for burgers. Two rug rats collided with Andre on their way out to the playground, and the woman ahead of them in line jiggled a screaming baby. Any minute Andre expected Lena to laugh and tell him this was all a big joke, but she moved steadily up toward the counter, as if she really intended to place an order.

Still, he couldn't believe it. When they'd nearly reached the head of the line, she turned to him, and he figured she'd come clean at last.

"The place is really full," she said.

Okay, here came the punch line. "I noticed." He smiled at her. "Think maybe we should try another restaurant?'' Like one that didn't serve dinner on a plastic tray?

"No, this will work, but maybe you'd better go hold down a table for us while I order. What do you want?"

He stared at her. "We're really eating here?"

"I thought we would. Don't you like it?" She looked completely sincere, and more than a little embarrassed.

And he was totally at sea, unable to figure out what was going on. Maybe she was up to her eyeballs in debt and this was all she could afford. Whatever the reason, it seemed that if he wanted to share a meal with Lena, he'd be doing it fast-food style.

If this was dinner, he wondered what she had in mind for the dancing and entertainment part of the evening. If she continued on this frugality kick, she might be taking him to her apartment where she'd crank up some tunes on her CD player. Hmm. He could live with that. Oh, yeah, he could definitely live with that.

He scanned the familiar menu. "A double cheeseburger, chocolate shake and a large order of fries would be great."

"My pleasure. There's a table over in the corner. If you hurry you should be able to snag it for us."

"I'm your guy." He worked his way out of line and over to the vacant table. One swipe of his hand got rid of the crumbs on the seat, but as he sat down he noticed that the collision with the rug rats earlier had left him with ketchup on his best slacks.

This wasn't at all the way he'd pictured this date, but maybe he'd be smart to let the chips—or in this case, fries—fall where they may. He had no idea why they were here. It could be a budget thing, or maybe Lena was into surprises and unconventional ideas. He liked that explanation better. Tightwads weren't his style.

He watched her move up to the counter and noticed the way the blue gauze skirt swirled around her long legs. She was wearing an ankle bracelet, and he'd always liked the way those looked on a woman. Oh, yeah, all sorts of exciting possibilities were swirling in the air tonight. His body began to hum in anticipation.

CHAPTER THREE

LENA WAS REASONABLY CERTAIN that Andre considered her a lunatic but was too polite to say so. Meanwhile, she was dying of embarrassment as she watched him pretend enthusiasm for a burger when he'd undoubtedly expected filet mignon. Surely he was counting the minutes until this weird date was over.

Even so, she had to admit there were advantages to this setup that wouldn't have come with your typical upscale eatery. For one thing, with such cramped quarters, her knees kept touching his under the table and their hands bumped as they reached for their shakes or grabbed for a fry.

Plus they were both eating with their hands, which gave an earthiness to the experience that knives and forks would have taken away. He licked his fingers and so did she. Watching him do that certainly gave her a sensual thrill. If only she knew whether the gleam in his eyes came from interest in her or because he was controlling hysterical laughter. Probably the second.

She'd always thought sitting across from a man at a table for two with candlelight, wine and soft music was the most intimate setting. Turns out she was wrong. Sure, kids at the next table were staging a loud battle with a squadron of action figures, and to her left a couple of teenage girls were shouting into their cell phones, but that meant she and Andre had to lean in close to carry on a conversation.

He was being a good sport, obviously using his salesman skills to try and put her at ease. As if she'd ever be at ease in this situation. First there was this ridiculous restaurant choice, and then there was the reality of leaning close to Andre, the hottest thing since sliced jalapeños. Those dark eyes and longish hair made her think of a bistro in Paris and walks by the Seine. She'd never been to France, but she could imagine being there with a man like Andre.

She'd admired his smile for weeks, but from eighteen inches away it made her weak with desire. Such a sensuous mouth. Such even white teeth. To kiss that mouth would be heaven. To feel it moving over her body would change her world forever. Too bad this nightmare date would kill any possibility of that happening.

"I think I know why you wanted to eat here," he said.

She'd been so preoccupied that she had to reconstruct his sentence in her head before she could answer. "You do?" He couldn't possibly know about the April Fools. She didn't want him to know, either. At least, not until later, much later. Maybe they could laugh about it one day. Yeah, right. And maybe Town Lake would freeze over.

"It's a brilliant idea. Usually when two people go on a date they're feeling a little awkward with each other. I was counting on a bottle of wine to help out with that, but this is better. The barriers are disappearing and yet we're both completely sober.''

The barriers are disappearing. Was he serious? Maybe he wasn't putting on an act, wasn't pretending to be having fun. What an amazing concept.

"You really took me by surprise, though," Andre said. "I was sure you'd start laughing any minute and tell me it was all a big joke."

"No. This was the plan." She couldn't believe he actually liked the idea, though. No doubt he was still being nice.

"But you didn't want to tell me that, and I get it. If you'd invited me out for fast food, that would have seemed very weird."

And this didn't? "So…would you have said yes?"

He looked into her eyes. "Uh-huh. If you'd asked me to share a bag of pretzels outside a convenience store, I would have said yes. But I would have thought you were strange. Sexy, but very strange.''

"You must still think I'm strange." But he'd called her sexy. A flush spread through her. *Sexy.*

"Innovative." He reached out and traced a finger along her arm. "You played it right, asking me to dinner and then surprising me with a burger and fries. Plus I don't feel bad because you ended up paying. It's been fun."

She couldn't believe how well this was working out. If she could skip the belly-dancing class, they might be on their way to a most excellent dating experience, in spite of the fast food, maybe even *because* of the fast food. But the April Fools were all about being uncomfortable, and she was getting way too comfortable with Andre. That meant it was time to push the boundaries some more, damn it.

She glanced at the empty cardboard burger container in front of him. "Are you about ready to go?"

"Sure am. I can hardly wait to see what else you have in store for me."

"A little dancing, if that's okay with you." Her tummy twisted with anxiety. If only she could take him to a trendy night spot. But that wasn't the assignment the April Fools had given her.

"Dancing sounds awesome." He glanced down at his slacks. "But I hope the lighting's not too good. I was tagged with some ketchup."

She flinched when she saw the stain on what looked like a very expensive pair of pants. "Oops, sorry. I don't suppose you could sponge it off."

"These are dry-clean only." He shrugged. "I'll bet nobody will even notice."

"I'll pay for the dry cleaning. I'm sure you wouldn't have worn those if you'd known where we were heading."

"Forget about the dry cleaning. The surprise value was worth it." He ushered her through the door and into the mild April night. "Listen, can I take off this tie before somebody asks if we perform our act locally?"

That made her laugh, in spite of being extremely nervous about phase two. "You can ditch the tie." She pulled her keys out of her purse and pushed the button on her key chain that unlocked the car.

"Good deal." Immediately he stripped off the tie, stuffed it in his pocket and unfastened the top two buttons of his shirt. Then he paused to look at her.

Her skin heated as she realized he'd caught her staring at him. She'd never seen Andre with his shirt unbuttoned. He had a sexy throat, the kind she'd love to nuzzle. Drawing in the scent of his aftershave, she hummed softly with delight.

He continued to hold her gaze. "I'm so glad you asked me out on this date."

"Me, too." She struggled to breathe normally. When a guy looked at you like that, it usually meant he was about to make a move.

He rested his hands lightly on her shoulders. Yep, he was making a move. And she so wanted him to. Once they got to the belly-dancing class, he'd lose all interest in making moves, except to run for the nearest exit.

His voice deepened. "To think we've been working in the same building for six months. What a colossal waste of valuable time."

"I know." Her heart thudded in anticipation. She'd imagined kissing Andre—what woman with a pulse wouldn't?—but she'd never imagined kissing him while standing next to a statue of a clown.

He lowered his head. "Let's not waste any more valuable time."

Let's not. She closed her eyes and lifted her mouth in invitation. When his lips touched hers, she recognized immediately that he was very good at this. His aim was dead-on perfect—no sliding around looking for the right position. He owned this position, and the steady pressure of his mouth there was slowly coaxing a surrender she could hardly wait to give. By the time she felt the slide of his tongue, she was aching for the next step, a *very* French kiss.

"Mommy, Mommy! Those peoples are kissing! Ooo, gross!"

With a groan, Andre released her. "Maybe this isn't the place."

"I...don't know." She gasped for breath and managed a wobbly grin. "Where are we?"

His answering smile made her knees quiver. "Now there's a compliment I can live with. Come on, let's get out of here. Want me to drive?"

With great reluctance, Lena shook her head. "Um, thanks, but I'll drive." She had to follow the plan, because that's what friends did when they'd made a pact with each other. Brandy and Meg would follow their instructions, so she could do no less. Fair was fair.

If she turned over the keys, Andre might take that as a signal to go somewhere private and continue with what they'd started. And she would love to do that. But she wouldn't let down her friends.

Still, she had to admit this date was already more potent than she ever could have imagined. Only an hour into it and they'd shared a kiss of epic proportions. She could hardly wait to find out what a second round would be like. Unfortunately, they had a belly-dancing class to attend first, and that might put an end to any more kissing, ever.

"Want to skip the dancing?" Andre's voice was laced with suggestive undertones.

More than you know. Lena took a deep breath and started the car. "No," she said. "I promised you dancing, and dancing you'll get."

He laughed. "Sounds as if you have this all scripted."

"I, uh…well…" She scrambled for an explanation.

"That's okay. I'll go with the flow."

Dear Lord, I hope so. She pulled the car into traffic and headed for the dance studio.

DESPITE BEING FRUSTRATED by the urge to go on kissing Lena, to do a whole lot more than kissing, Andre thought it was kind of cute the way she was sticking to her program. And maybe she had the right idea. That kiss had been super-charged, obviously throwing them both for a loop. One or two more like that and they might start ripping off each other's clothes.

He thought about the condom he'd stuck in the pocket of his slacks after getting dressed. He wasn't sure why he'd grabbed it. He certainly didn't expect to have sex with Lena on this first date. But that kiss had him wondering if they'd even be able to hold off until some future time. At the moment he didn't want to postpone a darned thing.

Maybe he should see how she stood on the matter. "From the way we reacted, I guess we've both been anticipating that moment for a while," he said.

Her hands tightened on the wheel. "You could say that." She swallowed. "But don't get the wrong idea. I don't generally—"

"Me, either. Not generally."

"I think it's good to get to know each other first."

"Absolutely."

They spoke in unison. "Tell me about your fam—" They broke off, laughing.

"You first," he said.

"But it's typical and boring."

"Mine, too."

She glanced at him. "With a name like Andre Dumont? I doubt it. Trust me, there's nothing exotic about my family."

"There's nothing exotic about mine, either." And for the first time in years, he threw away his trump card. "I'm not French."

"What do you mean, not French? Are you saying that's not really your name?"

"No, it's my name, but you'd have to go back about six generations before you'd get to a bona fide French guy from France." And then he confessed what he'd never told anyone else, that he'd been named after a brand of champagne. He waited for her to start laughing.

"But that's so cool!" she said. "Champagne is all about celebrating, the drink you serve at special occasions. I think it's a great thing to be named after."

"You do?" Suddenly he began to like the concept a little bit, himself.

"And it goes perfectly with your last name. Your mom must be fun."

"Well, she is." And he'd taken this name business way too seriously. He could see that now. How interesting that he'd been worried about Lena being too uptight, when it was apparently an issue for him, too. "So you're okay with the idea that I'm not really French?"

"I'm relieved, to tell the truth. I've always been afraid you were too sophisticated for me."

He glanced at her in admiration. "So you met that

head-on with a fast-food meal. I'm impressed. That takes guts."

"But you don't understand. I'm a coward."

"Not from where I'm sitting."

"But I am. From the cradle on I was conditioned to play it safe."

He blinked. "A woman who plays it safe doesn't march into a guy's office and ask him out."

"She does if she's trying to overcome that handicap."

A rush of tenderness caught him by surprise. He pictured her repairing her makeup and working up her courage to come to his office on Tuesday afternoon. "Thank you," he said. "Thank you for being brave."

"Thank you for saying yes."

He heard the quiver in her voice and remembered how nervous she'd been that day. "You didn't think I would, did you?"

She shook her head.

"That makes you braver yet."

"Yeah." She chuckled. "I'm a regular Joan of Arc."

"I'm beginning to think so. I—" He paused when she turned into the parking lot of the YWCA. "Okay, I'm confused. I thought we were going dancing."

"We are. This is the place."

"O…kay." He unsnapped his seat belt and opened the car door, all the while picturing Big Band music and orange sherbet punch. "Might be a little more wholesome than what I had in mind, but I can deal." He waited until she'd locked the car and joined him on the sidewalk. "I need to ask one thing, though."

"What's that?"

"I know you said all that about liking my name because champagne is so festive, but we seem to be hitting all the spots where drinking wouldn't be possible. Is that on purpose?"

"No." She smiled at him as they walked toward the building. "Pure coincidence. I drink champagne. I like all sorts of alcohol, in fact. I'm especially fond of Chianti."

"No kidding? I love Italian food, and I haven't had any in forever. There's this place I've been meaning to try—Caesar's. We should go there sometime." Then he hesitated, realizing he'd just made an assumption. "That is, if you think you want to go out again."

"I would like to go out again," she said softly. "But maybe you'd better wait and see how tonight turns out before you commit yourself."

He laughed as he held the door for her. "What are you planning to do, put me through a Jazzercise class?"

When she didn't answer, he experienced a tingle of anxiety. But the muted music filtering down the hallway wasn't exercise music. Nope, this stuff was in a minor key and reminded him of snake charmers, spicy food and....

No, it couldn't be. Surely not. Guys didn't do that kind of thing. Then she opened the door, allowing him a glimpse inside. *Belly dancing.*

CHAPTER FOUR

FROM THE DOORWAY at the back of the room, Lena peeked inside. The warmup had begun, and all eight women were facing the wall of mirrors at the front. Lena's gaze halted abruptly as she spotted two familiar figures in the far corner. *Brandy and Meg.* They'd crashed the lesson. She'd kill them.

The instructor, an olive-skinned woman named Diana, turned and beckoned to Lena and Andre. "Welcome, Andre, Lena," she said in a sultry voice while she continued undulating to the music. "Take off your shoes and join us."

"She means just you, right?" Andre muttered.

"She means both of us." Lena glared at her soon-to-be-ex-friends standing in the front row. By looking in the mirror, they could see her perfectly. Their faces were red, as though they were both ready to crack up, but they somehow managed to gaze straight ahead, as if the music had put them in a trance.

"But I don't know how to do this," Andre said under his breath.

"Me, either," she murmured, slipping off her shoes to stand barefoot on the smooth wooden floor. She was so ticked off at Brandy and Meg that she forgot to be embarrassed that she'd brought Andre here. In fact, she was utterly determined to follow

through now. She would show them who else had
solid brass ones. "It's a class. She'll teach us."

"But there aren't any guys."

The hint of panic in his voice finally registered,
and instantly her determination vanished. She might
have something to prove to Brandy and Meg, but he
shouldn't have to suffer to help her accomplish that.
She'd brought him to a belly-dancing class. He must
be freaking out.

She swallowed. "Let's forget it," she said, wondering if there was any way she could erase his impression that she was nuttier than a Baby Ruth. "It
was a silly idea."

He studied her for a moment. Then he glanced
over at the women rotating their hips. "You really
don't know how, either?"

"I've had one class, last week. I'm still very much
a beginner." Which was the whole point for the
April Fools, to humiliate herself. But enough was
enough. "It's no big deal. We can leave."

He nudged off his expensive-looking loafers.
"You were right about the fast food. You're probably right about this, too."

Her heart gave a jolt. He trusted her to make the
right call. That was huge, and she felt the responsibility of it, especially considering the way their job
situation would change on Monday. She felt dishon-
est for not telling him about that, yet. "Listen, you
really don't have to."

"I'm guessing I should also take off the socks."

"Yes, but—"

"The bonus is that I get to watch you doing those
sexy moves." He winked at her, pulled off both

socks and tucked them inside his shoes. "Let's boo-gie."

"You have nice feet." Ai-yi-yi! Had she really said that out loud?

"Thanks. So do you."

Apparently she *had* said it out loud. And apparently they were going to spend an hour together learning to belly dance. "Thank you," she mumbled, her face hot as she walked quickly over to a spot behind the second row of four women.

Andre positioned himself beside her. "Just don't spread the word about this to any of the people at work," he whispered. "I'd never hear the end of it."

"I won't." Guilt threatened to swamp her. But she couldn't think of a graceful way out.

"Roll those hips," Diana crooned. "Get loose. Get supple."

Andre swung his pelvis in a circle, glanced at Lena and smiled. "Come on. Get with the program."

"Right." She tried to swivel her hips the way she'd been taught last week, but self-consciousness made her stiff and awkward. She couldn't *believe* she'd dragged Andre into this, or that she was actu-ally dancing in front of him.

He watched her in the mirror. "Loosen up," he murmured.

"I shouldn't have brought you here."

"Hey, don't give up on the idea, yet."

Apparently he was accepting the concept better than she was. "You're picking up on this really well, better than I did the first time."

"Ah, I'm just fooling around."

She worked to adopt his attitude, making a concentrated effort to relax and have fun.

"That's better," he said.

"Thanks." She decided to focus her attention on him instead of watching herself, which was painful. And boy, did he have moves.

"Very nice, Andre," Diana called out. "A little more bend to the knees. That's it. Now a little shimmy. Good!"

Lena's scarf tied at her hips rippled as she moved, which had been her intention back when she'd fantasized she could actually do this thing without fainting. Andre couldn't seem to take his eyes off that scarf, while she was totally engrossed in the subtle movement of his hips. He had no right to be so good at belly dancing.

And then it came to her. He had the loose hips of an outstanding lover. Watching him in the mirror, she barely had to use her imagination to picture him backing her up against that mirror and having his way with her. This class, which was supposed to be a joke, was morphing from a major embarrassment to an incredible turn-on.

"Hip, hip, shimmy, drop," Diana chanted, demonstrating the motion as she began to circle the room. "Use your butt. That's it. Excellent. *Everyone* is doing a fabulous job."

Lena couldn't speak for herself or anyone else in the class, but Andre had it going on. When he grinned at her in the mirror, she came to the surprising conclusion that, once again, he was having a blast. Meanwhile, Brandy and Meg were so busy watching him that they danced right into each other, colliding with a smack of bodies and a yelp of pain. Served them right.

"Body awareness." Diana's dulcet tones drifted through the erotic music. "Body awareness is everything."

Isn't that the truth? As Lena's self-consciousness faded, she realized that she'd never felt this sexy in her life. Maybe it had something to do with the messages Andre flashed when he caught her gaze in the mirror.

At the rate the dancing was going, they would both need that round of goofy golf to cool down. Without it, they were liable to climb in the back seat of her car and go to it. She couldn't let that happen.

In the mirror, she watched his swiveling hips. Sex must be second nature to him. He might not think he was very French, but he danced as though he was free of the inhibitions most American men had.

And for tonight, he was all hers.

ANDRE WAS LEARNING more than belly dancing tonight. He was also discovering that following the normal dating script led to predictable and boring evenings. Lena wasn't into that, and because of her creative approach he was fast becoming her slave, ready to do anything she asked of him.

Who knew that belly dancing in a class at the Y would be more like foreplay than any smoky dance floor in the city? Instead of the usual routine—fast dancing followed by slow dancing followed by even slower dancing and suggestive body contact—he was gyrating side-by-side with Lena and watching her in a mirror. And the effect on his libido was ten times greater than if they'd gone to a nightclub.

The longer they danced like this, the looser and more aroused he became. Fortunately the intense concentration on the instruction kept his bad boy under control, but once they were out of this studio, he planned to talk Lena into a visit to his apartment. Yes, it was probably too soon, but he was willing to take the chance. He had a hunch she might be willing, too.

Sex on the first date wasn't *always* a mistake, especially if two people had been fantasizing about each other for months, and if the date was designed to rip off the masks most couples wore on a first date.

Lena was obviously willing to be less than perfect in front of him.

"Now let's work on our arm positions," the instructor said. "Lift them like this, as if you're giving an invisible person a big hug."

Andre tried, but this wasn't quite as natural as swiveling his hips. Lena excelled at this part, lifting her arms with the grace of a ballet dancer. He looked as if he was holding an imaginary garbage can.

He was concentrating so hard on his arm position that he didn't realize the instructor had circled the room and moved in behind him.

"That's good, Andre, but you need to lift your elbows a little more, and raise your rib cage. Thrust your chest out." She cupped his elbows and positioned them. "There you go. Isn't that better?"

He felt like an imbecile. "I don't think men's arms are engineered to do this."

"Oh, but they are," the instructor said. "Haven't you ever seen male gypsies dance?"

"Can't say that I have."

"Very potent."

Potent. He liked the sound of that. If lifting his elbows and throwing out his chest made him look potent, he'd give it a shot.

"Wonderful. Keep it up." The instructor glided over toward Lena. "You have lots of potential," she said. "I hope you continue with the classes."

Andre hoped she would, too. He had a sudden image of Lena dancing privately for him. He'd like to see her in an outfit like the instructor wore—her belly bare and her cleavage emphasized by a sequined halter. Maybe it would have fringe on it that shook when she—

"Now lift your arms and rotate your wrists like this," said the instructor. "Pretend your have finger cymbals that you're using to keep time with the music. Undulating movements."

Watching himself in the mirror, Andre thought he looked like a man who'd stumbled on a hive of bees. But he wasn't any worse than the blonde and the redhead in the far corner, who kept giggling and crashing into each other. Lena was amazing, though. After riding out that rough spot in the beginning, she'd gradually turned into a temptress in blue, her bracelets tinkling as she moved. She made his mouth water.

He doubted his arm-wiggling routine was doing much for her, though. He'd felt damned studly when all they had going on was the hip shimmy, but getting his arms to do the snaky thing the instructor wanted interfered with his shimmy. Therefore he was immensely grateful when the instructor finally raised her arms high in the air, did a dramatic spin timed to the ending of the song, and declared the class over.

Lena turned to him, still breathing fast from the exercise. Her face was flushed and her eyes bright. He wanted to kiss her so much he couldn't see straight.

"Thank you for putting up with that," she said, her voice breathless. "You were—"

"Waving my arms like a crazed symphony conductor," he said. "But it doesn't matter." Nothing mattered but getting her alone. He wanted to hold her, kiss her, lose himself in her. She looked delicious right now, all worked up and trembly.

But the blonde and the redhead rushed up as he was about to suggest beating a fast retreat. The blonde spoke first. "What a good sport you are!" She stuck out her hand. "Hi. I'm Brandy. I'm a friend of Lena's."

"That's a matter of opinion," Lena said.

"Oh, Lena," said the redhead. "You knew we'd want to meet Andre. I'm Meg, by the way."

Andre shook her hand, too. God, he hoped these two weren't about to horn in and suggest they all go out for coffee. But he wanted to be polite, in case these were people Lena cared about. "Are you both beginners like me?"

"Gee, could you tell?" Meg grinned. "Brand new. Never tried this before. But we heard Lena was bringing you so we signed up for the class. Otherwise, no telling when she'd see fit to introduce us. She's very close-mouthed, that one."

"For good reason, obviously," Lena said.

Brandy didn't look the least bit sorry. "If you'd mentioned Andre before this, we might not have had to sneak around to meet him." She turned to Andre. "And it's been a pleasure. You were awesome to stick out the whole class."

"I absolutely agree," Meg said. "Well, we have to toddle along. You two have a good time with the rest of your evening."

"Thanks." With a sense of relief that his plans to be alone with Lena weren't ruined, Andre braced himself against the wall so he could put on his socks and shoes. "So you told them you were bringing me to this class?"

"They knew about it." Lena seemed uneasy. "But I never in a million years expected them to show up."

"Hey, it's okay. I have nothing against getting to know your friends." *Especially when they have the good sense to leave us alone.* "Ready to go?"

"Yes. Just let me speak with Diana a minute."

"Sure." Shoving his hands in his pockets, he watched her walk barefoot across the polished wood floor, and lust sucker-punched him in the gut. He thought about her plans for the night—the fast food, the belly dancing, and something she'd called *light entertainment.* It all added up to a planned seduction, didn't it?

The more he considered the chain of events, the more he was convinced that Lena had specifically designed this date to make him drool, and he was slobbering for sure. He hoped that her idea of light entertainment coincided with his. Light entertainment had to mean cruising back to her apartment, putting some tunes on the sound system, finally cracking open a bottle of wine, and cuddling on her sofa.

And once they were alone in a setting like that, the outcome was inevitable. At the thought that he might be less than an hour away from getting naked with Lena, he struggled to control a natural reaction. He didn't want her to turn around and discover he had a noticeable bulge in his pants. He didn't want to come across as lustful and crude, even though that pretty much described his condition at the moment.

Her conversation with the instructor seemed to take forever, but at last she walked back to him, a soft smile on her face. "Diana congratulates you. She says you're welcome in the class anytime."

He felt ridiculously pleased by that. Of course he probably wouldn't come back, but he liked being wanted. "It was fun, but I'm not sure it's my thing."

"I thought you did very well." She slipped on her shoes and her cute little ankle bracelet jiggled.

"I thought you were spectacular."

She laughed. "I have a long way to go."

"But you'll keep up with it?"

"I might. Ready to leave?"

He was definitely ready to leave. "Sure." He followed her through the open classroom door and down the hall. "Friday night seems like kind of a strange time to have a class like that, though." He was already thinking ahead to taking long weekends with Lena this summer, maybe over to San Diego.

She didn't respond until they were outside and walking toward the car. "I should probably tell you that the class isn't normally on a Friday night. It's scheduled for Wednesday.''

Something in her voice made him glance over at her. "So why the switch?" He had a hunch he knew, although it seemed incredible.

"I, um, set it up as a special deal."

"Just for our date?" He still couldn't quite believe it.

She nodded.

"So everyone in that room took an extra class this week so that you could bring me in on it?" In a way he was flattered that she'd go to so much trouble, but he didn't appreciate being part of an experiment, either.

"Trust me, it was no hardship. They were all curious as to how you'd react."

He turned to face her. "Lena, are you *testing* me?"

"No! I promise I'm not testing you."

"It sure seems that way."

"I'll bet it does. But I'm not. I just want this date to be…different."

He gazed at her, and realized that no matter what her motives were, she'd succeeded in getting his complete attention. "Mission accomplished," he said softly. "So what's next?" He mentally crossed his fingers and hoped she'd suggest going back to her place.

"Goofy golf."

CHAPTER FIVE

LENA CRINGED at Andre's expression of dismay. Of course he didn't want to play goofy golf. Only an idiot would want to cap off the evening dodging whirling windmills and navigating bumpy artificial turf. She could guess what he wanted to do instead. Something adult, like a makeout session on a soft couch.

She wanted to do the exact same thing, especially after getting hot and bothered in the dance class. A cool evening breeze caressed her damp skin, reminding her of another activity that also would bathe her in sweat. Oh, yeah, she wanted to do that...someday. But it wouldn't be happening tonight.

"Goofy golf." Andre repeated her answer in a monotone.

"Sure!" Oh, God, this was so ridiculous. He might have been interested before, but this would kill it for sure. "When was the last time you played a round?" She unlocked the car and walked over to the driver's side.

"I think I was sixteen." He climbed into the car.

She slid into her seat and closed the door. "I'll bet you had fun." She tried to calculate whether Brandy and Meg's surprise appearance at the dance class canceled her obligation to follow through with goofy golf. Probably not, damn it.

"Well, sure I had fun. I mean, how much is there to do when you're a clueless sixteen-year-old?"

Yep, he hated this idea. Lena started the car and pulled out of the parking lot. She doubted he'd been clueless at sixteen, doubted he'd ever been clueless. "Did you have a girlfriend?"

"Uh-huh. And what a disaster that was. I thought she'd broken my heart for good."

She looked over at him, relieved to be talking about something other than this dumb golf gig. "So what happened? Did she leave you for the star quarterback?"

"Are you kidding? I *was* the star quarterback."

She should have known. He'd been a cool guy back then, too. "So how did she break your heart?"

"She dumped me because I was a desperate virgin who wanted to have sex with the first girl I'd ever loved. I tried not to let on what I was after, but she could tell. She said I was a nasty boy."

"And were you?"

"Guess so. Still am."

His implication was obvious. And she was more excited than she cared to admit, wondering what this nasty boy might have in mind for her. Instead she was required to derail all his nasty impulses by forcing him to play goofy golf. "So what about you?" he asked. "Did you break some poor teenager's heart?"

If only she had, then she'd appear more worldly. But she was a terrible liar. "I didn't have a serious boyfriend in high school."

"That's hard to believe."

She gave him an A-plus for gallantry. "Not if you met my parents. They scared me to death with stories of girls who got pregnant and ruined their lives. They said the only form of birth control guaranteed to work was keeping your legs crossed."

"Oh, God, you sound like my first girlfriend! She used to say that to me all the time. So I'd try to control myself and pretend that kissing her didn't drive me insane, but every Saturday night make-out session produced an obvious physical reaction and she was offended. She said if I respected her I wouldn't get that way."

"My parents used to say that nice boys didn't have those kinds of ideas."

"Then I've never met a nice boy, because any guy I've ever known, especially at that age, is completely focused on getting some…well, anyway." He cleared his throat. "You know, I always wondered if Ellen got as worked up as I did during those nights we'd go parking out on some lonely road. I never got my hand close enough to her panties to find out."

"She probably did." Lena had no doubt. It was happening to her, just talking about make-out sessions with Andre.

His voice grew husky. "What makes you say that?"

"No fair."

"Sure it's fair. I'll play goofy golf if that's what you want to do. But I have to tell you, that belly-dancing class had quite an effect on me. I'm in better control of myself than I was at sixteen, but I still want to know if you're messing with my mind."

Lena was glad that they'd arrived at the entrance for the miniature golf course, because his direct question had her shaking. She parked the car and turned off the engine before facing him. "I had no idea how you'd react to any of this."

"I believe that." His gaze burned into hers. "So I'm telling you my reaction, straight out. I want you, Lena."

A tremor passed through her. "This is our first date."

His expression softened immediately. "Yeah. Yeah, you're right. I'm coming on too strong. I—"

"It's okay." She couldn't let him take the blame. "I'm…I'm more involved than I thought I'd be at this stage." Understatement of the year. She wanted him desperately. If they didn't leave the car soon, she'd either attack him or start chewing on the steering wheel. "But it *is* still our first date." That was her story and she was sticking to it.

"Maybe miniature golf is a good idea." He opened his door. "I'll even give you a handicap."

AS IT TURNED OUT, Andre struggled to keep the score even. On the first hole he let her putt first, figuring it was the gentlemanly thing to do. He hadn't counted on lust kicking in when she leaned over to place her red ball on the rubber mat. Cleavage city.

He was still thinking about that outstanding view when he positioned his blue ball on the mat, whacked it right past the hole, over the brick border and into the bushes.

His game never recovered. He became mesmerized by the way Lena moistened her lips before she stroked the ball into the hole—so mesmerized that he had to be reminded to take his turn. Her fingers curled around the shaft of the club created even more sensual images.

Grabbing a kiss was out of the question with chaperones to the front of them and chaperones to the rear. They followed a family with two little girls, and behind them three rowdy teenage boys kept him on the straight and narrow.

Left with little choice, he pretended to care about the game, when all he wanted was to see the marker for the eighteenth hole. Maybe he wouldn't get what he really wanted at the end of this golf game, but he'd settle for being allowed to kiss those full lips of hers. If she wanted to keep things light on the first date, he'd work with that. And he'd start making plans for the second date, and the third and the fourth.

He was so involved in the potential of future dates that he didn't notice the configuration of the sixteenth hole until after Lena hit her ball into a dimly lit cave and followed it inside. A quick glance told Andre the cup was inside the cave, too.

After turning back to check the position of the high-school jocks, he discovered that horsing around had left them a full hole behind. He might have a good sixty seconds in the cave with Lena. If he had his way, they would be a *very* good sixty seconds. Pocketing his ball, he walked into the cave.

She looked surprised. "I didn't see you putt in."

"That's because I'm conceding this one." He stepped closer and dropped his club to the artificial turf. "Instead I thought we could do a little fooling around."

"Andre, I don't think—"

"Just one kiss, Lena. One kiss to keep me going. That's all I ask."

Her mouth, the object of his quest, turned up at the corners. "Okay."

Green light. He pulled her into his arms and closed the distance between his lips and hers with a groan of impatience. Briefly he wondered if deprivation had made him exaggerate the effect of her kiss. Nope. Once he made contact he was in the pleasure zone.

Time stopped. His focus narrowed to the sensation of the kiss, so erotic it made his knees weak. Her mouth promised, teased and finally opened to the thrust of his tongue. His erection bloomed, and he cupped her tight bottom, settling her against him so that she'd have no doubt of his ultimate intentions.

And she wiggled closer.

Lost to everything but the hot woman snuggling in his arms, he backed her up against the wall of the cave. His brain swirled with thoughts of cleavage and damp panties. God knows what he might have tried next if a golf ball hadn't hit his foot with a solid thump.

Muttering a soft curse, he released her. "We have company. Let's go." He picked up the ball and tossed it back through the opening.

The response from outside the cave was immediate. "Whoa, dude, check it out! Major rebound!"

Stuffing Lena's ball in his other pocket, Andre grabbed both clubs in one hand and her arm in the other. "Let's get out of here."

She was breathing hard. "But we haven't finished this hole."

"Ask me if I care."

"We need to—"

"No, we don't."

At first it looked as if she might actually pull away from him, but at last she allowed him to lead her out of the cave. "We'll just go on to seventeen, then."

He stared at her, unable to believe after melting his circuits she'd want to keep playing this silly game. "How about if we bag the whole program?"

"We have to finish."

"Let's not and say we did! Lena, what difference does it make?"

"After we play the last two holes, I'll explain. I promise I will."

He knew he was getting cranky and took a deep breath. "I'm confused," he said more gently. "When I kiss you, you seem ready for anything, but then…then you act like we're following some blueprint."

"I can see why you'd think that." She angled her head toward the next hole. "Can you humor me a little longer? It's only two more and then I'll explain."

"After this explanation, *then* can we have a little private time?"

"Well…" She looked uncertain. "I'm worried about what you'll think of me if we take it too fast."

He reached out and touched her arm. "I'm worried about what you'll think of me, too, okay? I promise not to think poorly of you if you won't think poorly of me. Lena, we have fireworks going on here. I don't have a first-date rule, but if you do, then maybe after we finish the game you should take me home.''

"That would be the sensible thing, huh?''

"Guess so.'' His sense of humor came back. "Hey, what if you took me home, said goodbye and then drove around the block? Could we start on our second date if you came back in ten minutes?''

She laughed. "It does seem kind of ridiculous, doesn't it? If either one of us had been more assertive, we'd have started dating months ago.''

"Right. So by now, we'd be on our fifty-second date, at least.''

She smiled and held out her hand. "I can see why you're one of Thunderbird's top salesmen. Now give me my ball so we can wrap up this match.''

He handed it over. "We really have to finish?''

"We really do.''

He sighed and shook his head. "I don't get it.''

"I'll explain.''

He didn't want explanations. He wanted Lena, naked.

AS LENA WATCHED Andre struggle through the last two holes of goofy golf, she knew she had to tell him about the April Fools. That might ruin everything between them, but if she didn't tell him, he'd think she was some sort of anal dweeb who stuck to her plan no matter what. Besides, with the way this date was going, she'd eventually want him to know about the April Fools. She'd want him to know everything about her.

Including the fact that you'll soon be his boss? nagged the voice of her conscience. Yes, but she couldn't dump everything on him at once, could she? The April Fools were the least explosive of the two pieces of information. She'd see how he reacted to that, first.

His score for the last two holes was even worse than it had been for the previous sixteen.

"Are you sure you've done this before?" she teased as they turned in their putters at the front counter.

"Yeah, but never under such challenging conditions." He took her hand as they walked out to the car.

The snug feel of his fingers laced through hers made her think of bodies intertwined, wrapped together, fervently seeking satisfaction. "What do you mean? The weather's perfect."

"I happen to think it's hotter than the inside of a pizza oven around here."

In the glow of the parking-lot lights she caught the gleam in his eye. "Are you hinting that you were distracted?"

"Forget the hints. I'll just say it. You took advantage of me. Ruined my short game. If there had been a long game involved, you would have ruined that, too."

She grinned and realized she was having a fantastic time, better than she ever would have envisioned when she'd thought about this dating challenge. "But I didn't even flirt with you!"

"Hell, no, you didn't flirt. Flirting's for sissies. You skipped that completely in favor of flashing me some cleavage every time you positioned your ball. You'll never convince me that was an accident."

"Not exactly." Not after the first time, when she'd heard his quick gasp and had realized she'd been the cause of it. She'd been fascinated by her own power and couldn't resist testing it again…and again. She knew it wasn't fair to tease him when they wouldn't be having sex tonight, but they would have sex sometime, as long as he didn't blow a fuse when he heard the two secrets she was keeping.

"Just as I thought. You've been intentionally driving me nuts." Although his voice was light, there was an underlying huskiness to it. "And I'm afraid that, by the end of this date, I'm going to be certifiable."

If only she could invite him over to her apartment and be done with it. Maybe next week she would, after the promotion had taken effect and they knew how it affected their relationship. During the golf game she'd had time to think about that. Dating her might change Andre's life in ways he wouldn't appreciate. Dana could insist on transferring him out of the office, and he might not want to make that kind of sacrifice for the privilege of having a relationship with her.

She glanced at him. "Want to go for coffee?"

"Not particularly." As they reached the car he stepped around in front of her, blocking her path. "I want to be alone with you."

She gulped. "Before we make that kind of move, I need to talk to you about something." *A couple of things, actually.*

Briefly he looked uncertain, but he quickly covered it with a smile. "Please don't tell me you used to be a guy named Leroy. I'm too fragile to handle that kind of news.''

"No gender switches, I promise."

"Then whatever it is, I'm sure we can deal with it.'' He brought her hand up to his lips and kissed her fingers. "I'd like to deal with it. I'm so ready to deal with it.''

"Well…'' She wondered how best to tell him about the April Fools. They'd been able to talk freely in the car, so maybe that was the answer. "Let's take a little drive,'' she said.

"Great. My apartment qualifies as a little drive from here.''

"Um, I want to drive around some before…'' She gazed into his gorgeous eyes and wondered if she was the biggest fool in the world to put off the inevitable. Good sex could make a guy very mellow. Maybe he'd take her revelations much better after a nice satisfying roll in the hay. And if not, at least she'd have one hot memory as her consolation prize. "You know, maybe you're right. Maybe—''

"Let's drive around,'' he said softly. "When we get together, I want you to feel good about it. I want it to be right.''

Reality check. So did she. She'd been trying to rationalize the issue because she wanted him as much as he wanted her. "Thank you for not pushing your advantage.''

"You're welcome. But I need to give you fair warning…next time, I'm pushing.''

CHAPTER SIX

As THEY CLIMBED into the car, Andre was going nuts trying to imagine what Lena had to tell him before they could have sex. In the time she took to start the car and drive out of the parking lot, he envisioned a dozen horrible scenarios, all of them guaranteed to turn heaven into hell. Meanwhile he tried to act relaxed, as if he could accept anything she cared to throw at him. And that was pretty much true, considering the intensity of his lust.

Lena cleared her throat. "Okay, remember those two women we met at the belly-dancing class?"

"Yep." What if she was involved with one of them and he was her practice date to see if she could like guys? Well, he was up to that challenge. Bring it on.

"When we met four years ago we decided to start our own special group."

"Uh-huh." Maybe involving kinky stuff. Well, some kinky stuff was okay with him, but he had limits. Or did he? She looked so good sitting there in the darkened car, so luscious, so tempting. Ah, limits, schlimits.

"The group is designed to push us out of our comfort zones," Lena said.

"Oh, really?" Thinking of what that could mean

made his voice squeak with eagerness. He hated it when that happened, when his suave got all screwed up. He cleared his throat and lowered his voice to a manly pitch. "Like how?"

Lena stopped the car at a red light. "Sometime around April Fool's Day every year, we assign each other an activity that is potentially embarrassing. In other words, we agree to make fools of ourselves. It's amazing how much more confident we've all become in our business lives, and how our careers have benefited from taking those risks."

"Oh." Slowly his image of sex orgies faded, replaced by the suspicion that he'd been a means to an end. "So that's what the fast food and belly dancing and goofy golf were all about? Career advancement?"

"No!" She looked flustered. "No, I said it wrong. This is about personal growth, too, and—"

"So I'm like a workshop exercise?" Disappointment settled in his gut.

"No!"

"But the April Fool's thing made you ask me out, not the sudden urge to get together." Here he'd thought he'd pulled her in on the tractor beam of his manly appeal when in reality all she'd needed was a guy to go along with the program.

"It's not like that. I've been wanting to ask you out for months, but I didn't have the nerve. Then along came my assignment from Brandy and Meg, giving me the push I needed to do what I've wanted to do for a long time."

He felt a little better hearing that she'd been

dreaming about him for months. "So they thought up the activities?"

"They did."

Too bad. He'd enjoyed the idea that she was a little wild and unconventional.

"You've been a good sport, going along with this craziness."

He took a deep breath. "Well, I must be crazy, myself, because I had a good time. A great time. I thought the plan was some brilliant strategy to cut through the usual dating garbage."

She met that with a moment of silence. "In other words, I'd have been ahead of the game if I hadn't admitted anything."

And she'd been under no obligation to do that, either. The possible significance of her confession finally made an impression on him. "Why *did* you tell me?"

Her shoulder moved in a slight shrug. "I decided I had to."

"You had to...because?"

"Because a moment ago it seemed like we were heading toward...oh, never mind. Maybe I should just take you home."

Oh, excellent. They were back on the right track. So what if she'd been following orders? "We were heading exactly where you thought we were heading, and I don't want you to take me home." He had a sudden inspiration. "In fact, I have an idea that would fit in perfectly with the spirit of this date."

Her throat moved in a slow swallow. "What?"

"Let's go parking."

PARKING. Lena couldn't remember the last time she'd done that. "You mean go somewhere and make out a little?" She quivered with eagerness.

"Or a lot." He reached over and laid his hand on her thigh. "We've been acting like high-school kids all night." He rubbed her thigh and the thin material of her skirt shifted under his palm. "Why not stay in character?"

"It's an insane idea." And she was all for it. Sure, it was risky to her plan of containment. Alone in a dark car with Andre, she might abandon all caution. But if one hand on her thigh felt this exciting, she could imagine the results if he brought both hands into the equation.

Maybe she was rationalizing, but kissing in the car sounded manageable. With no bed in sight, she wouldn't allow herself to get too carried away, as in total sexual immersion. They were too old for back-seat sex, for heaven's sake. It wasn't seemly.

A sense of dignity would keep her from taking that ultimate step until after she revealed Secret Number Two, that she was about to become his boss. She could tell him now, of course. Man, talk about a mood breaker.

No, they could fool around a little, and maybe then she'd tell him.

Or not. She'd really prefer to have that conversation on the phone.

He squeezed her thigh. "Turn right here."

Hormones took over her brain. If she didn't get some mouth-to-mouth with this guy soon, she'd be a danger to herself and others. She flipped on the turn signal and headed down the street.

"Right at the next light."

Her skirt had scrunched up, either by accident or design, and now his hand lay on her bare thigh. The heat generated by his palm against her skin was enough to get an Alaskan through the winter.

Somehow she maintained control of the car as he directed her up a winding road that ended at what would soon be a new housing development. A few lots had been graded and one foundation poured. Lena circled the cul-de-sac and parked facing the way they'd come. The lights of Phoenix lay spread out before them.

She shut off the engine and took a shaky breath. "Nice view." If he moved his hand up about six inches, the view would be wasted on her.

"I looked at property here." His fingers brushed her inner thigh, but his tone was conversational, as if he had no idea he was turning her inside out with anticipation. "A little too rich for my blood at the moment, but maybe someday."

"You want a house?" She turned to look at him. The interior of the car was dark, but she could still make out his features, still catch the reflected sparkle of the city lights in his eyes.

"I don't want a house right now." He ended his subtle caress and unfastened his seat belt. Then he faced her. "Right now I have other things on my mind. Like getting you out of that harness."

"Oh!" She realized she'd been staring at him without moving, hypnotized by the possibilities. She glanced down, fumbling for the latch of her seat belt.

Gently he guided her hand away. "Let me."

Her gaze locked with his and her breath caught as

he slowly released the buckle. Apparently this man knew his way around a seduction. She needed to be extremely careful.

Holding the metal fastening, he glanced at where the shoulder strap lay between her breasts. "Has anyone ever told you that you do wonders for a seat belt?"

Her answer was breathy. "No."

He allowed the seat belt's tension to draw the strap up, bringing his hand with it. "This night's put all kinds of ideas in my head. Just now I was thinking what it would be like to make out with you while you were still belted in." His hand rested just below her breast. "Sort of Bondage Light."

Her heart thundered with excitement. She'd imagined Andre as a daring lover, and he was proving her right.

He moved the strap back and forth so it rubbed her breast. "But we can save that for another time."

The friction teased her already tight nipple and she began to quiver in anticipation.

He leaned closer, still using the strap to caress her as he slipped his free hand beneath the hair at the nape of her neck. "Mmm, you're damp here."

She was damp in other places, too. She wondered if he guessed. "It seems you're turning me on."

He smiled. "It seems you're turning me on, too. Kissing you has become my favorite thing."

Kissing me where, exactly? She'd have to watch herself. She was consumed with thoughts that went way beyond a simple make-out session. Well, he'd started it with the seat belt bondage comment.

"I knew I couldn't let you get away tonight without another taste." He drifted closer, only inches from her mouth.

She struggled for breath. "As it happens, I'm...getting rather fond of your kisses, too."

"That's good. Because I plan to give you all you can handle." His mouth brushed hers as he continued to rub the seat belt strap against her breast.

The scent of him—showered, shaved and very aroused—sent tingles through her system and moisture between her thighs. She leaned into the kiss, wanting more.

With a low chuckle, he gave her what she wanted—his mouth, his tongue, and at long last, his hand cradling her breast.

And still that wasn't enough. She gripped his head in both hands and deepened the kiss, breathing in the musky tang of sexual promise. As she tried to maneuver closer, the awkward bucket seats and the console between them became her bitter enemies.

The solid clunk of his knee connecting with the console clinched the deal; they needed to move. Easing away from his hungry mouth, she whispered "back seat" and reached behind her for the door handle.

"I'm there," he murmured.

In seconds they'd both exited the front seat, slammed the doors and climbed into the back, where they slid across the leather seat toward each other as if magnetized. Lena had had some teenage experience with back seat make-out sessions, but in those days she'd been consorting with boys. Now she had a fully aroused man thrusting his tongue into her mouth, untying the scarf from her hips, slipping his hand under her blouse to unhook her bra.

A wiser woman might have tried to stop him, knowing she could easily lose control of the situation. But desire was consuming Lena's brain cells at an alarming rate. And Andre operated with such expertise that a girl could only swoon and give in. To do otherwise would be interrupting the work of a sexual artist.

That explained why she eventually found herself naked from the waist up, even her bangle bracelets gone, with her legs sprawled over his thighs. She leaned her head back and sighed with delight while he used his talented mouth on her breasts. She had a hunch that her dignity was suffering.

The rest of her, however, was having a great time. There were men who knew how to pleasure a woman's nipples and men who did not. Andre belonged solidly in group A. He was working her into a frenzy, and from the bulge nudging her right thigh, she gathered the frenzy was mutual.

Oh, dear. Now she was thinking the unthinkable again, namely, making use of that exciting bulge for even greater pleasure. She'd told herself not to want that. She shouldn't want that. Not yet.

A coyote yipped in the distance. She'd never had sex with a man while coyotes howled nearby. She wouldn't be doing it now, either, if she knew what was good for her. Then again, Andre could be *very* good for her.

He licked and nibbled his way back to her mouth. "You're so delicious." He continued to stroke her breasts as he moved his lips to her ear. "I want the rest of your clothes off. I want you naked in my arms, wearing only your ankle bracelet.''

She liked that picture, too, but it sounded dangerous. She clutched his shoulders and tried to think. ''Andre, we're not going to—''

''We won't do anything you don't want.'' His breath tickled her ear.

With him, she wanted everything. But that was a mistake, at least for now. A huge mistake. Something else was huge, though, and it pressed relentlessly against her thigh. What normal woman wouldn't want to turn that bad boy loose?

Andre made good use of her inner-debate time to work the elastic waist of her skirt down over her hips. Somehow her black thong came along for the ride, and presto, she was exactly the way he'd said he wanted her.

He caressed the curve of her hip. ''You're gorgeous. If only I had more light, so I could see as well as touch.''

Lena had turned into a river of molten need. She gulped for air as he propped her against the door and ran both hands over her breasts, down her tummy and along her inner thighs. Dignity be damned. ''Touching…works for me.''

''I'm glad.'' His voice had grown thick and his caress more deliberate. With a hand massaging each thigh, he used easy pressure to guide her legs apart.

''Andre…''

''Only what you want.'' His thumbs stroked the outer folds of her vagina, grown plump and moist, giving him ample evidence of what she wanted.

In a few short moments in this darkened car, he'd

pulled her in way over her head. Now she was drowning in her own urges. When he moved relentlessly toward the center peak of her heated cleft, she whimpered softly.

"Is that a yes?"

She could barely speak. "A...definite...maybe."

"Let me make you come."

Sounded great to her. He was in the perfect position. She was in the perfect position. She managed a nod.

He slid a thumb over that strategic spot. "You're close, aren't you?" he murmured.

She trembled, hoping for another caress exactly like the last one. "Mmph." It was the best she could do.

A groan rumbled from his chest. "Lena, I want...I need to..." He lifted her legs from his lap and sank to his knees on the floor.

For one heart-stopping moment she thought he intended to rip open his pants and enter her. In her fevered state she wasn't sure she would have stopped him. Instead he wedged his shoulders under her thighs, lowered his head and settled his hot mouth on the exact spot guaranteed to drive her around the bend.

She'd known from his kiss that he had a devil's tongue, and now he was using it in a way that was probably illegal in some states. Seconds ago she'd wanted an orgasm more than anything. Now she wanted to experience this tongue bath for about a hundred years and *then* enjoy her orgasm. She clenched her hands and tightened her jaw, trying to rein in the climax that surged nearer with every swipe and flutter of his tongue.

Faintly the yap of a coyote penetrated the fog of sensuality surrounding her. The eager barking, rising in pitch, seemed to time itself to the rapid movement of his tongue, until she could hold back no longer. Her cries joined the yipping of the coyotes as her hips lifted and her body quaked under the onslaught of a violent orgasm.

He stayed right there as she drifted back to reality. He moved only to kiss her trembling inner thighs and her dew-drenched curls as he murmured soft words she couldn't make out because her heartbeat still thudded in her ears like bongos. At last he gently eased her back to the seat, all the while stroking her hips and thighs, her quivering tummy and her sensitive nipples.

She swore she could feel each individual nerve ending, could trace their pathways just beneath her moist skin. No man had ever put her so in touch with her body, from the roots of her hair to the sensitive space between each toe. When she'd debated the pros and cons of sex with Andre, she hadn't factored in complete ecstasy.

He kissed his way up the length of her body until he cupped her face in both hands. "I think you liked that." Male pride echoed in his voice.

She thought he deserved to feel proud of himself. "I loved that. I think you're more French than you imagine."

His laugh was strained. "Lena…" He put a bucketful of yearning into those two syllables.

It didn't take a genius to understand what he

wanted. "I'll be happy to return the favor," she murmured, reaching for his belt buckle.

He shook his head. "That's not what I want. Oh, I'd love you to do that sometime, but right now, right now I need... I need desperately to be inside you."

Her heartbeat had slowed, but it quickly started racing again. She'd had an important reason for not taking this step, but damned if she could think of it. Only one immediate problem came to mind. "But I didn't bring...I don't have..."

"I do."

CHAPTER SEVEN

ANDRE HELD HIS BREATH. A bed would have been wonderful, but right now he didn't have the time to spare. He was fairly sure that if he didn't sink into Lena's hot, slick vagina in the next couple of minutes, he'd lose what was left of his mind.

Begging wasn't cool. He liked to be in more control than that. But he did it, anyway. "Please."

"It's...it's too soon."

Her protest sounded weak enough that he knew she was barely convinced by her own argument. "I understand what you're saying," he murmured, nibbling at her delicious mouth. "But I figure we passed that objection sometime during your climax."

"Mmm." She responded to his kiss, parting her lips and sighing.

"I want to make you come again, the old-fashioned way." He felt her resistance ebbing, but he needed to get rid of it for good. "I want to be deep inside you, stroking, feeling you tighten around me."

"Mmm." Her breathing grew shallow.

He used more ammunition, painting a picture of future delight. "Think of me filling you, rubbing against every sensitive spot, bringing you nearer to—"

"Uh-huh."

He wasn't dumb enough to ask for clarification. In no time he'd pulled the condom from his pocket and shucked his pants and boxers. She was moving, too, repositioning herself with one foot braced on the side window and one on the floor. He still wasn't sure how they'd fit—he'd grown taller since the last time he'd tried this at seventeen.

She tried to help, lifting her hips while he maneuvered, but he couldn't figure out where to put his knees. He swore softly. They couldn't go outside where there was nothing but prickly pear cactus and mounds of dirt.

"Here." With amazing agility, she switched her position, kneeling on the seat with her bottom facing him. "Like this."

He sucked in a breath. If that wouldn't make his package happy, nothing would. Before she could change her mind, he knelt behind her and cupped the smooth curve of her backside in both hands. Then he urged her knees a little farther apart and homed right in. Sliding into her moist channel was pure ecstasy.

Wanting a repeat of that sensation, he pulled back and plunged forward again...and again, unable to resist the temptation of that glorious friction down the entire length of his penis. Then he forced himself to take shorter strokes and pay more attention to what was going on with her.

He'd promised her another orgasm, and he planned to deliver on that promise. Because she was panting and making little whimpering noises, he expected success. He changed his angle slightly and her panting grew heavier.

He needed to talk to her, but his vocal chords seemed welded in place by the heat they were generating in the back seat. He'd hoped to have sex with her, but in his wildest dreams he'd never imagined this scenario.

He swallowed and croaked out one word. ''Good?''

''Yes!'' She undulated against him in a move that reminded him of their belly-dancing escapade. ''More!''

More he could do. He picked up the rhythm. The firm slap of his thighs against hers mixed with her lilting cries and his heavy groans. He'd never heard sweeter music in his life.

He didn't have to ask—he knew she was nearly there from the hitch in her breathing and the way her muscles tightened. He stroked faster, wanting her to come even more than he wanted his own cherished orgasm.

And she did, loudly and spectacularly as he continued to pump. At last he was free to seek relief from the incredible pressure building in his groin. By the time he erupted, he was blind and deaf with lust. The force of his climax nearly knocked him from the seat, and he clung to Lena to keep from falling.

Gasping for breath, he clutched her slick body and closed his eyes, reveling in the sense of connection, of peace, of rightness. Something significant had just happened here. He was positive of that. With luck, she believed that, too.

SO MUCH FOR DIGNITY, Lena thought as she and Andre slowly untangled themselves. She was grateful for the darkness, which allowed them some privacy to regroup. In the heat of the moment, she'd abandoned every last inhibition, but now her natural modesty came creeping back. She picked up her long skirt from the floor and draped it over her.

Andre glanced her way. "Please don't tell me you're sorry."

"No." She owed him an honest reply. "I don't regret anything." Maybe she should, but she didn't.

"Good. I would hate that."

"Although I'm a little embarrassed that I got so carried away, that I acted so..." She searched for the word to describe her behavior.

"Liberated?" He leaned toward her and ran a finger over her lower lip.

She *had* felt liberated by the rush of passion, and some of that adrenaline was still hanging around, begging to be put to good use. Just the subtle touch of his finger against her lip was stirring her up again.

"Let's go back to my place," he murmured, "where there's a king-sized bed and a supply of condoms."

She couldn't think of anything she'd rather do. "But I told myself I wouldn't go this far on our first date." So much for self-control.

"I'm sure you did, but now that we have, we might as well enjoy ourselves in comfort," he said with a soft smile.

"You have a point." Then again, she was ready to agree that the Earth was square and made of cheddar.

"Great." He lifted his hips and pulled up his boxers and pants. "Let's get out of here."

She groped for her clothes, found her black thong and shimmied into it. She'd just finished slipping her skirt over her hips when she realized he was already dressed and watching her finish up. "No fair. You had a head start."

"I'm not complaining. I love watching you, although seeing you undress would be even better."

She found her top but was still minus her black bra. "Is that a suggestion for later?" She wondered if she had the nerve to strip for him.

"Yeah," he said softly. "I'll light some candles."

The prospect made her more addled than ever. Where was that damned bra, anyway?

"Looking for this?" Her bra dangled from his fingertips.

"So there it is." She was so glad she'd worn her laciest one, a delicate underwire that closed in front. "I think I can manage." She reached for it.

He pulled it back. "Let me."

"Um, okay." The sexual excitement that had been nibbling slowly at her restraint took an aggressive bite that left her aching. Just like that she was once again trembling in the grip of desire.

"Lift your arms over your head." He drew in a sharp breath as she followed his instructions. "Even in the dark, I can tell how amazing your breasts are. I can hardly wait to see you in candlelight."

"Then you'd better finish dressing me." Her voice came out low and husky. "So I can have something to take off later."

"Right." He slipped the straps over her wrists and drew the cups down. But instead of fastening the bra in place, he started playing, rubbing the underwire up and down over her nipples.

And like clockwork, her body tightened, gearing up for another orgasm. "Andre…"

"I can't help it." He abandoned the bra completely and cupped her breasts in both hands. "I love how your breathing changes when I stroke your nipples." He brushed his thumbs back and forth. "You're so incredibly responsive."

She moaned softly. "Maybe too responsive."

"No such thing." Dipping his head, he captured her nipple between his teeth.

The sharp delight of it made her gasp and sent a ringing message to the pleasure center between her legs.

He raked his teeth gently over the tip of her breast before circling it with his tongue. "I love making you react," he whispered against her damp skin. Then he opened his mouth over her breast and began to suck in a slow, easy rhythm.

She was his puppet. When he slipped his hand under her skirt, she opened her thighs, wanting whatever he offered. In moments he'd worked his way around the thong and pushed two fingers deep. And what he offered was heaven, created by his clever mouth and talented fingers.

She gave herself up to pure sensation, and he coaxed her to the brink so quickly it was embarrassing. Arching against his fingers, she clutched his head to her breast and cried out as tremors shook her.

With his fingers still buried deep, he kissed his way back to her mouth. "Want more?" he asked as he nipped at her lower lip and continued to caress her with those magic fingers. His touch demonstrated clearly that where there was one more climax there could be two...or three.... All she had to do was say the word.

And *yes* seemed the only word worth saying. Dimly she realized that he had complete control of the situation. He'd just proven he could reduce her to a mass of quivering needs in no time at all.

She felt the need to take back some of that control, difficult though it would be. She'd spent four years learning to be more assertive. She hated to think all that progress could be erased by a series of orgasms, outstanding though they'd been.

"Not here." Her voice was thick with passion. She eased away from him.

"My place, then."

"Yes." She fumbled a little getting her bra fastened, but she accomplished it. Then she pulled her top over her head.

"Want me to drive?"

She was tempted to let him. Feeling positively boneless, she would love to collapse against the seat and be swept away to his lair. But that would be too passive.

"I'll drive," she said. "Meet you up front." Somehow she managed to get out of the back seat and behind the steering wheel. Fortunately she'd left the keys in the ignition, because fitting that key into a narrow slot would have been beyond her abilities. She adjusted her position on the seat and tried to calm down.

But when she pulled her seat belt over and fastened it, she remembered his comment about Bondage Light, and she was a basket case again.

Gripping the steering wheel, she took a deep breath.

"I really will drive," he said.

"I'm fine."

"You remember how to get back to my apartment?"

She was lucky to remember her name, but if she concentrated very hard, she'd be able to find his apartment again. She had a great motivation to find his apartment. That's where the condoms were. "I remember."

"All righty, then. If you're sure."

"I'll be okay." She cleared the huskiness from her throat. "I'm just…"

"I know. Me, too." He held his hand out. "See that? I'm shaking."

"So you're not in any better shape to drive than I am."

"Probably not, but driving is what guys do, no matter what's going on. I'm conditioned to drive under stress."

She wasn't about to let him get away with that. "So am I." She started the car. "Just don't touch me, and I'll make it."

"Can I talk to you?" Laughter rippled through his question.

"Depends on the subject." She put the car in gear and headed back down the winding road.

"Okay, picnics."

"Picnics?"

"How do you stand on the subject of picnics?"

All she could think of was the company picnic last summer, which had been such a dating disaster. "What kind?"

"The kind where you leave in the morning with a basket of goodies and some wine, drive up to the White Mountains, find a secluded little spot well away from the road and spread out a blanket."

"Oh. That kind." It didn't take a genius to know what he had in mind for the blanket. Thinking of that, she nearly missed her turn. "Scratch that subject."

"You don't like picnics?" He sounded disappointed.

"I didn't say that." She pressed her thighs together, trying to settle herself down. "I just said we couldn't talk about them right now, okay?"

"Ah. Then I'll take that as a yes, that you're willing to go on one tomorrow."

"Yes. Now talk about something else." She knew what the picnic date meant. Any couple who headed from the first date into the second date with only a few hours in between was probably about to have a relationship. She needed to tell him about the work situation they'd both face on Monday. But she was worried about how he'd interpret the fact that she'd known all along and hadn't confided in him.

"How do you stand on the subject of a cozy little B and B?" he asked.

Yes, definitely a relationship. "I don't think we can talk about that, either."

"I'm going to assume that whatever topic you reject turns you on."

"Good assumption."

"So if I made a reservation at a B and B for to-morrow night, there's an excellent chance you'd go there with me after the picnic."

"I'd say so." The prospect of an entire weekend with Andre shimmered in front of her, a weekend in which work was the furthest thing from either of their minds. Once she'd spent that much time with him, they'd have created a bond that might see them through any problems with her promotion.

Telling him about everything now would change his attitude toward her—that much she could be sure of. He couldn't possibly make love to her all week-end without also remembering that on Monday she'd be in charge of his performance review at work. They needed this time to establish their connection, which logically shouldn't have anything to do with their jobs.

Exactly. They were two people who happened to work for the same company. By a curious set of events, on Monday she'd be in a position to oversee his production. They shouldn't allow themselves to be ruled by that.

She was convinced that after a weekend together, the news wouldn't be such a big deal. By Monday they'd like each other a lot, maybe even have some leanings toward the *L* word, and a silly work com-plication wouldn't matter. So it was settled. She'd tell him Sunday night, while they were cud-dling...somewhere.

"You passed the apartment complex."

"I did? Seriously?"

"Seriously. Take a right at this street and we can come in from the back."

"O...kay." She doubted he'd meant that statement to have a double meaning, doubted he'd intended a reference to what had been a life-changing event for her, but her mind was firmly planted in the Land of Sexual Innuendoes, so she thought of it immediately.

"I'll never forget that moment, you know," he said softly.

"What moment?" she chirped, as if she would never have those kind of thoughts.

"The moment when you scooted around on the seat and—"

"Oh, *that* moment." Her pulse raced.

"Yes, *that* moment. Incredible. Turn in here."

She squealed the tires, giving herself away.

"You're priceless." He laughed and reached over to squeeze her knee.

"Don't do that or I'm liable to take out several bumpers going through this parking lot."

He laughed again. "I can hardly wait until we're behind closed doors. There's a spot. Park right there."

She managed to fit her car into the space without dinging anything, which she considered a major accomplishment. They quickly exited the car and ran, hand-in-hand, to the door of Andre's first-floor apartment.

"Thank goodness I'm not up a couple of flights." He fitted the key in the lock and in a flash led her inside the darkened apartment.

Before she could move he'd flattened her against the closed door, thrusting his tongue into her mouth and tugging at her clothes. She fumbled with the buttons of his shirt just as desperately. So much for the striptease. Neither of them had the time.

The phone rang.

She wrenched her mouth from his. "Phone," she said gasping. Then she clutched a fistful of his shirt and pulled it from his pants.

"Answering machine." He whipped her top over her head and went back to kissing her while he reached for the fastening of her bra.

A loud male voice drifted through the apartment. Noise in the background indicated someone calling from a public place. "Andre, buddy, it's Jed."

Good. Not an emergency. Lena stopped worrying about the caller and redoubled her efforts to unbuckle Andre's belt.

"Listen, I know you're out with Lena for that big date you two had planned. Well, I'm here drinkin' with some of the guys and decided to call."

"Idiot," Andre murmured against Lena's mouth.

Jed's voice continued, even louder than before. "I just heard a rumor about her regarding work I think you should check out."

No! Dear God, no! She wanted to clap both hands over Andre's ears.

His frantic kissing stopped and he drew back. His face was in shadow, his expression unreadable. "Lena...."

She tried to catch her breath and prayed for a miracle. None arrived.

"This comes from a good source, old buddy. Apparently on Monday she's going to be your boss. So if I were you, I'd ask her about that before you get into any funny business, if you know what I mean. Company policy, and all that. Hope I'm not too late with this. Talk to you later. Bye.''

CHAPTER EIGHT

ANDRE SHOOK HIS HEAD, as if doing that would erase what he's just heard.

Her voice trembled, which seemed like a dead giveaway that she was guilty. "I can explain."

"It's true, then." He sounded cold and formal, but hell, what did she expect? Right when he'd let his guard down, he'd been kicked in the cojones.

"Yes, it's true, but—"

"How long have you known?" If she'd been notified before she asked him out, he'd never forgive her.

"Dana called me into her office this afternoon and told me about it. I thought about saying something to you. I thought about canceling the date. But I...wanted to go out with you."

He still didn't have this worked out. His mind was a jumble of betrayal and sexual frustration. "So before that you had no idea you were up for a promotion, one that could potentially have this result?" Total ignorance didn't compute. She must have had some idea.

She hesitated.

"Hey, Lena, let's have it straight. You owe me that much."

"All right, I knew something might be coming

along, but I've been so caught up in my April Fool's project that I forgot about it.''

"How convenient.'' Earlier he'd felt as if she'd used him, but he'd dismissed that feeling. It was back. "I guess we know who the fool is around here, don't we? And you're looking at him.''

"No, Andre!'' She put a hand on his arm. When he flinched, she pulled away. "Damn it, I was going to tell you before Monday morning. I swear to you that I wasn't about to let you go into work without a clue.''

"But you'd let me have sex with you without a clue.''

"Ouch. I think you just drew blood.''

"I think I wanted to.'' He wasn't sure which made him angrier—that she hadn't told him about her promotion or the fact of the promotion itself. He didn't mind working for a woman, but company policy said he couldn't work with a woman he had a relationship with. He was pretty damn sure that having back-seat sex counted as a relationship. Or was she figuring this as a one-night stand?

"Can you look at it from my side?'' She crossed her arms over her lace-covered breasts.

He noticed that she was shivering. "Are you cold?''

"No, just uncomfortable.''

Wordlessly he leaned down and picked up her top from the carpet where he'd thrown it in his rush to get her naked again. He handed it to her.

"Thanks.''

He waited until she'd pulled it over her head. "Okay, I'll listen to your side.'' He couldn't imagine it would make a difference, but on the off-chance that she had a reasonable explanation, he wanted to hear what she had to say.

"Dana told me I couldn't mention the promotion to anyone at Thunderbird until Monday. So even if I'd canceled the date, I would have had to make up some phony excuse about why I was doing that." She drew in a breath. "You would have seen right through me and jumped to the conclusion I'd changed my mind about dating you."

"Probably. But you see how carefully this so-called secret was guarded. As of seven tonight, I'll bet I was the only person left in the company who didn't know about it, and that was because I was spending the evening with the one employee at Thunderbird who won't talk."

"That should be a point in my favor!"

"As far as Dana's concerned, absolutely. You get a gold star. As for me, you should have told me, at least before we had sex." Man, did he sound judgmental. But he hated not having all the information he needed before he made a move. He'd thought he had all the necessary facts, so he'd jumped right in with both feet, or rather, with one significant part of his anatomy.

"So you're sorry we had sex?" She sounded troubled.

He didn't like hearing the distress in her voice, even if she deserved to feel that way. "No! Yes! I mean, I wasn't sorry before, but now I'm wondering how we'll deal with the office situation. I don't like sneaking around, and I'd rather not get transferred, either. I would have liked to know what I was getting into." The more he talked, the more indignant he became. "What were you thinking, letting me coax you into the back seat before telling me about this?"

"I wasn't thinking, okay? I told you I hadn't expected to get so involved on this first date, but you kept pushing!"

"Don't try to blame this on me. You were sending me the signals all night. You wanted me to push, so don't pretend you had nothing to do with what happened."

"Of course I had something to do with it, but we both seemed to want the same thing tonight, so what's so wrong with that?"

Her admission of responsibility caused him to throttle back a notch on his anger. "What's wrong is that I was operating with a lack of vital information."

Her chin came up. "The job shouldn't be what we're all about. I think if we'd spent the whole weekend together, as you planned, and I'd told you about this myself on Sunday night instead of you hearing it from Jed on the answering machine, you'd have had a completely different reaction."

"That's when you planned to tell me? Sunday night?" Well, now he was well and truly pissed.

"Um, yes. I thought—"

"You would have let me go the whole damned weekend, getting in deeper and deeper, and *then* dropped the bombshell?"

"What bombshell? Why should this be such a big fat deal?"

"Oh, no reason. No reason at all. Only that you've

put me in a very awkward position, forced to choose between you and a transfer.''

"Maybe not. Maybe—"

"And if I decide to stay put," he interrupted, in no mood to hear theories of how this *might* work out, "then you'll be supervising my every move, writing up my performance reviews, influencing my entire effing career. Other than that, it's no big deal at all!" He glared at her in total frustration. She hadn't intended to tell him until *Sunday,* damn it. He should have known she was too good to be true.

She glared back at him. Finally she shrugged. "Well, that's it, then. I guess this evening is over."

"I would certainly say so."

She picked up the purse she'd dropped beside the door. "For your information, I would never let what happened between us tonight influence how I deal with you at work."

His patience was completely gone. "That's ridiculous. Of course it will influence you. You might say it won't, but it will. You can't treat me the same as the other salesmen, no matter how much you want to. In fact, I've just decided. I won't leave it up to Dana. On Monday I'll put in for a transfer."

"Please don't do that."

"Don't worry. I'll put a spin on it that eliminates potential gossip. I'm a salesman. I'm good at manipulating situations."

She blew out a breath. "That is *not* why I'm worried about you asking for a transfer. Gossip doesn't scare me. This isn't about me, it's about the good of the company."

"Oh, my God, here we go again. You deserve some sort of plaque for loyalty, you know that?"

"And you deserve an award for being terminally obnoxious! But the fact is, you're a leader in that office. Much as it pains me to say it in my current frame of mind, they'd miss you."

He stopped himself from asking if *she'd* miss him. That was a cheap shot and they were both miserable enough as it was.

"Besides, Dana might refuse to transfer you," she added.

"Then I'll just have to convince Dana that it's the best thing to do."

"It's not the best thing, Andre."

"Yes, it is. I wish I could think of an alternative, but I can't. I'm not going to be able to be around you without remembering…everything." He would remember whether he was around her or not, and that was the worst part. Although he felt betrayed, he still wanted her, even now.

"I'd better go."

"Yes." He wondered if she'd read his mind, or if he was giving off non-verbal signals. If she made the slightest move in his direction, his control would snap and he'd haul her off to the bedroom. It wouldn't be tender, but it would be satisfying. And after what they'd already had together, another sexual incident or two with his soon-to-be boss wouldn't make much difference, now would it?

The more he thought about that, the more he felt justified in wanting another round. Why not? She'd enjoyed herself before, and she'd enjoy herself again.

And he could use some release from the tension caused by this new turn of events.

When she hesitated at the door, he held his breath. Once she was out that door, it was goodbye to the greatest sex he'd ever had.

If he transferred out of the office, technically they could continue to date, but he wouldn't want to, not after the way she'd misled him. Of course he wouldn't want to date her after that. But he could do with some more skin-to-skin contact with Lena before he gave up the chance forever.

"Goodbye, Andre. I'm sorry it turned out this way."

"Me, too." He watched her twist the knob and open the door. "Lena…"

"What?"

He cleared his throat. "You, um, don't have to leave, you know."

She whirled to face him. For one wild moment he thought she was about to rush back into his arms. Then she spoke, and he knew right off that he'd misjudged the situation.

"You want me to stay and have more sex with you?" Her voice rose. "After accusing me of deliberately fooling you and creating huge problems at work, you want me to follow you into the bedroom so we can carry on some more?"

He shrugged. "The horse is already out of the barn, so I thought we might as well—"

"If that isn't *exactly* like a man!" She stepped out and slammed the door in his face.

He heaved a sigh. Well, he *was* a man. Apparently, at the moment, that wasn't a good thing.

LENA HAD NEVER been much of a crier, but as she banged around her apartment after getting home from Andre's place, she wished she could cry. A real gully-washer might make her feel better. As it was, she wondered if she'd ever feel better.

What a mess. What a documented, certified, signed, sealed and delivered mess. Resisting the urge to call either Brandy or Meg, who by all rights would be asleep by now, she rummaged around for something to soothe her frazzled nerves. In the far corner of her refrigerator she found an open bottle of Bailey's and poured herself an eight-ounce glass of it.

Then she sprawled on her sofa and stared into space through the first four ounces. By the fifth ounce she no longer cared if Andre was the most amazing lover in the universe, or that he'd given her three, count 'em *three,* orgasms in under forty-five minutes. So what? He'd refused to understand why she hadn't told him about the promotion, which made him an insensitive jerk.

By the sixth ounce she'd not only sworn off Andre, she'd sworn off the entire male population. Never again would she be tempted by that certain smile, that tongue-wise kiss, those searching fingers that…uh-oh. She was heading down the wrong road with that train of thought.

After seven ounces she could finally admit to herself that she'd come *this close* to taking him up on his offer of more sex, even after he'd raked her over the coals for keeping the promotion a secret. She'd been weak, but she would be weak no longer.

Never mind that he was an outstanding nipple

man. Never mind that he was hung like a prize stallion. Never mind that he knew how to use that equipment to…uh-oh. Detour. Hazards ahead.

After she'd drained the glass, she started remembering all the adorable things he'd done. He'd eaten fast food without complaint and given belly dancing the old college try. He'd even forced himself to play goofy golf when all he'd really wanted to do was kiss her until they both went crazy with lust. She could still feel the urgency with which he'd pushed her inside his apartment and backed her up against the door, all the while thrusting his tongue inside her mouth and…uh-oh.

Good thing Andre wouldn't be walking in her door, because he'd find a pretty close to drunk woman who was ready to do anything he asked. And she wished with all her heart he would walk in the door. Yes, he was impossible. Yes, he was way too judgmental. But he was the sexiest, most lovable guy she'd ever met.

Unfortunately, even though he still wanted her, he didn't like her anymore.

Lena scooted down on the sofa, put her glass on the floor, rested her head on a throw pillow and went to sleep, leaving all the lights on. She dreamed that she was in charge of a muscled work crew that included Andre. And during their lunch breaks they would sneak away to have sex.

The phone woke her from that dream, and she put the pillow over her head in a desperate attempt to block out the morning light and get back to dreamland. No luck. Her answering machine picked up and she heard Meg's voice asking about her date.

Meg, one half of the traitorous duo who'd crashed the belly-dancing gig, had the nerve to call her. Meg, who had advised her to go for it now, before her job status changed. She didn't want to talk to Meg and certainly not about her date. Not ever, and especially not now, when she had a thumping headache and a crick in her neck from sleeping in a cramped position.

Oh, hell. If she didn't get up and call Meg back, Meg would call Brandy and they'd start speculating that Lena was still with Andre, that she'd slept over. Lena needed to squelch that rumor before it got started. Come to think of it, she was spoiling for a cat fight with Meg and Brandy. She was in the perfect mood for it.

Stumbling to the phone, she speed-dialed Meg.

"Lena!" Meg yelled into the phone.

Lena winced. "I take it somebody's had her quota of caffeine this morning."

"Oh, sweetie, you sound exhausted, you lucky woman." Meg chuckled. "Listen, I'm on the other line with Brandy. Just a sec, and I'll set us up with a three-way."

Perfect. Lena massaged her temple and prepared her speech about traitorous friends. But then, wasn't that the same speech Andre had given her a few hours ago? Whoops. Looks like she had a serious case of pot-calling-the-kettle-black syndrome.

"Okay," Meg said. "We're both here. Spill. We want details."

"Lots of details," Brandy said. "That was the yummiest guy I've ever seen! Except for Eric, of course. Scratch that. Honesty compels me to say that

Eric is not as cute as Andre. But looks aren't everything, so—''

"Be quiet, Brandy," Meg said. "Give Lena a chance to talk."

Lena took a deep breath. "The bottom line is that Andre and I are finished."

"Finished?" Brandy squealed. "But you barely got started!"

Lena's head threatened to explode as she described Jed's call and the resulting fallout. Reliving that moment was torture.

"We'll have this Jed person killed," Meg said.

"Poor Lena. So you left after that?" Brandy asked, her voice soft with sympathy.

"Yes, but…uh, he wanted me to stay, so we could have more sex."

"*More* sex?" Meg's squeal sailed over the line like a javelin aimed straight at Lena's temple. "You had sex before that?"

"Um, yeah. In the car."

Brandy sounded like she was hyperventilating. "Oh…my…God. He was so hot that you couldn't make it back to either apartment and ended up having car sex. I'm fanning myself over here."

Lena struggled to maintain her role as outraged woman. "But can you imagine that? He was really mad at me, but he thought we should have sex again, because, as he put it, *the horse is already out of the barn.* Can you believe he'd suggest such a thing?"

"Was the car sex good?" Brandy asked.

"Well, yes." The understatement of the millennium.

"Did you climb in the back seat or did you—''

"Brandy!" Meg sounded completely exasperated. "The issue here is whether this guy is slime for wanting more, when he was clearly furious with Lena for not telling him about her promotion. Now, Lena, you might have walked out on make-up sex. You do realize that."

"Oh, I don't think so," Lena said. "He's very upset about the promotion. He talked about transferring, he's so upset. He pretty much hates me."

"Hmm." Meg blew out a breath. "I don't think you should jump to conclusions. Maybe he was reacting to getting slapped in the face with the news. But if he still wanted to have sex, he might have hoped to keep the connection going, somehow."

"Yeah," Brandy added, "or he's a dog going after whatever he can get, in which case you're well rid of him."

"But what do I do now?" Lena wailed.

"Nothing," Meg said. "Absolutely nothing. Give this a chance to settle out. See how he is on Monday."

"Monday," Brandy's voice quivered. "Dear Lord, that's when I'm supposed to kidnap Eric. In all the commotion about Lena, I forgot."

Lena could hardly wait for the attention to shift away from her. "And tomorrow is Meg's sail on Tempe Town Lake." For the first time in several hours her mood brightened. "Brandy, how do you feel about spending a little time with me on the lake Sunday? And renting a camcorder to film the locals?"

"Hold on a minute," Meg said. "All Brandy and

I did was show up at the dance class. We didn't take pictures, so no fair—''

"I'm on it, Lena," Brandy said. "Way to up the stakes, Lena. You rock."

"Thanks." Lena smiled as she contemplated her revenge. "Now all I have to do is figure out a way to spy on your Dance of the Seven Veils, Brandy, and my life will be complete."

"Ha! Go ahead and try. I have excellent security in my building."

"If you and Lena make a video of me singing the theme from *Titanic,*" Meg said, "then I am finding a way around the security in your building. Just giving you fair warning."

"And I'll be your trusty accomplice," Lena said. "So e-mail me. In fact, both of you need to e-mail me. I'm now a double agent. Bye."

As Lena hung up, she decided that focusing on the other two April Fools was her best strategy to avoid thinking about Andre. And she didn't want to think about him, because she knew Meg was right. She couldn't do anything about the situation now. The ball was squarely in his court.

Unfortunately, she'd become used to being active instead of passive. Wondering what Andre would do next could make her crazy between now and Monday. Still, she had little choice but to wait and see what happened when they met at the office and she accepted her position as his supervisor. She thought of her dream and sighed. Chances were they would not be sneaking away during their lunch hour to have sex.

CHAPTER NINE

ANDRE SHOT SOME HOOPS with Jed and his buddies on Saturday afternoon because it beat sitting around his apartment thinking about Lena. Sweating on the court felt good, and afterward they all went out for beer, which felt even better. Andre wished he could shoot hoops and drink beer for the next few weeks, instead of going in to work on Monday.

Jed didn't mention Lena until he and Andre were walking back to their cars after the others had left. "So, did you ask her about that rumor, yet?"

"Yeah, I asked her. It's true."

"Seriously? She asked you out, knowing this was coming down?"

"Not exactly. She was sort of caught in the middle." Andre was amazed to hear himself say that. He'd figured that, given a chance, he'd lay blame. But he hadn't been able to rat her out, after all.

Jed leaned against the fender of his Corvette and gazed at Andre. "But you can't go on dating, right? I mean, the company won't allow it."

"That's right." Unless he transferred. He'd been so hot for that idea on Friday night, thinking he wanted to get away from her. Now he wasn't so sure.

"I think the company policy makes sense, dude. I mean, would you like your girlfriend writing up your performance review? Suppose she gets pissed off because you forgot her birthday or something? Boom, she nails you on the review.''

"Lena wouldn't do that." There he was defending her again. Yet he'd told her last night that the performance review was one of his big concerns.

"You sound like you're thinking of dating her on the QT. You know Dana would have a cow if she found out."

Maybe a part of his brain, unknown to him, had been working on this problem, because he had an answer. "We started dating before she got promoted, so there might be a way around company policy."

"There might be, but I wouldn't take it, buddy. You'll be putting yourself in a vulnerable spot. You know how these office romances go. One minute they're blazing and the next they're ashes. Watch out for a woman scorned, and all that stuff. Be smart. Don't stick your neck out.''

"If she were anybody else, you'd be right. But Lena's different. She wouldn't mess with my job because we had personal problems." Ironically, it was her dedication to the April Fools that made him so sure of that. She'd been determined to finish the stupid golf game, no matter what, because she'd given her word to her friends.

And right after that, she'd told him about the group and its goals. She hadn't mentioned her promotion, true, but she'd promised Dana she wouldn't. She was possibly the most ethical person he knew. Her only weakness seemed to be wanting him. That was a weakness he could forgive.

The sun slipped down behind Camelback Mountain, and Jed pushed his shades to the top of his head. "You know what you sound like?"

"A complete fool?"

"Well, yeah, that, too. But you sound like a guy who might find himself picking out china and silverware patterns before too much longer."

"Hey, I'm not that far gone." But despite the protest, he wondered if he might be.

"Listen to yourself, is all I'm saying. And be careful. Anyway, later, dude. Glad you could make it today. Don't do anything too stupid, okay?"

"Okay." But Andre had a feeling that warning had come way too late.

A WILD SUNDAY spent with Brandy videotaping Meg doing her thing on Town Lake kept Lena from brooding about Andre. She and Meg had also figured out how to smuggle a voice-activated tape recorder into Brandy's apartment. A delivery of a flower arrangement timed for the exact moment Brandy was leaving for work wouldn't have given her a chance to check for the tiny recorder slipped into the foliage by one of Meg's good friends who worked for the florist.

Lena tried to concentrate on that devious plan as she drove to work Monday morning, but her thoughts kept sliding over to her likely meeting with Andre. If Dana followed her usual pattern, she'd gather the sales force Lena would be supervising and make an announcement soon after everyone arrived. Maybe Andre would call in sick.

Or maybe he'd already requested a transfer. If he'd done that, Lena would have to tell Dana why. Andre shouldn't have to take the heat. There was a good chance Dana would put up a fight over losing one of her top salesmen.

Lena made it into her office without running into Andre, but then again, maybe he wasn't even here. The thought deflated her. Much as she worried about their first encounter, not having any encounter at all would be worse.

Sure enough, a memo lay on her desk—Dana had scheduled a meeting with the sales force in the conference room at ten. This should be a proud moment, Lena realized, not one filled with tension. The idea of turning down the promotion niggled at her. Maybe she was the one who should request a transfer.

But both Meg and Brandy had advised doing nothing yet. They thought a guy who'd made it through an entire belly-dancing class might have the ability to handle this turn of events, once he'd been given a chance to assimilate the information. Lena wasn't so sure. Meg and Brandy hadn't seen Andre's initial reaction or felt his fury.

"Lena Walsh?"

She glanced up to discover a delivery guy holding a clear vase filled with a dozen red rosebuds just beginning to open. At first she wondered if Meg and Brandy had decided to bug her office today, too. But the leaves of the roses wouldn't support a tape recorder. For Brandy's event Lena and Meg had chosen a dense glob of blooms and greenery tailor-made for the purpose.

Lena signed for the roses and set the vase on her desk. The scent filled her office, and she realized only one person could have sent them. Although she might hope they were a romantic gesture, they could merely be an apology. They could also serve as a classy goodbye.

Her chest tight with anxiety, she opened the small envelope and pulled out the card inside.

Of all the things I said Friday night, I forgot the most important. Congratulations.

Andre

She read the card a second time and a third. How had he meant that? Sincerely, sarcastically, ironically? She had no way of knowing, and she was more confused than ever.

The roses taunted her with their rich fragrance while she turned on her computer and answered e-mail. Every few minutes she glanced at the digital clock in the bottom corner of the screen as if watching the countdown of a bomb set to explode at ten.

Finally, with five minutes to go, she picked up her leather-bound notebook and left for the conference room. She should be thinking of something inspirational to say to the sales force, something that would make it obvious why Dana had promoted her to this position. Instead she rehearsed lines she'd love to use with Andre but wouldn't.

She'd feel more in command of the situation if she could walk into the conference room and get the upper hand over Andre with a zinger, something along the lines of How was your weekend? Or even better, How's your golf game coming along? Then there was her personal favorite, I've been impressed by your excellent performance recently.

She managed to distract herself long enough to walk through the conference-room door, but once inside, her gaze immediately swept the room, found Andre and locked on him. She forgot everything and everyone else.

If she'd thought this meeting would fill her with embarrassment or uncertainty, she'd been wrong. Maybe this last April Fool's stunt had made her more socially secure, after all. Or maybe she was falling in love.

The second explanation seemed the most likely, because seeing Andre swamped her with longing. Looking into those brown eyes had a far greater impact than she'd expected. Andre wasn't a problem she would have to work through. Corny and old-fashioned though it sounded, he might be the man she'd been searching for all her life.

Only the sound of Dana noisily clearing her throat brought Lena out of her trance. She turned to Dana, suddenly sure of what she had to do. "I need to talk with you for a minute before we get started," she said.

Dana glanced from Lena to Andre. "Okay. Let's just step outside the door, shall we?"

As Lena walked into the hall with Dana, she thought of the grief she'd catch from Meg and Brandy, who would totally disagree with this move. It couldn't be helped. She turned to Dana. "I can't accept this promotion."

Dana smiled. "I think you can."

"You don't understand. By accepting it, I'm jeopardizing the performance, maybe even the career, of one of your top salesmen."

"Andre? He told me this morning he's delighted to be working with you."

Lena stared at her. "But—"

"He explained that you'd asked him out before you realized the promotion would be coming through. He also mentioned that you kept our conversation Friday afternoon in complete confidence. He has total faith in your ability to separate your personal relationship with him from your professional one."

Lena struggled to get her bearings. Dana made it sound as if Andre intended to keep seeing her. Surely Dana had misunderstood.

"Ordinarily we don't approve of dating in circumstances like this," Dana continued, "but in view of how you've handled things up to this point, those rules seem unnecessary. I'd even go as far as to say I wouldn't want the company to stand in the way of you and Andre getting together. I can see why you'd be attracted to each other. You have many traits in common."

"We do?"

Dana laughed. "You don't think so?"

"I...I hadn't thought about it." She'd been too focused on sex, but she couldn't say that to Dana.

"You're both dedicated to doing a good job, for one thing."

Immediately Lena thought about the dedication Andre brought to great sex, and she blushed. "I suppose."

"You're too modest for your own good, Lena."

You wouldn't think so if you'd seen me in the back seat of the car on Friday night.

"You're one of the hardest workers in the building," Dana said. "Oh, and here's another similarity—both you and Andre like to be firmly in charge of your destiny. Andre admitted that at first he imagined the promotion could affect your relationship, but now he sees it differently."

"He does?" Lena was beginning to wonder if aliens had taken over Andre's body in the past forty-eight hours. He was sounding way too reasonable about this.

"He's out to win your admiration, which means he'll be performing at peak levels for Thunderbird. His sales record is completely in his control, and he plans to knock your socks off with his effort every month. It's a win-win situation for the company."

"Did he really say he planned to knock my socks off?"

"Yes, he did." Dana winked at her. "Now let's go back in. I'm sure the natives are getting restless without us."

Dazed and confused, afraid to hope for too much, Lena followed Dana back into the conference room. Once again she sought out Andre, and he gave her a broad smile. She wondered what the hell he was up to.

Somehow she got through the meeting, mostly by avoiding Andre's gaze. She had no idea what she said to the sales force, but it must have made some kind of sense, because afterward everyone came up to offer their congratulations.

Finally it was Andre's turn. He held out his hand, a sparkle in his eyes. "Congratulations. You're going to be awesome." His grip was warm and very firm, but he didn't hold her hand any longer than was polite.

Even so, her skin tingled. "Thank you for the…" She paused and lowered her voice. "For the flowers."

"My pleasure. Any plans for lunch?"

Her heart started beating in triple-time. "Nothing specific. Why?"

"I thought we could grab a bite somewhere. Would you be free around noon?" His tone was conversational, but his eyes told a different story.

"I think so."

"Great. I'll come by your office."

Her world seemed whirling out of control. "Why don't I come by your office?"

He grinned. "Either way. Just so we end up going to lunch together. See you then." He left the conference room.

Lena had no idea how she functioned coherently after that. Yet she heard herself making small talk with the remaining sales people and then she walked back to her office with Dana, who wanted to discuss sales strategy. Once Lena made it to her desk and said goodbye to Dana, she immediately wrote down everything Dana had discussed before it left her mind totally.

The next hour passed in a blur. She returned phone calls and even initiated a few, but she wasn't operating on all cylinders. How could she, when Andre was taking her to lunch? And there was that pesky dream she'd had the other night running through her mind.

When she appeared in the doorway of Andre's office a few minutes before noon, he was on the phone, but he quickly ended the call and stood. "Ready?"

"I guess so." If only she knew what she was supposed to be ready for.

"I thought we could take my car." He gestured for her to go ahead of him.

She thought of suggesting her car but changed her mind. Her car had too many potent memories attached to it. "Do we have time to drive somewhere?" She'd thought they'd walk to the sandwich shop right down the street from the office.

"I cleared a couple of hours with Dana. I told her we needed to iron out our new working arrangement." He waved to the receptionist as they breezed through the outer office and out the front door.

A couple of hours? Her imagination ran wild. The rest of her ran even more wild. Surely he wasn't thinking what she was thinking.

The parking lot had covered spaces for those who qualified through position or sales records. Everyone else got to bake in the sun. Lena rated a shaded parking spot and she guessed that Andre did, too. He walked toward a low-slung blue convertible parked in the preferred area. The top was down.

"This is it." He held the passenger door for her. "Top up or down?"

"Down is fine." She was positive she'd imagined his suggestive tone. This was a work day, and he'd recently told Dana that they'd keep their professional and personal lives separate.

She waited until he slid behind the wheel and started the car's powerful engine. "Andre, what's going on?"

"I'll tell you what, sweet thing, we have it *all* going on." He backed out of the space with practiced ease and was soon out on the street.

"What do you mean by that?" She had to raise her voice to be heard over the wind, which whipped her hair around her face. But she liked the feeling of freedom. She liked it way too much for a work day.

"I'll explain once we get there." He reached for the cell phone he'd slipped into a holder on the dash and punched in a number. "What do you want for lunch?"

"I don't know. Why, are we getting take-out?"

"No, we're having it delivered."

She didn't understand, but she decided to go along. "Okay, a salad, then."

"Chicken, tuna, veggie?"

"Chicken."

He spoke into the phone. "I'll soon be in Room 312, if you'll have room service send up—"

"*Room service?* Andre, what on earth are you—"

"One chicken salad," he continued, ignoring her completely, "one roast beef sandwich and a couple of iced teas. We should be there by the time you arrive."

"Andre Dumont, what are you up to?"

He disconnected the cell phone. "I'm kidnapping you. We're going to a resort for a two-hour lunch. After work, we can go back again if you want. I've booked the room for the night."

She opened her mouth, tried to think of something to say, and closed it again. He'd taken her completely by surprise. She was speechless.

"Meg gave me the idea," he said.

"Meg? You talked to Meg?"

"Yep. Or rather, she talked to me. Got my number from information and called me Saturday night." He smiled. "She demanded to know my intentions toward you. We danced around the subject for about half an hour, and in that time I figured out my intentions toward you are strictly honorable."

"You call this honorable? Kidnapping me in the middle of the work day?"

"Absolutely. I'm whisking you away from the hustle and bustle of our job, separating work from pleasure, exactly as I promised Dana."

"I can't believe Dana would approve of this." And the farther they went from the office, the less she cared. Andre was in super-salesman mode, and he was thrilling her down to her toes.

"I think she would. She's a fan of the grand gesture if it clinches the deal."

"What deal?"

He pulled into the entrance to one of Scottsdale's finest resorts and parked beneath the portico. Then he shut off the engine, took off his sunglasses and turned to her. "I'm falling in love with you."

"You are?" Suddenly the colors surrounding them seemed more vivid. She heard the tinkle of a fountain and smelled the fragrance of all the brilliant flowers nearby.

"Yes."

Her heart beat crazily as she looked into his eyes. "I'm falling in love with you, too."

"I was hoping." Eyes shining, he took her hand and brought it to his lips. Then he kissed her fingers and took a deep breath. "Be my girl, Lena. I promise that during work hours, you'll be the head honcho and I'll be the best damned salesman on your team, but during our off hours, I want you to be my girl.''

Filled with eagerness, she reached for him, but the seat belt held her prisoner. She fumbled for the buckle.

"Let me.'' He unfastened her seat belt without breaking eye contact. "I think I knew we were meant to be when I unhooked your seat belt on Friday night.''

She began to tremble. "The Bondage Light thing.''

"Yeah.'' He leaned toward her. "And instead of being shocked, your eyes got all sparkly with interest.''

"Andre, sex isn't everything.'' Maybe Cautious Girl hadn't completely left the building.

"I know.'' His mouth drew nearer. "We have lots of other things in common, too.''

"So Dana said.'' Then again, caution was highly overrated.

"So will you? Be my girl?''

She threw caution out the window and into the nearest flower bed. "Yes. If you'll be my guy.''

"It's a deal.'' And there, in front of a startled valet parking attendant, Andre sealed the deal. As his lips met hers, Lena had no doubt that he would be knocking her socks off…forever.

EPILOGUE

"I LOVE YOU. I love your bridesmaids, Meg and Brandy, and your parents, and my parents, and your crazy brother, and my sisters, and the minister and the pilot on this plane. I love everybody in the world." Andre leaned over and kissed her. "But you're the only one I want to fool around with. Tell me, do you like fooling around?"

"Under the right conditions." Lena smiled. "But I think somebody had way too much champagne at the reception. I'll bet you couldn't fool around if you wanted to."

"Wanna bet?" He wiggled his eyebrows at her. "Mile-high club, here we come. Meet you in the back."

She started laughing as she pictured trying to maneuver with her tipsy husband in the airplane bathroom. "Just let me give you my seriously considered, well-thought-out answer. No."

"I'll bet by the time we get to Hawaii, I'll have used my excellent skills of persuasion to convince you to do it."

She grinned at him. "You're good, but you're not that good."

"We'll see." He picked up her left hand and planted kisses all around the diamond ring he'd placed there four hours ago. "I love you. Did I mention that yet?"

"I think you might have made some reference to it." Skimming over the clouds, she could easily believe she was in heaven. To think that three months ago she'd been afraid to ask this gorgeous man for a date.

"I hope I've made *tons* of references to it. I don't want there to be any doubt. I love you."

She reached over and stroked his cheek with her free hand. "And I love you. More every second."

"Do you love me enough to join the mile-high club?" He gave her a sly smile.

"That's not about love. That's about all the glasses of champagne you consumed. We wouldn't fit in that bathroom, Andre. I think our first married sex should be more dignified than that."

"I don't. Our first sex ever was in the back seat of a car, with you—"

She clapped a hand over his mouth. "Shh."

He licked her palm, making slow circles that sent delicious sensations up her arm.

"Stop that."

He gave her one last swipe with his tongue and turned to her. "Am I getting to you?"

"No," she lied.

"Yes, I am. I can tell. C'mon. Meet me in the back."

"No." Every time she looked at him, she grinned like a fool. Nobody deserved to be this happy, but she wasn't about to question her good luck. They worked beautifully together at Thunderbird Savings, but it was the hours she spent at home in his arms that made her world such a beautiful place.

"We should be members of the mile-high club."

She gazed at him and sighed. "You are one persistent guy."

"And you love that about me."

"Mostly."

"We should start our baby there."

"No, we should not. We should start our baby lying on three-hundred-thread-count sheets on a king-size bed in a room overlooking the ocean."

"I think an airplane bathroom is way more interesting. C'mon. Let's do it."

She did her best to glare at him, but she broke into laughter halfway through the glare. "Are you going to keep this up for the entire flight?"

"Uh-huh. So we might as well do it and get it over with." He unfastened his seat belt. "I'll go first. Right side of the plane. Tap on the door and I'll let you in."

"Someone will see us."

He skewered her with a look, and suddenly he didn't seem quite as tipsy as before. "Don't tell me that one of the April Fools is worried about being embarrassed."

She groaned. "Are you going to use that line every time you want me to do something stupid?"

"Yep. After all, doing something stupid brought us together, so why stop now?"

She met the challenge in his eyes. Maybe he was right. "Okay. I'll probably regret this, but okay."

As it turned out, she didn't regret it as much as she'd expected to. And that's how she ended up getting pregnant in an airplane bathroom. Nine months later she presented Andre with a dark-haired baby girl on April Fool's Day.

Among other baby presents, Meg and Brandy presented little Delta with an engraved invitation to join the April Fools on her sixteenth birthday. Considering that without the April Fools Lena wouldn't have the man of her dreams or a sweet baby girl, she couldn't think of a better gift.

NOBODY'S FOOL

Stephanie Bond

For Chris, whose foolish errand
to put a card on the windshield of my car at the
airport made me fall head over heels in love.

CHAPTER ONE

Let us be thankful for the fools. But for them
the rest of us could not succeed.
—Mark Twain

"ARE YOU nervous?"

Kate Randall looked up at her assistant Patsy and extended a stack of folders. Her jumpy stomach vaulted higher. "Nervous about the staff meeting?" Her throat constricted. "Why should I be nervous?"

Patsy shook her head, causing her gray curls to bounce, then put a calming hand over Kate's trembling one and relieved her of the rattling folders. "You shouldn't be."

Kate nodded. "After all, I've known most of these people for my entire career."

"Right."

"Why would I be nervous simply because this will be my first time sitting at the head of the table?"

"There's no need to be."

"I'm not."

"Good." Patsy set a small box on the desk and beamed like a proud parent. "Here are your new business cards to go along with your new office."

Kate lifted the lid of the box and withdrew one of the crisp white cards.

Kate Randall
Vice President of Sales & Marketing
Handley Toys
Birmingham, AL
Handley Toys—Come play with us.

As always, she winced at the company slogan, a
point of contention among many of the staff members…especially the women. But CEO John Handley
failed to see the innuendo that might be construed—
the older man's gentle and brilliant mind simply
didn't work that way.

As Kate ran her finger over the raised type of her
new title, her chest filled with happiness and pride.
John Handley had hired her fresh out of college as a
marketing research assistant, and for the past ten
years, she'd put in countless hours working her way
up through product management and into brand management. There she'd championed the purchase of a
1970s toy from a rival company, Mixxo. It had run
way past its life cycle with them but she'd resur-
rected the product with big sales results. As an en-
core, she'd repeated the scenario the following year
with another Mixxo has-been toy and had been elevated into senior management as Handley, once a
fledgling game and toy company, became an official
contender in the industry.

Mixxo had responded to the humiliation by woo-
ing away her male predecessor and a third of Handley's sales reps, all men. She suspected that no one
at Mixxo would believe that a woman had orches-
trated the product coup. Known as the frat house of
the industry, Mixxo was all about the good-ole-boy

network and high-end entertainment for their customers. All the playboys worked there...well, except for one.

"More coffee?" Patsy asked, breaking into Kate's thoughts.

Kate frowned into her empty mug, thinking she should have reached for decaf this morning when she arrived. "I'll get it. I should stretch my legs since the meeting will likely last awhile." She stood and strode out of her office, slowing at the unfamiliar perspective she now had of the cubicles and ten-by-ten offices on this floor. On Friday they had belonged to her colleagues; now they belonged to her subordinates. She knew that most were happy for her, but some probably doubted her capability to operate at this level, and a few possibly resented her appointment to the position. Her back straightened when she thought of the challenge John had lain at her feet: rebuild the sales organization while sustaining the morale of the reps and the support staff that remained.

Much of her task, she knew, meant winning over one sales rep in particular. If truth be known, *he* was the source of her agitated stomach, and worse, he probably knew it. For the past six years she had wondered if their professional paths might cross again, and here she was, minutes away from living her fantasy. And this time, *she* would be in control. It was enough to make a woman smile.

"Careful," Lesley Major said, falling into step with Kate. "Someone might think you're gloating."

Kate could laugh because Lesley, who ran the information technology department, was her best friend. "Thanks for the new computer—Patsy told me you personally supervised the installation."

"I did, and you're welcome." Then Lesley grinned. "Actually, I wanted to scope out your new office—wow, what a view!"

"Thanks."

"As much time as you spend at this place, you should have something nice to see when you look up."

Kate angled her head. "If you're finished, Mom, I need to get to a meeting."

"Ooh, your first staff meeting—are you nervous?"

"I wish people would stop asking me that."

"Will you-know-who be there?"

Kate gave her friend a warning look, and Lesley lifted her hands in defense.

"I only came by to see if you wanted to have dinner with the Majors tonight."

Lesley and her husband Hank and their two kids were always good for a fun evening, but Kate's desk was piled high. "Can I get a rain check?"

"Only if you have a hot date."

Kate laughed. "I do—with my new computer."

Lesley sighed. "Of course you can have a rain check, but Kate, you need to get out."

"I get out."

"More than just to my house."

Lesley looked so worried, Kate wanted to hug her. She and Lesley used to hang out when they were both single. In the years since, Lesley had married and given birth twice. Kate, on the other hand, was harried and been *promoted* twice. Kate thought they were even, but Lesley disagreed.

"Look," Lesley said, leaning in, "the truth is, I invited Neil Powers to join us."

Kate frowned. "Neil Powers?"

Lesley sighed. "Give the guy a break, Kate—he has a crush on you."

Kate shook her finger. "I don't date coworkers."

"There's no policy against it. Besides, his company maintains our Web site—the two of you are hardly coworkers. And he's so cute!"

Kate glanced at her watch, which she kept set ten minutes fast to make sure she arrived everywhere on time. "I'm running behind, so I don't have time to chastise you about the Golden Rule."

"I know, I know—thou shalt not set up thy best friend on a blind date. But this isn't a blind date!"

"Goodbye."

Lesley frowned. "You're going to grow old alone."

Kate grinned and backed away. "I have Bernadette."

"Oh, yeah, *that* girl is a lot of company."

Kate smiled, turned, and kept walking to the coffee station at the end of the hall to replenish her cup. When she found the pot of decaf depleted, she sighed and walked around the corner to retrieve a grounds filter packet from a supply closet. She thought of Neil Powers and pushed her tongue into her cheek. Lesley was right—she did need to get out more, and Neil *was* cute. Maybe she would let her friend arrange a casual meeting. Later...after she became acclimated to her new job.

While Kate rummaged for the coffee, two male voices became louder and stopped when they reached the coffee station. They couldn't see her and she couldn't see them, but she recognized one of the voices immediately, and her pulse ratcheted higher.

"Damn inconvenient time for a meeting," the familiar voice grumbled. "I'm on the verge of closing a huge deal with Lexan Electronics, and I had to come here to play nice-nice for the new boss."

The other man, who sounded younger, made a sympathetic noise. "I don't know much about this Kate Randall, do you?"

A grunt sounded. "Paper pusher, came up through marketing. Never even been on a sales call."

At the derision in his voice, hot anger bolted through her. How dare he?

"But she's been with the company for a long time," his companion said. "I heard ten years."

A laugh sounded. "Yeah, ten years behind a desk."

Kate's eyes narrowed as she contemplated whether to confront the men or to ignore them.

"Well, she must be qualified or Handley wouldn't have given her the job, right?"

She silently applauded the younger man who was willing to give her the benefit of the doubt if only due to John's endorsement.

The first man scoffed. "Kate Randall just happened to be in the wrong place at the right time."

That did it. Kate conjured up a big smile before walking around the corner. "Good morning, gentlemen."

In one glance, she acknowledged that Eric McDaniels hadn't changed much in six years. Same steel-blue eyes, maybe bracketed with a few more lines. Same blue-black hair, but more closely cropped. Same strong features, softened with dimples and a lethal smile, filled out with maturity, and still too handsome for any woman's good. Tall as ever. Beneath his dark-colored jacket, his shoulders were a little wider, his stance a little cockier.

He had recovered from his initial split-second of shock and was sizing her up. Kate was glad she'd worn the army-green skirt and jacket that flattered her auburn hair and dark complexion. She had filled in over the last few years, too, but was pleased about the fact that her mirror now reflected a woman instead of a girl—instead of a naive twenty-six-year-old girl who had foolishly indulged in a one-night stand with the company's most notorious playboy, Eric McDaniels, and more foolishly, had mistaken good sex for true feelings.

"Hello, Eric," she said in as neutral tone as she could manage.

His chin lowered ever so slightly. "Hello, Kate." He gestured toward his sandy haired companion, as yet unaware of the turn of events. "This is Warren Woods."

"How do you do, Warren?" Kate extended her hand. "I'm Kate Randall."

Warren's greeting died on his lips. "I...*you're* Kate Randall?"

She nodded.

The young man looked stricken, then his expression relaxed and he pointed a finger at Eric. "Wait a minute, McDaniels, this is one of your practical jokes, isn't it? I've heard about you, how you're always trying to pull off a gag." He looked back to

Kate. "Come on, you're a secretary or something, aren't you?"

Kate pursed her mouth and shook her head.

Eric appeared to be enjoying the misunderstanding. "Um, Woods, this isn't a gag, although it's good to know my reputation precedes me." Then he looked at Kate and shrugged affably. "I didn't know you were back there, Kate."

She gave Eric her most tolerant smile. "That's okay—I have a knack for being in the wrong place at the right time." She held out her mug and after hesitating, he emptied the last of the coffee that he'd been about to pour into his own cup into hers instead. She sipped the hot brew, not caring that it wasn't decaffeinated, then she glanced at her watch. "Don't be late for our meeting, gentlemen."

As she walked away, she heard the younger man sputter and felt Eric's gaze bore into her back. She felt triumphant...until apprehension crowded in. Considering her history with Eric McDaniels, this situation was bound to get worse before it got better.

CHAPTER TWO

The best way to convince a fool that he is
wrong is to let him have his own way.
—Josh Billings

ERIC BIT DOWN on the inside of his cheek and tasted
the tang of badly chosen words as he waited for a
new pot of coffee to dispense. Apparently Kate Randall hadn't lost her figure, or her ability to catch him
off guard, although her tongue was sharper than he
remembered. Woods had already scampered off to
the meeting, afraid of further offending the new boss.
He, on the other hand, needed strong black coffee to
get through the next couple of hours of bureaucratic
bull.

He pinched the bridge of his nose between thumb
and forefinger, wishing he were anywhere but here,
fighting a hangover and the inexplicable image of
Kate's face superimposed over the face of the woman
he'd taken home last night. As much as he enjoyed
sales, he hated the rah-rah team-spirit propaganda
that most companies spouted. He had carved out a
nice corner of independence at Handley Toys—he
worked their major and national accounts, bringing
huge deals to fruition, and his superiors left him the

hell alone. The last thing he needed was a green boss looking over his shoulder.

He grimaced. A green boss with green eyes that could make a man forget to breathe.

He curled his hand around a Handley coffee mug. Damn it, it wasn't as if he hadn't thought about crossing paths—and maybe sharing a bed—with Kate Randall again. But *working* for her? What had John Handley been thinking when he'd promoted her to VP? She didn't have a clue about what made sales people tick.

She certainly didn't have a clue about what made *him* tick.

Eric frowned as he filled his coffee cup. John had offered him the VP position, but he'd turned it down because he'd never thought of himself as the home-office type. But the news that he would be working for Kate Randall had been enough to sever the loyalty he felt toward John and the company. Last night he'd called his former boss who now worked for Mixxo and told him he'd changed his mind about their offer. Two weeks from now, on April 5, he would have a new job.

He drank from the cup and swore under his breath as the searing liquid scalded his tongue. Then he made his way to the boardroom where the meeting was already in progress. He entered, not bothering to try to be quiet as he closed the door and leaned against the wall opposite from where Kate sat, addressing the seated group of about two dozen. Everyone glanced in his direction and he was filled with the satisfaction of knowing he was regarded as the leader of the pack.

"—pleasure to be working with all of you," Kate was saying. "My background with the company is product- and brand-management, so I have a good grasp of sales as seen from inside the business, but I'm committed to learning everything about external sales as quickly as possible." Then she stopped and leveled her green gaze on him. "Eric, there's an empty chair," she said, pointing.

He lifted his coffee mug. "I'd rather stand, thanks. This isn't going to last too long, is it?"

Her mouth tightened and the color rose becomingly in her cheeks—reason enough to keep goading her, in his estimation. In fact, if he kept pushing, maybe she'd fire him and then he wouldn't feel so guilty when he told John Handley he was leaving the company.

"That depends," she said evenly, "on how quickly we get through introductions and objectives for the quarter."

"Objectives?" he asked, then glanced at his watch. "My objective is to get out of here and back to the account I was pulled away from to attend this meeting."

The silence in the room stretched taut and for a split second, he felt bad about wielding his informal power. Until a taunting memory rose in his mind. A conversation that *he* had overheard the morning after their one-night stand.

Kate, a young woman had said in a panicky voice,

your reputation will be ruined if anyone knows you're involved with Eric McDaniels.

Involved? Kate had responded in a scathing tone. *I slept with him, but trust me—I have absolutely no intention of becoming involved with the likes of Eric McDaniels.*

Though exact details about that moment may have escaped his memory, he could still hear the stinging derision in her voice—as if she were referring to an invertebrate. And suddenly, he didn't feel bad at all about usurping her bogus authority.

The silence loomed larger in the room. His ears began to buzz and it seemed as if everyone else in the room fell away, leaving a channel of electricity running from him to Kate. He realized with a sinking stomach that the chemistry between them remained intact. Her gaze was full of defiance, and he suspected his expression was no different.

Finally, she wet her lips. "I might be new to this position, Eric, but I'm aware that your accounts are the single largest contributor to the company's revenue."

His backbone eased a fraction.

"So," she continued, lifting her hands, "educate me. Tell me about this account and what you've done to get to this point." Her smile was congenial, but didn't reach her cool eyes. "I'm sure we can all learn something from the company's top salesman."

Was it his imagination, or had she added a mocking inflection on those last words?

Eric shrugged and maintained his position on the wall. "The client is Lexan Electronics in Pensacola,

Florida. They have two hundred and forty locations in thirty-five states, and the product is our line of handheld electronic games.''

''What size order are we talking about?''

He gave her a dry smile. ''The size order that would mean adding an extra shift at our Huntsville factory.''

Kate nodded curtly. ''Whose line of games do they currently carry?'' she asked, making notes on a clean pad of paper. That pad of paper irritated him beyond reason, probably because it seemed to symbolize Kate's squeaky-clean desk presence. He contrasted it to his home office, where his desk was buried in spreadsheets, product-fact sheets, and expense reports.

''Travister Games,'' he said.

''And where are you in the process of closing the deal?''

Stalled, although he wasn't about to admit that. ''I was supposed to follow up with the entertainment buyer today,'' he fibbed. ''But now it looks like it'll be next week before I can get back there.'' Actually, the buyer was hedging, and he was hoping to wrangle an appointment on the tail end of his trip through Georgia and northern Florida.

''Are you trying to convince Lexan to expand or to replace their current line?''

He hated answering questions. ''Replace.''

She made a rueful noise in her throat and scribbled another note. Eric pushed away from the wall and managed a fake little laugh. ''You don't approve of my sales tactics?''

Kate looked up, her winged eyebrows raised. "It's not for me to approve or disapprove."

"But?"

She stopped writing and shrugged. "But if the customer isn't inclined to replace their entire line, why not start small and let them expand with our products?"

His blood pressure spiked, and he enunciated slowly. "Because...I...don't...do...things...*small.*"

Her mouth parted and her eyes narrowed ever so slightly. A sliver of satisfaction drilled through him because he knew she was remembering something else about him that wasn't so small.

She averted her gaze, then seemed to collect herself and looked back. "I assume you're shooting to close the deal by next Wednesday, the last day of March?"

"Sales people live and die by the quarter's end," he said. "But then you probably know that, being VP of sales and all."

Her jaw hardened. "I do know that. But this deal is big enough to swing profits from one quarter to the next. Are you sure you can make things happen next week?"

"Plenty of time," he said with confidence to spare.

"Just keep me posted, okay?"

She might as well have swatted him on the behind. He conceded that he could take a hit from anyone other than Kate, but after the way she'd dismissed him years ago, he had the perverse desire to take her down a notch.

"Why don't you come with me?"

She looked up, her expression wary. "What do you mean?"

"Go on the road with me for a few days," he challenged. "I can't think of a better way to learn the external sales side of the business."

She shifted in her chair under the gaze of everyone in the room. "I don't—"

"Maybe you can even help me close the Lexan deal," then he smiled and added, "boss."

Kate wet her lips, glancing all around the room. When the silence became uncomfortable, she gave a little laugh and shrugged. "Sure—in fact, I think it's a great idea."

Everyone in the room exhaled and nodded their approval, some chuckling and making remarks about what a good sport she was. Eric wanted to chuckle himself because the glint in her eyes when she looked up at him had nothing to do with sportsmanship and everything to do with retaliation. He sipped his coffee and half listened as she returned to her agenda, discussing individual territories and objectives for the quarter to begin April 1. Her plans didn't matter to him because he'd be gone shortly. Instead, he observed the precise way she moved her head and her hands, wondering from where she had acquired such reserve, such detachment, and remembering it was her aloofness that had first attracted him.

They'd been in Vegas at a trade show—he was a top salesman striking deals with clients, and she was one of the newbies who'd come to help work the company booth. Kate had confounded him from the beginning because she wasn't the type of woman he normally was attracted to. Other than her spectacular coloring, there was nothing flamboyant about Kate— her manner and her clothing were understated, and she'd seemed more irritated than flattered when he'd flirted with her.

Never one to back down from a challenge, Eric had pursued her relentlessly over the next few days of the trade show, and because he'd had to work to draw her out, he'd found out more about her than almost any woman he'd ever...bedded. Strange, the details he remembered after all this time—that she was an only child and her parents lived in Florida, that she disliked olives and traveling by plane, and that she had the most beautiful shoulders he'd ever seen. He had worn down her defenses, but by the time they had wound up in bed, he was the one seduced by the dichotomy of her cool air and her fiery beauty. Her disregard of him the next morning had injured his pride more than he or anyone else would have thought possible. He was, after all, happy-go-lucky Eric, salesman extraordinaire, ladies' man, practical joker.

He was suddenly distracted by the idea of having Kate Randall in close proximity for an extended period of time, and started thinking about all the wonderful ways in which he could plague her before he left the company. A smile tugged at his mouth. This occasion called for the practical joke of all practical jokes. A public humiliation, a personal vindication.

Kate looked up and caught him staring at her. Lasers flashed from her green eyes, and then she checked her watch and addressed the room. "I think it's time for a break. Let's meet back in twenty minutes."

Eric maintained his lean on the wall and waited until all the other sales reps had filed past him before pushing off to approach Kate. She walked up and glanced toward the hall to make sure they were alone, then crossed her arms. "What was that all about?"

He lifted his shoulders in an innocent shrug. "What?"

Her mouth pursed into a cinnamon-colored bow. "You know exactly what—that bit about me going on the road with you."

He assumed an indignant stance. "I try to help ease your transition into your new position, and you think I'm up to something?"

"Yes."

He grinned. "Well, I'm not."

She glanced around again to ensure they were alone. "Good, because I wouldn't want you to confuse anything in the past with something that might happen again."

His gut clenched. "Past?" he asked lightly. "What past?"

She was a tall woman, but still a head shorter than he, so her chin was lifted. Her eyes glittered like jewels and the barest hint of a smile skimmed her mouth. "I'm glad we understand each other. I expect you to treat me like anyone else in this position. And while I appreciate the opportunity to learn more

about external sales, I want to you know, Eric, that
I'm nobody's fool.''

Eric maintained a neutral expression until she
walked out of the room, leaving behind a disturbance
of spice-scented air. He closed his eyes briefly
against the stir of desire in his belly, then watched
her stride away from him. Nobody's fool?

A smile curved his mouth and he murmured,
''We'll see about that.''

CHAPTER THREE

A fool can no more see his own folly than he
can see his ears.
—William Makepeace Thackeray

"I FEEL LIKE a fool," Kate said into the phone.
"Lesley, I don't know why I let that man make me
so flustered. Do you think I made a mistake by agree-
ing to go with him?"

Lesley hummed. "Only if you wind up in bed with
him again."

Kate guffawed and, suddenly restless, got up from
her couch and walked across the red looped rug in
her living room, digging her toes into the thick yarn.
"Well, *that's* not going to happen."

"Then I don't see the problem. You said the only
part of your job that makes you uncomfortable is not
knowing the outside sales business—here's your
chance to learn from the best. Eric McDaniels may
be a ladies' man and a practical joker, but he could
sell condoms to a nun."

Kate laughed, then sobered. "Les, you ought to
see the way the other reps look up to him—like he's
some kind of god." Suddenly the responsibility that
John Handley had assigned to her seemed overwhelming. If sales dropped, every department in the

company would suffer. "For me to be an effective leader, it's important that I have Eric as an ally."

"Then you'd better go," Lesley said. "Look, whatever you want to say about Eric, he's not an idiot—he's not going to jeopardize his career by making a pass at his boss."

Kate's shoulders fell in relief…and something else that felt vaguely like disappointment. "You're right. I'm overreacting. Sorry to be such a downer. How was dinner?"

"We missed you."

Kate dragged a pedicured toe across the rug. "Was Neil there?"

"Yup."

"I've been thinking…"

"I'm listening."

"Maybe when I get back, I'll join the three of you for dinner some night."

"Good," Lesley said lightly, as if she were afraid if she sounded too enthusiastic, Kate might renege. "When do you leave on the sales trip?"

"Wednesday."

"And when will you return?"

"Next Wednesday, the thirty-first."

"Maybe we can get together the weekend after you return. I'm taking a couple of days off to go camping with the boys, so I won't see you before you leave. Will you be able to stay in touch?"

"I'm taking my laptop, so I'll be checking my e-mail. And I'll have my cell phone, although I don't know what kind of service coverage we'll have for some of the trip."

"Check in and let me know how things are going. I'll look in on your place every couple of days."

"Thanks, Les. You're such a good friend."

"Yes, I am. Try to enjoy yourself, okay?"

"I will," Kate said, although both of them knew the improbability of that happening. "Talk to you soon." Kate disconnected the call and walked to the kitchen to grab a bottle of water from the refrigerator—dinner had been shrimp-fried rice at her desk, and the soy sauce had left her with a thirst. She carried the water to her home office and winced at the stack of reading material she'd brought home. None of it seemed appealing. Instead she walked over to a cabinet and opened the doors to reveal her private indulgence—her collection of Bernadette dolls, with all the accessories she'd been able to gather for the 60s pint-sized fashionista.

Less popular and more petite than her counterpart Barbie, Bernadette had enjoyed only a short run on the toy shelf and had not evolved into bendable limbs and styleable hair. She remained frozen in her original state of rigid arms and legs, with a short auburn-colored bouffant and painted-on freckles across her tiny nose. Kate had seen her first Bernadette doll at a flea market when she was ten, and had been mesmerized by the similarity between the doll's coloring and her own. She had emptied her change purse to buy that first doll, dressed in dingy yellow clam-diggers and a blue-and-white striped sweater. The shoes that had gone with the outfit (white criss-cross sandals, she later discovered) were long gone, but astonishingly, a tiny mesh bag full of even tinier sand dollars was intact, its handle looped around the doll's arm. Bernadette had launched Kate's imagination. The insight she'd had into how attached children could become to toys had benefited her immensely in her job with Handley.

The glass display case held over thirty of the red-haired Bernadette dolls in varying stages of condition, in a half-dozen different outfits. Bernadette's closet hadn't been as deep as Barbie's. Kate smiled—she always thought of Bernadette as the poor relative, the late bloomer, the loner. Instead of a sports car, Bernadette had a bicycle, instead of friends, Bernadette had a bag of books, instead of a boyfriend, Bernadette had a little plastic cat.

"Meow."

Kate looked down and smiled at her Siamese cat Lenka who sat on her gray haunches, politely waiting for attention. "Meow yourself," Kate said, then closed the cabinet door and picked up the cat, stroking the spot behind her shoulder that she seemed to like best. Kate's mind drifted back to the morning's encounter with Eric and she replayed the scenes, reliving the mix of dread and thrill at seeing him again and sparring, this time on more equal footing. It was impossible to look at him and not remember the night they'd spent together in Vegas, and worse, she had known he was reliving those memories too. But to him, their one-night stand had been a conquest. To her...

She bent and released Lenka onto the smooth wood floor. To her, their lovemaking had been a sexual awakening—her first inkling of the connection a man and a woman could experience. In the wee hours of the morning, wrapped in Eric's strong arms, listening to his deep breathing, it had been easy to fool herself into thinking she'd fallen in love with him, and that he might feel the same way about her. Surely he had felt it—that strange welling in the chest, a mixture of fear and excitement, the intense ache when their bodies joined, the feeling of languid isolation from the outside world.

But as she had lain there, her limbs entwined with his, panic had pooled in her stomach, then risen in her chest to crowd out all other emotion. One person's earth-shattering experience was another person's roll in the hay. She'd seen her mother turn a blind eye to her father's stepping out off and on during their marriage, had seen her mother's bubbly personality shrink a little more each time her father found a new "friend." Hadn't she vowed not to become involved with a ladies' man? Hadn't she felt a pang of pity for the women who flitted around Eric McDaniels like birds waiting for a crumb of his attention? Instead she had become one of the flock, and within a few days' time, Eric wouldn't remember her name.

She had thought back over their conversations on the trade-show floor and over cups of bad concession coffee and realized that he'd played her for a fool. He hadn't been interested in getting to know her. It had all been foreplay for him, a means to an end. A *sale*. Like a pliable customer, she had bought his act—his flashing eyes and charming tongue and raucous sense of humor.

Kate remembered being overwhelmed with remorse, and had wondered if her behavior would affect the one thing in her life she felt confident about—her job. She had slipped from the bed inch by inch so as not to awaken Eric, and fled his room. The next morning at breakfast, Lesley had grilled her, but she had denied having any feelings for him, had dismissed the encounter as meaningless. And she had studiously avoided Eric the remainder of the trade show. As she recalled, he hadn't seemed to mind, no doubt grateful to be spared the awkwardness of explaining that he wasn't looking for a girlfriend.

To her credit, she thought she'd done a good job of pretending the one-night stand hadn't affected her. She had returned to Birmingham, immersed herself in work, and found the distraction a balm to her psyche. In truth, it was during that time that she'd developed a habit for working late, taking projects no one else wanted, haunting other departments on weekends. How ironic that overcompensating in defense of her encounter with Eric had ultimately fixed her directly in his path again.

She walked over to her desk and picked up one of the books she'd bought on the way home: *How to Make an Effective Sales Call*. The only way she was going to be able to maintain the upper hand on Eric was if she knew at least half as much as he did.

Their road trip loomed before her, rife with potential predicaments. Lesley was right—Eric wouldn't jeopardize his job by making an advance towards his boss. Besides, for all she knew, he could be happily cohabitating with someone, or even be engaged. No, she wasn't nearly as worried about any ulterior motives that Eric might have as she was about her own vulnerability where he was concerned.

Because, she conceded, hugging the book to her chest and looking around her painfully neat office in her painfully neat apartment—she was, heaven help her, *lonely*. Nail-gnawingly, teary-eyed, tissue-drenchingly, chest-achingly lonely. She leaned her head back and sighed at the ceiling. She didn't often stop moving long enough to acknowledge that ghost, but it lurked behind every late night at the office, every weeknight TV dinner, every Saturday-morning run in the park. She was ready for someone to come into her life, ready for love.

Kate bit her lip. She should've taken Lesley up on the invitation to dinner with Neil Powers—even *pretending* that she had someone in her life over the next few days would be a welcome distraction for her vulnerable heart.

"THIS GAG has to be good," Eric said to his pal Winston, then took a swig from a bottle of beer. "I mean really elaborate."

"Something that will have people talking about you long after you're gone?" Winston asked, mopping his forehead with a handkerchief.

Eric grinned. "Yeah. And something that will bring Kate Randall down from her high horse."

"What did this woman ever do to you?"

Eric tipped his bottle for a drink and considered his buddy's question. "Not enough."

Winston's eyebrows climbed over his glasses. "You two were involved?"

"Not exactly."

"Ah. Well…is she involved with someone now?"

Eric laughed. "The woman is married to her job. There are rumors that she might be a lesbian."

"Is she?"

"No." He frowned. "I don't think so." Her response to his lovemaking all those years ago came back in a rush. A sweat broke on his upper lip, and he shook his head. "No, definitely not." And he'd die before he'd admit it aloud, but he'd avoided the company holiday parties and summer picnics because he couldn't stand the thought of seeing fiery Kate with a mannequin boyfriend...or husband. Until today he'd been able to fantasize that she'd harbored a small amount of regret for writing him off all those years ago. She'd been the first woman to make him want...more.

"Is she a looker?"

Eric nodded, then caught himself and shrugged. "If you like the ice-princess type." A facade, because he knew the heat that simmered just beneath the surface.

"How about setting up a bucket of paint to fall on her?"

Eric shook his head. "I did that a couple of years ago to a sales guy in another division."

"Mice in her briefcase?"

"Did that to lady in production."

"Nail her office furniture to the ceiling?"

"Guy in customer service."

"Set her up for a radio phone scam?"

"Stockbroker buddy of mine." Eric lifted his index finger. "And *that* was funny, but his wife still won't talk to me." He sighed. "Besides, this has to be something more...cerebral."

"Well," Winston said, scratching his neck, "if she doesn't have a boyfriend, how about sending her an anonymous love note over e-mail?"

Eric worked his mouth back and forth and nodded. "That's good, but it needs something..." He snapped his fingers. "A secret admirer!"

"Yeah, string her along until—"

"April Fool's Day!" Eric crowed. "I'll be on my way out the door and no one will be able to touch me!" Then he frowned. "But how can we let everyone else in on the joke?"

Winston leaned forward. "We keep a log of the notes and her replies, and then on April Fool's Day, we send the log to everyone at Handley!"

Eric's conscience stirred. "I don't know about that."

"Okay, just the sales team then."

Eric hesitated, and his own hesitation irritated him.

"I'll make sure the notes are untraceable," Winston cajoled, warming up to the idea. "If she's as uptight as you say she is, she probably won't respond anyway. But if she does respond and says something juicy—man, oh, man, you'll be a legend." Eric's friend laughed, then wiped his forehead again.

Eric pulled on his bottle of beer, mulling the idea, trying to control that swell of anticipation that accompanied the planning of a good joke. "It's a great idea, and the timing *would* be perfect." He nodded. "I could give you our itinerary so you can send the notes while we're on the road."

"That's good—she'll never even suspect you."

Eric worked his mouth back and forth again, trying to decipher the dull niggling in his chest. "Still..."

Winston snorted. "You'd do it if she were a man, wouldn't you?"

"Hell, yes."

"Then there's your answer."

Eric looked at his buddy and nodded. Kate had told him herself that she expected him to treat her the way he'd treat anyone else in her position. He grinned. "Okay, let's see how the ice princess responds to having a secret admirer."

He wasn't any more interested in Kate's reaction to a secret love interest than he would be if she were anybody else.

Really.

CHAPTER FOUR

Fools grow without watering.
—Thomas Fuller

TWO DAYS LATER, Kate squinted at the computer screen, trying to make sense of what she was reading.

Kate,
So that you don't think I'm some kind of weirdo, I want you to know that I've never done anything like this before, but here goes…. You are a beautiful, fascinating woman, and I'd like to have the chance for us to get to know each other better. Since your business is toys and games, I'm hoping this note will appeal to your sense of romance and adventure. Waiting for your reply…

Fool for You

She glanced at the sender's address—FoolforYou, with an e-mail extension of letters and numbers that gave no hint of the source. She supposed in case she didn't reply, the man didn't want to be identified. If he hadn't used her first name and referenced the toy company, she might have thought the note was spam.

Doubt and pleasure warred in her chest—whether a woman was thirteen or over thirty, the idea of having a secret admirer probably never lost its appeal. She indulged the fantasy for a few seconds, frowning when the impossibility of the note originating from a certain dark-eyed, dimpled salesman flitted through her mind. Then realization dawned—of course: Neil Powers. The man was a computer whiz and Lesley had told her that he had a crush on her—what better way to break the ice than via e-mail?

She thought of Neil's sandy-haired, boyish good looks and conceded that his friendly smile held more appeal than her dolls and her cat and her paperwork. She couldn't put her finger on exactly when it had happened, but lately she had begun to long for... more. Male companionship, yes, but something more intangible—like the loving way Lesley and Hank looked at each other over their children's heads, or touched hands when they passed in the kitchen. It was as if one picked up where the other one left off, and even though they were both interesting, intellectual individuals in their own right, to think of them apart was almost inconceivable.

That's what she wanted—unity. Harmony. A strong physical attraction, of course, but also a foundation of caring that would stand when the attraction cooled. When Hank looked at Lesley, there was a certainty in his expression that he would endure torture before he would allow something bad to happen to her, or do something to cause her shame, like have an affair. Kate knew it was that cloak of love that made Lesley in turn devoted to Hank and to her children.

Kate looked back to the computer screen and acknowledged there was something very sweet and in-
genuous about a secret admirer. Here was a man who
was truly interested in getting to know a woman first,
rather than asking a few rote questions in prelude to
his conquest, as Eric McDaniels had.

A knock sounded on her office door and she
looked up to see the man himself, as if her thoughts
had conjured up his presence. He smiled widely, and
she was unprepared for her physical reaction to his
obvious good cheer. Eric was breathtakingly handsome and seeing him standing there, his shoulders
spanning the doorway, charisma emanating from
him, it was easy to see why he enjoyed such success
as a salesman—men wanted to be him, women
wanted to be *with* him. He was irresistible.

Almost.

She blinked and tried to rein in her wayward
thoughts. ''Yes?''

He strode casually into her office, taking in the
view of the Birmingham skyline with his mouth
pursed. ''Nice.''

''Thank you,'' she said in a neutral tone, noticing
that the roomy office seemed to shrink from the sheer
volume of him. ''Eric, did you need something?''

He walked closer to her desk and she lurched forward to block the message on her computer screen—
he'd be the last person she'd want to see the anonymous note. His gaze flicked in the direction of the
screen, then back. ''I was going to suggest that we
get an early start, maybe have lunch before we hit
the road, but it looks like you're busy.''

''Just answering e-mail,'' she said with a little

wave. "Lunch sounds fine. Give me about ten minutes, and I'll meet you in the lobby."

His gaze wandered back in the direction of her screen and she leaned farther, fighting the impulse to turn around and hit a screen saver button to hide the message. That would look too...*guilty,* she thought guiltily. "Okay?" Her voice sounded high and brittle.

Eric looked back to her and shrugged. "Okay. See you in ten."

She remained frozen in her unnatural position until he cleared the doorway, then heaved a sigh of relief and turned back to her screen. She hesitated, then hit the reply button and quickly typed:

Fool,
From your note, I gather that we already know each other. I am intrigued, but you have the advantage—identify yourself and perhaps we can talk.

K

Then before she could change her mind, she clicked the send button, and exhaled. At least she'd put the ball back in his court. She imagined Neil sitting at his computer, waiting for a reply to pop up in his in-box. A smile would play over his serious mouth, and for a few moments, he too would be caught up in the excitement of the anonymous flirting.

Kate smiled herself, absurdly grateful for the distraction before going on the road with Eric. Still, her heart thudded in her ears now that the moment of departure was near. She tabbed through the rest of her messages, deleting a few, forwarding a couple to Patsy for administrative follow-up, and saving most to file for future reference. Then she packed up her laptop, retrieved her weighty briefcase, and wheeled her suitcase through the doorway of her office, closing the door behind her.

Eric sat on the corner of Patsy's desk, trying to coax a smile from the older woman, who, from her body language, was having none of it. Kate bit back a smile because her assistant was the only woman she'd ever seen who was immune to the man's considerable appeal.

"And kindly remove yourself from the corner of my desk," Patsy was saying sternly, and Kate felt sure if the woman had had a ruler, she would have rapped his big knuckles.

Eric unfolded himself lazily, then looked at Kate and grinned. "She loves me."

Kate shook her head. "I don't think the McDaniels charm works around here."

He raked his gaze over her pale blue pantsuit, then made a clicking noise with his cheek. "Yet."

A warm thrill skittered over her shoulders, though she outwardly ignored him.

Patsy huffed and turned to Kate. "You're leaving early?"

Kate nodded, then extended a sheet of paper. "Here's our itinerary. If everything goes as planned, we'll be driving to Atlanta today, then on to Jacksonville, Florida, tomorrow for an electronics show on the weekend, then to Pensacola Monday to meet with Lexan Tuesday, and make our way back to Birmingham Wednesday.''

Patsy glanced at the sheet. "Are your hotels listed?" she asked suspiciously, as if she might call and make sure that Eric had secured separate rooms.

"Yes," Kate said evenly, her defenses rising, although she knew her secretary meant well. What Patsy couldn't know was that her anxiety about their road trip was pushing Kate's anxiety higher as well. She just wanted to get going—the sooner they got on the road, the sooner they'd return, on firmer ground she hoped. "Patsy, I appreciate you holding down the fort while I'm gone. Call me on my cell phone if you need to. Oh, and I'll be checking e-mail often.''

Patsy looked up. "Since when?''

Heat suffused Kate's cheeks guiltily when she thought about her secret admirer. Would he reply? "Since now," she said lightly. "Goodbye."

Patsy glanced at Eric, then back, and gave a curt nod. "Good luck."

Kate had the feeling Patsy wasn't referring to the Lexan Electronics account.

"I'll take your suitcase," Eric said, reaching for the handle.

"No, thank you," Kate said, stepping past him and walking down the hallway. On this trip she would have to seize every opportunity to exert her authority. "Let's get going."

Eric watched her walk away from him, the flare of her hips accentuated perfectly by the pale-colored slacks that fit snugly in the rear, then gave way to full, draping trouser legs. Nice.

He smiled to himself, wondering if Kate's earlier preoccupation with her e-mail had anything to do with the note Winston was supposed to send today. She had certainly seemed jumpy when he was in her office, as if she was trying to prevent him from seeing something on her computer screen. Had she succumbed so quickly to the idea of having a secret admirer? It would seem so, else wouldn't she simply have deleted the message and been done with it? And even her secretary had found it odd that she would be checking her e-mail often. Was Kate hoping for another note from her mystery man? He and Winston hadn't discussed the frequency of notes, just that he would respond as often as she did, using the basic wording that Eric had written on a cocktail napkin.

Eric's smile deepened. This trip might prove to be more interesting than he'd anticipated. He was going to enjoy watching Kate squirm while she decided whether or not she wanted to strike up a virtual romance with a virtual stranger.

When she stopped and bent over to adjust a strap on her suitcase, causing the fabric of her slacks to tighten across her rear, his groin tightened involuntarily. Ah, hell, who was he kidding? He was going to enjoy watching Kate, period.

At the sound of a deliberate throat-clearing, he turned his head to find Kate's secretary staring at him pointedly. He grinned and saluted, then strode after his fiery, unflappable boss.

Well...unflappable for *now,* anyway.

CHAPTER FIVE

The heart of a fool is in his mouth.
—Benjamin Franklin

"THERE'S A SECRET to direct sales," Eric said loudly over the rushing wind, gesturing with one hand. He was sprawled in the camel-colored leather driver's seat of his black convertible Porsche Targa, and Kate was holding on to her hair to keep it from flying off her head.

She glanced at the instrument panel, lifted one eyebrow, and shouted, "Driving twenty miles an hour over the speed limit?"

He grinned, his closely cropped hair barely lifting in the wind. "That's number two. Number one is establishing a long-term relationship."

She nodded, thinking how ironic it was to hear that from a man who seemed resistant to the idea of having a long-term relationship in his personal life. She was also thinking she might have taken notes if not for the fact that they were zooming down the road at eighty miles an hour, topless.

"Don't you think it's a little cool to have the top down?" Kate yelled, shivering in her coat, wishing she'd brought her gloves. They were barely an hour down the interstate toward Atlanta, and she was already feeling high maintenance.

"The temperature is perfect," Eric shouted. He was minus a jacket and seemed comfortable, his tie flapping happily past his left shoulder. "Just this side of brisk—it's good for the skin."

"But not the hair," Kate muttered, spitting out a hank of it and skimming her medusa locks into a hand-held ponytail. She longed for sunglasses to shield her stinging eyes. She should've known Eric McDaniels wouldn't drive a typical salesman's car—a sedan or a van or an SUV. What was it he'd said? *I don't do things small.* It followed, of course, that even his car had to make a statement—fast, sleek, sexy.

It suited him, the cad.

She studied the steel-gray sky, hanging low enough to touch. "It looks like rain," she shouted.

"Naw," he said with a dismissive wave. "It'll blow over—you'll see."

She saw all right—she was looking straight up when the first big drop of rain hit her in the eye. Within seconds, they were being pelted with a cold spring downpour. Eric pumped the brake, flipped on his turn signal, and eased to the right shoulder of the road. Kate held her arms over her head to make an ineffective hat. She groaned as icy water dripped under her collar and down between her shoulder blades.

He brought the car to a sliding halt, flipped on the hazard lights, yanked up the lever for the parking brake, then hit a button that brought the rag top up and over them like a clam shell closing.

Eric locked down the top with a handle on his side,

then reached across Kate to pull another handle into place. She flattened herself against her seat, but could not completely escape the brush of his wet shoulder as he worked with the lever. The simple movement brought the musk of his cologne to her nostrils and hinted at the power of his body. Kate swallowed hard against her physical response to his nearness, telling herself it was sheer biology. She closed her eyes briefly to suppress the anger and frustration that he could still affect her, and that she had even agreed to accompany him on this trip in the first place.

The lever he turned in front of her sealed the car with a vacuum that pulled at her ears. Eric sat back in his seat and grinned like a boy who'd been caught in a rainstorm while riding his bike. Indeed, with water dripping from his hair and nose, he looked every inch the mischievous imp. Her anger spiked, and her expression must have said so.

"What?" he asked.

"Look at me," she said, holding her arms down so the water could drip off. "Why didn't you just put up the top as I asked?"

He had the nerve to shrug. "Because I didn't think it would rain."

She gestured violently. "All you had to do was look up!"

"I'm sorry, all right?"

She glared at him. "If I didn't know better, Eric, I might think you were trying to make me look foolish." She raked her dripping hair back from her face. Her mascara, she knew, was sliding down her face with the rest of her makeup. Her slacks were water-marked and probably ruined.

"How do you think I feel?" he asked irritably. "It'll take days for the interior of the car to dry out."

She shot him an evil look and shook her arms in a futile attempt to shed more water.

He sighed, then said, "Kate, I *am* sorry about getting you wet." He stopped and his words seemed to echo around them in innuendo, resurrecting old memories. Her chest tightened, and she averted her gaze, wanting to scream. The tiny car was suddenly confining and steamy and way too intimate with the two of them huddled inside while the rain outside beat down on the roof and windshield.

"Look," Eric said, "I think I'll wait until this lets up some before I pull back out on the highway. So…maybe this would be a good time to clear the air."

Kate glanced back, struck anew by how handsome Eric was, his steel-blue eyes rimmed with thick lashes, his nose strong and shot with character, his chin square but ready to yield to a smile. "Clear the air about what?" she asked suspiciously.

"About that night in Vegas."

"I don't want to talk about it," she said quickly, and shifted in her seat a fraction of an inch closer to the door, away from him.

"I know you don't want to, but don't you think we should?"

"There's nothing to say," she declared, "except that I'm sure we're both able to put our mistakes behind us."

He pursed his mouth slightly, but she couldn't read his expression.

"In other words, Eric, I have no intention of allowing what happened between us years ago to affect our working relationship now, and I hope you feel the same.''

He spread his hands. "I do. I thought I was doing you a favor by offering to teach you the ropes.''

She lifted her chin. "Fine. As long as this isn't some kind of ploy for us to be alone." There...she'd said it. Voiced the thought—fantasy?—burrowed in the recesses of her mind. She held her breath in the warm, steamy cocoon.

His jaw hardened a split second before humor returned to his eyes. "Don't worry, Kate—I have no intention of trying to seduce you.''

Her lungs squeezed, forcing her to exhale. "Good," she said evenly. "Because I have no intention of being seduced.''

He nodded good-naturedly, then grinned. "In sales, we call this a meeting of the minds.''

Grateful for the lighter mood, Kate tried to relax and finally managed a conciliatory smile. "If I weren't waterlogged, I'd write that down.''

He snapped his fingers. "I almost forgot—I put a thermal blanket under the seat for, um, emergencies.''

She caught his gaffe—right. Ten dollars said the thermal blanket was for emergency *trysts,* but at this point, she didn't care.

He leaned sideways and reached under Kate's seat. Unfortunately, the movement placed his head down by her knee, conjuring up too many intimate situations for her comfort. She inched away, but he moved into the extra space, grunting in his effort, his arm brushing her leg while he groped around the floor. Through her clothing, her skin burned every time he touched her. Instead of clearing the air, their conversation about their past seemed to have keened her senses.

"Eric," she said, gritting her teeth, "I'll get it."

"Found it," he said, then straightened, dragging a blue cotton blanket with him. He handed it to Kate. "Maybe this will help absorb some of the water until we can make it to the rest area a few miles ahead."

She took the blanket and their fingers touched, sending bolts of awareness up her arm. He felt it, too, she could tell by the momentary slip of his trademark grin. She practically snatched the blanket out of his hands, then set about soaking up as much water from the surface of her clothing, hair and skin as possible. Eric turned on the air conditioner and while the blast of cold air sent her into a spasm of chills, it was better than the steamy heat that had developed in the interior of the car.

She flipped down the visor and braved the mirror, groaning at the creases in her makeup and the dots and dashes of mascara on her cheeks. "I don't think I'm going to make a very good impression on our first customer."

Eric scoffed. "You look great."

Unbidden pleasure shot through her, but she pivoted her head and gave him a warning look.

He raised his big shoulders in a shrug and loosened his water-spotted tie. "I mean you look…fine. We'll be calling on a mega toy store in the Atlanta suburbs—it'll be pretty casual."

She looked back to the mirror, satisfied that Eric seemed prepared to behave himself. But she was horrified to see something foreign in her eyes…a spark that hadn't been there this morning. Kate lifted the end of the blanket and blotted, choosing to attribute the new light to her secret admirer and not to… anyone else.

From the corner of his eye, Eric watched his boss repair her makeup as best as possible under the circumstances. As if she needed it. He bit down on the inside of his cheek to keep from staring outright. Kate Randall had remained his favorite fantasy, but his mind had failed to retain the potency of her beauty. He'd forgotten how truly extraordinary her coloring was, and the way her bottle-green eyes leapt with fire when she was angry—or aroused.

He shifted in his seat, wondering why he'd pushed her into discussing their one-night stand. It was history. Ancient history. Since that time, many women had come and gone in his life. And Kate? His eyes ached from straining not to look at her. Had men come and gone in her life, or were the rumors true— that she was a workaholic, more bent on climbing the corporate ladder than on climbing into anyone's bed?

"Earth to Eric."

He started and turned his head. "Huh?"

Kate gave him an odd look and extended the blanket. "I said the rain has stopped."

He looked around—she was right. A chill had settled over his wet arms and face. He took the blanket, remembering when he'd put it under the seat he'd had other plans for sharing it with a beautiful woman. Now he'd never be able to look at the blanket without thinking about Kate. He remembered her words,

Good. Because I have no intention of being seduced.
If he were a less experienced man, her aversion to
him might make him think that their night together
had been less than satisfying. But he'd been there,
and she had been satisfied. Three times, damn it. So
what had made her decide that he was too inferior to
become involved with?

And perhaps more significantly, why did he care?

Shaking off his uncharacteristically foul mood,
Eric managed a laugh. "This isn't the most promising start to our trip, but it gives you an idea of what
life on the road is like." He stuffed the damp blanket
under his seat, then fastened his seat belt and waited
for Kate to do the same.

"How much are you on the road?" she asked.

"About two weeks a month, rotating my territories. I typically drive this route, especially when the
weather is nice. This will be a light week leading up
to meeting with Lexan. Mostly, I'll be visiting flag
ship stores for goodwill and to get some advance
copies of our products into the market. And there's
the electronics show on Saturday."

She turned in her seat to face him. "Eric, I don't
believe I ever told you how much I appreciate that
you didn't jump ship to Mixxo, because I'm sure
they made you an offer."

Her expression was so genuine that a guilty pang
struck behind his breast bone. What would she think
of him once she learned that he *had* jumped ship?
But there was too much at stake for him to grow a
conscience now, so he tried to make light of her comment. "No, you never told me."

"Do you think you'll always be in sales?"

He shifted uncomfortably. His plan was to close the deal with Lexan before the end of the quarter to qualify for a bonus. Then in a few months, he'd be back at Lexan Electronics pushing the line of Mixxo products—that was the crazy, competitive, and lucrative world of sales. "I can't imagine being anything but a salesman."

"I'm looking forward to seeing you in action," she said, her tone slightly mocking. "John told me that you give quite a performance."

Eric turned on the left-turn signal and waited for an opening in the traffic before merging. "I have my own bag of tricks."

Kate looked at her watch.

"What, are you bored already?" he asked.

"Hmm? No, I was trying to figure out what time we'd arrive at the hotel this evening."

Despite his previous denial of plans to seduce her, his pulse spiked at the thought of being alone with Kate in a building full of beds. "Are you in a hurry to experience bland food and be overcharged for parking?"

"Actually, I was wondering when I might be able to check my e-mail."

Satisfaction curled in his stomach, but he forced himself to sound offhand. "Expecting an urgent memo?"

Kate studied her manicure, her expression detached. "Something like that."

Eric's good humor returned full force, and he shifted the car into a higher gear. "Don't worry— we'll be at the hotel in plenty of time for you to check your e-mail."

CHAPTER SIX

Tricks and treachery are the practice of fools,
that don't have brains enough to be honest.
                                    —Benjamin Franklin

Kate,
I promise to divulge my identity soon, although
when you discover who I am, I don't think
you'll be so surprised. I do want to make one
thing perfectly clear—I have a lot of female
friends, and I'm not looking for another one.
I'm ready for a woman who wants to have a
grown-up romantic relationship, with an eye to
ward a long-term commitment. Are you game?
                                    Fool for You

KATE GAVE IN to a little thrill of flattery to be singled
out. And the things he said spoke to her—she, too,
was looking for a grown-up romantic relationship
with an eye toward commitment. Over the years
there had been a handful of guys she'd met through
friends and dated for a few months, but the relation-
ships had eventually petered out for no good reason—perhaps lack of interest on both sides. She often wondered if she had unrealistic expectations of

physical chemistry leading to a deeper bond, but Lesley had assured her over and over that love would hit her out of the blue.

Years ago, Eric had been that hit. Right between the eyes. Right between the thighs. And right through the heart. On some level, had she been comparing her feelings toward other men to the powerful attraction she'd felt for Eric? It was long past time for letting go of that fantasy. Even if Eric suddenly turned into a deep, caring individual willing to make a lifetime commitment, their positions alone made a relationship impossible. One side of her mouth slid back in a wry frown. Since the idea of Eric undergoing a personality transplant seemed highly unlikely, the rest was a moot point.

Kate mentally went down the short list of possible names for the sender of the notes, but kept coming back to Neil Powers. The sender wanted them to get to know each other, so that seemed to rule out old boyfriends. He knew what she did for a living, and intimated that she knew who he was. The note had been sent at 3:30 in the afternoon, about the time she and Eric had been shaking hands with the manager of the largest toy store in Atlanta.

She had marveled over the way Eric had greeted most of the employees by name, had helped to relocate a display of Handley toys, and had rounded out the customer call by challenging a group of twelve-year-olds to an impromptu tournament on a new Handley electronic hand-held game. Seeing him sitting cross-legged on the floor with his dress-shirt sleeves rolled up, working the small buttons of the game with his big thumbs, it was easy to imagine him as a boy—tousled hair, laughing eyes, winning grin. In those few minutes, Kate had realized why Eric McDaniels was the best salesperson in Handley's history—selling toys and games gave him an excuse to *be* a kid. It was the perfect occupation for the man who didn't want to grow up.

Kate shook her head free of Eric and reread the e-mail message from FoolforYou. She wet her lips, then put her hands on the keyboard and began to type.

Fool,
For now I'll go along with your anonymity, but you have to share a few things with me—what do you do for a living? Do you live in Birmingham? And most importantly, are you a NASCAR fan?

K

She hit the send button, then exhaled and checked her watch. Almost time to meet Eric for dinner. She changed from her water-marked pantsuit to a pair of black slacks and a lightweight yellow sweater, then made her way to the hotel restaurant. She frowned wryly when she saw that Eric was already there flirting with the busty bartender. He was leaning on the bar, and the young woman was studiously polishing the knob of the beer tap with a towel. Talk about Freudian.

Kate sauntered over, watching Eric trying to make what might be his biggest sale of the day. He was gesturing with a bottle of beer in one hand, and the coed seemed to be buying whatever he was saying, which must have been hilarious since they both burst out laughing. When Eric turned his head and saw her, he straightened, his trademark grin faltering.

Kate felt slightly vindicated since her heart did the same thing at the sight of him. He still wore the rumpled slacks, shirt and tie that had been doused in the downpour, except now the knot of his tie hung low and the top two buttons of his shirt were undone, revealing the peek of a white T-shirt, and a few dark chest hairs. Unbidden, an image of his bare chest flashed through her mind—well-defined pecs covered with a mat of black hair.

"Kate," he greeted boisterously, then nodded toward the bartender. "This is Hillary. Hill, this is my boss, Kate."

Hill gave her the once-over. "You're his boss?"

"She's much older than she looks," Eric assured his young admirer.

Kate rolled her eyes, and then a thought crossed her mind and she frowned—how old was her own admirer? What if it wasn't Neil, but some teenager who had somehow hacked into her employee profile? Suddenly undone, she crossed her arms. "Eric, is our table ready?"

"Why don't we check?" He tossed a generous tip for Hillary onto the bar.

"Will I see you later?" the woman asked hopefully.

"Not this trip," he said ruefully, then cut his eyes indiscreetly toward Kate, as if she were the whip-cracking boss who brooked no fun on company time. Hillary nodded knowingly and went back to her polishing. Eric finished his beer in one drink, then swept his arm in front of Kate. "Shall we?"

She gave him a wry smile. "Don't leave on my account."

"I'm not—I happen to be starving." He sniffed. "Speaking of which, do you realize that you always smell like food?"

She bristled with mixed reactions. "If you mean my cologne, it's vanilla…and spice."

He wagged his eyebrows. "And everything nice?"

Kate frowned. "Are you drunk?"

"Not yet," he said happily. "But that's a very good idea."

Warning bells were going off in Kate's head as they were shown to a table—as she recalled, alcohol had played a role in their one-night stand all those years ago. Not that she could blame it all on the wine—Eric had primed the pump with a liberal dose of come-on. In hindsight, she had probably looked as starry-eyed as Hillary the knob-polisher.

The maître d' smiled as he stopped at a cozy table tucked away in a corner. "The best seat in the house, Mr. McDaniels."

"Thanks, Gordon," Eric said, discreetly passing a ten-dollar bill as he shook the man's hand. Eric pulled out Kate's seat and she hesitated. "I can't be a gentleman?" he asked, then grinned. "My mother would kill me if I didn't mind my manners."

Kate smiled. She was being foolish, reading too much into his actions—Eric would pull out a chair for any woman. She slid into the chair and allowed him to shift her chair closer to the table, keenly aware of his body pressed against the back of it. "You must stay in this hotel often. Everyone seems to know you.''

''Another sales trick,'' he said, taking his own seat. ''Find a nice hotel with a good restaurant, and become a regular. When I bring clients here, the staff treats me like family.''

And so they did. A waiter appeared, calling him by name and lighting a luminary on their table for ambiance. Eric ordered another beer. Kate hesitated, then, determined not to look as if she were trying to avoid temptation, ordered a glass of merlot. For dinner, he ordered steak and she ordered fish. When they were alone with their drinks, Kate sipped from her glass and experienced a few seconds of pure panic when she wondered what they could talk about. Thankfully, sanity dawned and she settled on the obvious subject: work. ''So, Eric, what attracted you to sales?''

Eric drew from his beer, then settled back in his chair and shrugged, his face wreathed in smiles. ''Can't remember exactly, the money I suppose.''

''Did you go to college?''

He nodded. ''Auburn.''

''What did you study?''

He hesitated, then leaned forward. ''Psychology.''

She lifted her eyebrows in surprise.

Eric seemed almost sheepish. ''When you think about it, I guess it's as good a preparation as any for sales.'' He lifted the bottle to his mouth. ''I've certainly met my share of personalities—John Handley being one of them.''

She nodded in agreement, then decided to cut to the chase. ''Eric, you don't think John should have offered me this job, do you? Because I'm a 'paper-pusher' as I overheard you say?''

He shrugged slowly, as if trying to gauge whether she wanted an honest answer. ''It doesn't matter what I think.''

''Actually, it does.''

''How so?''

''You know the situation I'm in here, Eric. You're the top salesman, and the other reps take their cues from you.''

He laughed. ''I think you give me way too much credit, Kate.''

''Eric, I need your support. Let's try to find some kind of common ground. It's in both our best interests to work together, not to mention the rest of the sales organization.''

He lifted both arms. ''I thought that's what we were doing—working together.''

She bit down on the inside of her jaw. ''But I sense a certain...resentment.''

He lifted his eyebrows. ''Maybe you're not as good at reading people as you think. Ah—here's our food.''

Kate frowned, perplexed by his comment. But he was completely distracted by the food, becoming animated, making a show of inhaling the aroma of the calamari appetizer and sighing in satisfaction. ''Rob, tell Chef Aaron that this is *fine*-looking squid.''

''I will, Mr. McDaniels.''

He divided the food between their plates, and Kate watched as he ate with gusto, his gaze suspiciously averted—she knew a sidestep when she saw one. A few feet away, a man with a Spanish guitar began to strum and sing quietly, effectively filling the silence as they ate. Their entrees arrived shortly. Eric didn't seem eager to resume their conversation and, in fact, had fallen into an uncharacteristically serious mood. Kate forked in mouthfuls of buttery sea bass and rice pilaf and studied him under her lashes.

A furrow had developed between his thick dark eyebrows, and the corners of his mouth were turned down as he chewed. Her conversation had obviously stirred some deep-seated concerns—apparently Eric did have reservations about her ability to lead the sales organization, more than his offhand comments to a young sales rep had revealed. In fact, if he would make jokes about her lack of experience, she might feel better. It was his lack of teasing that concerned her, because it seemed to represent something deeper.

They were sitting scarcely three feet apart, but they might as well have been on opposite sides of the room. Even the air between them seemed to clash, bursting with unsaid words, resentment, and…something else. Something dark and disturbing. Was it dislike…or desire?

Did Eric consider her to be weak because she had succumbed to his flirtation all those years ago? She swallowed a mouthful of wine, savoring the slight burn as it slid down her throat. Did she consider *herself* weak for succumbing to his flirtation?

Their eye contact was sparse and awkward. Under the table, their legs brushed occasionally, prompting shifting and murmured apologies. She hadn't felt this awkward since ninth grade, and frankly, she didn't know what to do about it.

Because as much as she wanted to move past their former sexual encounter and get on with their professional relationship, they couldn't. Not, she realized with a sinking heart, when the electricity they still felt when they were together was like a big white elephant sitting between them. Ignoring it seemed childish, but giving it a name, well, that seemed dangerous.

The guitarist took a break just as the waiter cleared their dishes. "May I bring you a dessert menu?" the man asked, and they talked over each other in their haste to decline.

"No, thank you—"

"I need to—"

"—I'm full."

"—turn in early."

The waiter nodded, then set a small leather folder on the table between them. "I'll take the check whenever you're ready."

They both reached for it at the same time, although her hand closed around it first. Eric's hand covered hers a half-second later.

"I'll get it," she said.

"No, I'll get it," he said.

Neither of them budged. The warmth of his big hand consumed her much smaller one. The feeling unnerved her, rekindling memories of the heat they could generate together. She locked gazes with him and was alarmed to find something akin to desire in the depths of his stare. Seconds ticked off, and she blamed her sudden headiness on the wine and the intimate surroundings. She moved her hand, but he resisted. Panicked, she blurted, "Eric, you should always let the boss pay."

That did it. After a heartbeat, he lifted his hand abruptly, then scooted his seat back and stood, his mood changing from serious to congenial in an instant. "I think I'll call it a night. Thanks for dinner…boss. See you in the morning." Then he nodded and strode back toward the bar.

Kate gave her credit card to the bemused waiter and waited for a receipt. That hadn't gone well. The man certainly brought all of her insecurities to the surface, which frustrated her even more. She was in a position to put Eric in his place, but that place wasn't as well defined as it should be. It wasn't enough that she had decades of a male-dominated society's conventions to battle, but her own lapse as well. Sex transcended titles. Good or bad, the fact was that Eric had seen her naked, and that would always color his judgment where she was concerned.

And vice versa.

She didn't glance his way when she walked past the bar on the way out of the restaurant, but she heard the young bartender's laugh. Apparently, they had picked up where they'd left off, and apparently, Eric still had a girl in every port. Which had nothing to do with his ability to sell, she reminded herself on the elevator ride to her room.

And his ability to sell was the extent of her interest in Eric McDaniels.

Really.

CHAPTER SEVEN

Life is one fool thing after another
whereas love is two fool things after each other.
—Oscar Wilde

AT THE SIGHT OF Kate standing next to the valet station with her roll-along suitcase, Eric scrubbed his hand down his face. She was perfectly coiffed, perfectly beautiful in an orangey-colored jacket and long, swishy skirt that revealed her fine ankles. She hadn't yet noticed him and pulled back her sleeve to check her watch, her expression cool and calm.

Apparently she had slept well. He, on the other hand, had closed down the bar, then sat on his bed in his underwear and watched ESPN. It was supposed to have taken his mind off the fact that he was experiencing some strange feelings toward Kate that he shouldn't be having toward his boss. Feelings that he'd never had toward any woman that he could recall. Wait, there had been a woman in Vegas...

He frowned—no, that was *Kate.*

She looked up and gave him a tight smile. "Good morning."

"Are you always early?" he asked irritably.

Her eyebrows shot up. "Usually."

He handed his ticket to the valet. "Hiya, Mick."

"Hiya, Mr. McDaniels." The man wagged his finger. "You really had me going last time—I really thought someone had been joyriding in your car."

Eric started laughing and turned to Kate. "I went to a collision place and rented a wrecked black Porsche and switched it out with my car in the valet parking lot." He laughed harder. "Mick here almost had a stroke when he went to get it."

Mick laughed until they were both leaning on each other and wiping tears, but Kate seemed less amused.

"I guess you had to be there," Eric said, his laughter petering out.

Kate smiled to humor him, he was sure, and he had another flash of irritation for the people in the world who couldn't take a joke. If a person couldn't laugh once in a while, what was the use in living? He gave Mick the "women—sheesh" look and the man jogged off to get the car.

"What's on the schedule today?" Kate asked, all business.

"We'll head on down to Jacksonville to meet with the buyer for Lincoln Toys."

"They're a chain of independently owned toy stores?"

"Right."

"How long will we be on the road?"

"Six hours, give or take, depending on traffic." He walked out when the car arrived at the door, helped Mick to settle their luggage in the tight trunk, then gave the man a generous tip. When he slid into the driver's seat, Kate was already buckled in, a notepad and pen on her lap.

"Let's keep the top up today."

Not a question—an order. He pursed his mouth and snapped his own seat belt into place. "Whatever you say."

"Tell me about Lincoln Toys."

Maybe it was because he hadn't had his second cup of coffee, but Eric didn't feel like talking about business. "What did you do last night after dinner?"

She looked surprised. "Me? I...went back to my room and got caught up on e-mail."

He checked the smile that came to his face. He'd phoned Winston this morning, eager to know if Kate had indeed responded to the notes they'd concocted and, more importantly, if she'd revealed anything interesting, but he'd gotten his buddy's voice mail. "E-mail has definitely changed the way that people communicate, hasn't it?" he asked, keeping his tone offhand.

"Yes, although I admit I'm not as proficient at it as I should be." She shrugged. "I guess I'd still rather hear the person's voice or talk to them face to face."

Was she referring to communication in general, or to her secret admirer? He nodded, going along. "Nothing can replace personal interaction."

Kate gave him a wary look and he realized that his words could be construed as having a more intimate meaning than he'd intended.

"In sales," he added quickly, not sure why he was suddenly restless—innuendo had never bothered him before. He'd practically made a career out of it. Eric flipped on his signal, then eased into the choking rush-hour traffic heading south into the city. Feeling anti-social, he turned up the radio to fill the silence, although with Kate sitting close enough to touch, he had a hard time concentrating on the driving. She seemed oblivious to his agitation, which aggravated him further.

The woman was driving him crazy. His attention span was nonexistent. His mind ran in circles and figure-eights, crisscrossing memories from six years ago with more recent impressions until he could almost believe they had slept together only last night.

While he concentrated on keeping space between his car and the cars around him, Kate returned calls on her cell phone. He told himself he wasn't interested, but he found himself strangely riveted. There was something voyeuristic about watching her while she was unaware, but he was shameless. And he was hoping she'd call that girlfriend of hers and mention something about her secret admirer.

The first call was to her assistant, Patsy—the one who hated him, he thought wryly. Kate went down a laundry list of items, giving succinct follow-up instructions with self-assurance and a well-rounded knowledge base that surprised him. John Handley had credited Kate with acquiring and reestablishing two defunct toys from the Mixxo lineup, but frankly, he'd thought the old man was being generous. He remembered Kate as being extremely beautiful and quietly intelligent, but not particularly driven.

Maybe he'd underestimated her. Or maybe she'd simply changed a great deal since he'd known her.

He liked listening to her voice, he conceded, her precise diction softened by the slightest accent. Her assistant must have said something funny because

Kate laughed, a surprising burst of happiness that lit her face and made him instantly want to hear it again.

The next few calls were to people whose names he recognized but with whom he had never worked directly. Some of the information she dispensed sounded out of her realm as VP of sales, then he realized that she was answering questions from former colleagues in other departments—product management and branding. They must have relied heavily on her if they were still calling for her opinions. She handled everything with aplomb and finesse, acting as arbitrator during one call that he gathered was a three-way conversation.

Her next call was to John, which gave him pause. He talked to John maybe once a quarter, and in between only when there was a problem. But Kate addressed John in a tone and with shorthand phrases that told him they spoke often—perhaps every day. And if he'd expected her to gush or to shrink to appease the boss, he was wrong; she handled John with the same composure and ease with which she handled peers and subordinates. Eric's respect for her nudged higher—maybe the lady knew what she was doing after all.

Suddenly, her tone changed and she looked in his direction. "Yes, he's right here…okay, let me activate the hands-free feature." Then her expression changed. "Oh…okay." She extended the phone. "John wants to talk to you."

Panic blipped in his chest—had John somehow heard about him accepting the job at Mixxo? That didn't seem likely, and besides, some crazy part of him reasoned in a split second that if John knew and fired him on the spot, there would be no obstacle to sleeping with Kate.

Well, except for Kate herself.

He took the phone. "Hello, John."

"Hello, Eric. I wanted to congratulate you."

His heart dropped. "On what?"

"Silverstein's voted you their sales rep of the year."

One of his most hard-won accounts. He exhaled with relief and pleasure. "Wow, that's great. What did I win?" He glanced over and Kate was looking at him with open interest.

He liked it.

"A weekend in Vegas."

"No kidding?"

"I'm not a practical joker like you," John said with a chuckle.

"Thanks for the bulletin."

"Sure thing. Oh, and Eric?"

"Yes, sir?"

The older man's tone ratcheted lower. "I probably don't have to say this, but…you will behave yourself around Kate, won't you?"

Eric scoffed. "Of course, John."

"It's just that I can't afford to have my new VP made to feel…uncomfortable."

"No problem."

"I mean, I've heard that you're quite the ladies' man, and Kate *is* so lovely—"

"Say no more," Eric cut in with a little laugh, despite the clench in his stomach. "Is that all, sir?"

"Yes. Tell Kate goodbye for me."

"I will. Goodbye."

Kate took the phone that Eric extended to her, burning with curiosity about their exchange. The men had worked together for so long, it was hard not to feel left out.

"John told me to say goodbye."

"What was that all about?" she asked lightly.

"One of my accounts named me sales rep of the year."

She smiled. "That's great."

"And John is concerned that I might be misbehaving around you."

Her smile faltered. "You mean the practical jokes?"

"Among other things." He sighed with melodrama. "For some reason, he thinks you won't be able to resist me."

Kate's stomach jumped. If John had concerns about her and Eric traveling together, why hadn't he mentioned it to her?

"That was a joke, Kate. John knows you'd never do anything inappropriate."

She closed the phone, glad for an excuse to look away. "You make it sound like a shortcoming."

He shrugged. "It just doesn't sound like much fun."

"Maybe 'fun' isn't my objective."

"Maybe it should be."

She looked up sharply and saw the glow of desire in his gaze before he adopted his trademark jauntiness and looked back to the road. Longing hit her midsection, and she hated herself for not being able to stop it. She shouldn't want him. The reasons to stay away from him were too numerous to count. Yet she'd lain awake most of the night, wondering if he was sleeping alone, and berating herself for caring. For reasons she didn't quite understand, she was drawn to Eric with an intensity that suggested something deeper than a physical attraction. It was as if on some level she craved the very characteristics about him that she railed against, to counter her own extremes.

The air hummed with sexual awareness. He shifted gears and she was engrossed by the rippling of his thigh muscle beneath his dark slacks. Her chest welled with yearning to the point of pain, and she desperately tried to distract herself from a sinking realization that she very much wanted to sleep with Eric. The fact that she was entertaining thoughts that might jeopardize her job shook her to the core.

She flipped open her phone and dialed Lesley's office number, willing her friend to be at her desk. On the fourth ring, her friend answered. "Handley Toys. This is Lesley Major."

"Hi, it's me."

"Hey! I've been waiting for you to call."

"I tried to get through last night, but the phone was busy."

"Oh, Hank was on the Internet most of the evening. One of these days we're going to join the rest of the world and get DSL. How are things going?"

"Oh, fine." She could feel Eric's heated gaze on her and strained not to look at him.

"Is McDaniels behaving himself?"

Kate swallowed, miserable she was the one having rampantly improper thoughts. "Yes."

"Oh, he's right there with you, isn't he?"

"Yes. Did you get a chance to swing by my place?"

"Yeah, I stopped on the way home from our camping trip last night. Lenka seemed glad to see me, and all is well. I gave your fern a drink."

"Thanks."

"I saw Neil Powers this morning."

Her mind flew to the anonymous notes. "Oh? Did he mention anything…out of the ordinary?"

"He asked about you and I told him you were out of town. Then he asked when you were coming back." She made a cooing noise. "He seemed eager to see you."

Kate squirmed in her seat. "I'm looking forward to having dinner when I get back." She darted a glance toward Eric and even though he drummed his fingers on the steering wheel to the beat of the song on the radio, she was sure he was listening. "Look, I'd better go." Before Lesley could plan an engagement party. "I'll talk to you soon, okay?" She disconnected the phone call and racked her brain for someone else to call—not her parents, unless she really wanted Eric to get an earful of her life.

"Sounds like you're missing out on something," Eric remarked, nodding toward the phone.

So he *had* been listening. She stared at his profile for a few seconds, fighting a flood of desire and the urge to laugh hysterically and declare that, in fact, she was missing out on a lot and that he could help her fix that right here and now. A second later, sanity returned. She was an independent, accomplished woman entrusted with her company's revenue stream.

"I'm not missing anything I can't live without," she returned, her tone more vehement than she intended. Then she pulled out her notepad, determined that the drive to Jacksonville would be productive. "So, like I said, tell me about Lincoln Toys."

By focusing on work with laser concentration, she was able to push thoughts of Eric to the recesses of her mind and get through the day and through dinner. On impulse, she invited the Lincoln Toys buyer and store manager—both men—to dine with them, removing temptation to steer the conversation into personal territory. She felt Eric's gaze on her throughout the meal, but she studiously avoided all but courteous eye contact. When the meal ended, to avoid a private moment with Eric, she excused herself from the group and escaped to her room. After a quick shower, she prepared a cup of herbal tea and booted up her laptop to access her e-mail. When she saw a note in her electronic in-box from FoolforYou, her pulse picked up.

Kate,
If I tell you what I do for a living, I'll give away my identity. Suffice it to say that I work in a professional environment and there are occasions for our paths to cross. And yes, I live in the Birmingham area. I'm not too familiar with NASCAR, but I am willing to learn. My vice, if you can call it that, is fantasy. I read fantasy fiction and graphic novels, and I've tried my hand at illustration. I hope this doesn't make you uncomfortable, but you've been the topic of more than one fantasy of mine.

Fool for You

An Important Message from the Editors

Dear Reader,

Because you've chosen to read one of our fine romance novels, we'd like to say "thank you!" And, as a **special** way to thank you, we've selected <u>two more</u> of the books you love so well **plus** an exciting Mystery Gift to send you — absolutely <u>FREE</u>!

Please enjoy them with our compliments...

Pam Powers

How to validate your Editor's "Thank You" FREE GIFT

1. Peel off gift seal from front cover. Place it in space provided at right. This automatically entitles you to receive 2 FREE BOOKS and a fabulous mystery gift.

2. Send back this card and you'll get 2 brand-new *Romance* novels. These books have a cover price of $5.99 or more each in the U.S. and $6.99 or more each in Canada, but they are yours to keep absolutely free.

3. There's no catch. You're under no obligation to buy anything. We charge nothing—ZERO—for your first shipment. And you don't have to make any minimum number of purchases— not even one!

4. The fact is, thousands of readers enjoy receiving their books by mail from The Reader Service. They enjoy the convenience of home delivery...they like getting the best new novels at discount prices BEFORE they're available in stores... and they love their Heart to Heart subscriber newsletter featuring author news, horoscopes, recipes, book reviews and much more!

5. We hope that after receiving your free books you'll want to remain a subscriber. But the choice is yours— to continue or cancel, any time at all! So why not take us up on our invitation, with no risk of any kind. You'll be glad you did!

GET A *Free* MYSTERY GIFT...

SURPRISE MYSTERY GIFT COULD BE YOURS **FREE** *AS A SPECIAL "THANK YOU" FROM THE EDITORS*

The Editor's "Thank You" Free Gifts Include:

- *Two BRAND-NEW Romance novels!*
- *An exciting mystery gift!*

▼ DETACH AND MAIL CARD TODAY! ▼

393 MDL DVFG   193 MDL DVFF

FIRST NAME	LAST NAME

ADDRESS

APT.#	CITY

STATE/PROV.	ZIP/POSTAL CODE

(PR-R-04)

Thank You!

The Reader Service — Here's How It Works:

Accepting your 2 free books and gift places you under no obligation to buy anything. You may keep the books and gift and return the shipping statement marked "cancel." If you do not cancel, about a month later we'll send you 3 additional books and bill you just $4.74 each in the U.S., or $5.24 each in Canada, plus 25¢ shipping & handling per book and applicable taxes if any.* That's the complete price and — compared to cover prices starting from $5.99 each in the U.S. and $6.99 each in Canada — it's quite a bargain! You may cancel at any time, but if you choose to continue, every month we'll send you 3 more books, which you may either purchase at the discount price or return to us and cancel your subscription.

*Terms and prices subject to change without notice. Sales tax applicable in N.Y. Canadian residents will be charged applicable provincial taxes and GST.

A little thrill passed over her, which might have had something to do with the fact that she'd been in hyper-sex mode all day in proximity to Eric.

So Neil Powers was into the fantasy genre? The thought of him drawing her as a buxom, leather-clad femme fatale was more amusing than titillating, but a woman who worked in the toy business could do worse than hook up with a man who liked fantasy. Besides, it might grow on her.

Fully aware that their correspondence was on the verge of veering into a much more personal realm, Kate placed her hands on the keyboard. She could put on the brakes, play coy or barrel ahead.

As her fingers hovered over the keys, a knock sounded at her door, and she pivoted her head, frowning. She pushed to her feet and padded to the door, drawing the belt on her white cotton robe tighter as she looked through the peephole.

At the sight of intense blue eyes and deep dimples, she sucked in a sharp breath. What was Eric doing here?

CHAPTER EIGHT

Looking foolish does the spirit good.
                                    —John Updike

ANOTHER KNOCK sounded at the door, causing her to jump. "Kate, it's me, Eric. Open up."

Kate checked to make sure the long robe covered her, knotted the belt again, then smoothed a hand over her damp hair and opened the door. "Yes?"

He straightened and his gaze swept from her hair to her bare feet. "Oh…I…*wow*."

She couldn't help it—she was female. A tickle of pleasure traveled up her spine. Still, she crossed her arms and maintained a staid expression. "Eric, what do you want?"

She wanted the words back as soon as they left her mouth, but they were already out there to be responded to or to be ignored. And Eric wasn't the kind of man to let something slip by.

He wet his lips and adopted a wide-legged stance. "Gee, Kate, I don't think it would be appropriate for me to say what I want right now."

She swallowed, terrified of the little bolts of awareness traveling over her body. She wished he would laugh or crack a joke. Eric was easier to deal with when he was acting a fool than when he was the way he looked now—eyes hooded with passion, lips parted and hands poised to touch her. He was waiting for her to make the next move, and she knew from his elevated breathing that he'd be happy to spend the night in her bed.

And then what? She blinked and dragged in a cleansing breath. "Eric, what are you doing here?"

He averted his gaze, knowing the moment had passed, and then he reached into his back pocket and pulled out a credit card. "You left your card at the restaurant. After our guests left, I walked back past the restaurant, and the maître d' stopped me. He thought that we were…together."

She took the card. "Thank you, but you could have slipped it under my door."

"I wasn't sure this was your room."

"You could have asked at the front desk."

One side of his mouth lifted. "I guess I wanted to see for myself." He craned to look past her into her room. "Checking your e-mail?"

At this distance, he couldn't possibly see the words on the screen, but Kate was jumpy all the same. "Catching up on work, that's all."

He made a tsking noise. "You know what they say about all work and no play."

"Makes Jane a vice president?" Kate asked, her head angled.

He smiled and pointed his finger. "That's pretty good. Did I ever tell you that you're the best-looking boss I've ever had?"

She squinted. "Are you drunk?"

"Can't I pay you a compliment without being drunk?"

"Sure, but since all of your bosses at Handley have been middle-aged balding men, I'm not so sure it's a compliment."

"Trust me, I meant it as a compliment."

She laughed. "Trust you? I lost count of the people in the hotel who came by our table tonight to recount some practical joke you'd pulled."

He shrugged. "I'm a legend."

She shook her head and scoffed. "I'll see you in the morning, Legend."

"Oh, that was the other thing—I came to tell you that I'll be playing golf with the Lincoln guys tomorrow. Jacksonville is a great place, so I'm sure you'll find something interesting to do."

She arched an eyebrow. "I'm sure I will, too. I'll be rounding out your foursome."

His eyes widened. "You play golf?"

"Occasionally. What time are we meeting?"

"Eight o'clock in the lobby," he said with obvious reluctance, then frowned. "But you'll have to play from the men's tees."

"Good," she said with a little smile. "I always do."

The look on his face was so priceless, she almost hated to close the door on it. Just before he disappeared from view, he said, "Kate?"

She relented and swung the door open a foot.

He leaned in. "Tell me again why we can't do this," he said, pointing his finger back and forth between them.

His mouth was close enough to smell on his breath the musky red wine they'd shared at dinner. Her senses stirred and her body strained toward him. She held on to the door for strength. "The fact that you have to ask is pretty much reason in itself, don't you think? Good night, Eric."

She closed the door and turned the dead bolt, then leaned against the door until her vital signs slowed. That man was going to be the death of her.

Across the room, her computer screen glowed.

Her mood buoyed. Unless she found another man first.

She reclaimed her seat in front of the laptop, then began to type.

> Fool,
> Your hobbies piqued my interest, but we'll have to meet face-to-face to discuss them more fully. I'm eager to explore the diversions we have in common. When can we meet?
>
> K

The note was more daring than she'd meant it to be and no doubt was influenced by her feelings toward Eric, but she hit the send button anyway. A few seconds later she felt oddly deflated and even though she settled in a chair to read, she kept glancing toward the door, remembering Eric standing there, teasing her, almost daring her to let him in. She only hoped that her raging libido wasn't as obvious to him as it felt to her.

She puffed her cheeks out in frustration and laid back her head. Then she thought of tomorrow and smiled. Eric might have the edge when it came to sex appeal, but she could hold her own on the golf course.

ERIC WATCHED with mixed feelings as Kate walked up to the tee. When he and the other men had claimed a handicap of ten and she'd chimed in the same, he had guffawed. But she had persisted, probably because she felt as if she couldn't back down at that point. And even though he wouldn't mind seeing her make a fool of herself, watching an overconfident golfer could be downright painful—not to mention dangerous if the person wasn't careful with their shots. But as his boss assumed her stance, he took in her snug khaki-colored shorts and long, brown legs and conceded that the scenery wasn't half bad. Then he pursed his mouth—actually her stance and grip looked pretty decent, too.

When she started her backswing, he had the first inkling that he'd been had. Her swing was picture perfect and, according to the *ping* of the club hitting the ball, she'd found the sweet spot on the driver she'd rented at the pro shop. He watched the ball climb and climb, then he yanked off his sunglasses to get a better look. When the ball dropped in the middle of the fairway, he couldn't believe his eyes. "That's a two-hundred-and-fifty-yard drive," he muttered.

Shep Lightly and Tom Atlas from Lincoln Toys turned on him. "Damn it, McDaniels, is this another one of your practical jokes?"

"You made us think she's your boss, but she's some kind of golf pro, right?"

He held up his hands. "Whoa, boys, she really is my boss."

Shep started back to the golf cart. "Yeah, right."

Tom was behind Shep. "McDaniels, I've had about enough of your gags—"

"Gentlemen," Kate said behind them.

They all turned.

A little smile played over her mouth. "This joke's on Eric. I am his boss, but he didn't know that I played on the University of Alabama's golf team when I was in college."

The men perked up instantly. "You don't say?"

Eric gave her a murderous glare. "I guess you forgot to mention that little detail, *boss*." The scrap of doubt he'd harbored about carrying on with the practical joke that he and Winston had planned vanished.

The men howled with laughter. "Well, it's about time someone got one on McDaniels," Shep said, coming back to Eric and slapping him on the back. Tom picked up his driver and shook Kate's hand, then asked for pointers when he assumed his own stance.

Eric and Shep were standing in the tee box about ten feet behind them. "Damn," Shep whispered, "she's a smart dame, a knockout *and* she can play golf. Will she marry me?"

Eric scowled.

And the day went downhill from there. Kate moved like a graceful athlete, turning heads at every hole with her perfect putt *and* her perfect butt. Distracted as hell and feeling pressured to be on his best game, Eric hooked and sliced his way to one of his worst scores in recent history. Meanwhile, Kate, Shep and Tom shot their handicaps and seemed to have a rollicking good time in the process. Not only that, Kate had managed to pick their brains about licensing older-brand toys for children's books and comics. She was...perfect. And Eric wanted to wrap his driver around something.

He gritted his way through lunch and listened while Kate charmed Shep and Tom into expanding their book program throughout the seven Florida locations. "Your demographics indicate an older customer—grandparents shopping for grandchildren— and those customers will buy more traditional products such as books. We just signed an agreement to distribute Weeping Willow books—and at least three more Weeping Willow movies will be released in the next two years. We think the franchise will be a gold mine for stores like yours."

The men didn't know what hit them. And the more Eric watched Kate, he was feeling as though something had hit *him*. His moods around Kate vacillated between wanting to teach her a lesson to wanting to touch her all over. Friday night found him lying in bed in his boxers, trying to think of ways he might accomplish both at the same time. Leaving Handley to go work for Mixxo was looking like a better decision all the time. He would never be able to work for Kate when every time he looked at her, all he could think about was how much he would like to see her with her clothes off.

A few days ago, he would have thought that if he'd given John Handley an ultimatum—either Kate goes, or he goes—the old man would have chosen him. But after seeing Kate in action for only a couple of days, he could see that she was more valuable to Handley Toys than he was. He was a hack salesman with a good product, and salesmen were a dime a dozen.

He looked around the hotel room, almost unidentifiable from the thousands of other hotel rooms he'd stayed in during his career. Many mornings he had opened the drawer of the nightstand to glance at the phone book to remind him what city he was in. Lately, being on the road appealed to him less and less. One of the attractive qualities of the Mixxo job was a more concentrated territory that would have him crossing fewer time zones.

Wow, had Kate ever trounced him on the golf course today. His ego still smarted when he thought about the men ribbing him, saying he should get his boss to give him some pointers on how to keep his head down when he swung. From the smug smile on Kate's face, she had enjoyed every minute.

He smiled now. She certainly couldn't cry foul when her correspondence with a secret admirer was exposed. He was sure that's what she'd been doing last night when he'd stopped by her room to return the credit card, but it was killing him not knowing for sure. He reached for his cell phone and called Winston again. When his friend's voice mail kicked on, he said, "Hey, man, it's Eric. I was calling to see how the joke is going and if you-know-who is taking the bait. Call me when you get a chance."

At least tomorrow would be a no-brainer—he and Kate would be attending a regional electronics show to check out competitors' products. Electronics was his forte, so he would be on solid ground. Unless

Kate wore something incredibly sexy, like a burlap sack.

He frowned wryly—or unless she had a robotics degree that she'd forgotten to mention.

CHAPTER NINE

Nothing fools people as much as extreme passion.
—Bishop Hall

KATE CLOSED HER EYES and touched her tender eyelids.

"Are you okay?" Eric asked.

She opened her eyes wide and nodded. "My eyes are just tired, and I have a touch of a headache." She gestured vaguely to the overwhelming display of elaborate booths, some of them enormous and fitted with enough flashing lights and robotic arms to rival a Hollywood movie set. "So much to look at, I suppose."

"It's been a long day," Eric said. "Why don't we head back?"

She shook her head. "I don't want to keep you from doing what you need to do. I think I'll try to find a bottle of cold water and sit down for a few minutes. I'll meet you back here in say, an hour?"

He glanced at his watch, then nodded. "That will give me time to see the last couple of people I need to meet with." Then a wrinkle formed between his eyes. "Are you sure you'll be okay?"

Kate was touched by his uncharacteristic compassion and nodded. "I'll be fine." She turned and walked away toward the concessions area, wishing she'd worn more comfortable shoes and wondering where she might nab a couple of aspirin. A few minutes later she found a water vendor and a stiff plastic chair to sit in near the concession stands. She lowered herself to the chair, grateful for the break.

Eric was relentless. The man was an electronics maniac, eager to try every new gadget and toy at every booth. It was really quite a marvel. The excitement on his face when he discovered something new or "cool" gave her more pleasure than seeing the product itself, and she marveled at the ease with which he interacted with other salespeople. Everyone, male and female, gravitated toward him. Seven hours in, though, her insoles were giving out and she'd had her fill of gadgets, gewgaws and wingdings.

Sipping the cool water, she wondered how much of her sudden restlessness had to do with the fact that she hadn't heard from her e-mail admirer yesterday. Maybe her request to meet face-to-face had been too forward, too soon. Maybe she'd never hear from him again. Or maybe he'd simply been too busy to answer. Or maybe he was having computer problems.

She didn't want it to be over. She willed Neil Powers to keep their correspondence going because she was feeling a little desperate for any kind of distraction.

She was starting to suspect that if her heart was left to its own devices, it would fall for Eric. Again. When she'd awakened this morning, the anticipation she'd felt at sharing the day with him went beyond normal boss-subordinate feelings. And when he'd walked into the lobby wearing chinos and a red shirt, her chest had swelled with appreciation—and she couldn't attribute her enthusiasm to the Handley Toys emblem on the left pocket of his shirt.

By the time she'd reached the bottom of the water bottle, she felt somewhat refreshed. Since she still had a few minutes to kill before meeting up with Eric, she meandered around a few booths they hadn't yet gotten to.

She stopped by a booth of new electronic pets and watched the ten-minute demonstration. The adults were riveted, but after a few minutes, the younger attendees walked away. She made a mental note, then moved on to a digital device that operated like a hard sketch pad with different-colored stylus pens. The drawing could be saved or printed, or "torn off" by pushing a button that made the noise of paper being torn and then wiped the screen clean. Kids were congregating there, and staying. She made another mental note. While standing in the next booth, she heard a man's voice on the other side of the tall wall say, "Eric McDaniels, you old dog—how's it going?"

"Good, Tag, how's it going with you?"

"Fine. Hey, I heard through the grapevine that you're going to be a Mixxo man starting next Monday."

Kate froze and waited for Eric to set the man straight. Instead, the silence dragged on too long for her comfort. "Listen," Eric finally said, "that's not public knowledge yet. I'm here with my boss, so mum's the word, okay?"

Kate's heart dropped. John would be devastated.

"Sure, man, I won't say anything. When are you breaking the news?"

"I have a big deal I'm trying to close before Wednesday. I figured I'd break the news after that and at least go out on a good note."

"Sounds like a plan. How's your golf game these days?"

"I'd rather not talk about it," Eric muttered, and their voices grew more dim as they moved away from the wall.

Kate leaned against a table, besieged with a dozen thoughts and emotions—betrayal and hurt among them. Which was silly because Eric owed her nothing, not professionally—since they'd been working together barely a week—and certainly not personally. Still, when she'd expressed appreciation that he hadn't gone to Mixxo, he could have said something.

Which wasn't entirely fair, she conceded, since technically she would've had to fire him on the spot. This way at least he had a shot at getting the Lexan business for Handley before he left. And even though a quarterly bonus was probably his motivation, it was a win-win situation under the circumstances. Eric had no doubt considered all possible scenarios before deciding on this course of action. And it was in her company's best interests if she didn't say anything until after the Lexan account had either been won or lost.

She acknowledged a tightness in her chest at the prospect of not working with Eric in the future, which only reinforced her fears that she had developed intense feelings for him. Then on the heels of her musings, another thought occurred to her.

If she weren't Eric's boss—

"Ma'am, could I interest you in a demo?" a man asked, gesturing to the digital camera display she'd been standing next to.

She jumped, realizing that Eric could come around the corner at any moment. "No, thank you." She scooted out of the booth and walked in the opposite direction, her mind spinning with the ramifications of Eric leaving Handley.

"Check your e-mail! Right here—use our new lightweight laptop to check your e-mail! Free of charge! Privacy guaranteed—all Web browsers available!" The man running the booth gestured to her, waving her into a small cubicle. "Give it a try, ma'am. Take as long as you want. Here's a brochure."

She acquiesced because it would give her a nice, quiet place to sit and collect herself before she had to meet Eric. She waited until the man disappeared before pulling up her preferred browser and accessing her e-mail through several secured servers. When her messages loaded, she scanned the addresses, smiling when she spotted a note from FoolforYou. She glanced over her shoulder, then pulled up the note.

Kate,
Yes, I'd very much like to meet face-to-face to explore our "diversions." I'm trying to figure out how someone as amazing as you can still be single. Is there by chance a broken heart in

your background? My schedule is flexible, so
let me know when and where you'd like to
meet.

Fool for You

"Interesting," a man said into her ear.

Kate started and turned to see Eric standing at her
shoulder, peering at the screen. Heat flooded her face
and she fumbled for the keys to remove the e-mail
from the screen, furious. "How dare you spy on
me!"

He backed away, lifting his hands, laughing. "I
wasn't spying on you. I saw the top of your red head
and I wondered how you were feeling."

She gritted her teeth. "You're insufferable."

He gave her a wry smile. "If it makes you feel
better, I didn't read the note."

She turned back and exhaled, then stabbed keys to
log off the system.

"Wow," he said, "it must have been personal for
you to get so upset."

She stood and marched past Eric. "I'm going back
to the hotel."

"I'll go with you."

She turned. "Don't, Eric." She lifted her finger,
dismayed to see it shaking. *"Don't."*

Kate left the show and grabbed a taxi back to the
hotel, taking refuge in her room, berating herself for
letting Eric get to her…again. She called room service and ordered a salad. While she waited, she emptied her briefcase and studied reports until her eyes
were practically crossed. Feeling restless and a little
homesick, she called Lesley, who, gauging from the

sounds in the background, was in the middle of a family pillow fight.

"Kate! Hold on." She covered the mouthpiece. "Everybody, cool it until Mommy gets off the phone!"

Kate smiled at the ease with which her friend governed her household, and, for the first time ever, experienced a little pang of envy.

Lesley uncovered the mouthpiece. "Okay, I'm back. What's up?"

"Oh, nothing, really, I'm just checking in."

"You sound funny—do you have a cold?"

"Just a touch of a headache. I was at an electronics show all day."

"Ugh. Should have been with me at the kiddy jungle gym all day that's only slightly less harrowing. Seriously, how are things going?"

"Fine, really. Fine."

"'Fine, really. Fine.'? Me thinks thou doth protest too much. Is McDaniels giving you a hard time?"

"Nothing I can't handle."

"Hmm. I hope so."

"What's that supposed to mean?"

Her friend sighed. "It means that I know you were head over heels in love with him once, and old habits are hard to break."

Kate touched her temple and, incredibly, felt tears pressing on her eyelids. "Lesley, I really don't want to talk about this right now. I just needed to hear a familiar voice."

"I could give you Neil's number."

Kate hesitated, considering telling her friend that

she suspected Neil was her anonymous e-mailing "Fool." But how crazy would that sound?

A knock sounded on her door. "Oh—gotta go, Les. That's room service."

"Good timing. Take care of yourself."

"Bye." Kate hung up the phone, grabbed the tip money she'd set on the desk, then opened the door.

Eric stood in the hallway, looking contrite. "I came to do something."

She crossed her arms. "Apologize?"

He stepped forward. "No." Then before she could process what was happening, he put one arm around her back, pulled her against him and lowered his mouth on hers. In a split second she registered the familiarity of his lips, the musky, masculine scent of him, the instant desire rising in her limbs. Then sanity snapped back like a broken rubber band, and with much effort, she wrenched away. She stepped back, bumping the door, and covered her mouth. Anger— at herself—coursed through her veins. Her chest heaved as she tried to get enough air. "You shouldn't have done that."

"Like hell," he said, his expression dark. "It needed to be done before now."

"We can't do this," she said, shaking her head. "I'm your boss." Remembering that wouldn't be the case for long, she added, "And it would never work between us."

He frowned. "Why not?"

She drew herself up and flung out her arm. "Be-cause...because you're...*you* and I'm...*me*. We're like oil and water."

"Maybe," he said, then he leaned in. "But there's

something between us, Kate, and it's inevitable that we get together. Forget that you're my boss—we're man and woman first.''

Kate stared, and was at a loss to do anything but laugh. ''Are you *kidding* me? Eric, I've fought role stereotypes my entire life, and you're one of the biggest male chauvinists I've ever met. Don't forget that I overheard you telling a coworker that I wasn't qualified for this job. You were condescending to me during my first staff meeting, and during this trip, you've patronized me like I was one of your 'women.''' She poked him in the chest to emphasize her words, causing him to back up. ''Well. I'm. Not. One. Of. Your. Women. And I'm not going to take a step backward in my career just to climb into bed with you.''

Eric jammed his hands on his hips and looked as if he wanted to refute her, but couldn't. Finally he donned what she was sure he thought was his most swaggering, most adorable expression. ''So you're low enough to resort to the truth—is that the best you got?''

She wanted to kill him. Instead she spied the room service server wheeling her dinner down the hall. The man stopped at her door, and she gave him the tip she was still holding. Then she took the lid off the chef salad, happy to find it drenched in ranch dressing. She picked up the salad plate and smashed it against Eric's chest, grinding it into his red shirt for good, gooey measure. ''How's that?'' She smiled, then slammed the door in his face.

CHAPTER TEN

You will do foolish things, but do them with
enthusiasm.
—Sidonie Gabrielle Colette

Fool,
I'm flattered by your compliments, and I suppose that everyone past the age of fifteen has a
broken heart in their background. My heart is
no exception. I'm traveling for business, but
will be returning Wednesday. Would you be
available to meet for coffee Thursday or Friday?

K

KATE REREAD the note and sipped her tea. She was
glad she had waited until this morning to reply to the
note, waited until she had recovered from Eric's lat-
est assault on her senses so she could think more
clearly.

She bit her lip. So Neil Powers wasn't the most
exciting man she'd ever met—at least he was insight-
ful and attentive. And accommodating. She had a
feeling that dating Neil would be conflict-free. Unlike…

Kate frowned and hit the send button, then settled

back with her tea to watch a Sunday news magazine on TV. The anchor's mouth moved, but unfortunately it was Eric's words that kept creeping into her head like a bad song. *There's something between us, Kate, and it's inevitable that we get together. Forget that you're my boss—we're man and woman first.*

She emitted a dry laugh. The man's ego was big enough to be taxed. And that kiss…

She gave herself a mental shake and decided to take a book to the pool. They weren't scheduled to depart for Pensacola until late this afternoon, and she was feeling confined. Unfortunately, the only book she had with her was *How to Make an Effective Sales Call*. She donned a modest green one-piece bathing suit and a pair of shorts and headed to the outdoor pool, which was crowded. She found a chaise in a semi-shady spot a few feet away from the activity and tilted her face up to enjoy a few minutes of sun before diving into her less-than-riveting reading material.

And that kiss…well, Eric had really overstepped his bounds there. Did he think she would be receptive to him after the way he'd behaved? That she'd be willing to hitch her reputation to his runaway train? She wet her lips, reliving the intense pressure of his determined kiss. Hard, skilled…promising.

"With that smile on your face, you must be thinking about something good."

Her eyes flew open. Eric stood over her, brown and buff and wearing black trunks.

"Nice day, eh?"

At the sight of his bare broad shoulders, she swallowed. "You're blocking the sun."

He moved and walked over a few feet to grab an empty chaise. "Mind if I pull up a chair?"

She frowned. "Actually, I'd rather be alone."

"That's no fun," he said, dragging the chaise close, then dropping into the chair. "I hope you know that my dry cleaner is going to charge me a small fortune to get the food stains out of my clothes."

She turned over on her stomach and reached for the book. "Don't even think about trying to expense it."

"Need some lotion on your back?"

"No."

"Towel?"

"No."

"Cocktail?"

"No."

"Whatcha reading?"

Without looking in his direction, she held up the cover, then reread the same paragraph for the third time.

"Do you work *all* the time?" he asked.

She looked up. "Do you talk *all* the time?"

"Pretty much—it's my only flaw."

She lowered her sunglasses. "Is that supposed to be funny?"

"Yes." He sighed. "Kate, I want to call a truce."

She arched an eyebrow. "A truce?"

He nodded. "I really want to land this deal with Lexan."

At the uncharacteristically genuine tone of his voice, her mouth softened. "And?"

"And...I need your help."

She frowned, wary. "How so?"

"I'm not connecting with the buyer."

"Can you be more specific?"

"He doesn't like me." He shrugged. "Go figure."

One side of her mouth slid back. "How do you know he doesn't like you?"

He winked. "Believe me, I can tell when someone does or doesn't like me. Besides, he called this morning to cancel our meeting tomorrow."

She blinked. "We're not going to get the business this quarter?" With Eric leaving, it could be a while before someone could take over major accounts. She hadn't even thought about a replacement.

"I did talk the guy into rescheduling to Tuesday." His grin was sheepish. "I told him I had my boss with me and I couldn't leave town without bringing you by."

The smallest of smiles lifted the corners of her mouth. "I'm your Trojan horse?"

"Something like that. The thing is, the buyer really does like our line of electronic games, I can tell. So, I'm thinking our odds of getting the business will improve if we hit him with a tag team presentation."

She weighed the benefit of the business to Handley versus having to work closely with Eric on a presentation. Since he was leaving the company soon, this would be a good way to find out as much as possible about Lexan and his other accounts without raising his suspicion. And she had agreed to accompany him on this trip to learn more about direct sales—this might be her only chance to pitch directly to the customer. Then she frowned. "Do I have your word that there will be no funny business?"

He held up his hand. "Scout's honor, boss."

She turned over and sat up. "What would I have to do?"

ERIC COULDN'T REMEMBER the last time he'd been nervous on a sales call, but his hands were sweaty as he held open the door and allowed Kate to precede him into the building that housed Lexan Electronics' headquarters. Some of his apprehension was due to the fact that he did want to close this business—his bonus was riding on a healthy order, and he preferred to leave Handley with a bang. But he conceded that much of the tightness in his chest was due to the fact that Kate would witness him either close the deal, or crash and burn.

Talk about performance anxiety.

The lobby was an impressive display of tile, glass and chrome, but Eric only had eyes for the woman who walked in front of him.

In the last day and a half, they had gotten along better than he could have imagined because they'd been focused on one objective. He wanted the account badly enough to repress his natural urge to flirt with Kate, and in return, he'd watched Kate slowly let down her defenses. The drive to Pensacola yesterday had been downright enjoyable. He had shared his approach to other major accounts, and together they'd assembled a dynamite presentation for Lexan.

Although in his opinion, the vision of Kate in a cream-colored suit was enough to clinch the deal.

The problem was, while his respect for her over the past couple of days had grown exponentially, so had his lust. He had no choice now but to leave

Handley because he knew for certain he wouldn't be able to hide his desire every time he saw her.

The buyer, David Jyles, greeted them with his normal brittle tone, but as Eric predicted, Kate had him eating out of her hand in no time. She asked endless questions about their operation, using her relative ignorance of sales to her advantage. At the end of their allotted thirty minutes, the buyer called his secretary and asked that his schedule be cleared so he could spend more time with the "good people from Handley."

Pangs of jealousy barbed through Eric's chest when the man swept appreciative glances over Kate, but he could tell Jyles was also responding to her genuine manner and her savvy questions.

He remembered a couple of sentences he'd read in the secret admirer note that he'd seen when he was looking over Kate's shoulder at the electronics show—why *was* someone as amazing as Kate still single? And did she have a broken heart in her background?

Funny, but he'd never thought about Kate having broken his heart when they were in Vegas. She'd gotten under his skin, into his brain, and she continued to plague various other parts of his body…but his heart?

"Eric," Kate said in a tone that indicated he had missed something.

He blinked. "I'm sorry—yes?"

"Mr. Jyles asked to see our samples."

Eric leapt into action, unlocking his sample case and lapsing into the presentation he and Kate had perfected. He demonstrated the twelve handheld games while she took on the role of liaison, seemingly as skeptical as Jyles at first, asking lots of questions to help guide the buyer toward "yes." An hour later, Jyles was exhibiting signs of wanting to be asked for a deal. Eric went for the close and waited.

Jyles clasped his hands on his desk and twiddled his thumbs. He glanced back and forth between Kate and Eric. "I have to be honest with you—I'm really happy with Travister, the line of games we carry."

Eric's stomach twisted in disappointment.

"But," Jyles continued, "I'm willing to supplement our current product line with, say, four Handley games."

Supplement, not replace. A strategy, Eric recalled, that Kate had suggested in her sales meeting. And his response, he recalled, had been *I don't do things small.*

His mind raced. Even if Jyles placed an excellent order for the four games, it wouldn't be enough for him to hit his numbers for a sales bonus. He'd been complacent this quarter, counting on his ability to land this account in a big way—the McDaniels way. It would be the same end result for him if Jyles bought four games or none. And if he bought four, that would make it harder to sell Mixxo games to him a few months down the road.

But four games would give Handley a toehold with a big player.

Eric swallowed. He felt Kate's gaze on him, unaware of his inner turmoil.

"Four games would be a great beginning," he heard himself say, then he stood and extended his hand to Jyles.

"I'M SORRY you won't get your bonus this quarter," Kate said, sipping the dessert wine they'd ordered. She *had* felt for him during the presentation to Jyles. She'd understood it was hard for him to swallow his pride and take the lesser deal—the deal she had suggested...especially since he wouldn't see the benefit of the business.

"That's okay," he said lightly. "There's always next quarter."

She sipped again, fighting the urge to tell him that she knew he wouldn't be around next quarter. He'd made a sacrifice today for Handley, so she owed him the courtesy of letting him announce his departure.

"We were good together," he said, his eyes twinkling. He lifted his glass. "To us."

She hesitated, then clinked her glass against his. As they sipped, the atmosphere changed. The smile left his eyes and was replaced by desire. Longing pooled in her stomach, sending warning signals to her brain. The last few days had been too enjoyable, too relaxed. She'd let down her guard, and he'd managed to slip past her defenses.

"I guess this is it," he said. "Our last night."

She nodded, unable to speak. Certainly unable to respond to his subtle invitation. *Our last night on the road. No one has to know.*

Her heart pounded against her rib cage, her pulse throbbed in her ears. She wanted him more than she'd ever wanted any man, more than she'd wanted him six years ago. There was no good end to the sexual fascination she had for Eric McDaniels. The wisest alternative seemed to be evasion.

"I think I'm going to call it a night," she said

abruptly, setting down her glass and rummaging for her credit card.

"Go ahead," he said, his voice gruff. "Let me get the check tonight."

She looked up and saw the message in his eyes: Go. *Now.* "Okay," she murmured. "Good night." Kate didn't wait for him to respond and practically race-walked out of the restaurant and to the elevator. She stabbed at the up button, feeling the pull of his body calling to hers.

When the doors opened, she rushed inside the elevator and leaned into the wall until she was delivered to her floor. She fumbled with her electronic door key, but eventually got in. The air-conditioning was a blast of relief to her fevered face. One more night—she only had to get through one more night.

But she kept looking back to the door, wavering. Would she forever regret not taking Eric up on his subtle offer? Maybe making love with him again would be the one thing that would release her from the hold he seemed to have on her. In her present state of mind, the ramifications seemed hazy and obscure, but she reasoned that nothing could be as bad as this unbearable longing.

She walked to the door and took a deep breath. Just as she reached for the knob, she heard a rustle of footsteps on the other side. She looked through the peephole and at the sight of Eric, his jacket slung over his shoulder and his head down in thought, her heart soared. When she opened the door, his arm was up in the knocking position.

He blinked in surprise. "Kate. I…um…"

She exhaled and bit into her lip. "Me, too." Then she stepped aside to let him in.

CHAPTER ELEVEN

You ask whether I have ever been in love:
fool as I am, I am not such a fool as that.
——C. S. Lewis

THEY WERE LOCKED in a frantic kiss before the door
closed. Kate opened her mouth to receive his tongue,
heady with the knowledge of what was to come. His
jacket fell on the floor. She splayed her hands on his
back, frustrated at the fabric barrier between her
hands and his skin. They began to undress each
other, still kissing, touching, murmuring. She reveled
in the warm, smooth skin of his biceps, explored his
back and waist. He slipped her bra strap down her
shoulder, kissing a trail of fire across her collar bone.

Kate gave in to his touch, arching into his body,
hurrying his mouth to her breasts. He unhooked her
bra and covered her nipple with his lips, licking and
drawing her into his warm mouth, kneading her flesh
with his hand. She cried out, pushing her hands into
his thick hair, skimming her nails across the nape of
his neck. He pulled away long enough to tug at the
waistband of her skirt. She took over to speed things
along, and by the time she had stripped down to her
lacy cream-colored panties, he was completely nude,

his erection hard, the velvety knob already wet with wanting her.

He held her at arm's length and emitted a groan of appreciation that weakened her knees. She went into his arms for a full-body-contact kiss. His arousal pressed into her stomach, sending moisture to the V of her thighs. He brushed his hand against her stomach, then lower to tease her wet curls with his fingers, fondling the tiny nub that resided there. She gasped and leaned into him, pulling on his shoulders and arms, raking his back.

He scooped her up and carried her the few steps to the bed, lowering himself on top of her, moving her hair aside to kiss her neck and her ear. She undulated against him and he moaned, then clasped a budded nipple in his mouth. Age-old desire flooded her midsection, and she captured his erection in her hand. He inhaled sharply against her breast, then kissed her again, hard, using his tongue and teeth to kindle a like response.

Their feverish fingers and tongues were tinged with desperation, as if they both knew they might never get the chance to touch each other again. Suddenly he reached down to clasp her stroking hand. "Enough," he said hoarsely, his eyes hooded. "I can't take much more, Kate."

"Then make love to me," she murmured.

His breath rasped out and he kissed her again, briefly. "Don't move." He pulled away and left the bed, grabbing his pants off the ground, getting protection, she realized. Seeing his hands shake filled her with warm satisfaction—she affected him as much as he affected her. She took the condom from him and rolled it on. He lay down next to her and turned her over to face him, then pulled her knee over his hip, aligning them sex to sex.

"You are so beautiful," he whispered, kissing her neck and inhaling. "You smell so good. Kate, do you know how long I've wanted you?"

Any response she might have had was obliterated when he cupped his hand behind her hip and thrust into her ready body. She gasped and clawed at his shoulder. He rocked into her fully, breathing hard, then was still, allowing her to become accustomed to his length. She reveled in the exquisite fullness and contracted around him, pulsing slowly at first, then moving against him with more intensity. He slid into the rhythm she chose, using his thumb to stroke her sensitive folds.

Kate was powerless against the passion that consumed her. Eric instinctively knew her body and her needs. She buried her face against his shoulder, inhaling the scent of him, resurrecting a buried memory that she had been there before, had kissed this very patch of skin, had loved it then and loved it now.

Loved *him* now.

The realization of her feelings for Eric fueled her desire, sent her to a higher physical plane. She moved her hips in a deliciously slow dance, clasping the length of him, delaying the stroke of his hand against her. She felt her climax building from that unidentifiable, mysterious place that is nowhere, then suddenly everywhere at once. She nipped at his ear. "I'm going to come," she breathed.

He flicked his tongue against her ear. "I want to hear you, Kate."

The hum in her body suddenly converged into one point, shooting to the surface, bringing spasms of pleasure that sent her body bucking against his. She cried his name over and over. Just as she was descending, floating, he rolled her beneath him and plunged into her with a guttural noise. He whispered her name against her breasts, and gathered her close. Their bodies were perfectly attuned. She met him stroke for stroke, faster and deeper until he shuddered and collapsed into her. "Kate...Kate."

She sighed and held his head against her neck as he recovered, wanting to fold herself into him. How could she have fallen for him...again? What about this man made her want to risk everything? He kissed her neck, her chin, then pulled her over to face him and smiled. "Wow."

"Yeah, wow," was all she could say.

"So," he said with a little laugh, "are we going to get together and do this every six years?"

She wasn't sure what she expected—a profession of undying love? A request to take her out sometime? His class ring?—but her heart shook with disappointment anyway. It was great, it was quick, it was over. She conjured up a smile. "Who knows where we'll be in six years?"

"True," he murmured, and she waited for him to tell her he was leaving Handley. He didn't. Instead he left the bed and went into the bathroom—to dispose of the condom, she assumed.

She lay there, her sweat-covered body now chilled,

a dull ache in her chest, dreading what was to come. She got up and quickly redressed, then placed his clothes on the foot of the bed.

Eric emerged from the bathroom, took in her state of dress and gave a little laugh. "I guess you don't want me to spend the night."

Kate hugged herself. "I don't think that's a good idea. Let's not make this more awkward than it has to be."

He looked at her, his expression unreadable, then lifted his hands. "Okay." She turned away while he dressed.

"You can dispense with the false modesty, Kate. We've just seen everything there is to see."

She refused to turn around, though, mostly because she was afraid her face wore a telltale expression. "What time are we leaving tomorrow?" she asked over her shoulder.

He grunted. "How about nine o'clock? That way I can drop you off at the office before three in the afternoon. I assume you want to get back to work ASAP?"

"Of course," she said, sounding prim even to her own ears. "After all, we're finished here."

"Yes, we are," he said. "Good night, Kate."

She turned, suddenly panicky. "Eric?"

He was at the door, but turned back. "Yeah?"

"I'm sure you understand how…that is, I wouldn't want everyone—"

"Relax, Kate," he said with a laugh. The Mc-Daniels charisma was back—carefree, nonchalant, casual. "This stays between us. Trust me."

Kate,
What better day for you to meet your Fool than on April Fool's Day? I'll be at Comet Coffee Thursday morning at 7:00. This will be so great!
Fool for You

KATE STUDIED the screen and exhaled slowly to ease the guilt pangs in her chest. So she'd be using Neil Powers to get over Eric—men did it all the time. Besides, if given the chance, Neil might turn out to be the man of her dreams. If last night's episode had taught her anything, it was that she was wasting time—and love—on Eric McDaniels.

She signed off her computer, packed it up, and wheeled her luggage toward the elevator, wincing when her overused hip and calf muscles contracted. It wasn't bad enough that Eric was the first man she'd slept with in a long time—if he knew that she'd fallen in love with him, he'd never let her live it down.

In Eric's eyes, it would be the ultimate joke. On her.

ERIC STABBED a button on his cell phone, listening to the ring while keeping an eye out for Kate. His bad mood was getting worse every minute. When Winston's voice mail kicked on, he swore under his breath. After the beep, he said, "Winston, it's Eric. Where the hell are you? Look, man, I changed my mind about the April Fool's gag on my boss, okay? So cancel the e-mail that was supposed to go out tomorrow to the distribution list I gave you. Got that? *Cancel the e-mail.* And give me a call to let me know you got this message." He hit the end key, and returned the phone to his inside jacket pocket, irritation guiding his every movement.

Then make love to me, she'd said.

Damn, what a fine damn mess he'd gotten himself into. Damn it. Setting up his boss for a humiliating stunt. Sleeping with her. And now…damn it, damn it, damn it, he was having all these weird *feelings* for her. Protective. Concerned. *Loving.* He pulled his hand down his face. This was bad.

When the elevator doors opened and Kate alighted looking every inch the smart, successful, sexy woman she was, Eric's gut clenched.

This was very, very bad.

CHAPTER TWELVE

The first of April is the day we remember what
we are the other 364 days of the year.
—Mark Twain

KATE STOPPED outside Comet Coffee and took a
deep breath before pushing the door open and walking inside. The smoky, nutty aromas of freshly
ground coffee tickled her nose...and her dancing
nerves. She surveyed the seating area, looking for a
familiar face, but she didn't see anyone she knew.
For a few panicky seconds, she wondered if Fool was
indeed a stranger. Or a stalker. Or if the entire thing
was a big, fat joke—it was, after all, April Fool's
Day.

She checked her watch again, then gave a little
laugh—sometimes setting her watch ten minutes fast
got her into trouble.

Her pulse was still tapping overtime as she joined
the line to get a cup of coffee. She kept an eye on
the door, but reached the counter without seeing anyone familiar. She ordered a cup of decaf with cream,
remembering only last week she'd been standing behind the coffeemaker at work when she'd first heard
Eric's voice again after so many years. So much had
happened in so few days' time.

The drive home yesterday had been painful—for her. Eric had been his normal jovial self, reinforcing her notion that their night together had meant little to him. He'd spent a lot of time pushing speed dial buttons on his cell phone, but since he never talked to anyone, she assumed he was checking messages. They'd driven in and out of rain, and the drive had seemed interminably long. When they began to see signs for Birmingham, even Eric showed signs of restlessness. Her concerns about how they would part were allayed when they pulled into the parking lot at the same time John Handley was coming out of the building. He had stopped to get an update on Lexan, and Kate had left the men to chat. She suspected that Eric had taken the opportunity to tell John he was leaving Handley, and she expected to get a visit from John this morning.

All evening she had hoped that Eric would call her to tell her himself. Instead she had walked around her apartment carrying Lenka and doing something she never did—drinking wine alone. Between her second and third glass, she had opened her Bernadette cabinet and informed the dolls they didn't know how good they had it to be manless.

When she'd realized she was talking to dolls, she'd put down the wineglass and gone to bed.

"Ma'am?"

Kate blinked.

"Here's your coffee," the young girl behind the counter said.

Kate took the coffee and moved aside, blowing on the top of the liquid. Just as she looked up, the door opened and she froze.

Neil Powers gave her a shy smile and a wave. He was wearing gray corduroy pants and a navy shirt, his hair fashionably shaggy. When he walked up, she realized that she'd never noticed his eyes were brown. They were nice eyes.

"Hi, Kate," he said, his voice tentative.

"Hi," she said with a little smile. "So it *was* you."

He looked at her, his eyebrows raised, and a few seconds passed. Then he exhaled and laughed at the same time. "Yeah, it was me. I'm Fool for You." His cheeks reddened slightly. "You must think I'm weird."

She laughed and shook her head. "No, I don't think you're weird. I think that you're incredibly…" She looked into his nice brown eyes and felt her smile fall—they weren't the eyes of the man she loved. "Sweet."

She closed her eyes briefly and when she opened them, Neil was staring at her. He angled his head, then he squinted. "Something just happened, and I have a feeling it doesn't bode well for me."

She pressed her lips together. "Do you remember asking if my heart had been broken?"

"Yeah. You said anyone over fifteen has had their heart broken and your heart was no exception."

"Well…I just realized that it's more broken than I'd thought."

He shrugged. "I'm a patient man."

"Let me work on this," she said softly. "I'll keep you posted."

He nodded, then sighed and gestured toward the counter. "I think I'll drown my sorrows in a latte."

She smiled. "I need to get back to work. I'll see you around." She waved and watched him walk away, wondering when she'd get to the point where she could entertain the thought of letting another man near her heart.

She sipped her coffee on the walk back to Handley's building, thinking right now she had bigger problems than losing Eric McDaniels, like the fact that she was losing her best salesman and major account rep. That wasn't going to reflect well on her, one week into the job. And if John got a whiff of their personal involvement, he was likely to demote her to the mailroom.

When Kate walked down the hallway to her office, her assistant wore a sour frown. "Good morning, Patsy. Is something wrong?"

Patsy nodded toward Kate's office and harrumphed.

Kate strode into her office and her pulse jumped at the sight of Eric standing next to her window with his back to her. He wore jeans and a sport coat. His shoulders looked tense and his hair hand-ruffled.

"Eric?" She closed the door behind her.

He turned and his handsome face wore a troubled expression so uncharacteristic, it was startling. "Hello, Kate. We need to talk."

Her stomach churned, but she felt compelled to put him at ease. She held up her hand. "Look, Eric, I know why you're here."

"You do?" he asked, looking more distressed. He pushed his hand into his hair. "What am I saying? Of course you do. It probably came through while I was driving over here."

She frowned—his resignation? "I'm not sure when it came through, but I know all about it."

He came over and stood in front of her, his eyes a little wild. "Kate, I'm so sorry—I tried to stop it, but I couldn't. It was supposed to be a stupid joke to make you look bad in front of the sales team, but it got out of hand."

Her mind spun in confusion.

He emitted a harsh laugh. "I just want you to know the secret admirer thing was all my crazy idea—I know you must be humiliated."

"*Your* idea?"

"Yeah." He sighed and paced the area in front of her desk. "I was angry about having to work for you, and…and then you made that comment about being nobody's fool, and I…" He lifted his hands. "I'm sorry, Kate. For some reason, I thought that exposing the notes between you and a secret admirer would be funny."

She squinted. "You hacked into my e-mail?"

He stopped pacing. "No, *I* arranged for the notes to be sent."

She touched her temple, still trying to make sense of what he was saying. "You know Neil Powers?"

He frowned. "Who? My buddy Winston sent the notes."

"Does Winston know Neil?"

Eric studied Kate's expression and realized she seemed more confused than angry. And right now, he was pretty confused himself. "*Who* is Neil?"

A ring sounded from his jacket pocket and he withdrew his cell phone. The display read Winston Grant. "About damn time," Eric muttered, then flipped open the phone. "Winston? What the hell is going on?"

"Sorry, buddy. I know I really let you down, but it couldn't be helped."

Eric frowned. "Let me down?"

"The notes—I couldn't send them. I was feeling kind of bad that night we were together, and as it turns out, I had the chicken pox. I've been in the hospital for a freaking week, sick as a dog."

When Winston's words sank in, Eric's stomach bottomed out. "You didn't send the notes?"

"No," Winston said dryly. "And did I mention that I've been in the hospital?"

Holy relief swept through Eric...until he lifted his gaze to Kate's face, and realized she now seemed more angry than confused.

"I'll call you back," he said into the phone, then snapped it closed. He turned his most charming smile on Kate and shrugged. "My mistake."

She crossed her arms, her cutting green eyes dismembering him. "Let me get this straight—you put a buddy up to sending me e-mail as a secret admirer? And my correspondence with your friend was going to be distributed to the sales team?"

He winced. "But...he didn't do it, so...no harm, no foul?"

He expected her to throw something at him, to fire him on the spot, to slap his face. But he didn't expect her eyes to fill with tears.

"Kate?" A lump formed in his throat and he crossed the space between them.

She held up her hand. "Don't. You. Dare. Touch. Me."

He let his hands fall uselessly by his sides. "Kate, there's something else I need to tell you."

When she finally looked at him, she'd regained control, her eyes dry again. "What?"

"I, uh...." Damn, now that the moment had come, he was as nervous as a schoolboy. "I love you." There.

But instead of bringing her lovely self over and falling into his arms, Kate lifted her eyebrows. "You love me?"

He smiled. "That's right."

She burst out laughing. "That's a good one, Eric—what, do you have my office wired?" She turned and waved to the corners. "Did you rig up a hidden camera?"

He frowned. "No."

"Really? Because you couldn't possibly think that I'd believe something so ludicrous on April Fool's Day, could you?"

"Well...yeah."

"Ha! From the biggest practical joker in the business? And after you told me that you were willing to humiliate me in front of my colleagues just to get a laugh? Why don't you just tell me why you really came to see me, Eric?"

He shook his head, confused. "What?"

"That Monday you'll be working for Mixxo Toys."

He felt the blood leave his face. "How did you know?"

"I overheard you talking to someone at the electronics show."

"And you didn't say anything?"

"No—I was waiting for you to do the honorable thing and tell *me*."

He set his jaw. "I was trying to close business for Handley before I left."

"You were trying to qualify for your bonus."

That he couldn't deny. And he couldn't miss the way that Kate had spoken to him—with disappointment and disgust. Like the tone she'd used years ago to tell her friend she'd never get involved with the likes of him.

He'd never felt so worthless in his life.

Kate pursed her mouth. "Just tell me one thing, Eric—did you take the Mixxo job before or after John made me VP?"

He decided not to lie. "After."

She gave a curt nod and averted her gaze. When she looked up again, her face was placid and professional. "Well, to show there are no hard feelings, we'll have a going-away party for you in the boardroom tomorrow." She dropped into her chair and flipped the switch on her computer. "Close the door when you leave."

He looked at her bent head, realizing suddenly how bleak his future seemed without Kate. And why should she believe his pathetic declaration? Had he done anything that would make the woman believe he loved her?

Recognizing a bed of his own making, Eric left, stewing in the knowledge that, today, he was the world's biggest fool.

CHAPTER THIRTEEN

"Fool! Don't you see now that I could have
poisoned you a hundred times had I been able
to live without you?"
—Cleopatra to Marc Antony
Anthony and Cleopatra, William Shakespeare

KATE SURVEYED the boardroom, decorated with
streamers and a few balloons. Someone had written
Good luck, Eric on the board and a side table was
stocked with soft drinks and snacks. A big white
sheet cake with the word Congratulations written in
blue sat on the end of the table. She'd ordered the
cake herself to keep up the image that she was happy
for him. The entire sales team was assembling today
in honor of Eric, their leader.

"Hey."

Kate turned to see Lesley, smiling tentatively. "Is
this a bad time?"

"No, come on in. I'm just…getting ready for the
sendoff."

"I tried to call you last night."

"I went to bed early," Kate lied. "I'm still trying
to catch up on my sleep from the trip."

Lesley walked up to her friend and lowered her

voice. "Was there a particular reason you didn't get a lot of sleep?"

Kate looked up. "No."

Lesley simply nodded, but Kate suspected her friend didn't believe her. Kate wet her lips, then spoke quietly. "Well…there was this *one* night."

Lesley nodded. "Thought so."

"Did you talk to Neil?"

"Yup."

"I feel terrible."

"Don't," Lesley said, shaking her head. "Do you love Eric?"

Kate sighed, then nodded.

"And how does he feel about you?"

Kate tried to laugh, but it came out as a strangled sound. "Eric will never love anyone as much as he loves himself. He took this job with Mixxo because he couldn't bear to work for me."

"He told you that?"

Kate nodded. "How can I be in love with a man who's that chauvinistic?"

Lesley shrugged. "Because love isn't reasonable. It's…love." She made a rueful noise in her throat. "I have to get back to my desk, but I'll come around when the party starts."

Kate smiled and waved goodbye, but Lesley's words stayed with her. *Because love isn't reasonable.*

Is that how her mother, an educated and attractive woman, could still look at her philandering father with abject adoration? It was a distressing and depressing thought.

The first few salespeople arrived for the party, distracting Kate from her musings and reminding her that she had a job to do, that people were counting on her to lead. She and John had spoken yesterday afternoon about who could fill Eric's shoes. Unfortunately, as John had pointed out, the best people in the industry were networked to Eric, and his departure would be enough to keep them away. She had looked at John and point-blank asked him if he had offered the VP job to Eric first, and he'd admitted that he had.

"But only because Eric had seniority," John had added. "Eric would have done a good job, but you were my first choice, Kate. You're the visionary."

Nice words from a nice man who had been her mentor for so many years. She loved Handley Toys almost as much as John Handley himself.

The room slowly filled to capacity, then to overflowing. Love him or hate him, it seemed that everyone in the company was fascinated by Eric McDaniels. Kate wryly noted there was no shortage of females more dressed up than normal for a casual Friday. The time dragged by and everyone started looking at their watches. Lesley came up next to her. "Where's the guest of honor?"

Kate shook her head. "Who knows? Maybe he's waiting to make a grand entrance."

"Speak of the devil," Lesley said, nodding toward the door.

Eric walked in, wearing his trademark dimpled grin. The room burst into applause and low cheers as people moved forward to shake Eric's hand or slap him on the back. Her heart squeezed at the sight of him, but she took solace in the knowledge that soon he'd be away from Handley and the likelihood of their paths crossing would be almost nil.

He made the rounds, slowly moving in her direction. John Handley slipped into the room and nodded to her. Kate decided that she'd say a few words in Eric's honor, and then turn it over to John and Eric. When Eric stepped up to her, her heart was beating ridiculously fast.

He wore a little smile, his eyes unreadable... maybe a little sad. The gathering was probably making him feel nostalgic.

"Hi, Kate."

"Hi, Eric."

He gestured to the crowd. "This is nice—thank you."

"No problem." So they wouldn't be forced to make more small talk, Kate waved her arms. "Everyone, may I have your attention, please?"

The room quieted, and everybody turned toward her and Eric. She pasted on a big fake smile and said, "As you know, we're here today to say goodbye to one of our true legends at Handley." She looked at Eric for the sake of presentation, which was a mistake because she almost faltered. Her gaze met his eyes...the eyes of the man she loved. She swallowed hard and forged ahead. "Eric, we're all going to miss you and we wish you luck at the competition." Then she smiled. "Well, not *too* much luck."

Everyone laughed, including Eric.

"Speech, speech!" chorused around the room.

Eric's grin deepened, then he put his hands on his hips, and the room quieted. "Well, anyone who knows me knows I'm not much of a talker." Everyone laughed because no one could outtalk Eric. "But," he said, his voice turning more serious, "I do have something important to say today." He paused. "I've done a lot of fool things in my career, and some of you have been on the receiving end." More laughter sounded.

Then he turned toward Kate. "But this week I out-did myself. I alienated the woman that I love."

Her fake smile evaporated, and her skin tingled. The room grew dead quiet except for a collective intake of breath. Kate blinked and knew everyone was thinking what she was thinking: Had Eric really just said that?

"I've been an idiot," Eric said. "I didn't think that Kate was qualified for this job, when, in fact, she's taught me a thing or two about being a good salesperson...and about being a good person."

Her vital signs escalated—where was this going?

"I was condescending toward Kate because I thought she didn't deserve to be my boss." He gave a little laugh. "The truth is, she's the smartest, most classy person I know, and I'm fully prepared to do her bidding for the rest of my life." He reached into his pocket and withdrew a ring box. "If she's willing to have me."

Gasps sounded around the room, then shrieks of disbelief, then silence as they waited for Kate's re-sponse.

Her heartbeat thudded in her ears, and her mouth opened. She was still unable to comprehend what was happening. Eric McDaniels was willing to make a fool out of himself in front of everyone...for her? She stared at him, her mind reeling.

"I love you, Kate," he said, then got down on one knee, and opened the ring box to the background of more gasps as everyone craned for a better look. There were no two ways about it—the square-cut diamond was huge. "I don't do things small," he said, his eyes crinkling at the corners. "Marry me, Kate."

Her heart swelled with happiness, but complications crowded the corners of her mind. "But...our jobs...how..."

"I'm not taking the Mixxo job," he said.

"I believe I need to speak up here," John Handley said, stepping forward. "Kate, Eric is staying, but you don't have to worry about working too closely with him because I've decided that Eric will have your job."

Disappointment hit her hard, but she was determined not to show it.

"Because, Kate," John continued, "I've decided it's time for me to retire, and I want you to have *my* job. What do you think of that?"

Murmurs traveled around the room and cheers sounded, but the noise reached her ears dimly as though through a filter. Her emotions were a wreck. "I don't know what to say, John."

John laughed. "You'd better tackle one question at a time. I believe you have a marriage proposal on the table."

Everyone laughed and Kate looked down at Eric with love for him burning in her heart. "This isn't one of your practical jokes, is it?"

"No," he said, his eyes dark and serious. "You'll have to trust me on this."

She looked into his eyes and decided that if it *was* one of Eric's gags and she fell for it, the worst that could happen is that she would look like a fool. And the best…

Her heart filled with pure joy. "I do, and…I will." She smiled through her tears, and laughed. "Marry you, I mean."

The room erupted in a roar of cheers and applause. Lesley picked up the marker and corrected the message on the board to read Good luck, Eric and Kate. Across the room, her friend winked at her and gave her the thumbs-up.

Kate waited until Eric slid the ring onto her finger, then sailed into his arms. He kissed her soundly, then picked her up and spun her around. When he set her on her feet, he whispered, "You know that Vegas trip I won? I was thinking we could go this weekend…make new memories."

She smiled up at him. "Sounds wonderful."

Suddenly he frowned. "But I do have one question before we take this too far. *Who* is Neil?"

Kate threw her head back and laughed until she cried. "Don't worry, Eric—you're my favorite fool."

He grinned and zeroed in for a kiss. "What more could a man ask for?"

EPILOGUE

PATSY SET A SMALL BOX on the desk and beamed like a proud parent. "It's taken a while, but finally, here are your new business cards to go along with your new office."

Kate lifted the lid of the box and withdrew one of the crisp white cards.

Kate Randall
President and Chief Executive Officer
Handley Toys
Birmingham, AL
Handley Toys—Fun for life.

Her first undertaking as CEO had been to change the company slogan to one she thought reflected the ageless appeal of their products.

"Thank you, Patsy."

"Oh, and Mr. McDaniels—I mean, *Eric*—is waiting outside."

Kate bit back a smile at her assistant's formality. "Did he say if this was a business matter or personal?"

"Considering his arms are full of baby paraphernalia," Patsy said with a wry smile, "I'd say it's personal."

Kate unconsciously touched her growing stomach and grinned. "Send him in."

Suddenly her door burst open and all she could see was Eric's legs—a mountain of toys obscured him from the waist up. "Sorry," he mumbled from behind the armload. "My arms were getting ready to give out." He walked unsteadily over to the table in the corner of Kate's office and dumped the goods there, a mind-boggling array of stuffed animals, mobiles, balls, rattles and who knew what else. Eric grinned, dimples deep, eyes flashing, so obviously proud of himself he could scarcely stand it. He held up a fuzzy pink giraffe. "What do you think?"

Patsy scooted out and Kate stood and came around her desk, shaking her head. "I think we're going to have to buy a bigger house if you keep buying toys." She was also thinking, for the hundredth time, that she was glad they were having a girl because she wasn't sure she could survive two male McDaniels in one house.

He looked over his shoulder to make sure her office door was closed, then asked, "Can we break our 'no kissing at the office' rule just this once?"

She smiled and nodded, then went into his arms for a long, sensual kiss. When his kiss began to stir her senses to life, she pulled away, wagging her finger. "Don't you think I'm pregnant enough for now?"

Eric laughed and touched her stomach. "I can't *wait,* Kate—I can't wait until our baby is here."

She nodded and smiled up at him. "Me, too."

"I love you," he murmured, then squeezed her. Her heart welled. "I love you, too."

Then his eyes widened, and he turned back to the jumble of toys on the table. "I almost forgot. I was told explicitly by one of your former coworkers in production that you were to have the first one of these to roll off the assembly line." He rummaged, then came up with a box and extended it to her.

Kate took the cardboard and cellophane box, and bit into her lip to keep her hormonal tears at bay. "Bernadette." Same cropped red hair and freckles, but with a spiffy new teen ensemble, complete with baggy jeans and graffiti'd skateboard. She looked up. "What's your expert opinion on our new product, Mr. VP of Sales?"

His dark eyebrows went up. "Well, considering you were able to secure licensing for Bernadette books and there's a TV series in the works, I'd say you've struck gold, Kate...again."

She smiled, thinking she and Bernadette had come full circle together, and how wonderful that her own daughter would be able to enjoy the next generation of Bernadette dolls.

She set the box aside and looped her arms around her husband's neck. "How did life get so perfect?"

He pulled her against him. "I don't know. All I know is that in a couple of months, I'm going to be an absolute fool for *two* women."

Kate tilted her face up. "Would you mind if we broke our 'no kissing at the office' rule again?"

"Would I mind?" Eric grinned, then lowered his mouth to hers, and murmured, "Are you joking?"

FOOLS RUSH IN

Judith Arnold

To Ted, who still makes me laugh
after all these years

CHAPTER ONE

MOST PEOPLE would have been annoyed to find themselves stuck in bumper-to-bumper traffic during morning rush hour on the Fitzgerald Expressway. But Mark Lavin wasn't most people.

For him, being stuck in traffic meant being stuck in his SLK Roadster, which was not exactly a hardship. Six weeks old, the car still smelled new. The seat cradled his back, the steering wheel curved sweetly against his palms, and even though the engine had been built for zipping around hairpin turns at high speeds, it tolerated gridlock with grace.

Until this car, he'd always owned old clunkers. But he was past thirty now, he had a big title and a salary to match—and then he'd gotten that recognition from *Boston's Best* magazine. A silly honor, but definitely worth celebrating. So he'd ventured into a Mercedes-Benz showroom and found true love in the form of a pewter-silver metallic dream machine with charcoal-leather interior, a retractable roof, a six-speed manual transmission and power everything. He'd earned this car, it was his, and if he had to be crawling along the expressway at two miles an hour, surrounded by thousands of other morning commuters, well, there were far worse ways to do it than in a Benz.

Besides, he could actually do his job while he stared through the windshield at the glowing red rows of brake lights ahead of him. His stereo was tuned to WBKX, "Boston Kool X-treme," and his quadraphonic door-mounted speakers were pumping Rex in the Morning's drive-time show.

Mark was Rex's boss. And it hadn't always been smooth sailing. One year ago, on April Fool's Day, he'd nearly fired Rex because the deejay had issued a news report on a devastating earthquake in Los Angeles. No earthquake had occurred; the news story had been Rex's idea of an April Fool's Day prank. But it had ignited panic all over Boston. People had tied up the city's phone lines trying to reach friends and relatives in southern California. The mayor had issued a statement proclaiming the news report a hoax, and Mark had received a phone call from City Hall asking him to shut his shock jock up.

Mark had ultimately let Rex keep his job. The guy ranked number one in his time slot—mostly because his show veered so close to the line of tastelessness. The earthquake report, complete with damage estimates and casualty figures, had crossed that line, however. Mark had reamed Rex out, suspended him without pay for a week and warned him never, ever to pull a stunt like that again.

Now it was one year later, another April Fool's Day. The sky was a springtime mix of sun and clouds, the traffic crept toward downtown Boston, and Rex was playing Warren Zevon's "Werewolves of London." A good choice, Mark decided, trying to let the ergonomic splendor of his car soothe his anxiety over what might pop out of Rex's mouth in the remaining two hours of his show.

He reached the Mass Pike exit just as Zevon issued his last musical howl. "That was Celine Dion," Rex announced, "doing her cover of 'Dirty Water.' In her version, of course, Leonardo diCaprio dies. I don't know about you, but it makes me tear up a little." He sniffled dramatically.

Mark rolled his eyes. As long as Rex's jokes continued in that vein—no false alarms about natural disasters—Mark would be happy.

"And now for the news," Rex announced in his trademark baritone. Mark sat a little straighter and tightened his hands around the steering wheel, bracing himself. "In this morning's top story, the mayor of Runyon Poke, Vermont, has issued a proclamation declaring cows within its borders sacred. 'If they can worship cows in India, I don't see why we can't worship them here in Runyon Poke,' Mayor Crouton was quoted as saying. Runyon Poke boasts a population of two hundred thirty-seven, not counting the cows. Its chief export is cottage cheese."

Mark let out a long breath.

"Down in Washington," Rex continued, "both houses of Congress have passed a bill requiring all newly elected senators and representatives to wear propeller beanies for their first three months in office. 'People take Congress much too seriously,' the Speaker of the House said in defense of the bill. 'We want to introduce a little levity.' The President is expected to sign the bill into law."

Mark smiled.

"Closer to home, Boston's mayor has declared a

moratorium on snow. 'I know we get snow in April sometimes,' the mayor explained, 'but we don't want it. Enough is enough. Snow will be illegal until next November fifteenth.'''

Mark chuckled.

''Time to pay some bills, and then I'll be back with more music and noise,'' Rex said, segueing into an advertisement for a muffler repair company.

Okay. Mark wasn't going to have to fire Rex this year. He exited the expressway and cruised down the street to the garage under the skyscraper that housed WBKX's broadcast studio. At the bottom of the ramp, he inserted his card into the slot at the entry gate and entered the gloom of the garage. Even though the station's broadcast antenna was positioned at the top of the building, the reception was lousy amid all the concrete. His car filled with hissing static and he turned the radio off.

Once he was parked, he lifted his leather bomber jacket from the seat next to him, tossed it over his shoulder and headed for the elevator, humming ''Werewolves of London.'' He couldn't hit Zevon's high-note howls, but he didn't care. Rex had kept things under control this year, and Mark was feeling great.

As soon as he entered WBKX's headquarters on the thirtieth floor, he was surrounded by Rex in the Morning again. Ceiling speakers in the reception area broadcast the station's programming nonstop. He smiled at the receptionist and ambled down the hall to the studio from which Rex was broadcasting. The jingle of a national hamburger chain chased ''Werewolves'' from his mind. That jingle represented big bucks to the station. Mark's smile expanded.

Rex's voice returned when Mark was just steps from the door. ''This news just in. Get out your hankies, ladies, because it's going to make you weep.''

Mark paused in the hallway and held his breath.

''It was just two and a half months ago, on Valentine's Day, that *Boston Best* magazine named Mark Lavin, our general manager here at WBKX, one of the five most desirable bachelors in Boston. Tragedy struck this morning when Lavin announced his engagement to comely Claire O'Connor. How's that for a word, folks? *Comely.* Think about it.'' He paused, leaving five seconds—an eternity in radio time—of dead air. ''So cross Mark off your lists, ladies. But don't forget, I'm still available. Give me a call here at the station if you want to explore the meaning of the word *comely* with me. And say good-bye and good luck to my boss, Mark Lavin, because Claire O'Connor is from this day forward the only *comely* he'll be experiencing.''

Mark swore under his breath. That was not funny. Not funny at all.

He yanked open the control booth door and glared through the soundproof glass that separated Rex from his producer. Rex's long mop of salt-and-pepper hair was partly restrained by his headset, and he kept his beard trimmed so it wouldn't interfere with the microphone, but he still gave the appearance of someone who'd hit adolescence in the late 1960s and never outgrown either that decade or that life stage. ''Weather update,'' he intoned into the mike. ''No snow forecast for today. Looks like the mayor's word

is law in this town. In honor of my boss's engagement, let's spin a tune about the joys of marriage."
"Wedding Bell Blues" spilled through the speakers
into the control booth. Eyeing Mark through the
glass, Rex grinned and signaled with a thumbs-up.

Mark signaled back with a thumbs-down. "What
the hell is he doing?" he asked Rex's producer,
Gary, who sat at the controls, feeding Rex whatever
he needed, from commercials to sound effects to
questions and cues. "What was that crap about my
being engaged?"

"April Fool's Day," Gary answered calmly. He
was as mellow as Rex was hyper. "You're supposed
to laugh."

"I'm not laughing. Tell him." Mark gestured toward the microphone through which Gary commu-
nicated with Rex in the broadcast booth.

"Mark says he's not laughing," Gary reported
into the mike. Rex shrugged, his grin unflagging.

"Ask him who this person is—this woman he's
announced to all of Boston that I'm marrying. I've
never even heard of her!"

"He wants to know who his fiancée is," Gary re-
layed to Rex. Rex winked, then swiveled around on
his stool and busied himself with the CD racks along
the back wall.

Mark gritted his teeth to keep from cursing. "Tell
him his ass is toast," he finally said.

Gary leaned toward his mike and said, "Mark
would like to drink a toast to you." Mark whacked
Gary's arm, but Gary was too busy laughing to care.

And Rex was smart enough to keep his back to the window until Mark stormed out of the control booth.

CLAIRE HAD her coat off before she reached her office. A typical April day—not quite warm, not quite cold, almost sunny but the meteorologists were forecasting a chance of sprinkles. She'd dressed for every possibility, in a sweater set, lightweight wool slacks and her trench coat with its removable lining zipped in. She'd been too hot while riding the T, too cold while strolling across the plaza to City Hall. This must be what menopause was like: springtime in Boston.

"Hey, Claire!" Denise greeted her as she passed through the reception area. "Congratulations!"

Claire smiled vaguely. She had no idea what Denise was congratulating her for, but she'd been raised to acknowledge kind words with a smile. Inside her own tiny office, she flipped the light switch, turned on her computer and hooked her coat over a limb of the coat tree in the corner. Her computer issued a predictable chorus of buzzes and clicks as it warmed up.

"Claire?" Steve LaPina, one of the department's staff engineers, peered into her office. His mouth spread into a huge grin as he spotted her behind her desk, on the verge of settling into her chair. "Get over here, you little sneak!"

"What?" She and Steve were certainly friendly enough to call each other names, but a little sneak? Claire was the least sneaky person she knew. And she was five-eight, hardly little. But Steve's smile was infectious and his arms were spread wide. She circled her desk and accepted his hug. "What's this all about?"

"What's this all about?" he echoed, then laughed. "It's no secret anymore! Wonderful news! I'm so happy for you!"

Before she could ask him what wonderful news he was so happy about, he released her, gave her chin an affectionate nudge with his knuckles, murmured, "You comely thing, you!" and strolled away, an extra bounce in his step.

Frowning, she returned to her desk and sank into her chair. Her computer monitor displayed the usual array of icons. Her desk calendar lay open to April 1, with a notation about a demolition hearing scheduled for one-thirty that afternoon. Her pens and pencils stood neatly in her beloved Red Sox mug, her framed posters of Faneuil Hall and the Old North Church hung on the wall opposite her… Everything was exactly as she'd left it yesterday. She hadn't won the lottery, hadn't received a promotion, hadn't changed her hairstyle.

So why had Steve and Denise congratulated her?

She swiveled in her chair to reach her radio on the shelf behind her desk, and tuned the dial to WGBH, the public radio station. She needed the soothing strains of classical music to help her clear her thoughts. A Corelli concerto filled her office; she closed her eyes and let the music wash over her.

"Claire!"

She opened her eyes to find her doorway filled with a bouquet of silver helium balloons with "Congratulations!" printed on their shiny surfaces. The balloons entered the room and then she saw who was carrying them: Meryl, Beryl and JoAnn from Human Resources, all of them grinning so brightly she had to shut her eyes again. Too much silver. Too much joy.

The three women swept into her office, chattering excitedly, pressing the knotted strings of the balloons into her hand. Meryl mentioned something about a shower. Beryl cooed that her mother must be so thrilled. JoAnn issued a lovesick sigh and admitted to being terribly jealous. Then they swept out of her office, leaving her alone, clinging to the balloons.

What? she thought, panic creeping up her spine into her skull and down into her stomach, churning both her thoughts and the remnants of her breakfast. What was going on?

Maybe she was suffering from amnesia. Maybe she was dreaming this entire morning. Maybe she'd slipped through a wormhole and wound up in an alternate universe. *Why was everyone congratulating her?*

"Claire!" yet another well-wisher bellowed through her open door. This visitor was Maggie, one of her closest friends at the Landmarks Commission. "Oh, look at those balloons! Aren't they cute?"

Claire gaped at the balloons, still in a queasy state of disbelief edged with panic. "What am I supposed to do with them?" she asked. "If I let go, they'll fly up to the ceiling."

"Tie them onto something," Maggie said helpfully. She eased the strings out of Claire's clenched fist and knotted them around the arm of her desk chair. "Where'd you get them?"

"The trio from Human Resources gave them to

me,'' Claire said, shaking her head and lowering her voice. ''Maggie, you've got to help me. I have no idea why everyone is congratulating me.''

Maggie finished securing the balloons, then straightened up and stared at Claire. A bit shorter than Claire, a bit older and blessedly grounded, Maggie looked bemused. ''You haven't even made a formal announcement, and you've already forgotten?''

''Forgotten what? I don't know what I've forgotten!'' Claire realized she was babbling and pressed her lips together. She also closed her door. She didn't want Denise or anyone else outside her office to eavesdrop and conclude that she was demented.

''Your wedding engagement?'' Maggie suggested, studying Claire's face as she enunciated each syllable. ''Does that ring a bell?''

Her wedding engagement? ''What are you talking about? I'm not engaged!''

''It was on the radio, Claire.''

''My wedding engagement? On the *radio?*'' Pain throbbed inside her skull. ''What wedding engagement? And why in the world would it be on the radio?''

''Your fiancé,'' Maggie said, still speaking slowly, as if to an imbecile. ''Mark Lavin? The head honcho of a radio station? Does any of this sound familiar?''

''No.'' Claire dropped into her chair. Her elbow jostled the strings, and the balloons bobbed and rustled above her head.

''Well, if it makes you feel any better, he's quite a catch.''

''It doesn't.'' Claire gave her a hard look. ''How

would you happen to know he's a catch? Do you know him? Do *I* know him?''

"You're engaged to him, remember?''

"I'm not—'' Claire sighed. She'd already denied her engagement several times. Either the radio was wrong or she'd lost her mind.

"You haven't introduced me to him yet,'' Maggie continued. "But I know he's a catch thanks to the article in *Boston's Best* a couple of months ago.''

"What article?'' Claire asked warily. Her hands gripped the edge of her desk. She felt like one of the helium balloons—if she let go, she might just float away, completely out of this world, which she was no longer sure she recognized.

"Boston's most desirable bachelors,'' Maggie explained with forced patience. "They chose five, and he was one of them. Definitely the studliest of the bunch, too. I wonder if there's a copy of the magazine anywhere. It was the Valentine's Day issue.''

A Valentine's Day magazine. A radio announcement. None of this made sense. Why would Claire O'Connor, of all people, be engaged to some studly Boston bachelor? Especially one who ran a radio station?

"Oh, my God,'' she said as her memory stirred back to life.

"What? It's beginning to ring a bell now?''

"Oh yeah,'' Claire muttered. Her gaze drifted to the calendar open on her desk. April 1st. April Fool's Day, and alarms were clanging inside her brain.

MARK WASN'T SURE what pissed him off the most: Rex's attitude, his annoying practical joke or the idea of getting married. It wasn't as if he was militantly opposed to the concept of marriage. His parents were happily married and he assumed that eventually he would be happily married, too. But he'd just been named one of the city's hottest bachelors by *Boston's Best,* and he wanted to savor that status for a while. Although he'd been surprised that the magazine had chosen him, along with a successful fund manager at Fidelity, a celebrity chef at a fusion restaurant in the South End, an orthopedic surgeon at Mass General and a young Boston University professor, he'd appreciated his place on that short list. He'd appreciated even more the attention it brought, the fame and glory. *Boston's Best* had run a full-page photo of him sitting on a park bench in the Public Garden, a smaller shot of him at his desk, surrounded by stacks of CDs, and a five-paragraph profile making him sound pretty damned special. He knew better than to believe his own hype…but the hype was fun. He'd relished the sudden increase in flirting that came his way, and the good-natured jabs from envious colleagues and friends. He'd been pleased by the publicity the profile had brought to WBKX. And thinking of himself as one cool Boston dude? Yeah, he'd loved it.

And now Rex was marrying him off. The bastard!

Mountains of work awaited his attention, but he couldn't concentrate. Instead, he lifted his phone and punched in his secretary's extension. "Ellie?" he said when he heard her voice. "Do me a favor. Find out everything you can about Claire O'Connor."

"Your fiancée?"

He heard laughter in her voice, but he ignored the taunt. "Find out who the hell she is."

"You're marrying her and you don't know who she is?"

"Just do it," he snapped, then slammed down his phone.

"There you go," Maggie said, waltzing into Claire's office an hour later with a magazine in her hand, her index finger wedged between the pages. She slapped the magazine onto Claire's desk and flipped it open to the page she'd been marking with her finger. "There's your fiancé."

Claire stared. She'd been doing a lot of that since she'd settled at her desk—more specifically staring into space, contemplating why Rex Crandall had chosen her to make fun of and trying to figure out what to do about it. She'd be happy to ignore the bogus wedding announcement, but that was impossible when colleagues kept poking their heads into her office to shout their congratulations and question her about the time and place of the nuptials. How many other people had heard Rex's radio show? How many hundreds of thousands of Boston-area listeners believed she was engaged to this Mark Lavin person, whoever the hell he was?

She directed her gaze to the photo of Mark Lavin, which occupied a full, glossy page of *Boston's Best*. Oh, God—he was gorgeous. Thick, dark hair tumbled in waves around a face of angles and edges. His eyes were deep-set and the color of espresso, his nose long and narrow and his smile wickedly seductive. He wore a leather jacket with the collar turned up, faded jeans and sneakers—the kind of outfit rich people wore when they wanted to prove that despite their wealth they were really Average Joes.

He was no Average Joe, though. For one thing, he'd been declared one of the top five bachelors in the city, and for another…he was *gorgeous*.

The facing page contained a smaller photo of him, seated at a desk heaped with CD jewel cases. He wore a blue shirt with the collar open and the sleeves rolled up; a colorful tie hung loose below his throat. His hair was as tousled in the indoor photo as in the outdoor one. It wasn't exactly long, but it was long enough. Long enough for a woman to lose her fingers in its thick waves.

She wasn't that woman, though. She wasn't the type to lose her fingers in the hair of a breathtakingly handsome bachelor she didn't even know, even if she was supposedly engaged to him.

"You can see why everyone's congratulating you," Maggie remarked, ogling the larger photo of Mark Lavin. "This is a guy a lot of women would like to marry."

"How do you know that?" Claire retorted. "Maybe he's obnoxious. Maybe he picks his nose in public and tortures puppies for fun."

"Look at those eyes," Maggie argued, gesturing toward the photo. "Do they look like the eyes of a man who tortures puppies?"

No. They looked like the eyes of a man who enjoyed sex. Claire felt her cheeks heat as that unbidden thought drifted through her mind.

Her phone rang. She prayed the call wasn't another congratulations—although she'd have just as much difficulty getting through a conversation about any other subject. Sighing, she lifted the receiver. "Hello?"

"Claire Connor?" The voice was male and unfamiliar.

"I'm Claire *O'Connor,* if that's who you're trying to reach."

"Right. Sorry." He hesitated, then said, "This is Mark Lavin. Your fiancé."

Claire sent Maggie a frantic look and mouthed, *It's him.* Maggie jabbed her finger at the magazine photo with a wide-eyed questioning look and Claire nodded. Her gaze remained on the picture, as she tried to connect it to the dark, gravelly voice on the other end of the line.

"Are you still there?" he asked.

She cleared her throat. "Yes."

"Rough morning?"

An unexpected smile teased her lips. Shifting in her chair, she jostled the strings tied to the arm, causing the balloons to bob above her head. "It's been awful."

"That bad?"

"I've got friends angry with me for failing to tell them you and I were seeing each other. I've got other friends grilling me about where we've registered for our wedding presents. And I've got—" her elbow jostled the balloon strings again "—balloons."

"Balloons."

"Yes."

"This thing has obviously gotten out of control," he said grimly. For some reason, his solemn tone made Claire want to laugh. After a moment, he added, "We should probably get together and come up with a strategy to shut down this rumor. How about if I stop by your office so we can work something out?"

"No," Claire said quickly. "No, don't come here." Good God, if he came to her office, everyone would make a huge fuss. Meryl, Beryl and JoAnn might bring even more balloons.

"I'd ask you to come here…"

"No." If she went to Mark Lavin's office, she might run into Rex Crandall, and she didn't trust herself not to punch him in the nose.

"Can we meet somewhere, then?"

She eyed her calendar. There, right below the bright red April 1 was her note about the demolition hearing. "I've got a meeting at one-thirty. It could drag on for hours." And the odds were good that people at the meeting would have heard she was betrothed. Her gaze drifted from her calendar back to the magazine, to Mark Lavin's dark, mesmerizing eyes.

"Five-thirty," he suggested. "We can meet at the Kinsale. That's right near your office. You're in City Hall, right?"

She supposed she ought to be flattered that he'd made an effort to find out where his alleged bride-to-be worked. Of course, she knew more about him than he knew about her, thanks to the article in *Boston's Best*. She knew that he was the general manager of WBKX, he was thirty-two, he'd grown up in western Massachusetts but now lived in Somerville, he'd graduated from Wesleyan University and earned a master's degree at Emerson—and he loved being single. In case there was any doubt, the last line of the article quoted him as saying, "I love being single."

"Claire?"

She gave herself a shake. "Yes. The Kinsale at five-thirty."

"And we'll figure this mess out," he promised. "We'll come up with a way to set the record straight."

"And we'll hire a hit man to take care of Rex Crandall."

He laughed. "That, too."

CHAPTER TWO

HE SAT at a table in the Kinsale, nursing a Glenlivet and scrutinizing every woman who entered the pub. Which one had Rex linked him to? That skinny chick with the spiked pink hair? No, thank God—she bee-lined to a group of equally punky people at a table near the bar. One of those two matronly women lug-ging shopping bags? No, they were clearly tourists, with their cameras, their comfortable walking shoes and their shopping bags featuring the logos of Quincy Market shops. Ellie had ferreted out that Claire Connor—*O'Connor,* he'd have to remember that O—worked in City Hall, in the Landmarks Com-mission office. He doubted she would wear comfort-able walking shoes and carry a camera.

He sat up straighter when a buxom blonde sa-shayed in, but she waved at someone behind him and sauntered past his table without stopping. Then a group of beefy guys in duckbill caps came in, and an older guy in a fisherman's knit sweater…and a tall, slim redhead in an open trench coat and tailored slacks, a leather tote gripped in one hand and worry shadowing her eyes. Green eyes, he noted. Jade green. Pale skin, a tiny nose and wide cheeks. She searched the room, then zeroed in on him. A nervous smile twitched her lips.

If Rex were going to marry Mark off to someone, he could have done a lot worse than this.

Mark rose from his chair. She wove among the tables to reach him, the amber light from the overhead fixtures lifting golden highlights to the surface of her long, curly hair. She extended her right hand and he took it. It was cool and fine-boned. "Mark Lavin?" she asked.

"And you must be Claire O'Connor." With an O.

Another faint smile tugged at her lips. "I'm sorry I'm late. That demolition hearing ran on and on."

Releasing her hand, he gestured toward the chair across from him. She sat, then shrugged out of her coat and draped it over the back of the chair. As he resumed his seat, he studied her more closely. Her mouth reminded him of a kitten's, the corners tilted up even after her smile faded, and her upper lip was unbearably dainty. Her eyes were tired but intense. She fidgeted with the handles of her tote for a moment, then resolutely lowered it from her lap to the floor. She was obviously nervous, but her hand hadn't been clammy in his. It had felt velvety soft, with a hint of strength in her grip.

Mark beckoned a waitress over. "Would you like a drink?" he asked Claire.

"Just...a cup of tea, please," she requested. "Herbal, if you have it."

He wondered if she avoided liquor, then reminded himself that he shouldn't care. It wasn't as if he were going to marry her or anything. If she was a teetotaler, she could drink her total tea, and he could entertain himself by gazing into those dazzling green eyes of hers.

He took a sip of his single malt and leaned back. "Where are your balloons?" he asked once the waitress had departed.

"In my office. I popped a few with the point of a pencil. It was therapeutic." She flashed him a grin.

"Nobody sent me balloons," he told her, feigning disappointment. Then he grimaced. "The phone rang off the hook all day at the station, though."

She looked sympathetic. "Really?"

"Listeners. Women, mostly, moaning about how unfair it was that I let *Boston's Best* include me in their bachelor story when I was obviously involved with someone."

"What did you tell them?"

He snorted. "I didn't tell them anything. They called the station, not me. Rex put them on the air."

She pursed her lips. "Rex Crandall."

"I take it you know him?"

Before she could answer, the waitress returned with a cup, a small pot containing steaming water and a tray of teabags. Claire studied the selection like some kind of connoisseur, then plucked a lavender envelope from the tray and nodded her thanks to the waitress. She occupied herself opening the envelope and dipping the teabag into the pot.

"I also got a call from the magazine," he told her. "They're pretty ripped. Apparently it's a big deal to get picked as one of their annual top-five bachelors, and I seem to have tainted the honor."

"Did you tell them the story wasn't true?"

"Yeah. But it's kind of like saying, 'I don't beat my wife.' The minute you deny something like that, people assume you're lying." He watched her pour tea into the cup. Once she'd finished, he asked, "So you know Rex Crandall?"

"I'm afraid so."

"And...what? You insulted him? Questioned his manhood? I mean, I know why he targeted me. I'm his boss and I'm on his back all the time. But why you?"

She traced the handle of her cup with one slender finger. "I dated him last fall."

Mark labored not to show his astonishment. Claire O'Connor seemed way too classy for Rex. Her complexion was dewy, her clothing neat and perfectly tailored to her tall, slender body, and she had good manners. She was the sort of woman who unwound from a long day and a demolition hearing—whatever that might be—with a cup of herbal tea.

Rex, on the other hand, was a gonzo. No way could Mark see him with someone like Claire.

"He was hosting a free concert in front of Faneuil Hall," she said. "There were a few bands, T-shirts were given away—it was some sort of publicity thing for your radio station."

"Right. I remember that." WBKX sponsored numerous concerts during the year, many of them free outdoor shows to promote up-and-coming artists and the station.

"I wound up being his contact. Faneuil Hall is a landmark, so the station had to work through my office."

"And you went out with him?" Mark simply couldn't see it. The thought of Rex even looking at a woman as refined as Claire, let alone talking to her or—God forbid—touching her… No. The picture refused to come into focus

"A few times. He's an interesting man. He has a lot of energy."

Did he sleep with you? Mark wanted to ask. Not that it was any of his business who she slept with, but…damn, her eyes were something. And the delicate hollow at the base of her throat, and the wistful, inexplicably sexy curve of her smile…

"I could see it wasn't going to develop into anything, and after a few dates I told him so. I thought he took it all right. I mean—look at me. I'm not his type, am I?"

"Not in the least." He shouldn't have felt relieved, but he did.

"One evening, not long after we had that conversation, my phone rang. It was a friend of his, telling me he'd fallen off a ladder and suffered a head injury. This friend said that just before he passed out, he asked for me. He was in a coma at Metrowest Medical in Framingham, and I should come right away."

Mark frowned. He didn't recall Rex missing work due to a head injury last fall.

"Of course I raced to the hospital. I was so upset and frightened for him. I didn't know if he was near death, or why he'd asked for me. I just went. On Route 9, a policeman gave me a ticket, even after I told him why I was speeding. I got to the emergency room, ran inside and no one knew who Rex Crandall was. No one fitting his description had been admitted. So I went back outside—and there, in the parking lot, Rex and his friend were waiting for me.

They'd made a bet, apparently. Rex had told him that even if a woman broke up with him, she'd still come running if he needed her. He took fifty dollars from his friend. And I paid seventy-five dollars to the Framingham Police Department for that damned ticket.''

"Jeez."

"I let him know what I thought of his stupid practical joke. Right there in the hospital's parking lot. I didn't exactly censor myself," she added, smiling crookedly.

He imagined her cursing Rex out. He imagined her all flushed with anger, her eyes flashing, fiery emotion spilling from her pretty pink lips. The idea sent an unexpected heat humming along his nerves.

"I would have thought that settled the score for him," she went on. "I broke up with him, he cost me seventy-five dollars and made me feel like a fool, and so be it. I can't imagine why he's still bothering with me. It's been six months since he pulled that stunt."

"Rex's mind is a strange thing," Mark explained. "I don't know what's going on with him most of the time. Maybe marrying you off to me is his way of saying he's sorry."

"Because you're such a great catch?" She smiled wryly.

Well yeah, as a matter of fact. He *was* a great catch—*Boston's Best* sure thought so. But to come right out and say so would make him sound conceited, so he just shrugged.

She appraised him for a minute, then shrugged, too. "He does have a lot to apologize for. When I broke up with him, he said I was...well, never mind." She lowered her eyes, evidently discovering something riveting in the steam rising from her cup of tea.

"What?" Mark was far too curious—about her, about what Rex said she was, about the long, tawny lashes fringing her eyelids. "What did he say you were?"

"A dried up arctic bitch," she said.

Ouch. "He's got a way with words."

She raised her eyes to him, and they flashed with amusement. Still, Mark felt bad for her, bad that she'd received that kind of infantile abuse from Rex. Mark had broken up with a few women in his day, and a few women had broken up with him. It was never a pleasant experience, but when he was doing the breaking up he always tried to be gentle about it.

"Okay," he said, fortifying himself with a sip of Scotch. Rex might be a son of a bitch, but Claire seemed smart and game. Together, they could figure out a way to wiggle out of this make-believe marriage-to-be. "The way I see it, we've got several options. One would be to make a bold public statement declaring that we're not engaged."

"A bold public statement?" she asked dubiously.

"A press conference."

"A press conference!" She laughed. "Surely we're not that newsworthy."

As the general manager of one of the city's most popular radio stations, the sponsor of numerous benefit concerts and a highly esteemed eligible bachelor, according to Boston's top-selling local magazine, Mark considered himself reasonably newsworthy. Obviously Claire didn't view herself the same way.

Perhaps something more low-key would be appropriate. "We could issue a press release."

She shook her head. "Wouldn't that be like saying, 'I don't beat my wife'? If we deny it in a big way, people will think we're protesting too much."

Good point. "Another option," he suggested, "would be to ignore the whole thing and hope it goes away."

"That was more along the lines of what I was thinking."

"But if we go that route, you run the risk of getting more balloons," he warned her. "If we don't step forward and say we're not hooked up, some people are going to continue to think we are."

"But that's still better than a press release." She sipped some tea, lowered her cup and met his gaze. "Do you think it would be possible to get Rex to say something on his show tomorrow? If he admitted that he made the whole thing up..."

"For one thing, if we ask him to do that, he'll know he got us good. If I order him to do it, I've got an employer-employee situation, which I'd rather avoid. And frankly, unless I make an employer-employee situation out of it, I don't think he'd offer an on-air retraction. And I don't think getting one of the other announcers to do it would be particularly effective. Rex can be a real asshole."

"Indeed." She tapped her fingers together as she thought. Her eyes seemed brighter now, not so strained. Not jade, he decided, but shamrock-green. With those eyes and her red hair, and the O in her last name, she fit right into this Irish pub—except that she was drinking tea instead of Irish whiskey.

"There's got to be a middle ground in this," she said. "Something between a forceful denial and complete silence."

"Like what?"

She exhaled heavily, drained her cup and put on a brave face. "If those are my only choices, I think we should go with complete silence."

Mark nodded. He didn't mind letting it be her choice. He could deal with the consequences. He could make his own private statement to *Boston's Best,* so they wouldn't think they'd made a mistake in highlighting him in their Valentine's Day issue, and he could tighten the screws on Rex in ways only a general manager could tighten the screws on a deejay—even the most popular morning drive-time deejay in Boston.

Claire could pop her balloons and get on with her life. Someday, he thought, she'd make someone a lovely fiancée. What was the word Rex had used to describe her?

Comely.

Mark knew what *comely* meant, and he wasn't a teenager, snickering at a silly pun. But when he contemplated Claire O'Connor's lush hair and her long legs and everything in between...

No. He didn't even want to think about it. He was a desirable bachelor and Claire had been, until a half hour ago, a complete stranger, and this was all a stupid joke. If Mark was a gentleman—and he liked to believe he was—the best thing he could do, the *only* thing, was to extricate Claire from this ridiculous situation and let her get on with her life.

And let himself get on with his.

CHAPTER THREE

CLAIRE HAD JUST FINISHED pouring her coffee when her phone rang. At seven-thirty in the morning, the shrill sound would have been jarring even if she'd gotten a good night's rest. But she hadn't. How could she possibly sleep? She was *engaged*. To *Mark Lavin*.

All through the night, her mind had raced like an engine in neutral with the gas pedal floored—lots of noise but no forward motion. She couldn't pinpoint exactly what was causing her mental motor to race. Anger at being made the butt of a practical joke, for one thing. Worry about how to convince her colleagues that a wedding wasn't in her immediate future. Uneasiness about the public nature of the whole situation.

And Mark, her supposed intended. Every time he'd entered her thoughts, her mind had revved to the point of redlining.

He was much better-looking in person than in the photo in *Boston's Best,* which was saying a lot, given how handsome he'd appeared in the photo. In person, his dark eyes sweetened his face. His smile expressed a variety of emotions—emotions Claire could relate to. When he'd told her about Rex Crandall's addiction to beer nuts and they'd both burst into laughter

at exactly the same instant, when they'd both reached
for the check and his fingertips had brushed the back
of her hand, when he'd gazed into her eyes and she'd
felt as if he could see every intimate detail of her
life... And he was tall. Most men she met were her
height, or sometimes even shorter. Not that a man's
height mattered to her.

Not that *anything* about Mark mattered.

She carried her mug to the table by the window in
her compact kitchen, then grabbed the receiver from
the wall phone. "Hello?"

"Mary Claire." Her mother's voice crackled with
indignation. "When were you planning to tell me?"

"Tell you what?" she asked, settling into her chair
and stirring her spoon through the bowl of corn
flakes.

"That you're getting married. I'm your mother!
Was it supposed to be a secret? Something you were
going to spring on me the day of the wedding?"

How had her mother heard? Surely she didn't listen to Boston Kool X-treme radio. "It's not true,
Mom," she said, abandoning her spoon for her mug.
She needed caffeine more than carbohydrates. "I'm
not getting married."

"Are you telling me the *Boston Globe* is publish-
ing lies?"

"The *Boston Globe*?" The sip of coffee Claire
had managed to swallow threatened to return on her.
Setting down her mug, she reached for the newspaper, which she would have been reading right now
if her mother hadn't telephoned her. "Where is it in
the *Boston Globe*?"

"The Names column, in the Living section," her

mother told her. Claire tucked the receiver between her ear and her shoulder, freeing both hands to flip through the pages until she reached the column, which covered local gossip and promotional events.

Damn. There was her name, printed in boldface, along with Mark's. The paragraph's headline read "Boston's Best Bachelor Bites the Bullet." Grimacing, Claire silently read on: "When WBKX's Rex in the Morning announced the engagement of the station's general manager, Mark Lavin, hundreds of hopeful bachelorettes in the Hub sighed with dismay. So did *Boston's Best*, which had named him one of the five most desirable bachelors in Boston in its Valentine's Day issue. A magazine spokesman said Lavin denied he was engaged, but he was later spotted canoodling with his lovely bride-to-be, Claire O'Connor of the city's Landmarks Commission office, at the Kinsale Pub. Best wishes to the happy couple, and condolences to all those grieving bachelorettes."

"Canoodling?" she blurted out.

"If you want to canoodle, there's nothing I can do about it," her mother scolded. "You're twenty-eight years old and you live on your own. You can canoodle to your heart's content. But getting engaged, Mary Claire? I haven't even met this young man! I've never even *heard* of him."

That was the second time her mother had used her full name. Not a good sign. "*I* only met the young man yesterday," she told her mother. "I'm not engaged to him. I can't believe the *Globe* wrote about us." She sighed. "We weren't canoodling, either."

"Call it whatever you want."

"We were discussing how to make this silly rumor about our marriage go away." *And we touched hands that one time, going for the check, and maybe I spent a little too much time—like most of the night—wondering what it would be like if Mark touched my cheek, or my knee, or any other part of my anatomy.* Feeling her cheeks burn with a blush, Claire shoved that thought away.

"Why doesn't he want to marry you?" her mother asked.

Leave it to her to twist things around. "He doesn't *not* want to marry me, Mom, but—"

"So he *does* want to marry you?"

"No!" She shoved the newspaper away and reached for her mug again. Her cereal was inedible, the flakes soggy beyond salvation. "He doesn't want to marry me. I don't want to marry him."

"Why not? What's wrong with him?"

"Nothing. We don't even know each other, Mom."

"You could get to know each other. It could work. Stranger things have happened."

"Mom—"

"You're twenty-eight years old," her mother repeated. "It's time to stop canoodling and settle down. Your sisters are married. You should be married, too."

"I'm not going to get married just because Liz and Frannie are married."

"You should get married because it's wrong for you to be all alone, a beautiful girl like you, with so much to offer. This boyfriend of yours, Mark Lavin, it sounds like he's got a very good job."

"He's not my boyfriend."

Her mother ignored her. "Solid, respectable, he probably makes a good living. I'd prefer a church wedding, if I have anything to say in the matter."

Claire wondered if *she* had anything to say in the matter. It was *her* wedding, after all. Correction: her *non*-wedding. "Mom, listen to me. I'm not marrying Mark."

"And I'm asking why not," her mother repeated. "If it's in the *Globe*—"

Claire rolled her eyes. "How about if he told you? If Mark himself told you we weren't getting married, would you believe him?"

"Now, that's an idea. Why don't you bring him around? I'm roasting a chicken for dinner. I could roast two. If Frannie and Liz are available, with their families... Megan hates chicken, but I can always fix her a hot dog. That's all she's eating these days—hot dogs. I don't know how healthy it is. Liz says she sometimes eats a hot dog for breakfast, can you imagine? It's better than sweets, I suppose. The pediatrician says—"

Claire gave up on waiting for her mother to pause for a breath. "Mom," she interrupted in a near shout, "I'm not coming for dinner. Don't invite Frannie and Liz. And Megan. Don't invite anybody! I was just going to have Mark give you a call—"

"I want to meet him," her mother insisted. "I want to see with my own eyes just what's going on between the two of you."

"*Nothing's* going on between the two of us!"

"And I want to see that with my own eyes."

"We're not coming for dinner."

"Then you'll come after dinner," her mother resolved. "I'll roast just the one chicken. Come around eight."

"I don't know if he's free tonight," said Claire, now just wanting to get her mother off her back.

"You're engaged to him and you don't know if he's free?"

"I'm *not*—" Claire cut herself off. Like so many conversations with her mother, this one was heading over a cliff and straight to hell. "If you don't hear from me," she said, "we'll be at your house at eight. If he can't make it, I'll let you know."

"Oh, he can make it," her mother said with blithe certainty. "The least he can do is come and meet his fiancée's mother."

Claire managed a good-bye and hung up the phone. Then she returned to the table and reread the item in the Names column. She cursed soundly. So much for her and Mark's plan that they could ignore this thing and it would go away.

It was definitely not going away.

FOR SOME REASON, Mark was actually looking forward to meeting Claire O'Connor's mother.

Well, not exactly looking forward to it. But given the way the rest of his day had gone, a trip to West Roxbury to visit the O'Connor matriarch might wind up being the high point of the past twenty-four hours.

His "engagement" was still news. The *Boston Globe* had mentioned it in its Living section that morning—hard to miss, with his name and Claire's printed in boldface. The *Globe* had described them as "canoodling." Jeez. Tomorrow's *Herald* would probably include an item about them "billing and cooing." What century was it, anyway?

Because of the *Globe* piece, Claire's phone call hadn't been unexpected. She'd sounded worried. Unlike him, she wasn't used to appearing in the newspaper. He'd made appearances in the *Globe*'s Names column more than a few times since being named general manager at WBKX, usually in conjunction with a concert or promotion the station was sponsoring.

"I'm still not opposed to issuing a press release," he'd told her.

"That's not the biggest problem," she'd said. The biggest problem, apparently, was her mother, who refused to believe Claire wasn't engaged to Mark. "She said she wants to hear this from you—in person," Claire had explained.

He could have said no. He could have said the whole idea was ridiculous, which it was. But when he'd closed his eyes he'd pictured Claire, tall and willowy, with her rippling red hair and her kittenish mouth, and the lovely sound of her laughter, and those long, long legs of hers, and he'd said, "Sure, no problem."

Claire had suggested that they meet at her mother's house, but he'd insisted on picking her up at her apartment. They'd need time to prepare, to work out an effective strategy before they faced Mrs. O'Connor. Besides, he welcomed any excuse to drive someone else in his new car. Claire would probably enjoy taking a spin in the Benz-mobile.

After Claire's phone call, his day had gone downhill. Many more people had seen the blurb in the

Globe than had heard Rex's April Fool's Day prank yesterday—which said less about Rex's ratings than about the *Globe*'s enormous circulation. His phone hadn't stopped ringing, even after he'd asked Ellie to screen his calls. He'd wasted thirty precious minutes on the line with an editor from *Boston's Best* magazine, doing his damnedest to convince her that the whole thing was a gag and that he hadn't misrepresented himself to the magazine when they were putting together their Valentine's Day edition. He spent another half hour crafting a retraction for Rex to read on the air, if Claire would agree to such a maneuver. Personally, he'd like more than a public retraction from Rex. He'd like Rex to buy him a case of top-tier single-malt Scotch whisky—and a case of herbal tea for Claire, if that was her drink of choice. He'd like Rex to donate a hundred hours of effort to a charity of Mark's and Claire's choosing. Actually, he'd like Rex's balls on a silver platter, doused in Tabasco sauce.

He'd hoped to head to the gym after work for a pick-up basketball game—to let off some steam—then take a quick shower, grab a bite at the club's snack bar, and then drive down to the South End to pick up Claire. But just as he was shutting off his computer, Sherry Altamont pounded on his office door. If Ellie hadn't already left for the day, he might have been spared this intrusion, but without Ellie guarding his door, Sherry got through. Mark had met her a month ago at a shindig to raise money for a literacy program, and they'd hit it off. She was pretty, she was smart and the couple of dates they'd gone on had been enjoyable.

Sherry had stormed inside and sliced through him like a machete. "How could you be engaged to this woman? You were dating *me!*" she'd shrieked. "What kind of two-timing scum are you?"

"Is there more than one kind?" he'd asked.

"I thought we had a relationship!"

"We went out a few times," he'd said, not sure that qualified as a relationship.

"And I have to *read* in the *newspaper—*" she'd relied on emphasis to add drama to her tirade "—that you're *engaged* to *another woman!*"

"According to the newspaper, all we were doing was canoodling."

"You're scum!" she'd howled. "Two-timing scum!" Then she'd whacked him on the head with her purse, which, fortunately, was stylishly small and hadn't inflicted too much damage.

By the time she'd departed, he'd lost interest in the pick-up game. He'd lost interest in dinner, too, but he knew he ought to eat something so his stomach wouldn't growl in Mrs. O'Connor's presence. He wound up ordering take-out Thai and eating it at his desk—and chugging gallons of water from the cooler, because he'd forgotten to tell the chef to go light on the chili.

Convincing Claire's mother that he wasn't going to become her son-in-law ought to be easier than dealing with Sherry Altamont—or with Thai Haven's *Gai Pad Prik.* He popped an antacid, detoured to the men's room to tidy his hair, which had been mussed by Sherry's pocketbook assault, and took the elevator down to the basement garage.

Driving his car soothed him. The worst was over,

he assured himself. He would set Claire's mother
straight, the *Globe* piece would fade from the city's
collective memory as some juicy new scoop took its
place, and he'd get back to being one of the city's
most desirable bachelors. And maybe he'd let Rex
Crandall continue living with his body fully intact.

He felt even better when he drove down Bradford
Street, cruising past the neat three-story brick buildings until he found the one with Claire's address. No
parking spaces were open on the narrow street, but
before he could switch on his hazard lights and abandon his car long enough to ring the bell, she appeared
in the doorway, her hair vibrant in the glow of a
streetlamp, her hands plunged into the pockets of a
green wool blazer and her legs appearing wonder-
fully lanky in snug-fitting black jeans. Mark wondered what she'd look like in a dress, with her legs
exposed.

He wondered what she'd look like naked.

Forget it. She wasn't his fiancée, his girlfriend or
even his date for an evening. She was just a lady
having trouble communicating with her mother. Na-
kedness would not be a part of the evening's activities.

"I was watching for you," she said, pulling open
the passenger door before he could get out of the car
to open it for her. "I knew you'd never find a parking
space. It's awful on this block."

"Do you have a car?" He recalled her telling him
about the speeding ticket she'd gotten while rushing
to the hospital in Framingham to see Rex.

She nodded, set her purse on the floor at her feet
and buckled her seat belt. "I pay to park it in a lot.

I really should just get rid of it, for all the money I spend on parking.'' As he eased into gear, she seemed to become aware of her surroundings. ''It's an old Hyundai. Nothing like this.''

He tried to suppress his grin. ''You like this car?''

''It's spectacular. It smells new.''

''It is.'' The hell with suppressing his grin. ''First new car I ever owned. I thought it would fit the image of a top-five bachelor.''

''It does,'' she said, settling back into her seat.

He wondered if she meant that as a compliment. He wondered why he cared. He wondered why her legs kept drawing his attention when he had to stay focused on the traffic and the mission before them. He wondered why the new-car smell didn't appeal to him as much as Claire's smell—something faint and flowery and utterly feminine.

''What do I need to know about your mother?'' he asked to distract himself from her fragrance, her legs and all the rest of it.

Claire reflected for a minute before answering. ''She's stubborn. And she desperately wants me to get married. Both my sisters are married—and Frannie is younger than me. My mother considers it a tragedy that Frannie got married before I did.''

''So you have two sisters?''

''Frannie and Liz. Mary Frances and Mary Elizabeth. I'm Mary Claire. If my mother gets riled, she'll call me by my full name.''

Weird, he thought—three sisters all named Mary. ''How about your father?''

''He died six years ago,'' she said.

''I'm sorry.''

"He was a great guy. A city cop. He died in the line of duty."

"Really?" Mark wanted to pull off the road and give her a hug, just for having endured such a tragedy.

She smiled. "He wasn't murdered. He was directing traffic at the scene of an accident during a snowstorm. A passing motorist lost control of her car and hit him. I mean, it was terrible, but at least we didn't have to relive the whole thing in the newspapers and the courts."

"I guess." He still wanted to hug her.

"My mother is an administrative assistant at an insurance company, and she gets a widow's pension. She spends her free time worrying about when I'm going to get married. I wish she'd get married herself. It might make her stop obsessing about me."

"If you'd like, I can have Rex link her to someone during his next radio show."

"Please don't," she said dryly, then laughed.

He laughed, too. And spent the rest of the drive to West Roxbury thinking about how much he enjoyed the sound of her laughter and wondering what it would be like to hug her.

CHAPTER FOUR

CLAIRE'S MOTHER hadn't roasted an extra chicken for Mark, but she might as well have. She welcomed him into the modest Victorian house Claire had grown up in as if he were a long-lost relative. Of course, he *would* be a relative if he married Claire. But they'd journeyed here to make certain her mother understood that that wasn't going to happen.

"Come, sit in the living room," she said, practically ignoring Claire as she tucked her hand into the crook of Mark's arm and dragged him inside. Trying not to laugh at her mother's aggressive hospitality, Claire followed them into the living room. She found its shabby familiarity consoling. The furniture never changed, the carpet faded incrementally and the framed photos displayed on the fireplace mantel froze her sisters, her niece, Megan, and Claire herself in ages now long out of date. One photo featured her parents on their twenty-fifth anniversary—three years before her father's death. The air smelled faintly of lemon, not from her mother's chicken recipe but from furniture polish. She must have dusted the place today. In honor of Mark's visit, probably.

"I'm so pleased to meet you," her mother babbled, even though Claire hadn't yet introduced them.

"Mrs. O'Connor—"

"It's Mary Maude," she corrected him. "You can call me Maude. Now, would you like coffee, tea or sherry?"

"Nothing, really, I—"

"Fine. Sit down." Her mother nudged him toward the sofa. "I've got cookies."

"Cookies?" he whispered to Claire once her mother had disappeared. "And what's the thing with Mary?"

"She likes the name," Claire whispered back. "You'd better sit. She'll get mad at you if you don't."

"If she gets mad at me, will she call me Mary Mark?" he deadpanned, his dark eyes dancing with laughter.

Claire pressed her hand to her mouth to keep from giggling. This was serious—her mother actually believed she and Mark were getting married—but Mark's nearness, his smile, his good humor about the awkward position made her far too grateful and relieved to be concerned.

Her mother emerged through the dining-room doorway, grandly bearing a glass platter full of bakery cookies, which she placed at the center of the coffee table. Mark glanced at Claire and she tipped her head slightly toward the sofa before sitting. With a nearly imperceptible nod, he lowered himself onto the cushions next to her.

Claire's mother beamed at them as she settled into one of the armchairs on the other side of the coffee table. She crossed one wool-trousered leg over the other, smoothed the waistband of her sweater over her trim abdomen and patted her graying red hair into place. Then she gave Mark an expectant smile.

"Mrs. O'Connor," he began.

"Maude."

"Maude," he corrected himself, then smiled. When Claire's mother favored a person with one of her megawatt smiles, that person's best recourse was to smile back. Mark seemed to understand this instinctively.

"Have a cookie," she urged him.

He took one but didn't bite into it. "Claire told me you didn't believe her when she told you we weren't engaged."

"It said in the *Boston Globe* that you were engaged."

"What the *Globe* printed was accurate, up to a point," Mark conceded. "It said we were spotted together at the Kinsale."

"We weren't canoodling, though," Claire interjected.

"That's true. We weren't canoodling." Mark shot her an enigmatic look. His smile was still in place, but she sensed something solemn in his gaze, as if he wanted to debate the implications of the word *canoodling* with her.

After a moment, he broke his gaze away from Claire and turned his attention to the cookie in his hand. He flipped it over in his palm. He had large hands. Claire again recalled his touch when their hands had collided over the check at the tavern, and her unwanted response to that accidental contact.

"Claire and I are not engaged," he said, so firmly Claire wondered whether he was trying to convince her mother or her. "Yesterday at the Kinsale, that was the first time we'd ever met each other."

"Like a thunderbolt," Claire's mother announced. "That's how it was with me and my beloved Brian, may his soul rest. The first time we saw each other—in Mr. Giovanni's European history class at Marian High School—it was like a thunderbolt struck us both. From that moment, we knew we were meant to be together."

"Our situation is a little different," Mark said.

"We're not high-school kids," Claire pointed out.

"The whole thing started as a practical joke," Mark clarified.

"At our expense," Claire added.

"Look at you two." Claire's mother shook her head. "You're already finishing each other's sentences. I'm telling you, some things are just meant to be."

Claire knew well—and resented—her mother's habit of hearing only what she wanted to hear and ignoring everything else. But Maude looked so hopeful, so open to the outlandish possibility that her daughter could have fallen in love with the complete stranger sitting next to her on the sofa. How could Claire be angry when her mother was so profoundly convinced that her spinster daughter had found a man?

Mark finally popped the cookie into his mouth. "Mm," he grunted. "It's good."

"Have another." His mother inched the platter toward him.

He took two cookies and handed one to Claire. "They're really good," he insisted.

She lifted it to her lips, aware that he was watching her taste it, as if her enjoyment of it was important to him. She ate it, nodded and murmured, "Very good, yes."

Still watching her, he ate his cookie. Only after he'd swallowed did he turn back to her mother. "So, the thing is, Maude, we have no plans to get married."

"Meaning what? You're going to live in sin?"

"Mom!" Claire rolled her eyes.

"Meaning," Mark said, blessedly unruffled, "we don't even know each other. It's crazy to think we could be engaged."

"So, you'll get to know each other."

"That's not the point," Claire said, impatience finally stirring inside her. "I told you we weren't engaged, and you didn't believe me. You said you wanted to hear it from Mark himself. So here he is, telling you the same thing I told you. *We're not engaged.*"

"Fine. You're not engaged." Her mother leaned back in her chair and tapped her fingers together. "That will come in its own time. When you're ready, you'll get engaged."

Claire wanted to scream. Exercising extreme self-control, she said, "I don't think—"

"Claire," Mark murmured, covering her hand with his to silence her. "Your mother understands. We're not engaged."

He was right. The woman had acknowledged that essential fact about Claire and Mark. They'd accomplished their task.

His hand remained on hers, sending a pulse of heat

up her arm and through her body. She was seated too close to him on the sofa. She was far too aware of him, his clean scent, the breadth of his shoulders beneath his unzipped leather jacket. Far too aware of his unbearably sexy smile and the strength of his fingers woven through hers.

But they weren't engaged. And eventually, when an engagement wasn't forthcoming, when months passed without Claire's even mentioning Mark's name, her mother would acknowledge the truth. She'd forget about the *Boston Globe,* and Claire would forget about the April Fool's Day radio broadcast.

Claire doubted she would ever forget about Mark Lavin, of course, but there wasn't much she could do about that. Except, maybe, to free her hand from his grip.

But touching him felt much too good. So, like the biggest April fool in the world, she kept her hand right where it was.

THEY LEFT her mother's house an hour later. Claire would have been happy to leave as soon as they'd set her mother straight, but Maude was determined to regale Mark with stories of Claire's childhood: the Halloween she'd gone trick-or-treating dressed as a stop sign—"I've got to tell you, Mark, you've never seen a more adorable stop sign," her mother had boasted—and the Christmas she'd given her older sister half a deck of cards and her younger sister the other half, so they'd learn to play better together. "Only seven years old," her mother had boasted, "and our Claire had the makings of a U.N. negotiator."

Claire would hardly claim that her decision to divide the deck in half had indicated extraordinary diplomatic skills. As she recalled, she'd had only enough money to buy one deck of cards at the neighborhood dime store. A seven-year-old's allowance didn't stretch far in those days.

She doubted all these embarrassing stories about her past could interest Mark, but he was a polite guest and let her mother ramble while he munched on cookies. Finally, when her mother paused to catch her breath, he eyed Claire, arching one brow in a question. Claire took the cue and announced to her mother that they had to be on their way.

Maude walked them to the front door. She shook Mark's hand, hugged Claire, nagged her to phone more often and sent them off with the admonition that they should keep her informed of their plans, so she wouldn't have to learn such important things in the pages of the newspaper.

Claire didn't speak until they were driving down Washington Street, heading back to the city. Mark's car issued a subdued yet powerful hum, and the contoured seat hugged her back. She still felt the warmth of his hand holding hers, still felt the imprint of his fingers on her arm as they'd strolled down her mother's front walk to his car. His smile lingered, even though her mother was no longer with them and he didn't have to be polite anymore.

"You are a very nice man," she said, trying to persuade herself that his kindness was the only reason his casual touches had gotten to her.

"You think so?" He glanced her way, then brought his gaze back to the road.

"You were so sweet to my mother. I know she can be aggravating."

"All mothers can be aggravating. It's their job. It's *our* job not to let them succeed in aggravating us."

What a sensible attitude. And a generous one. God, she had to stop thinking of all the things she liked about him. He was about to disappear from her life, now that they'd put this engagement nonsense to rest.

"So tell me," he asked as he stopped for a red light, "how come your mother's so anxious to marry you off? It's not like you're that old."

"In my family, twenty-eight is old," she said. "My older sister got married when she was twenty-five, my younger sister when she was twenty-four."

"That still doesn't make twenty-eight old," he argued.

She shrugged. The light turned green and his car accelerated so smoothly, they might have been floating several inches above the asphalt. "I think my mother believes it's her fault I'm not married, and she feels guilty about it."

"How is it her fault?"

"It's not, but she thinks it is." Claire paused for a moment, unsure whether Mark could possibly be interested in hearing about this part of her life after he'd already sat through her mother's tales about Halloweens and Christmases past. The look he sent her implied that he was waiting for her to elaborate, so she did. "I was twenty-two when my father died. My sister Liz was in the midst of planning her wed-

ding, which was only six months away. And Frannie
was out in Chicago, at Northwestern University. I
was in graduate school at BU, but my situation was
pretty flexible at that time. My mother was a wreck,
so I moved back in with her and took care of everything.''

"Everything?"

"The bills. The will. The insurance. Setting up her
pension with the police department. Sorting through
my dad's clothing. Getting my mother some therapy
when the depression seemed to be winning. I spent
two years holding her together and getting her back
on track.'' She stared out at the cityscape blurring
past the window, letting the memories wash through
her. She felt no bitterness, no regret. Those two years
were simply a part of her life, like working in City
Hall, and going to school, and dressing up as a stop
sign for Halloween. ''My mother thinks those years
were my prime time for meeting guys. She thinks
that because I returned home to take care of her, I
missed my chance.''

"Do you think that?''

"Of course not. But it eats at her.''

He fell silent, weaving through the traffic, which
grew denser and slower the deeper into the city they
traveled. She wondered if he thought her family was
dysfunctional or co-dependent or just plain nuts. She
wondered if she'd said too much, if he thought she
was some sort of martyr—which she'd never considered herself being during that period when she'd put
her life on hold to help her mother through her grief.
She wondered if he was just counting the minutes

until they reached Bradford Street, where he could drop her off and be rid of her forever.

They reached her block, and to her amazement, a car pulled out of a space just as Mark turned the corner. Mark nosed his car into the space without asking Claire if she wanted him to walk her to her door. He turned off the engine and swung open his door before she could say anything.

He was a nice man, she reminded herself. Nice men walked women to their front doors, even if such chivalry wasn't necessary.

Her building was halfway down the block. She slung the strap of her purse over her shoulder and climbed out of the car as he edged between his front bumper and the car in front of his to reach the side-walk. He didn't take her hand or her elbow as they started down the street, which was fine. He'd prob-ably only done that earlier in the evening to impress her mother.

Claire was sure he'd impressed Mary Maude O'Connor. She'd be hearing from her mother about Mark: "Why aren't you seeing him? What did you do to scare him away? He was a fine man, Claire, and you're no spring chicken…" and she'd have to explain, all over again, about the April Fool's Day joke.

They reached the entry to her building, just far enough from the streetlamp to cast Mark's face into shadow. Even so, Claire could see its strong lines and sharp angles, the astonishing darkness of his eyes framed by short, thick lashes, the natural way his mouth settled into a smile.

"You know," she said, because someone had to

say something, "I'm not sure we convinced my mother of anything tonight. But I appreciate your willingness to try."

"Oh, I think we convinced her of plenty," he disputed her, his voice soft and tinged with laughter.

"Perhaps the question is, did we convince her of what we intended to convince her of?"

"That I can't say." His smile expanded. The muted light that reached them played across his lips, caused his teeth to glint and highlighted a dimple. "It was pretty painless, though. Of all the repercussions of this stupid joke, tonight wasn't so bad."

"You're sweet to say so."

"I'm not sweet," he told her. "I'm not even sure I'm nice." His smile faded. "I wish...I don't know, maybe I wish I could have made your mother really happy tonight by telling her I *was* going to marry you."

"That would have been—impossible," Claire said, blurting out the first word that came to her. Others followed: *ludicrous, unthinkable, insane, unrealistic, and back to impossible.*

"It's just..." He sighed. "I like being a bachelor. I mean, for now. Down the road, yeah, I'd like to get married. But I'm still getting the feel for this whole top-five Boston bachelor thing. It's a silly honor, but it's a big honor, too, and—"

"You don't have to justify yourself to me," she assured him with a smile.

He didn't smile back. "I know I don't, but..." He sighed again, his eyes radiant even in the shadows. Then he tilted his head slightly, leaned forward and touched his mouth to hers.

His kiss was even more miraculous than finding an available parking space on her block. It seemed like a whim, totally impulsive—and yet that one light caress of his lips lit a fire deep inside her, like a spark landing on a pile of dry leaves. She felt the crackle of energy, the sudden burst of heat, as the spark ignited.

She drew back, embarrassed to have reacted so strongly to what he'd surely intended only as a friendly little peck. He gazed down at her, searching her face, looking terribly serious, and then slid his hand to the nape of her neck and covered her mouth with his.

This was no friendly little peck. The heat that billowed through her was obviously surging through him as well. His fingers fisted in her hair, his tongue parted her lips and slid inside, and she clasped his upper arms, partly to hold herself steady and partly to keep him from pulling her even closer. If he did, she'd burn to ashes. This blaze would destroy her.

Her tongue tangled with his, her breath merged with his and she felt the flames licking through her. Had *Boston's Best* known what an effective kisser he was when they'd chosen him as one of their superstar bachelors? Had the reporters tried him out, just to see how good he was? If he was this good at kissing, was he as good at everything else?

And why was she thinking such X-rated thoughts?

Because kissing Mark Lavin made her want to do X-rated things with him. Even though she hardly knew him. Even though before yesterday she hadn't known him at all. Even though his idiot deejay had thrown them together as a ratings-boosting stunt.

Slowly, Mark drew back. His hand relaxed and he let his fingers stroke through her hair before he released her. She struggled not to let him see the effects of his kiss—her erratic breath, her shaky legs, her pounding pulse. He didn't seem as strongly affected, but when he spoke she heard a roughness in his voice. "I'm sorry. I shouldn't have done that."

"Why not?" she asked, sounding braver than she felt.

"Because I—" He shut his mouth. His expression was oddly pained. "I just shouldn't have." He reached out and ran his fingertips down her cheek and under her lower lip, then dropped his hand, spun away and stalked down the street without even saying good-bye.

His abrupt departure told her what his unfinished sentence hadn't: he shouldn't have done it because they were virtual strangers. He shouldn't have done it because a kiss like that held promises he didn't intend to honor. He shouldn't have done it because the way he'd kissed her was the way a man kissed a woman he was engaged to, not the way a man kissed a woman he was never going to see again.

CHAPTER FIVE

MARK SPENT a lonely weekend sampling the dozens of disks artist reps had sent him during the past week. He would have loved to get together with someone, but Sherry and her dangerous purse were out of the question, and when he phoned Jenna, another woman he'd been seeing, she said, "Oh, fabulous news, Mark! I'm so happy for you! Guess what? I just got engaged, too! How about we all get together, you and your fiancée and me and mine?"

"I'll pass," Mark said, because it was easier than explaining that he didn't have a fiancée.

Listening to assorted cuts by up-and-coming artists in the privacy of his Somerville condo was all the excitement he could hope for this weekend. In a few more days, maybe a week or two, the world of Boston would move on to some other gossip, people would forget Mark's name had ever appeared in the same sentence as the word *engaged,* and he'd get back to his regular bachelor life. And Claire would get back to her regular life, as well.

Claire.

He shouldn't have kissed her after bringing her home from her mother's house, but he'd been... curious. The kiss had more than satisfied his curiosity. It had assured him that if she wanted to be someone's fiancée, she'd have no trouble achieving that goal. Any woman with such gorgeous hair, such creamy skin and gentle eyes, such long legs and elegant shoulders and such a wickedly talented tongue should have no trouble snagging a commitment-ready man. Mark wouldn't be surprised if Claire made Mary Maude O'Connor a very happy mother in the not too distant future.

He was irked at how much of his weekend he actually spent thinking about Claire and the lucky bastard who would ultimately make her his bride. It was all Rex Crandall's fault for linking her and Mark together in the first place. Rex's idea of a joke had completely screwed up Mark's weekend. If not for him, Mark would never have met Claire, and he wouldn't have spent the weekend all alone except for a stack of CDs and memories of a kiss hot enough to melt steel.

Had Claire ever kissed Rex like that? If she had, Mark might just have to kill Rex. Torture him, at least. Assign him to the graveyard shift, 2:00 a.m. to 6:00 a.m., when a grand total of three desperate Boston insomniacs might be willing to listen to his show.

On Monday morning, Mark listened to Rex's voice through the speakers in his office as the guy made jokes about the Rolling Stones—"the Kidney Stones," he called them—and played Weezer, Beck and the Pogues, and fielded phone calls from "Barry in Quincy" and "Marlene in Woburn" who wanted to sound off on the governor's hairstyle. Hearing the usual smug tone of Rex's voice made Mark decide that the time for torture, or at least a confrontation, had arrived. Rex owed Mark an apology. He owed

Claire one, too. Maybe forcing the jerk to make an on-the-air retraction wasn't such a bad idea—although Mark still hadn't abandoned the notion of reassigning him to the overnight slot.

At his request, Ellie corralled Rex as he stepped out of the broadcast booth shortly after his show ended at ten o'clock, and escorted him down the hall to Mark's office. Mark looked up from the ad schedule as Ellie nudged Rex into his office and then left, shutting the door behind her. Rex slid his hands into the pockets of his baggy overalls and smiled out at Mark from behind his scraggly mane of hair. "How's it going, boss?" he asked amiably, his gaze deceptively innocent.

"How should it be going?"

Rex shrugged and leaned against the closed door. "Am I getting fired?" he asked, sounding not the least bit alarmed by the possibility.

Mark wasn't going to fire him. The guy's ratings were too damned good. Unfortunately, they were also too good for the graveyard shift.

In any case, Mark didn't want to come across as unable to laugh at himself. He *could* laugh at himself. He often did. He just hadn't done any laughing for the past forty-eight hours, and Rex deserved the blame for that. "Is that your way of telling me you want to quit?" he tested the deejay.

Rex laughed. He obviously felt pretty secure in his position.

Mark gestured toward a chair but Rex shook his head and remained standing. With a shrug that said "suit yourself," Mark spoke. "Okay, here's what I want to know: why her?"

"Why who?"

Rex seemed determined to make this as difficult as possible. Mark sighed. "Why Claire O'Connor? Of all the women in Boston you could have hooked me up with, why her?"

"What happened? Did you go and fall in love with her or something?"

"Of course not," Mark snapped, fresh anger building on the stockpile of anger he'd amassed over the weekend. "She's not my type."

"Well, yeah," Rex drawled.

Mark peered up at Rex. He couldn't miss the defiance in the guy's smirk. "That was the point, wasn't it?"

"She's so wrong for you, I just had to do it. The perfect mismatch. Sorry, boss," he added as an apparent afterthought. It was one of the most synthetic apologies Mark had ever heard.

"What made you so sure she was wrong for me?" he asked, aware that he was far too eager to hear Rex's answer.

"For one thing, she listens to classical music." Rex uttered the word *classical* as if it were a curse. "Public radio, that kind of stuff. Beethoven. Bach. *Dvorak!* You know? What kind of babe listens to *Dvorak?*"

Dvorak or no Dvorak, Mark would never consider Claire a "babe." She was too thoughtful, too considerate, too...tall. Her hair wasn't brassy enough, either. It was a muted red, the color of sugar maple leaves turning in autumn. And her kiss...very adult. Nothing babe-ish about it at all.

"Plus, she's a city bureaucrat," Rex went on. "A

paper pusher in City Hall. Major yawn. And of course she's seriously lacking in the sense-of-humor department. To say nothing of the mammary department.''

True, she wasn't exactly buxom—but a huge chest wouldn't look right on her. Mark thought her body was perfectly proportioned. ''I take it you became acquainted with her mammaries during your hot little affair with her?'' he asked, his stomach tensing slightly as he awaited Rex's reply.

''Our hot little affair? Is that what she told you?'' Rex let out a hoot. ''That girl was colder than the summit of Mount Washington in January. I spent a few evenings with her and realized, hell, I could shut myself up inside a refrigerator if I wanted to die of hypothermia.''

Cold was the last word Mark would use to describe Claire, especially after he'd kissed her. That she'd been cold to Rex pleased him enormously, though. His abs relaxed and his hand unfisted against his knee. ''No sense of humor, no breasts, colder than Mount Washington,'' he ticked off her flaws according to Rex. ''Okay. Just wanted to get a sense of your reasoning here.''

''It played out well,'' Rex said, his grin growing self-congratulatory. ''We got tons of phone calls on that show, and e-mails are still coming in. And who would've guessed the *Boston Globe* would pick it up? I mean, that was sweet.''

''The *Boston Globe*,'' Mark said dryly. ''How lucky can you get?''

''So, is that magazine going to sue you? The one that anointed you the top bachelor boy?''

"I think I've straightened things out with them. There have been some other repercussions, though. No lawsuits—yet—but repercussions." Mark recalled the cranial whack Sherry had given him with her purse, and his miserable weekend, one of the worst weekends he'd endured since hitting puberty. Amazing how such a bad weekend could have followed such a good kiss.

"Well, damn," Rex said, continuing in the fake-sympathy mode. "I'm real sorry to hear that."

"I can see how sorry you are. All right, get out of here. I just wanted an idea of what you were thinking when you pulled this stunt."

"I was thinking, it's April Fool's Day," Rex told him.

"And what an honor it is to have been chosen as your fool. We're not done yet, Rex, but for now I want you to go away."

Rex twisted the knob and opened the door. He appeared on the verge of saying something, but Mark's grimace must have silenced him, because he only shrugged sheepishly and exited, shutting the door behind him.

Once Mark was alone, he swiveled to his computer and punched the keys to call up the archives of the station's CD library. Just out of curiosity, he wanted to see if the station had any Dvorak CDs in stock. Hadn't the guy had a big hit with the *New World Symphony* back in the late 1800s? If Mark could spend the entire weekend listening to songs by bands named Linotype and Thumping Baboons, it wouldn't kill him to give old Dvorak a spin.

"SO," MAGGIE SAID, "what's the decision on that Hanover Street building? Are we granting the owner permission to put in new windows?"

Claire leaned back in her chair, closed her eyes and rubbed the knotted muscles at the base of her skull. She'd spent much of the day reading reports and arguing with Steve LaPina about the landlord's petition to install thermopane windows in the nine-teenth-century building in the North End. The ground floor of the structure was a decidedly twenty-first-century Italian restaurant, so Claire didn't see a sig-nificant issue of architectural integrity in installing the new windows for the tenants who lived upstairs. However, she sensed that the landlord was hoping the Landmarks Commission would turn down his ap-plication so he'd be spared the expense. His was one of the most slipshod applications Claire had ever seen. Steve thought they should reject it because of that, but she couldn't stop thinking of the tenants, shivering as icy winds seeped in the old windows in the winter and paying a fortune in electrical bills as their air-conditioning seeped out the old windows in the summer.

"No decision yet," Claire remembered to answer Maggie. "We're still bickering."

"Bickering's fun," Maggie said, dropping onto the chair across the desk from Claire. "Are you free tomorrow night? I know it's short notice, but I was wondering if you might want to come over for din-ner."

Claire opened her eyes and stared at her friend. The lilt in Maggie's voice implied that this was more than just a dinner invitation. "Why would I want to come over for dinner?" she asked warily.

"Because I'm a great cook?" Maggie shrugged and grinned. "Lowell's cousin Tom is in town—his company wants to relocate him to their Boston office, and he's spending a week looking around and checking out the housing market. We thought it might be nice if you could join us for dinner tomorrow."

"Tom is a single man, I take it? You and Lowell are doing a little matchmaking?"

"He's a great guy," Maggie said. "An accountant, but not the accountant type at all."

"What's the accountant type?" Claire asked, a stalling tactic. Much as she enjoyed Maggie's cooking, she didn't want to be set up with Maggie's husband's cousin. She didn't want to be set up with anyone. Given the odds that she'd ever meet another man who could insinuate his way into her consciousness, into her waking moments and her dreams, the way Mark Lavin could, she was figuring on remaining single for the foreseeable future, if not the rest of her life.

Of course, if she remained single she'd have to change her telephone number so her mother and sisters couldn't badger her.

Too shrewd to phone Claire and nag her personally, Claire's mother had delegated that task to Frannie and Liz. Frannie had called Saturday to ask about the guy she'd introduced their mother to; Liz had stepped up to the plate on Sunday, favoring Claire with a long phone conversation that covered the joys of motherhood and the importance of family. Claire loved her family, and she didn't doubt that motherhood was a noble pursuit. But before motherhood, before marriage, a woman needed a man. The right man.

Mark wasn't the right man. If Claire told herself that enough times, she might eventually come to believe it. Not that it mattered, since he'd walked out of her life.

Without even saying good-bye.

He was a bachelor—a top-rated one, as if bachelorhood deserved ratings. He drove an expensive bachelor car and lived in a bachelor world of rock stars, concerts and blurbs in the local newspapers and magazines. He kissed like a pro. And he'd regretted kissing her. He'd made it pretty damned clear, when he left her outside her building Friday night, that she would never see or hear from him again.

She ought to jump at the chance to have dinner with Tom the accountant. But Mark Lavin was like a virus, infecting her. Until she was cured, she didn't want to meet anyone else.

"I'm sorry, Maggie. I don't think so," she said.

"We could do it Wednesday, if that works better for you."

"No day works better for me." Claire forced a smile, hoping to forestall questioning from her friend. "I hate blind dates."

"It's not a blind date. It's just dinner at my house."

Still smiling, Claire shook her head. "Some other time, maybe. If this guy accepts the transfer and moves to Boston, I'll come for dinner then." Maybe she'd have recovered from the Mark Lavin disease by then.

Maggie scrutinized her. "Getting together with Tom—or with anyone, for that matter—would be a good way to reacquaint certain people with reality," she pointed out.

"What people?"

Maggie leaned forward. "Meryl, Beryl and Jo-Anne are still talking about hosting a bridal shower for you," she whispered, even though she and Claire were all alone in the office. "You're not supposed to know about it. It's going to be a surprise."

Claire groaned. "The only shower I want is the one in my bathroom at home," she said. "If you overhear them discussing this shower, please set them straight for me."

"If you socialized with guys—like Tom, for instance—that would set them straight."

"No, it wouldn't. They'd think I was cheating on my fiancé and report me to the *Boston Globe*," Claire argued. "When some people get an idea stuck in their heads, it's hard to unstick it." The way Mark was stuck in her head, she thought glumly.

Her phone rang. "Okay, I'm leaving," Maggie said, shoving herself to her feet. "Let me know if you change your mind about coming for dinner."

Claire nodded. She watched Maggie exit her office, then lifted the receiver. "Claire O'Connor," she said.

"Claire? It's Mark."

Her palm, wrapped around the molded plastic of the receiver, grew damp. Her breath caught in her throat. She closed her eyes again, and remembered the erotic pressure of his mouth on hers, the heat of his body so close to hers, the way he'd tangled his fingers into her hair. Why had he called? How was she going to get over him if he charged back into her life?

"Hello, Mark," she said in as calm a voice as she could muster.

"How are you?"

Had he called to chat? "I'm fine," she said, irritation dampening the mindless excitement she felt at hearing his voice. "And yourself?"

"I've got a problem," he told her, then reconsidered his answer. "Actually, Claire, *we've* got a problem."

CHAPTER SIX

MARK LOVED his parents. One thing he loved about them was that they generally kept their noses out of his business. They lived in western Massachusetts, nearly three hours away, and when he got together with them, they usually had enough to talk about—politics, their students, the house, their vacation trips and the summer season at the Williamstown Theater Festival—that questions concerning Mark's social life rarely arose.

So he was surprised when his mother phoned his office to say, "What's this about your getting married?"

"What's what about my getting married?"

"You know I don't always read the *Globe,*" she began. "But Noreen's sister—you remember Noreen, don't you? The history department secretary?"

He didn't, but he said, "Sure."

"Anyway, her sister lives in Roslindale and she read in the *Globe* last week that you were seen—I believe the word was *canoodling*—with a woman you were engaged to."

Jeez. Didn't they have anything better to talk about at Williams College than one brief, misleading item in last week's *Globe?* Mark took a deep, calming breath and said, "First of all, I'm not engaged to her.

And second of all, we weren't canoodling. We were just talking." And having a drink—although hers had been tea, which didn't count. And yeah, he'd been thinking she was damned pretty, and maybe he'd also been undressing her in his mind, because he was a healthy heterosexual male and that was what a healthy heterosexual male did when he was having a drink with a damned pretty woman.

But they hadn't been canoodling.

"I can't tell you how excited Noreen was, Mark," his mother said. "She still remembers the day you left for college. As I recall, she was very disappointed that you chose not to attend Williams."

No way would Mark have attended the school where both his parents taught, even though he could have gone there for free. At eighteen, he'd wanted only to put some distance between himself and his folks, to study at a school where everyone didn't know him as the son of professors Lavin and Lavin.

"Naturally, she was thrilled to read that you were finally settling down. I'm thrilled, too, Mark. I just wish I hadn't had to learn this news from Noreen."

"It's not news," Mark said. "It's not true. I'm not settling down."

"Oh." Disappointment added a tremor to the word.

So much for his parents keeping their noses out of his business. "It was an April Fool's Day prank. One of the deejays here at the station made the whole thing up."

"Why would he do that?"

"As an April Fool's Day prank," Mark repeated, figuring that was easier than explaining that Rex had done it as a petty rebellion, sticking his boss with a woman totally wrong for him, a woman he believed to be totally cold. Which Claire definitely wasn't. But Mark didn't want to think about that.

"According to Noreen," his mother continued, "this fiancée of yours works for Boston's Landmark Commission. My heart started pounding when I heard that."

"She's a bureaucrat," Mark insisted, although that word didn't seem to fit Claire any better than *cold*. "I don't know what her job entails. Tell Noreen not to believe everything she reads."

"Old buildings," his mother murmured blissfully. "You know how I adore old buildings. Does she save them from the wrecker's ball?"

He had no idea. The evening he'd met her at the Kinsale, she'd mentioned something about a demolition hearing. That didn't sound like saving buildings to him.

"Mark." His mother's tone was stern beneath a layer of maternal affection. "I know you're excited about being the top bachelor in Boston—"

"One of the top five," he corrected her.

"One of the top five. You've received this supposed honor, but you can't let it define you for the rest of your life. When Dad and I were your age, we already had our Ph.Ds, our marriage and our son. I know children take longer to grow up these days…"

Mark opened his mouth and then shut it. Why protest to his mother that he was no longer a child?

"…but if you opened yourself up to the possibility of meeting a nice woman…"

"I've met nice women," Mark broke in. Maybe

Sherry and her killer purse wouldn't qualify as nice, but Jenna was nice…and engaged to another man. He'd known other nice women, though. Claire was nice. She also claimed that he was nice. He shook his head to get himself back on track. Nice was irrelevant.

"Someone with an interesting career," his mother was saying. "Someone with intelligence and common sense and generosity. And a sense of humor. What more do you need?"

Big knockers, he thought, although in fact he'd never been obsessed with breast size. He wasn't Rex Crandall. He had no complaints when it came to Claire's bosom—not that her bosom had any significance to him whatsoever.

"I mean, really, Mark, is it so difficult to find a woman with those traits?"

"Mom." Impatience gnawed at him. He didn't want to think about the traits that made a woman desirable. He didn't want to think about how many of those traits Claire possessed. She didn't even listen to WBKX, for God's sake. And whether or not his mother considered being a top-five Boston bachelor worthwhile, *he* did. Was it a crime to want to enjoy his title for a little while? "You've never pressured me before," he said. "Why are you doing this now?"

"Because your engagement announcement appeared in the *Boston Globe.*"

"It wasn't an engagement announcement. And it was wrong."

"Was it?"

Actually, the blurb had contained no factual errors,

other than the canoodling part. "It was misleading," he corrected himself.

"And I'm not pressuring you. I'm just saying, so? Who's this woman? Why shouldn't she be the one?"

"It was an April Fool's Day joke!" he erupted. At that moment, it struck him as the most unfunny joke in the world.

Ignoring his outburst, his mother said, "I'd love to meet her. Why don't you bring her out to Williamstown for a day? We haven't seen you since the holidays. We could catch up, check out your new car—I know your father would love that—and meet this fiancée of yours."

"She's not—"

"Your fiancée. So you say, Mark. I'm not deaf."

"But you don't believe me," he complained.

"Well, if it appears in the *Globe*... That's a reputable newspaper. They don't usually get things wrong. Did they print a retraction?"

"No."

"So there was nothing to retract?"

"They never actually said she was my fiancée," he argued wearily. "We're not getting married."

"Why? She's not smart?"

"No, she's smart, but—"

"Not generous? Doesn't have a sense of humor? Please don't tell me it's something superficial like she's not pretty."

"She's beautiful," he said, then clamped his mouth shut to stifle a curse. "Her appearance has nothing to do with anything, Mom. The bottom line is, Claire and I are not getting married."

"So, you're not getting married. You could still

come out and visit us. We haven't seen you since last December. You could come and bring her along for the ride. It's a long drive by yourself, and this way we could meet her.''

''Why do you want to meet her if she isn't my fiancée?''

''Am I only allowed to meet women you're engaged to? I'd like to meet this woman you've been linked with. Is this a crime?''

Of course it wasn't a crime, any more than his mother's stubbornness was a crime. Maybe his mother's stubbornness *should* be a crime, but as of now, there were no laws against it.

''I can't imagine why she'd want to drive all the way to Williamstown with me,'' he said.

''Invite her. Maybe she'll say yes. Saturday would be best. You could get here early afternoon, we'll have a nice dinner, and we'll all get to know one another. Does she like fish? I'll make my bouillabaisse. That's always a hit with guests.''

He didn't want his mother to make her bouillabaisse. He didn't want to drive to Williamstown. He didn't want to telephone Claire and invite her to join him. He wanted to forget her hair, her emerald eyes and her soft lips, her hold on his imagination. He wanted to forget the way kissing her had almost been enough to make him abdicate his top-five bachelor throne.

But his mother would never back down. She wanted him to come to Williamstown with Claire, and she'd keep at him until he buckled. He knew she would.

''I'll talk to Claire,'' he said. ''I'm not making any

promises about this weekend, but I'll talk to her. I want it very clear, though—we're *not* engaged.''

"Of course not. Let me know once you're certain what your plans are. I can't wait to see you—and to meet this lovely woman.''

How did his mother know Claire was lovely? What if lovely Claire had something better to do on Saturday? What if she hated bouillabaisse?

He'd survived his encounter with her mother. He supposed she could survive an encounter with his. As soon as his mother got off the phone, he would call Claire at City Hall and run this ridiculous plan by her. If she was as smart as he thought, she'd say no. And he could go back to being a bachelor.

"YOU TOLD your mother we'd drive all the way to Williamstown to see her?" Claire blurted into the phone. Her office radio spilled Handel's "Water Music" into the air, but the mellow orchestral suite failed to calm her twitchy nerves. Above her a single balloon remained, hovering near the ceiling. The other balloons had leaked helium and by the end of last week she'd untied the droopy bouquet from the arm of her chair and discarded them. But one balloon had escaped and floated up to the ceiling. She could easily grab its cord and haul it down, but she admired its stamina. As long as it remained up there, she wasn't going to disturb it.

The string dangled within reach of her hand as Mark explained to her over the phone that they had a problem: his mother wanted to meet her and was hoping he would bring her with him to Williamstown on Saturday.

Claire had been just getting used to the idea that she would never see him again, and now she was supposed to spend all day Saturday driving across the state with him?

"If you don't want to go, I wouldn't blame you," Mark assured her. "I tried to explain to my mother that we aren't engaged, but she didn't get it."

Claire knew how that could be. She'd had the same experience with her own mother.

She should say no. Spending more time with Mark wasn't going to help her put him out of her mind. What if he kissed her again? What if, as he had on the night he'd met her mother, he kissed her and walked away? Why should she make herself vulnerable to him?

But Williamstown…the winding roads, the rolling hills, the scenery, the greenery. The chance to get out of the city for a day, far from her mother, her sisters, Maggie, and Meryl, Beryl and JoAnn with their shower plans… God, she really wanted to go.

She could protect herself, she resolved. She could fend off any more meaningless kisses from him. All he was asking was that she accompany him on a visit to his mother, just as he'd so generously accompanied her on a visit to hers. Williamstown was supposed to be gorgeous, and the long drive would be heavenly in Mark's slick sports car. The Saturday page of her desk calendar was blank.

Her father always used to say a person couldn't have too many friends. Why not let Mark become her friend? As long as he didn't kiss her again, she'd be all right.

"Fine," she said. "But I want to make sure your mother understands that we're not engaged."

"We can make sure she understands when we see her."

"The way we made sure my mother understood," Claire said, although she wasn't convinced that they'd accomplished that goal last Friday.

"Right," Mark said, sounding oddly tentative. His voice was steadier when he added, "If we leave the city at ten, we'll get there about one. We can spend a couple of hours and I'll have you back home by eight or nine at night."

"Okay." The plan in no way resembled a date. It entailed nothing romantic. In fact, she wondered why he hadn't simply turned down his mother's invitation. Did he want to inflict Claire on his mother, for some reason? Did he want to inflict his mother on Claire? Did he want company for the drive, and no one else was available? Did he want her to ooh and ahh over his car? Did he want to be friends with her?

Whatever his reason, he'd asked and she'd said yes. Call her a fool, but she'd agreed to the trip. She and Mark would be friends, and she'd get to spend a day far from the city, cruising the length of the state back and forth in his magnificent car. She wouldn't let him kiss her, wouldn't let him touch her, wouldn't let him send her any of his mixed signals—sexual overtures followed by panicked flight.

A day in the country with a friend. She could handle that.

CHAPTER SEVEN

"So, WHAT EXACTLY is a demolition hearing?" Mark asked.

Claire settled deeper into the bucket seat and clutched her hair. She'd fastened it into a ponytail as soon as she'd seen him driving up Bradford Street with the convertible top of his car open. But even with an elastic and her hand containing most of her hair, gusts of mild spring air whipped loose strands into a frenzy. By the time they reached his parents' house, her hair would resemble a fright wig.

She didn't care. The only impression she had to make on Mark's parents was as their son's non-fiancée. She could be his non-fiancée as definitively with wild hair as she could with neat hair.

His hair blew freely, the thick dark waves tossed back from his face. His eyes were hidden behind sunglasses and he wore an off-white cotton sweater and jeans. He looked like someone heading to the beach, even though it was barely sixty degrees out and they were driving in the opposite direction from the ocean. Claire had chosen to wear tailored wool slacks, a silk blouse and a blazer. Glancing at his faded jeans, she realized she was grossly overdressed.

He looked much too good in jeans, she acknowledged. Then again, she couldn't imagine anything he wouldn't look much too good in. Or out of.

She had to stop thinking that way. She had to accept that this relationship was going nowhere—other than to Williamstown for the day. In fact, she had to accept that it wasn't even a relationship. It was…a practical joke.

He tilted his head slightly, reminding her that she hadn't answered his question. "If someone wants to tear down a building," she said, raising her voice to be heard above the wind, "he has to deal with our office. Even if the building itself isn't a landmark, we need to consider the integrity of the neighborhood. Boston's historical architecture is one of its most important characteristics."

"So they have to get your permission to bulldoze a building? Even if it's an ugly old garage or something?"

"They have to go through lots of steps before they can bulldoze a building. My office is only one of the steps."

"My mother's going to want to discuss your work," he warned, accelerating to pass a slower car. "My parents' house is more than a hundred and fifty years old."

"Really?" Claire didn't want to love the Lavins any more than she wanted to love their son, but she might just let herself fall in love with their house. "Is it farmhouse style, or more of a town style?"

"Farmhouse. It's small."

"Of course." Early nineteenth-century farmers in western Massachusetts generally didn't build palaces for their families.

"Low ceilings, uneven floors, the whole bit. When I was a kid, I could never get my Matchbox cars to roll very far on the wood floors. The planks were too uneven."

"So you grew up in this antique farmhouse?"

"It didn't feel like an antique to me," Mark said, dissatisfaction mingling with fondness in his tone. "It felt like a rattletrap. Hot in the summer, drafty in the winter. Things were always falling apart. Whenever anything broke, my mother would head out to her garden and leave my dad and me to fix it."

"Antique houses are like that. Constantly in need of repair."

"I live in a condo now. If anything needs repairs, I call up the association and say, 'Fix this window,' or 'Rewire this outlet.' It's not that I can't do the repairs myself—I learned a hell of a lot about fixing things while I was growing up. I just love the luxury of having someone else do the fixing for me."

Claire studied him. In profile, with his sharp sunglasses and his sharper nose and chin, he looked sleek and modern. Yet she could imagine him in an old house, armed with a screwdriver and a can of putty, patching and restoring and grumbling good-naturedly the entire time.

"So, your mother gardens and your father does the repairs?" she asked.

"That about sums it up," he said. "My mother teaches history and my father teaches political science. My mother cooks and my father does the dishes. My mother's published four books and my father's published five—and that really bothers my mother. She's knocking herself out to get her fifth book finished so she can catch up to him.''

"They sound very accomplished." Claire glanced at his jeans again—damn, but he filled them nicely—and decided she was glad to have dressed a little more elegantly for the afternoon.

"They're down-to-earth," Mark said, "like your mother."

They didn't sound like her mother. They were professors at one of the nation's most prestigious colleges. Claire's mother was a secretary. But she did like to garden.

"They have a dog. You aren't allergic to dogs or anything, are you?"

"No," she assured him.

Mark passed another car, then slowed as Route 2 narrowed from four lanes to two. Claire had traveled west through the state before, but only on the Mass Pike, which remained a major highway from the New York state border all the way to Boston Harbor. Route 2 had started out as a highway, then had wandered through a few towns, then had widened into a highway again and now was back to two-lane wandering. Mark had to lower his speed to accommodate the traffic, much of which seemed to be pickup trucks and SUV's towing boats or carrying canoes and kayaks on their roofs. "Is there a lake around here?" she asked.

"Rivers, lakes and we're not too far from Quabbin," he told her, naming a huge reservoir at the center of the state. "It's finally warm enough for people to put their boats into the water."

Since they were no longer cruising so fast, Claire

could relax her grip on her ponytail. Above the roof-less car stretched a clear April sky, baby blue and fresh. The air smelled clean and piney from the for-ests that covered the gentle hills on either side of the road. She needed to get out of the city more often, she decided.

She also needed the company of good-looking men more often. The way Mark's wind-tousled hair fluttered in messy waves around his face softened its angles. "Tell me about your work," she said. "What exactly does a radio station's general manager do?"

"Everything except spin disks on the air," he an-swered. "Although I could do that, too, if I had to. I got interested in radio work at college, when I took a deejay slot on the school's station. It's a real power trip, you know? Just you and the mike, and you get to decide what everyone has to listen to. Listeners either accept your choices or turn you off. After col-lege, I moved into commercial radio and discovered that some program director got to decide what I should be playing. I wanted the power, so I did grad-uate work at Emerson College and got into radio management."

"And now you decide what everyone has to listen to again?"

"Actually, the program director does most of that. But I have input. I deal with musicians and their reps who are trying to get their songs on the air. I also oversee the business side of the station—ad revenues, ratings, promotion, community outreach." A loaded logging truck slowed to a crawl in front of them, but then took a wide turn off Route 2. Mark smiled and hit the gas, obviously glad for the stretch of open road before them. "Rumor has it you like Dvorak."

Startled, Claire eyed him sharply. The rumor happened to be true; she couldn't listen to Dvorak's *From the New World* without weeping over the symphony's transcendent beauty. Still, Mark's knowledge of her musical taste surprised her. "Where did you hear that?"

"Rex mentioned it."

That Mark had discussed her with Rex both flattered and unsettled her. "What else did he tell you about me?" she asked, not sure she'd like his answer.

Mark glanced her way, then turned back to the road. "Nothing much."

Oh, hell. The creep must have told Mark all sorts of things. She scrambled through her memory, trying to recall what, other than a speeding ticket and a sour aftertaste, she'd gotten from her acquaintanceship with Rex. They'd gone out for dinner in the North End one night, but by nine o'clock Rex had been yawning and complaining that he always got tired early because he had to wake up at 4:00 a.m. to do his show. On another occasion, they'd had a blistering argument over who was the greatest rock band out of Ireland—he'd claimed it was U2 and she'd contended it was Van Morrison, and Rex had scoffed that a solo performer like Van Morrison couldn't be compared to a rock band. She recalled a Saturday she and Rex had spent at a beach in Plymouth. They'd left early when the clouds unexpectedly opened up and drenched them, and Rex had kissed her and pawed her chest a bit in his car outside her building, his approach about as erotic as a horny high-school boy's. Unable even to fake a response, she'd extricated herself and said she really didn't think they should see each other anymore. Then she hadn't heard from him until more than a week later, when his friend had phoned and said Rex was in a coma and needed her. And she'd gotten that blasted speeding ticket.

She turned to Mark and caught him glancing at her again. "Really," he insisted. "He didn't say anything."

His discretion made her smile.

Route 2 grew narrower and twistier as they pushed farther west, climbing into the Berkshires. The woods on either side of the road grew thicker. A stream ran parallel to the road, tumbling over rocks and fallen trees. The gravel shoulders sprouted signs warning of deer crossings, bear crossings and a dangerous hairpin a few miles ahead. The air felt cooler, probably because of the higher altitude and the forest's shadows.

"We're really in the wilderness, aren't we," she said as they passed another Bear Crossing sign.

"Civilization returns on the other side of the hairpin turn," he promised. And it did. Once they'd eased around the treacherously sharp curve, they descended into a valley of old mills and modest houses. "North Adams," Mark informed her. "Williamstown is the next town up the road. The last town. After Williamstown, you're out of Massachusetts."

As they drove past the campus where Mark's parents taught, he pointed out some of the buildings to her. "You may feel you're in the sticks," he said, "but there's always something happening in a col-

lege town. Concerts, plays, lectures, visiting digni-
taries. Sports, too. My parents used to take me to all
the college home games—football, hockey, lacrosse.
It wasn't a bad place to grow up, although at this
stage I prefer city living."

"I imagine being one of the top five bachelors in
Williamstown wouldn't carry quite the same prestige
as being one of the top five bachelors in Boston."

He angled his head toward her, as if trying to as-
sess whether she was teasing him. She was, sort of.
But she was testing him, too, attempting to measure
just how important his top-bachelor ranking was to
him.

After a minute, he cracked a smile. "I always say,
if you're going to be something, you might as well
be tops at it. Why be a mediocre bachelor if you can
be a top-five bachelor? Why be a small-town bachelor when you can be a hub-of-the-universe bachelor?"

"The only people who think Boston is the hub of
the universe are people who live in Boston," she
noted.

"And they're right," he said as he slowed the car
and steered onto a gravel driveway.

The house at its end was charming: white clap-
board with black shutters flanking the windows and
a welcoming red front door. A plaque next to the
door identified the year of the house's construction
as 1848. Ancient oaks, sycamores and evergreens
stood sentry in the yard, and brave blades of new
grass struggled to poke through the earth. "Oh,
Mark! It's fabulous!"

"Trust me, it's a rattletrap," he muttered, though

his smile widened. He shut off the engine and they both climbed out of the car.

By the time they reached the door, Mark's parents had it open and the yard filled with spirited canine barking. Mark's mother had long, silver-laced black hair braided down her back and large gold hoops piercing her ears. His father looked like an older version of Mark, his thick, wavy hair streaked with gray, the lines in his face etched more deeply, but his eyes as dark and his smile as engaging. Like Mark, both his parents wore faded jeans and sweaters. Claire had to remind herself that they were both *Dr.* Lavin, because they looked like a couple of organic-farming hippies.

"Come in, come in!" Mark's mother urged them, swinging the door wider and nudging a medium-size tan dog back from the threshold with her knee. "Get back, Lovey," she scolded, then returned her attention to her son. "Mark! Give me a kiss." He didn't have a chance to object, because she wrapped him in a smothering embrace and pulled him down so she could kiss his cheek. As he straightened up and hugged his father, his mother gathered Claire's hands in her own and beamed at her. "Claire! It's such a pleasure!"

Claire found the greeting rather effusive, given that she wasn't Mark's fiancée or even his girlfriend. If all went well, she might emerge from this trip as his friend, period. Their drive that day was the longest time they'd ever spent in each other's company.

But she liked being enveloped in such familial warmth. She sensed nothing phony in his parents' behavior, nothing forced. They seemed genuinely happy to see their son and meet Claire.

"So that's the new car," his father said, stepping out onto the small porch and scrutinizing Mark's sports car. "I am…" he paused, then laughed "…green with envy."

"Go." His mother gestured toward the vehicle. "Go play with the car." She shooed her son and husband out to the driveway, then ushered Claire inside the cozy house.

In the Landmarks Commission office, Claire dealt almost exclusively with urban buildings. But she appreciated many of the features of the Lavin family farmhouse—the wide plank floors, the narrow halls and doorways, the multitude of fireplaces, the rippling settled glass in some of the twelve-over-twelve windows. A wood-burning stove occupied a corner of the huge farm kitchen, which was furnished with a massive table and four chairs of knotty pine. Braided rugs lay scattered across the floor. A dog's food and water dishes sat on a mat on the floor near the sink. The dog who'd barked so enthusiastically when she and Mark had arrived wandered over to the water dish and had a drink. Claire couldn't identify its breed, but it was the color of taffy and had floppy ears and a friendly face.

"Your house is wonderful," Claire said.

Mark's mother smiled. "Thanks. It keeps us busy." She moved to a large pot on the range. When she lifted the lid, a rich aroma of fish, sherry and spices filled the air. "I hope you like seafood, because I made bouillabaisse."

"I love it." Claire removed her blazer because the

room was so warm. "Is there anything I can do to help, Mrs. Lavin? Or is it Dr. Lavin?"

"It's Naomi, and if you really want to help, you can tear these greens for the salad." She lifted a wet head of romaine from the sink and handed it to Claire. "Let me get you a bowl."

Within a minute, Claire had rolled up her sleeves and was tearing romaine leaves. Naomi busied herself slicing a loaf of French bread onto a cookie sheet and sliding it into the oven to toast. "What a perfect day for a drive," she said cheerfully. "God knows when we'll ever see Mark and his dad again. If Mark lets Bob take a turn behind the wheel, they might be back by nightfall—or they might not. I wouldn't put it past them to keep driving until they hit Seattle. Little boys love their fancy wheels, don't they?"

Mark certainly loved his fancy wheels. Claire had grown up with sisters, who'd been much more obsessive about clothing, shoes and jewelry than about cars, and her father had never seemed unduly interested in them, either. "Mrs.—I mean, Naomi?" She shook the excess water from a leaf before adding it to the salad bowl. "I hope Mark made it clear to you that we're not getting married."

"He explained that the report in the *Boston Globe* was misleading. Leave Claire alone, Lovey," Naomi scolded the dog, who was giving Claire's loafers a thorough sniffing.

"He's not bothering me—or is it a she?"

"She. Her name is Lovey, and she understands English, so feel free to tell her to bug off if she's bothering you. She obviously likes you. If she didn't, she'd be growling. And her tail—that's always a giveaway.'' Lovey's tail wagged like a metronome set on allegro.

"Anyway…the piece in the *Boston Globe*…" Claire resumed tearing romaine leaves. "It was more than misleading. It left the impression that there was something going on between Mark and me. There's not."

"Nonsense," Naomi overruled her. "You're friends. If nothing else, you're drawn together by your victimhood, the shared embarrassment of this silly joke or whatever it is."

"All right," Claire conceded. "We're friends. But we're not engaged."

"Whatever you say." Naomi blithely handed her a tomato and a knife. "You can add that to the salad."

Claire couldn't guess what Naomi believed, what she suspected, what she hoped for. Did she want Claire to be Mark's fiancée? Did she want her celebrated single son to get married? To a woman he scarcely knew?

Claire had claimed that she and Mark were friends. She wanted that to be true. In all honesty, she wanted to be more than friends with him. It wasn't just because he was good company. It wasn't only that he seemed so at home with himself. It wasn't even because in a pair of dashing sunglasses, with the wind ripping through his hair, he was close to irresistible. It was because he was the kind of man who unflinchingly hugged and kissed his mother when he saw her.

That hadn't seemed like a particularly bachelorlike thing to do. It seemed much more like the behavior of a man who appreciated the bonds of family.

Mark wasn't a family man, Claire firmly reminded herself. He was a carefree guy with a hot car and a blissful lack of commitments. If not for Rex Crandall's obnoxious stunt, Claire wouldn't even be a blip on Mark's radar screen. Why waste energy imagining what his future as a family man would be like? Even after kissing her, Mark had made certain she understood that she would never be a part of that future by turning tail and walking away.

By the time the bread was done toasting, the menfolk had returned from their test drive. Bob Lavin seemed as excited as a child on his birthday. "Naomi, I'm telling you—the engine is so smooth on this baby," he babbled while Mark dropped into a chair and beckoned Lovey. He gave the dog's ears a vigorous scratching, while the dog panted contentedly and nuzzled his knees. Every now and then, Mark would bend his head to Lovey's and murmur something. Lovey seemed to understand him; she'd respond with a happy bark or a nod.

Claire forced herself to look away. As sexy as Mark's smile was, as attractive as his build, as mesmerizing as his eyes, none of them were as appealing as his obvious joy while playing with his parents' dog. He no longer seemed like a big-shot radio executive, a condo owner, a typical male infatuated with his fancy car—or a bachelor singled out for special mention in a glossy urban magazine. He seemed like a man with a heart.

Over their mid-afternoon dinner, Mark and his parents talked nonstop, doing their best to include Claire in the conversation. Naomi discussed her gardening—"I defy any animal-rights activist to explain to

me why grubs don't deserve to be killed''—and Bob
discussed the recent visit to the campus of a U.N.
diplomat. They talked about their students, their research, a trip they were considering taking to the Gal-
apagos Islands in August. They asked Mark how
things were going at the radio station, what fund-
raisers he was organizing and what charities those
fund-raisers would be supporting.

"I can't say I'm a big fan of the music they play
at WBKX," Bob Lavin confessed to Claire. "I'm an
old folkie. Bluegrass, acoustic music, that kind of
thing."

"Claire likes Dvorak," Mark told his parents, who
seemed to approve. Claire wondered why he'd mentioned her musical preferences. It wasn't as if he
needed to make his parents respect her. After today,
she would never see them again.

Even knowing that, she enjoyed the meal. She ordered herself to focus on the banter and the delicious
seafood stew, and tried not to think about how affectionate Mark's parents were, and how affectionate
Mark was with them. After clearing the table, Bob
and Naomi gave Claire a tour of the house, the upstairs of which was even quirkier than the downstairs,
full of oddly angled rooms, low doorways and
crooked floors. Then all of them, including the dog,
trooped out into the backyard to admire the vegetable
garden Naomi had only just started planting. Then
back inside for coffee and tea and a homemade apple
tart served with scoops of vanilla ice cream. "How
do you find the time to cook like this?" Claire asked
Naomi as she rubbed her full belly. "You're a college professor."

"She doesn't cook like this most of the time," Bob explained, sending his wife a teasing look. "She doesn't cook like this for me. Only for Mark, when he's visiting."

"And when he brings his friends over," Naomi added.

"Like hell," Mark complained. "When I was in high school, you never cooked like this for my friends."

"When you were in high school, your friends would descend upon the kitchen like locusts and eat everything in sight. My bouillabaisse would have been wasted on them."

"I hope you didn't go to all this trouble just for me," Claire said. "I've had a wonderful time, but…"

Naomi arched her eyebrows in a question. "But?"

Claire glanced at Mark for help, but he seemed as curious as his parents to hear what she had to say. "Well, as I said earlier, we're not getting married."

"Of course you aren't," Bob said

"We understand that," Naomi added.

"Before April Fool's Day, Mark and I had never even heard of each other."

"You would have heard of me if you read *Boston's Best*," Mark joked.

Ignoring him, she moved her gaze from Bob to Naomi. "You've made me feel so welcome here— like a part of the family. But I'm not."

"We want you to feel welcome," Naomi explained. "You're Mark's friend, so of course you're welcome."

"And you don't eat like a locust," Bob praised her, his smile uncannily like his son's.

"When that article appeared in the *Globe*," Naomi said, "we thought, well, maybe you were the one. Mark was adamant about your not being his fiancée, but we wanted to see for ourselves."

"You didn't believe me?" Mark looked indignant.

"It has nothing to do with believing you," Naomi said. "It has to do with a mother's intuition."

"And now that you've seen for yourselves?" Mark pressed her.

"As you've said, you're not getting married," Naomi answered.

"You made your point," Bob conceded.

"Okay," Mark said, sounding mollified. Claire ought to have been mollified, too, but she couldn't suppress her longing for things to be different. This outing hadn't helped her to clarify her own feelings. It had only made her aware of what a decent, generous man Mark was—or could be, if he ever got tired of being a bachelor. Claire had to accept that he was a long way from tired, though. She mustn't allow herself to think of him as a potential fiancé.

That one last balloon lingering against the ceiling of her office was bound to deflate eventually. The sooner she accepted that, the better.

In fact, she resolved, Monday morning she'd yank the damned balloon down from the ceiling, puncture it, and toss it in her trash can. Then she'd move on for good.

CHAPTER EIGHT

CLAIRE WAS unnaturally quiet once they left his parents' house. The only time she spoke was to ask him if he'd mind closing up the car's top, since dusk had drained the day of its heat as well as its light. He'd accommodated her, although he would have left the top open if she hadn't been cold. He was looking forward to taking long, nighttime top-down drives this summer, with the stars twinkling above him and all that darkness gusting through the car.

Other than mentioning the top, though, Claire didn't say a word. As they wound their way through North Adams and up into the hilly switchbacks of the Berkshires, she sat silently, minute after minute, her hands folded primly in her lap and her gaze glued to the SUV in front of them, its taillights glowing and a kayak strapped to its roof.

Mark wasn't a mind reader. If he'd been blessed with that particular talent, he might have guessed that Rex would stick one to him this past April Fool's Day to spite him for having been chewed out so royally over last year's show. Mark might have prepared himself somehow, or taken steps so Rex couldn't make him the butt of a joke. Or he might not have been so harsh after last year's show so Rex wouldn't have been so eager for revenge.

Like hell. Rex had deserved the dressing down and the hit to his wallet he'd received last year. And he deserved punishment this year, too, even if this year the mayor hadn't called Mark up to complain about the havoc Rex's show had wrought throughout the city. Rex had wrought havoc in the lives of only two people this year: Mark and the woman whose mind he wished he could read.

She seemed to have had a good time at his parents' house. Lovey had obviously adored her—the dog didn't rub her nose against the shins of people she didn't adore, and she'd rubbed her nose against Claire's shins so much, she'd probably come close to wearing a hole through the fabric of Claire's pants. He'd had no trouble reading the *dog's* mind. She thought Claire was just fine.

He had to agree with Lovey. Claire was fine. Better than fine. She was sharp and funny and gentle. She was passionate about preserving antique buildings like his parents' house, and when a drip of bouillabaisse broth had settled on her lower lip and she'd caught it with the tip of her tongue, he'd remembered, with a sharp twinge in his groin, that she was also passionate in other contexts.

When the time came for him to settle down, he'd want to settle down with a woman like Claire O'Connor, someone calm and steady and thoughtful, someone who could roll with the punches and hang on to her sense of humor. Someone with hair like hers, and legs like hers and wide, green eyes and a passionate pink tongue exactly like hers.

"Are you hungry?" he asked, trying to ignore his

own sudden hunger, which had nothing to do with food.

"God, no." She laughed weakly. "I'm stuffed. Your mother is a very good cook."

"I liked your mother's cookies, too."

"My mother bought those at a bakery."

"Doesn't matter. I think we should be grateful that our mothers are skilled when it comes to feeding our friends." Talking about their mothers helped to take the edge off his hunger. It was a hunger he couldn't satisfy, not with Claire. Not as long as he wasn't ready to settle down. He might not be able to read her mind, but after today he had a pretty clear idea of at least one aspect of it: Claire wasn't the sort of woman a bachelor could party with and part from. She was loyal, committed. Even after breaking up with a guy, if she believed that guy needed her, she came running, breaking the speed limit if necessary.

If Mark touched her—and with her hand resting on her knee, just inches to the right of the gear stick where his own hand rested, touching her would require only a small shift in his position—he would want her. If he kissed her, his hunger for her would overtake him. And then he'd break her heart, because he wasn't ready to be anyone's fiancé yet. If he were, she could easily be the one. *If.* But he wasn't. Not yet.

She glanced at him, smiled and turned back to stare at the SUV ahead of them on the narrow road.

What was she thinking?

"Was today horrible for you?" he asked, hoping to jostle a reaction out of her.

"What?" She looked confused. "No. It was lovely."

"I thought you were going to say, 'It was Lovey.'"

"No, the dog was fine. I liked the dog."

"She can be a little pushy. I saw her sniffing at your legs all afternoon."

"I didn't mind." She settled back in her seat. "Lovey's an awfully sentimental name for a dog."

"My parents consider it alliterative," he explained. "Lovey Lavin."

"That does have a nice ring to it."

Claire seemed to be loosening up, relaxing a little, her posture thawing. An hour into the drive, he finally had a conversation going. "We had another dog when I was growing up," he told her. "I got to pick his name."

"I take it you didn't name him Lovey."

"I named him Scamp," Mark said. "A manly name."

She smiled—and glimpsing her smile made him feel even more triumphant. "Scamp was a mutt," Mark recalled, shaking his head nostalgically. "We picked him up at the pound. He was a great dog." Scamp had joined the family when Mark was seven and had died when he was in college. As much as he liked Lovey, she would never replace Scamp in his heart.

"Mark?" Claire's voice had an edge to it.

"Yeah?"

"Look at the car ahead of us—the SUV. Doesn't it look like the boat is wobbling?"

The road was dark, but his headlights caught the

sway of the kayak on the SUV's roof, and the vibrations in the straps holding it in place. "Hard to say," he muttered, easing up on the gas. "I think—"

And then he stopped thinking—because the kayak snapped free of its restraints and shot backward like a fiberglass missile, slamming into the hood of his car, careening off it and crashing against the windshield. His air bag exploded in front of him, shoving him back into his seat as he floored the brake pedal. The Benz-mobile jerked to a halt and the air bag fizzled into a limp sack that dangled from the steering column.

He turned to Claire. She was pressed back into her own seat, her air bag also limp and emitting a metallic scent. Her eyes were closed and a red welt appeared on her chin. She wasn't moving.

"Oh, my God," he whispered, then said it louder as he yanked off his seat belt. "Oh, my God! Claire! Claire, are you all right?" He ran his hands over her face, her shoulders, her throat and then back up to her face. "Claire!"

Her eyes fluttered open. "I'm okay," she said in a shaky voice.

"Are you sure?" Leaning over her, he saw glints of something sparkling in her hair and on her knees. Chips of his windshield. The outer layer of the safety glass had spider-webbed from one end to the other, and some of the inner layer had splintered off into the car, onto Claire. "Don't move," he ordered her.

"I'm okay."

"You've got glass on you. You could be hurt. Don't move." He lifted his hand toward her hair and noticed that his fingers were trembling. Oh God, oh God. She could be hurt. *Claire.*

"I'm okay," she said, her voice a bit stronger. "I'm fine." She lifted her hands to her hair and plucked a couple of glass chips from the tangled waves. "It's not sharp."

"Don't." He grabbed her hands and pulled them away from her head. The insides of her wrists were unnaturally pink, like that raw spot on her chin. The air bag must have caused the abrasions.

He continued holding her hands, in part to keep her from groping for glass in her hair and in part because he couldn't bear to let go of her. Her flexing fingers reassured him that she was, indeed, okay. But his pulse pounded crazily in his skull, and an edge of hysteria was making his vision momentarily go red. *She could have been killed!*

She hadn't been killed. She was okay. His breathing slowed, his vision returned to normal, but he kept her hands clasped tightly within his. He wasn't about to let go.

"Mark. Look at your car."

"The hell with my car!" A car was just a car—even if it was a Mercedes SLK Roadster. Claire… God help him, if she'd gotten hurt…

Transferring both her hands into one of his, he used his free hand to open the console between the seats and pull out his cell phone. Clicking it on, he punched in the emergency number. After one ring, it was answered by a nasal woman who informed him he'd reached the police station of a town whose name he didn't recognize, and his call was being recorded.

"Yes," he said, still clinging to Claire's hands. "My car was just hit by a boat."

"By a boat? Are you in the water?"

"No. The boat's on land. It was on the roof of an SUV, and now—" He squinted through the dense lace of cracks obliterating his windshield. "—it's on the hood of my car."

"Is anyone hurt?"

He gazed at Claire, at that raw smudge on her chin, at her startled eyes and sweet, delicate mouth. "No," he said, feeling his heart heave in relief. "No one's hurt."

A HALF HOUR LATER, Claire remained standing along the shoulder of the road in the thickening night, her arms folded across her chest and her purse hanging by its strap over her shoulder. Beside his damaged car Mark huddled with a police officer, a tow-truck operator and the burly, bearded driver of the SUV. They all seemed remarkably calm under the circumstances. If an unsecured kayak had hit her car, she'd be pretty upset—and her car wasn't a brand-new Mercedes Benz.

Fortunately, the kayak didn't weigh much. It had dinged and dented the hood of the car, but most of the damage was to the windshield. Claire suffered a pang of grief for the car. Just hours ago, Mark and his father had taken it for a spin through the streets of Williamstown, two little boys flush with the thrill of tearing through town in a hot coupe. Now that hot coupe sat like roadkill on the side of Route 2.

After a few more moments of debate with the

other men, Mark broke from the group and strode over to her. "How are you?" he asked.

She was amazed that he seemed more concerned about her condition than his car's. She was in far better shape than the car was. Her chin stung a little—a glance in the side mirror had indicated a burn the size of a quarter on the edge of her jaw. But that would clear up in a day. "I'm fine," she told him for the umpteenth time. "How are *you?*"

He ran his hands along her arms from her elbows to her shoulders and back again, as if checking for fractures. Then he released her and shoved his hands into his pockets. "Here's the deal. The other driver is freaking out, pleading guilty left and right. He's told the cop the whole thing is his fault—"

"Which it is," Claire pointed out.

"I think he wants to keep his insurance company out of it. I don't know if he realizes how much the repair is going to cost, but for now, he's saying he'll take care of everything."

"Will he take care of getting us back to Boston?"

Mark sighed. "Yeah, but not tonight. I need to have the car towed back to Boston for repairs, and apparently it's next to impossible to get that done on a Saturday night. The local guy said he'd do it tomorrow—and he's the only tow operator in the area. He's willing to tow the car to his garage for the night, and then move it down to Boston tomorrow, even though that'll mean skipping church." Mark reached up and she felt a light tug on her scalp as he unsnagged a piece of glass, and then the soothing stroke of his fingers freeing the chip from a wavy lock.

"Actually, he sounded kind of pleased about skipping church."

She was so distracted by his hand moving through her hair that she momentarily lost track of what he was saying. Once he'd tossed the bit of glass onto the gravel at their feet, her mind cleared and she digested his words. "So what are we going to do tonight?"

"Well, Ray—that's the SUV driver—said his sister-in-law owns an inn in town, and she can put us up for the night. His treat."

Claire ruminated. Was the inn nice? A picturesque bed-and-breakfast or a dive? More important, would Ray's sister-in-law put them up in one room or two? "Do you think we'd be better off returning to your parents' house for the night?"

"We're sixty miles from their house. I can't see asking them to drive all this way to get us, and then drive home, and then have to bring us back here tomorrow."

Claire nodded. "And we're how far from Boston?"

"About seventy miles."

"Okay." She was tired, and it wasn't just from the stress of the accident. She also felt overwhelmed by the gracious reception his parents had given her, by the food and the company and the long drive…and most of all by the understanding that she had fallen for a man who had no intention of abandoning his bachelor ways. By the time they'd left his parents' house, she could no longer deny the unpleasant truth: she loved Mark Lavin. And he'd made it clear that he loved his swinging single status.

If only he would throw a fit over his battered car instead of gently fishing pieces of glass out of her hair, she'd be able to steel her heart against him. But he was being so kind, so considerate—as if she, a woman his obnoxious disk jockey had shoved into his life, was more important to him than his dream car.

"So should we take Ray up on his offer and stay at the inn?" he asked.

"Sure." She shrugged. She had no pressing business back in Boston, and returning to Mark's parents' house would only bring her back to the place where she'd been forced to acknowledge that she loved him.

He patted her shoulder, then pivoted and jogged back to the men clustered by the Mercedes. They conferred for a few more minutes, the bearded man spoke into his cell phone, and Mark returned to Claire. "Officer Beldon is going to drive us to Ray's sister-in-law's place. Ray is on the phone with her now. She's expecting us."

Claire nodded, gave the policeman a grateful smile, and warned herself that when Mark placed his hand at the small of her back, it was only to guide her over the uneven surface of the road's shoulder. As soon as they were both seated in the back of the cruiser—Claire did her best to ignore the cage-like divider installed to keep criminals from attacking the officers in the front seat—Mark pulled his hand from her and left a chaste space between them.

She twisted to peek out the rear window as Officer Beldon drove away from the scene. The tow-truck operator was busy hooking Mark's car up to his wrecker. "How bad is it?" she asked Mark. "How much damage?"

He shrugged. "I'm no expert. Windshields are an easy repair. The hood, I don't know."

"You seem to be taking it well."

"It's just a car," he said.

"It's a very expensive new car."

"You could have been hurt—or killed." His voice broke slightly on the last word.

She was touched by his concern. "So could you."

He shrugged again. "I never get hurt," he said. "But you... Thank God you're all right." His voice drifted off, and she felt a wave of emotion in its wake. Mark seemed more relieved than Claire herself that she hadn't been injured.

The inn Officer Beldon drove them to would not have received many stars from the Michelin Guide. A sprawling, dilapidated building surrounded by pine trees, it featured a well-lit front porch and lopsided shutters adorning the windows. A wooden plaque reading Lake Vue Inn hung from a post near the front steps. Claire wondered whether the misspelling was deliberate.

Officer Beldon dropped them off with a reminder that in the morning he'd transport them to the body shop where Mark's car had been towed, and he'd fax Mark a copy of his accident report once it had been processed. They watched him drive away, then climbed the porch steps and entered the building.

A sturdy, dark-haired woman no more than a few years older than Claire greeted them as they crossed the threshold. "Come on in, folks!" she bellowed, a welcome almost as enthusiastic as Mark's parents'.

"I'm Betty. This is such an honor, having a pair of celebrities like you staying here! I've set aside my best room for you."

"Celebrities?" Claire muttered. Mark scowled.

"When Ray gave me your name," Betty said, nodding to Mark, "I recognized it right away. The radio station, right? You're a famous bachelor, and *you*—" she turned to Claire "—are the woman who made him give up his wild bachelor life."

"How do you know this?" Claire asked as Mark's frown deepened.

"It was in the *Boston Globe*."

"You read the *Globe?*" Mark asked. "We're miles from Boston."

"To tell you the truth," Betty admitted, motioning for them to follow her up a crooked flight of stairs, "no, I don't read the *Globe*. But you're on the Web site."

"The *Globe* Web site?"

"No, the *Boston's Best* bachelor Web site. There's a whole bunch of us who've been following the *Boston's Best* bachelors over the years. A girl's allowed to dream, right?" She marched down a narrow hall as she prattled on. "When word got out that the City Hall woman lassoed you, well, I've got to tell you, the chat room just about exploded. Some people thought it was a betrayal of everything *Boston's Best* stands for. Others said, 'Hey, what are you gonna do? When Cupid's arrow pricks you, that's it. Today a bachelor, tomorrow a hubby.' Love can be that way. Me, I think the whole thing is awful romantic." She swung open a door at the end of the hall and flicked on a light. "Here it is—best accommodations in the place. I've stocked the bathroom with soap and shampoo, some toothbrushes and a little toothpaste sample. Ray explained the circumstances of your stay, and I figured you'd need some toiletries. Stranded so far from home, thanks to that turkey's stupid boat. I told my sister when she married him, I said, 'Donna, he loves kayaks more than he'll ever love you.' But did she listen to me?''

Apparently not, although Claire kept her mouth shut.

''I've only got one key for the room—'' She pressed it into Mark's hand ''—but that shouldn't be a problem for you two lovebirds. There are a couple of other guests here—the season hasn't started yet, so it's pretty quiet. If you need anything, I'm downstairs. Just pick up the phone and dial zero. There's coffee and muffins in the morning.''

Before Mark could respond, their garrulous hostess vanished down the hall.

Claire surveyed the room. Like the stairs, the floor was slightly crooked. The rug looked as if a dance troop had been holding step-dance rehearsals on it, and the bedspread was so faded she couldn't guess its original color. The curtains were equally faded, the dresser's surface scratched, and the light emerging through the bathroom door was a sickly yellow. A single queen-size bed extended from one wall.

''Do you think this building is a landmark?'' Mark asked with a sly smile.

''I think it deserves a demolition hearing,'' she shot back.

He moved to stand beside her. His gaze followed hers to the bed. ''If this is no good, Claire—''

"It's fine," she said curtly. The bed was large, and she was exhausted after this long, eventful day. All she wanted to do was wash the glass out of her hair and go to sleep. She definitely didn't want to have to explain to their hostess why a room with only one bed in it wasn't acceptable to the celebrity couple whose alleged engagement had been dissected and debated on the Internet.

"You're sure?"

Claire crossed to the bathroom. The ledge of the sink held two cellophane-wrapped toothbrushes and a mini tube of toothpaste, and a bottle of shampoo and a bar of soap were perched on the rim of the tub. "All I need is shampoo and a pillow."

"All right." Mark gave her a dubious look, then crossed to a lumpy-looking easy chair and settled into it. "You can have the bathroom first. Be careful with your hair. You could cut yourself on any glass splinters that might still be caught in it."

"Don't worry," she said. "I won't cut myself." She stepped into the bathroom and shut the door.

Was she crazy? She gazed at her distorted reflection in the warped mirror above the sink. She looked weary and pale, except for the scuff mark on her chin, but she didn't look crazy. She and Mark were adults and they'd been through a traumatic experience. They'd wash up, get some rest, and go back to Boston tomorrow. She'd sleep in her clothes. Nothing was going to happen. She didn't *want* anything to happen. Mark didn't love her, he didn't want to make a commitment to her, he hardly knew her...

Nothing was going to happen.

Turning from the mirror, she felt a shiver trip

down her spine. A memory of the instant the kayak had hit the car flashed through her, and she felt dizzy—not from pain but from shock. Mark had brought her to Williamstown to meet his parents—to convince his parents that he and she weren't lovers. And somewhere along the way, she'd realized she'd let herself fall in love with him, which made her the biggest fool the world had ever seen. And then his car had been hit by a kayak.

The whole trip seemed surreal.

It still seemed surreal after she'd showered, after she'd dressed again in the clothes she'd worn all day, brushed her teeth and wrestled the pocket comb she had in her purse through her wet, tangled locks. Surreal and exhausting. She was too drained to think about love or Mark or what might have been if he wasn't a famous Boston bachelor. She needed to get some sleep. And she needed to return to the life she'd had before April Fool's Day.

CHAPTER NINE

As SOON as he heard the shower spurt and hiss behind the closed bathroom door, Mark grabbed the room key and left. His brain was jangling, overcrowded, unable to sort itself out. He needed fresh air and solitude.

The inn sat on an unlit country road. He began a slow circuit around the rambling building. The night was crisp and cool and the ground was solid beneath his feet, loamy from the spring thaw. Just putting one foot in front of the other felt good.

He was a bachelor so famous that women across the state discussed his marital status on Web sites. He *liked* being a bachelor. He liked the freedom, the unabashed selfishness of it, the irresponsibility. The fast car.

Yet when that kayak had smashed into his roadster, all he'd been able to think about was Claire. Was she hurt? he'd wondered desperately. Why wasn't she opening her eyes? Had the glass shards from the windshield cut her? He hadn't even bothered to check whether he himself had been injured. His mind hadn't been cluttered then. It had contained only one thought, as clear as a laser piercing through all the crap that usually preoccupied him. *Claire.* If she'd been hurt...or killed... Just contemplating the

possibility caused his gut to knot and his vision
to blur.

What a day. What an insane, overwhelming day.
Why had he introduced her to his parents? Because
his mom had wanted to meet her. Because she'd
dragged him to *her* mother's. Because he owed his
parents a visit, and it was a long drive, and the trip
would be more pleasant with company. But if all
he'd wanted was company, he could have invited
Sherry to join him—well, maybe not Sherry, but he
knew other women. Or he could have invited a male
buddy. He had some close friends among the guys
he played pick-up basketball with at the gym, and a
couple of buddies from college and grad school who
lived in the Boston area, and his neighbor Pete. His
neighbor Lisa, too. She was sort-of-almost divorced,
and she'd been sending him looks ever since the *Boston's Best* article had appeared.

But it hadn't occurred to him to make the trip to
Williamstown with anyone but Claire. He'd wanted
her with him. Only her.

It had been unsettling to have Claire with him in
the company of his parents, who were arguably the
most happily married people he knew... He came
from a solid family, and he appreciated his good fortune in that. He understood what a loving marriage
was all about, what a magnificent gift it was. He
wanted a loving marriage himself—someday. Not
now. Not yet. Not while he was one of the most
desirable bachelors in Boston.

But...*Claire*. She meant more to him than anything he could think of, even his precious Mercedes.

After three orbits around the inn, he went back

inside, climbed the stairs and sauntered down the hall to the room. He unlocked the door, pushed it open and confronted yet another cause of his current agitation—the bed.

He could ask for a separate room. If Ray refused to pay for it, big deal. This place wasn't the Ritz; a second room couldn't possibly cost much, and even if it did, Mark could easily afford the expense. But then Betty the blabbermouth would go online and all her Internet friends would discuss the fact that Mark Lavin, one of *Boston's Best*'s top five, had declined to share a room with his intended. Mark didn't want to give that chat-room hen party anything more to cluck about.

He supposed he could sleep on the floor. Or he and Claire could share the bed. He could sleep with his back to her. He'd already kissed her once, and he'd seen the glow in her eyes when that kiss had ended, a glow that had asked far more of him than he was ready to give.

So he wouldn't kiss her again, because he wasn't ready to give more. He could spend a night in bed with her and not kiss her, because the last thing he wanted was for her to get hurt. She'd avoided injury in one collision tonight. He'd make sure she avoided injury in a second collision in this bed.

The room was quiet, no shower sounds filtering through the closed bathroom door. He couldn't wait to take a shower himself. He felt achy, not only from the accident but from hours of driving. He wanted to scrub off the fatigue that clung to him like a layer of grime, and then get some rest. He wanted to sleep without dreaming.

The bathroom door opened and Claire emerged, clothed except for her bare feet, a towel draped over her shoulders to keep her hair from soaking her blouse. She couldn't spend the night in that fancy blouse.

He pulled off his sweater. "Why don't you sleep in this?" he suggested.

She stared first at the sweater he extended to her and then at him. He had on a dark blue T-shirt and his jeans; it wasn't as if he'd stripped himself stark naked. But her eyes widened and she pressed her lips tight as if to hold back whatever she might have wanted to say.

"It'll be a lot more comfortable than sleeping in what you've got on now," he pointed out. "And if it gets wet from your hair, who cares? It's just an old sweater."

"Are you sure?"

"Yeah, I'm sure." She still hadn't taken the sweater, so he tossed it onto the bed and hoped the rest of the night wouldn't be as awkward as that particular moment. "I'm going to wash up," he said, moving past her and entering the steamy bathroom.

Standing under the shower's hot spray helped. If he thought about Claire putting on his sweater and crawling under the covers on the other side of the door, he'd have probably needed an ice-cold shower, so he distracted himself by thinking about the logistics of getting his car back to Boston tomorrow. He hoped that the tow truck transporting the car would have enough room in the cab for both him and Claire. Once the driver delivered them and the car to an auto body shop that specialized in Mercedes-Benzes,

Mark could call a cab. And he'd save the receipt for the cab fare. Ray was going to reimburse Mark for every damned penny this disaster was costing him.

He shut off the water, stepped out of the tub, and ran a bath towel over his body. He scrubbed his scalp with the towel, dug a comb from the hip pocket of his jeans and neatened his hair as best he could. His pockets contained a lot of necessities, but a razor wasn't among them. His cheeks, jaw and upper lip were dark with a stubble. Not much he could do about that.

The bedroom felt chilly after the humid warmth of the bathroom. Claire was already in bed, lying on her side near the edge, one arm resting atop the blanket. She'd cuffed the sleeve of his sweater to free her hand. He wondered how far down her legs the sweater fell, wondered whether she'd kept her underwear on underneath it—then shut down that thought before it could go anywhere.

The lamp on her side of the bed was turned off, but she'd thoughtfully left the other bedside lamp on for him. He lowered himself to the mattress, removed his jeans and left them on the floor beside the bed. Then he slid under the blanket and turned off the lamp, throwing the room into darkness. The sheets were cool and smooth and the room smelled of the shampoo they'd both used.

"Are you okay?" he asked. He'd already asked her if she was okay countless times, but he couldn't keep from asking one more time.

"I'm fine, Mark." Her voice sounded distant, probably because she was facing away from him.

He told himself to shut up and close his eyes, but

his body disobeyed. His eyes remained open, adjusting to the gloom until he could see Claire's outline, the rise of her shoulder, the spill of her hair across the pillow. His mouth opened, too. "I know this is...well...not what you were hoping for."

"Mark—"

"I feel lousy, dragging you out to Williamstown for the day, and then this mess."

"It's all right, Mark. Things happen."

"Yeah."

She was so close, yet she could have been miles away. The blanket sagged between their bodies, forming a woolen barrier, and beyond the blanket was her back. *Things happen,* he thought—maybe because they were supposed to happen. Maybe because of fate. Maybe because if they didn't happen, the people they might have happened to would miss a vital lesson.

"I love your hair," he said, reaching across those miles, across the barrier of the blanket, but unable to breach the greater barrier of her unwillingness to face him. Lying with her back to him meant presenting him with her hair, thick with rippling curls, cool and heavy and damp. He twirled his fingers through it and thought that if Claire were really his fiancée, he could touch her hair like this all the time, gather it, let it flow like rippling silk across his palms.

She turned, and her hair slipped out of his grasp. "Mark." Her voice was quiet and steady. Just like her.

He should apologize, but he wouldn't. The only thing he felt sorry about was that he was no longer touching her. He was a selfish son of a bitch, touching her because he wanted to, because he *had* to, and if he had a shred of decency in him he'd get out of bed and sleep on the floor. He'd leave her alone. She was too good a woman, and he wasn't a good enough man. Not yet.

"You're wrong," she murmured.

"About your hair?"

"About what I might or might not be hoping for."

Too cryptic. He didn't know what she was getting at. Once again, he wished he had mind-reading gifts. "What are you hoping for?" he asked.

She turned from him. "Things I can't have."

Her voice was almost too soft to hear—except that she'd said exactly what he was feeling. He was hoping for things he couldn't have: her. Tonight.

What did she want that she couldn't have? Something he could give her? Something he could do? After seeing her strapped into her car seat, helpless and unmoving, with broken glass strewn over her and that welt on her chin, he would have given anything, done anything for her, just to save her. Just to make her all right. Just to see her open her eyes and smile.

He still felt that way, that he would do anything she wanted. Give her anything she hoped for.

He slid his hand under her chin, careful to avoid the bruise, and steered her face back to him. Their gazes met, and in her eyes he saw what she hoped for, his own hopes reflected. *I'll do anything,* he thought, then pulled her into his arms and covered her mouth with his.

SHE'D BEEN HOPING for *this*. Actually, she'd been hoping for much more, but she was a realist. She knew that this was the closest she would ever get to Mark, while they were trapped in some limbo unconnected to the world of their everyday lives. In the morning they would accompany his damaged car back to Boston and he would resume his bachelor ways, and the balloon that lingered near the ceiling of her office would ultimately swoon to the floor.

She hoped—stupidly, futilely—that Mark could renounce his top-bachelor title for her. But no matter how sweetly he'd behaved toward her today, no matter how solicitous, no matter how loving a son he was, how playful a dog-lover, how charming a companion, she knew her hope would never be fulfilled. That didn't mean she couldn't have one night, just one night when they could belong to each other.

From the moment she'd pulled his warm, soft sweater over her head, she'd been at war with herself—wanting him and knowing he could break her heart simply by doing what she hoped he would do. If he hadn't made a move, she would have let that hope die.

But he'd kissed her. And she was kissing him back, promising herself that whatever happened tonight would be worth the heartbreak tomorrow.

His mouth moved on hers, hot and hungry. The kiss he'd given her outside her building a week ago might have been a mere handshake compared to this. It was possessive, demanding, consuming. His tongue took everything she had to give, and then took more, filling her, claiming her. His unshaven chin was scratchy, making her lips tingle. His hands cupped the sides of her face, his fingers weaving into her hair. She'd wished she had a hairdryer with her, because her hair never looked good if she didn't brush and blow-dry it after a shampoo. But Mark loved her hair. He'd said he did.

And she loved his kiss. She loved the heat of his body spreading under the covers, the lean length of him, the firm contours of his shoulders beneath the thin cotton of his T-shirt. She loved the fresh-showered scent of him. She loved the disheveled waves of his hair and the thick shadows of his eye-lashes, visible as her eyes grew accustomed to the dark. She loved the strength in his hands, in his tongue, the pressure of his chest bearing down on her, easing her onto her back.

He rose to his knees and the blanket skidded down the slope of his shoulders. For a long moment he gazed at her, as if he could read all the yearning in her face, in her heart. Then he reached for the ribbed edge of his sweater and dragged it up over her hips, over her waist. She'd left on her panties but removed her bra, and when he pulled the sweater high enough to expose her breasts, she heard him sigh.

That faint sound brought her mind into focus. "Mark?"

He bowed to kiss first one and then the other breast, and they both sighed this time. Her nipples grew tight, burning from the contact of his lips.

"Mark," she said again, forcing out the words, "I don't..." She lost her voice as he yanked the sweater's sleeves down and off her arms, as he hauled the sweater over her head and tossed it over the side of the bed.

"God, you're beautiful," he whispered, then bent to nuzzle her throat.

"I don't have anything." She had to force out the words.

He lifted his head and smiled. "You have everything I could ever possibly want."

She might take that either as an unbelievably romantic compliment or as a commentary on his rather limited wants. She chose the latter interpretation because it made her laugh, and laughing relaxed her. "I'm talking about protection, Mark."

"Oh." He touched his lips to the hollow between her collarbones, then the hollow between her breasts. "I have a condom."

"You do?"

"'Don't leave home without it,'" he said, quoting the old commercial. "I always carry one, just in case."

"Just in case." She pretended to disapprove. "Is that some bachelor thing?"

"I always carry my cell phone. I always carry an ATM card. You never know." He sat back on his haunches and stripped off his T-shirt, exposing the most beautiful male chest she had ever seen, streamlined with muscle and textured with a sparse patch of hair across his pectorals.

"So I qualify as 'just in case,'" she murmured.

"You qualify as 'you never know.'" He shimmied out of his boxers, then tugged her panties down her legs and off. He seemed oddly stunned at the sight of her. Yet she was sure that, given his "don't leave home without it" philosophy, he'd seen plenty of naked women before. She'd seen a couple of men herself. But no man had ever looked at her the way Mark was looking at her, his dark eyes luminous, his expression awed. "I only have one," he whispered, a rueful smile twisting his mouth. "We're going to have to make it count."

If the keen, worshipful anticipation in his gaze was anything to go by, one bout of lovemaking with Mark might be intense enough to kill her. She'd die happy, though.

She lifted her hand and flattened her palm against his chest. His skin was warm, and it flexed at her touch. He stretched out next to her so she could reach more of him, and she touched everything she could—his hard shoulders, the ridge of his rib cage, the soft hairs along his forearm, the taut expanse of his abdomen. His buttocks, as unyielding as his shoulders. His thighs, covered in coarser hair. His erection, full and pulsing against the curve of her hand.

That one intimate touch caused him to groan and push her hand away. He pinned her on her back, pressed her arms to the mattress so she couldn't touch him any more, and then kissed his way down her body, taking his time with her breasts, lingering at her navel, causing her stomach to clench and her hips to arch. He kissed lower, nudged her legs apart and took her with his mouth, licking and nipping until her entire body convulsed with pleasure.

"Mark…" His name tumbled from her lips, half a sob, half a plea. No one had ever made her feel so resplendently alive—and so utterly weak. "Mark—"

"Shh." He slid back up her body, slightly out of breath.

"That was—" What? She didn't think the English language had a word adequate to describe what she'd just experienced.

"Shh," he said again, then silenced her by brushing his lips against hers, tracing his tongue over her lower lip and pressing his arousal against her belly.

She wanted him to feel what she'd felt. She wanted him to be as deliriously grateful to her as she was to him. Mustering what little energy she had, she propped herself up on her elbows, then pushed herself to sit. Mark sat back on his haunches once more, and Claire wrapped her arms around him. He was solid yet graceful, his physique sinewy rather than bulky. She ran her hands down his back, savoring the smooth, hot surface of his skin, the subtle motions of his muscles. When she kissed his chest he moaned.

Operating on instinct—she'd never done this before—she kissed a path downward, pausing to dip her tongue into his navel and sensing a tremor in his breath, grazing even lower, touching her mouth to the tip of his penis.

He moaned again, dug his hands into her hair and eased back her head. She peered up at him, worried that he wasn't feeling anything as wonderful as what she'd felt when he'd made love to her with his mouth. "Am I doing it wrong?" she asked.

"No. Oh, no." A dazed laugh escaped him as he pulled her back up so he could stare into her eyes. "I want to be inside you when I come," he said.

His words turned her on as much as his kisses had, his touch, his gaze. He released her and reached over the side of the bed, where he'd abandoned his jeans. The heavy denim rustled as he rummaged through his pockets. When he returned to her, he was holding his one precious condom. In a matter of seconds, he had it unwrapped and unrolled. He drew her into his arms, guided her legs around his waist and pulled her down onto him.

She panicked. They were sitting up, and she didn't know what to do.

"Hold on," he murmured, his hands clamped to her hips. She clung to him and he rocked her, rocked them both, arching upward into her. As impossible as it seemed, this felt even more exquisite than what he'd done to her just minutes ago. Her body shivered, tensed, gathered him in. He slid his hands forward, his thumbs pressing lightly against where their bodies were joined, and she shattered inside, fierce pulses consuming her. He froze, barely breathing, embracing her as her throbbing body embraced him.

She buried her head in the curve of his neck and gulped in shaky breaths. As the storm ebbed, her hands relaxed against his shoulders. It was only then that he moved, guiding her onto her back and surging into her. This was for him. His thrusts were faster, harder; he no longer held anything back. She wrapped her arms and legs around him, wishing she could give him as much as he'd given her, wishing he could feel everything she'd felt, every magnificent, heart-stopping sensation.

He strained, his body tense and damp with sweat. She stroked his back, cupped his head and rose off the pillow to kiss him. Somehow that kiss unleashed something in them both. She heard his helpless groan an instant before yet another climax overtook her. He shuddered in her arms, his hips fused to hers, their souls merging for one blissful instant.

Slowly, slowly her soul pulled away from his and

retreated to a safe place inside herself. She remembered who she was, where she was, whom she was with and why. She remembered that today's mission had been to convince Mark's parents that she and Mark had no intention of forging a lifelong commitment to each other. In fact, to convince them of quite the opposite, that they were two strangers whose paths had crossed thanks to nothing more than a stupid practical joke.

Mark shifted onto his side next to her, one arm wedged under her and the other looped over her, his chin resting gently on the crown of her head. "Are you okay?" he whispered, the same question he'd asked her when he'd first climbed into bed with her, the question he'd been asking her ever since his car had been clobbered by a runaway kayak.

In terms of broken glass and air-bag burns, she was okay. In terms of being stranded overnight in some no-name village halfway between Williamstown and Boston, she was okay.

In terms of how she was going to recover from what she'd just shared with Mark, how she was going to get through the rest of her life without him—that she wasn't so sure of.

But that wasn't the answer he was looking for. So she said, "Yes, I'm okay."

CHAPTER TEN

HE COULDN'T SLEEP. At some point Claire drifted off; her head grew heavy against his shoulder and her breathing grew deep and steady. He envied her ability to slip into unconsciousness. He wished his brain would stop humming enough so he could rest.

It wasn't churning the way it had been earlier, when he'd taken his three-lap hike around the inn. Instead, it was still and bright, as if someone were beaming a high-intensity flashlight through his skull.

He didn't want this. He was one of Boston's top five bachelors, for God's sake. The new-car smell hadn't even faded from his Benz-mobile yet.

Now his new car was a mess.

And so was his life.

Sighing, he held Claire closer. Her legs felt sleek against his. He'd been thinking about her legs from the first time he'd met her—her legs, her hair, the whole damned package. And what was inside the package, too—the intelligence, the serenity, the sincerity. The sense of humor. The sympathy that would make a person risk a speeding ticket in order to reach a friend in need, even if that "friend" turned out to be a lying bastard. The passion for old buildings, old neighborhoods, old communities.

The passion she'd just shared with him. *Comely*...oh man, she was comely.

He held her closer. Her hair snagged in his day-old beard. Her breath whispered against his chest. It felt warm, right.

He didn't want this. It wasn't the plan. He was a freaking superstar bachelor, for crying out loud! What was that bull the innkeeper had said? Something about Cupid's arrow? The hell with Cupid. The only thing he'd been struck with was an air bag.

Claire had been thrust into his life and now his self-image, his future, his whole life—everything was on the line. What was he going to do?

MARK SEEMED distracted to Claire when they arose the next morning. Shadows underlined his eyes and his beard gave him a scruffy, dangerous look. He didn't talk as he gathered his clothes—the jeans on the floor by his side of the bed, the sweater on the floor by hers, the T-shirt and shorts tangled in the bedsheets. Claire had left her own clothes laid neatly over the back of the easy chair. She scooped them up and shut herself inside the bathroom so she wouldn't have to deal with his silence.

What they'd done last night was a mistake. Mark obviously knew that as well as she did. She could put his mind at ease by telling him she recognized that their lovemaking had been an anomaly, a one-time occurrence. No promises had been made, no strings attached, no future acknowledged. Surely that would cheer him up.

But she didn't want to cheer him up. She wasn't in a particularly cheery mood herself.

For all she knew, his gloomy disposition reflected his concern about his car and had nothing to do with her or last night's intimacy. Ahead of them lay a long trip home in a tow truck, after which she would return to her routine while he wasted days haggling with insurance companies, getting estimates, filing reports and contemplating whether to sue Ray. His car would ultimately be repaired, but it would never be new again. No wonder he was sulking.

They picked at the jumbo blueberry muffins Betty set before them in the dining room downstairs, sipped the coffee she poured for them and declined the orange juice. Officer Beldon showed up at nine and drove them to the auto shop where Mark's car had spent the night. In the hazy morning light, it looked wretched, the windshield a ghastly lace of cracks and the hood dented and scratched. Mark winced at the sight.

"Sure, I can fit you both in the cab," the tow-truck driver said once he and Mark had completed some paperwork. Mark gallantly took the center of the seat, as if to protect Claire from the driver. The man seemed pretty harmless, though, a skinny fellow in his thirties with a few acne scars pocking his cheeks, a wedding band on his left hand and a NASCAR cap perched on his head. The truck's cab smelled of gasoline and the seat's upholstery was as stiff as a wooden bench. "Mind if I turn on the radio?" he asked amiably once they were on Route 2, dragging the crippled Mercedes behind them. "Sometimes, when the weather patterns are right, I can pick up WBKX all the way out here. That's your station, ain't it?"

"Yeah," Mark grunted.

Claire gazed out the window. None of the scenery they passed looked familiar to her, even though she and Mark had driven this road less than twenty-four hours ago. Then, she'd been a different person: confident that they could become friends, amused that his parents seemed as hung up on their fictional engagement as her mother had been, absorbed by the rustic scenery and exhilarated by the top-down drive in the powerful sports car. Never had she imagined that the day would end as it had, and that she would be feeling so bereft today, so alone.

"That weekend show your station does isn't so good," the driver noted, punching buttons on the radio console and picking up only static. "Weekdays, that deejay Rex? He's great, when the station's coming in. Rex in the Morning. If it's just the right amount cloudy, we get pretty good reception in the shop."

"You think he's great?" Mark muttered.

"He's hilarious. Some of his jokes have me laughing so hard I've got to stop working for a minute to catch my breath."

"Some of his jokes are awful," Mark snapped.

"You think so?"

"Look—I'm sorry." Mark gave the radio's knob a sharp twist to turn off the static. "I need to talk to Claire for a minute, and I can't do it with that crackling noise."

"Suit yourself," the driver said with a shrug.

Claire braced herself for whatever Mark had to say. She hoped it wouldn't have anything to do with last night.

"About last night," he began.

While she doubted she'd ever see this tow-truck driver again, she didn't care to discuss her sex life in front of him. Public discussions of her private life were what had caused this entire disastrous situation, even though Rex had invented that private life just to needle her and his boss. "No, Mark. Please," she said, cutting him off.

"Claire." Mark pried one of her hands free of her purse, which she was clutching as if it were a life preserver, and folded his hands around her fingers.

She drew in a breath and turned from the vista of trees and hills and ponds blurring past the window to glance at him. No man deserved to look so good with mussed hair and an overnight shadow of beard, she thought. No man deserved to turn her life inside-out the way Mark had, and then run off to be a bachelor.

"I've been thinking," he said.

Wonderful. Should she contact *Boston's Best* and inform them that their esteemed bachelor had a brain?

"I've been thinking," he elaborated, "about where I am in my life, where I thought I was. Where I ought to be. There is always a choice, you know? Not a single answer. But a choice."

This was a bit too philosophical for her. Maybe she should have drunk a second cup of coffee, but even extra caffeine wouldn't have put her in the right frame of mind for a discussion on the concept of choice.

"Actually, that's wrong," he refuted himself. It occurred to her that he hadn't really worked out what he was trying to say. He was fumbling, struggling to put into words concepts that were far from clear in his mind. "I thought I had a choice. I guess I do, but it's not really a choice, because the choice is between clinging to a stupid idea or grabbing hold of something that will make me happy and fulfilled." He paused. "Does any of this make sense?"

"No," she said.

The tow-truck driver glanced toward them. "Doesn't make sense to me, either."

"I'm not talking to you," Mark said. "This is between me and Claire."

The driver shrugged and raised his eyebrows. Mark shifted on the seat to face Claire. "What I'm saying is, marry me."

"What?" She definitely should have had a second cup of coffee. Maybe a third and a fourth. She might have fantasized about such a moment last night while lying in the warm shelter of Mark's body, but this was the morning, the sun was burning through the windshield and the tow truck was carrying her back to reality.

"Marry me," he repeated. "That's the choice that will make me happy and fulfilled. The bachelor thing won't. It just won't."

"I thought she was your fiancée," the driver interjected. "Betty told my wife—"

"Stay out of this, would you?" Mark said, silencing him, then turned back to Claire. "You heard him. You're my fiancée." He smiled hesitantly. "We've already gotten to that point. We may as well go the rest of the distance. What do you say?"

She wanted to say yes. She wanted to believe he

meant every word, however incoherent most of those
words were. But he'd been in an accident last night.
Maybe he'd struck his head on something at the moment of impact and had suffered a brain injury. Or
he could be experiencing post-traumatic stress. "I
say you're crazy," she answered.

"No, I'm not. Really. Everyone who knows me
thinks I'm sane."

Her heart started pounding, the way it had
pounded last night when he'd kissed her, when he'd
told her he loved her hair, when he'd done everything
he'd done to her. "What about being one of Boston's
top-ranked bachelors?"

"The hell with that. I thought that was what I
wanted. But then we got engaged and I just don't
want to be a bachelor anymore. I want to want it, but
I don't. I can't make myself want what I don't
want."

Anyone who heard some of his convoluted state-
ments would definitely doubt his sanity. But she was
able to decipher his meaning. "Mark." She drew in
another breath, this one tremulous. His hands felt so
warm and strong around hers. His voice sounded so
positive. "We didn't get engaged. We never were
engaged. It was just a silly joke Rex played on us."

"I know. I'll deal with Rex," Mark promised.
"But he's not important right now. What's important
is that…" He sighed. "I love you."

"You hardly know me."

"I know everything I need to know." He lifted
her hand to his mouth and brushed her fingertips with
a kiss. "What I know is that the thought of going
home and being a bachelor depresses me. I don't

want that. I want *you*—everything you are, everything you'll ever be. I want to fall asleep every night with your hair touching me. I want to canoodle with you. Marry me, Mary Claire O'Connor."

Her eyes filled with tears. She no longer noticed the gasoline smell, the uncomfortable seat, the reflection of the truck's yellow flashing lights in the side mirror. She loved Mark. She wanted so badly to say yes. "You'd be giving up so much," she pointed out.

"What? My title as a prime bachelor? Ask me if I care."

"You're really serious?"

"He's serious," the driver chimed in. "You're already engaged to him, so you may as well marry him."

"Thank you," Mark said, sounding genuinely grateful for the driver's comment this time. He gazed at Claire. "You heard him. You may as well marry me."

"I may as well," Claire said, then laughed through her tears.

Mark arched his arm around her shoulders and pulled her close. She rested her head on his shoulder. Behind them trailed his battered sports car. Ahead of them lay a future filled with everything Claire could possibly desire. And next to her sat Mark, her fiancé, her wonderful April Fool's Day gift.

EPILOGUE

TRAFFIC ON THE Fitzgerald Expressway was bumper-to-bumper, as usual. Trucks idled noisily, impatient drivers honked and Mark never got out of first gear. Light rain fell from a dismal gray sky, misting the windshield. He clicked the wipers on to the intermittent setting.

Unlike the drivers crammed onto the road with him, he was smiling. He was in his Benz-mobile, Rex in the Morning was blasting through the speakers, and his beautiful wife was beside him, sipping coffee from a travel mug. Her demure wool pants suit and her raincoat contrasted sharply with what she'd been wearing an hour ago—nothing but soap suds and warm water when he'd joined her in the shower. "I don't have time for this," she'd protested half-heartedly, and he'd grinned and promised he'd be quick. He hadn't been, of course, and somehow she'd found she *did* have time for this, after all.

Wasn't that why travel mugs were invented? So that when the minutes set aside for breakfast wound up being spent on a far more pleasurable activity, a person could still enjoy her morning coffee before she reached her office?

"It's April Fool's Day," he reminded her as the car rolled a couple of inches forward.

"Don't remind me." She glanced at the radio. "Is Rex going to do anything awful this year?"

"I don't know."

"Last year's gag backfired, didn't it?" She grinned at Mark. "I think he was kind of disappointed that things turned out so well. Everyone else at the wedding seemed so happy, but he just moped."

"He was jealous," Mark explained. "You broke up with him and married me. Poor bastard. I feel sorry for him."

"You do not." Mark felt Claire's probing gaze on him. "Rex *is* going to do something this year, isn't he? You know more than you're telling me."

Mark guided the car ahead another inch and attempted a look of innocence. When Claire poked his arm, he shook his head. "Listen to the radio. That's the only way we'll find out if Rex has any April Fool's Day surprises on tap."

She did as Mark suggested, eyeing the radio as she sipped her coffee. "And in medical news," Rex said, "doctors have announced that, since most paper is made from wood fiber, it can be used as a dietary supplement. If you're constipated and tired of bran cereal, eating a few sheets of paper will solve the problem. Doctors advise people to avoid eating recycled paper, because you don't know what it's been recycled through."

"That's gross," Claire muttered.

Mark chuckled. "That's Rex."

"All right," Rex said. "How about this damp, dreary weather? Let's brighten things up with a song about sunshine." Less than a second later, the car's interior vibrated with the resonant opening chords of the *New World Symphony*.

Claire flinched. "Dvorak?"

"Is that what that is?" Mark asked, feigning ignorance.

"On WBKX?" Claire jabbed his arm again and started laughing. "Why is Rex playing Dvorak?"

"Beats me."

The music came to a sudden halt. "That sure doesn't sound like George Harrison singing 'Here Comes the Sun,'" Rex said. "How 'bout we try this again. I've got Peter Gabriel here, 'Red Rain.'" A pause, and the *New World Symphony* came on again.

"What did you do?" Claire asked sternly.

Mark coughed to keep from laughing. "Me? Why do you think I did something?"

"Because Rex would never play Dvorak. Not even on April Fool's Day."

"He would if all the disks in his queue are the *New World Symphony*."

"You didn't," she admonished, this time unable to suppress her laughter.

"I took a bunch of CDs of the *New World Symphony* and stuck different labels on them, and then I put them in Rex's stack. His director is in on it. Everything he plays for the next half hour is going to be Dvorak."

"Won't you lose listeners?"

"Nah. They'll all stick around to see how long the gag goes on, and how Rex handles it."

At the moment, Rex was handling it by stammering. "Something really weird's going on here, folks!" he said. "I'm being attacked by Dvorak.

Let's go to a commercial—'' and the largo movement of the *New World Symphony* came on.

"You are a very bad man," Claire scolded, still laughing.

"I am a very devoted husband," Mark defended myself. "Giving my wife her favorite music on the anniversary of the day we met."

"Yes," she said, this time not punching but caressing his arm. "You're a very bad, very romantic man."

"And you love me for it."

"I do," she said, but he already knew that. Which was just one more reason to smile on this rainy, happy April Fool's Day.

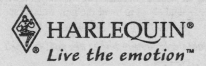

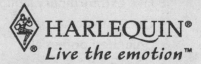

**Coming in April 2004
to Silhouette Books**

USA TODAY BESTSELLING AUTHOR
INGRID WEAVER

THE INSIDER

Gideon Faulkner had lived a life in captivity,
kidnapped and brainwashed years ago by the
Coalition. But he had found a way to sneak
into the outside world, and finally had a chance
to find his real family…and true love!

Five extraordinary siblings.
One dangerous past.
Unlimited potential.

**Return to the sexy Lone Star state
with *Trueblood, Texas*!**

Her Protector
by
LIZ IRELAND

Partially blind singer Jolene Daniels is being stalked,
and Texas Ranger Bobby Garcia is determined to
help the vulnerable beauty—and to recapture
a love they both thought was lost.

Finders Keepers: Bringing families together.

Available wherever books are sold in March 2004.

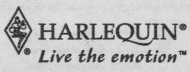

Visit us at www.eHarlequin.com

CPHP

**A brand-new story from the *USA TODAY*
bestselling series, The Fortunes of Texas!**

SHOTGUN *Vows*

by award-winning author
TERESA SOUTHWICK

After one night of indulgent passion leaves Dawson Prescott and
Matilda Fortune trembling—and married!—they must decide if
their shotgun vows have the promise of true love.

Look for *Shotgun Vows* in May 2004.

The Fortunes of Texas:
Membership in this family has its privileges...and its price.
But what a fortune can't buy, a true-bred Texas love is sure to bring!